The Gateway Chronicles

Book 2

To William,
The adventure continues...

The Oracle

By

K. B. Hoyle

TWCS
Publishing House

First published by The Writer's Coffee Shop, 2012

The Writer's Coffee Shop
(Australia) PO Box 447 Cherrybrook NSW 2126
(USA) PO Box 2116 Waxahachie TX 75168

Paperback ISBN- 978-1-61213-327-0
E-book ISBN- 978-1-61213-067-5

A CIP catalogue record for this book is available from the US Congress Library.

Cover image by: © Rceeh © Sergey Andrianov
Cover design by: Megan Dooley

www.thewriterscoffeeshop.com/khoyle

ABOUT THE AUTHOR

The Gateway Chronicles 2: The Oracle is K. B. Hoyle's second published novel. Ms. Hoyle lives outside of Birmingham, Alabama, with her husband and three children. She is a teacher at a local classical school and enjoys traveling, reading and, of course, writing.

Contact K. B. Hoyle via e-mail at kbhoyle@yahoo.com, like her on Facebook, or visit her blog at www.nightnark.blogspot.com.

Follow @kbhoyle_author on Twitter.

Dedication

To Caleb and Joshua

Special Thanks

Special thanks to Beth Mitchell, Yvonne Lovelady, Mariah Lawrence, Hannah Pryor, Bethany Carter, and Abby Shirer for the hours of selfless labor you put into helping me with this book. Thanks also to my husband Adam, my sister Julie, my brother-in-law Brad, and my friend Melissa Bell for all of your unflagging support. Thanks to my students for reading my books when you should be studying, and to my writers group for being the first to listen and offer insight. A very special thanks to Abby, Chris, Jesse, John P., John "Shooby," Jonathan, Katie, and Mark, the real "Cedar Cove" campers; without you these stories would not be possible. Thanks to author John Granger (*How Harry Cast His Spell*) for educating me in literary alchemy and for your correspondence. Finally, thanks to Donna Huber for your help, guidance, and advice, to Hayley German Fisher and Kathie Spitz for your expert editing skills, to Megan Dooley for the fabulous cover art, and to all the staff at TWCS Publishing House for making this dream a reality.

"The further up and the further in you go, the bigger everything gets. The inside is larger than the outside."

C. S. Lewis

CHAPTER 1
DARCY'S DREAM

Darcy started awake. Her heart was pounding in her ears and a fly beat idly against the windowpane next to her bed with an annoying *buzz* thunk, *buzz* thunk, *buzz* thunk. She rolled over and looked at her clock. *Seven-thirty! Too early for summer break.* She rubbed her face with both hands and tried to pinpoint what had woken her. She'd been having a bad dream, she knew that, but she didn't have any idea what it had been about now that she was awake.

With a sigh, Darcy sat up and stretched. Other than the sound of the fly beating against the window, the house was eerily silent. She frowned. Usually her mom was up by now, making breakfast for Roger, who rose with the sun. Darcy stood and opened her window to let the fly out and then padded across her carpet to crack open her door.

Nothing. Not a sound in the entire house. Her parents' door was still shut across the hall, as was Roger's just to the right of hers. She shrugged. *They must be sleeping in. Guess I'll get a head start on them.*

Darcy walked to the bathroom and shut the door gently. She went straight to the shower and turned on the faucet to get the water nice and hot before she got in. Going back to the sink, she brushed her teeth distractedly, unable to shake the feeling that something was amiss in her house. As steam began to fill the bathroom, she spit and took a drink to rinse out her mouth before glancing up in the mirror.

She froze.

No! She looked closer. It couldn't be. It must be the fog on the mirror obscuring her vision. She raised a shaking arm to wipe off the glass and brushed her hair out of her face with her right hand, the dead hand, as she often called it in secret.

She peered closer and felt herself go pale. It was undeniable. Her eyes were black, as if her pupils had enlarged to swallow up her usually grey irises.

She lurched against the sink as panic overtook her. Grabbing at the counter, she knocked the soap dispenser onto the floor. Shards of white ceramic flew everywhere and she stumbled backward in horror, stepping down hard on a jagged piece, but the pain didn't register. Instead, numb, she stared at her foot as her blood spread across the tiles in an ever-widening circle. But it wasn't red; it, too, was black.

Black and oily, it spurted and gushed out in nauseating waves. Darcy could feel herself hyperventilating. Her nightmare had come true. She was one of them, a *tsellodrin*.

The ever-present coldness in her right fingertips was spreading up her arm and into her chest. In a few moments it would cover her entire body. She screamed.

Back in her bed, her scream dissolved into the shrill ring of the house phone somewhere downstairs. The buzzing had been not a fly against her window but her cell phone on her bedside table.

Darcy sat up straight with a gasp and kicked the blankets off so that she could look at her foot. It wasn't cut. Her right hand was cold as ever, particularly in her fingertips, but the coldness had not spread to cover any other part of her body. She scrambled out of bed and dashed across her room to yank open the door.

"Darcy?" her mom called up the stairs. "Are you up? Do you want—"

Darcy lost the next thing her mom said as she flew into the bathroom and slammed the door. She peered in the mirror at her eyes. They were grey, as always. She breathed a deep sigh of relief and slouched back against the linen closet door. It was only a dream.

She returned to her bedroom. Now that she was awake and lucid, she remembered having had this dream before. All year long, ever since her return from the world of Alitheia last summer, Darcy had been plagued with nightmares in which she discovered she had become a tsellodrin, one of the poor souls who sold themselves to Tselloch for eternal servitude. But she was one of the Six, who were prophesied to destroy the evil reign of Tselloch. She couldn't be a tsellodrin.

Couldn't you, though? her conscience whispered to her. *You reached out for him in the end. You gave up.*

Darcy shuddered and massaged the fingers on her right hand as the memory came flooding back to her.

The panther spun back around, and Darcy, for the first time, clearly saw Tselloch in its eyes. She scrambled weakly on hands and knees over to him. "I'll do it," she breathed. "I want to live." As Darcy reached toward him, she heard the sound of crashing and shouting. Human voices. They were coming for her! With a gasp, she snatched her hand back a second time, but it was too late. Her fingertips were damp; she'd just brushed the tip of the panther's nose before she'd taken her hand away. She was going to become one of them. "No! No, no, no!" she gasped over and over. She held her hand out in front of her like it was contaminated. It felt strangely cold and dead to the touch. "I take it back!" she cried. "I didn't mean it!"

Darcy's cell phone buzzed again against the wood of her bedside table and she jumped, her thoughts interrupted. She picked it up and turned it over. She had two new text messages, both from Sam.

R U up yet? read the first one. Darcy looked at her clock. It was not really seven-thirty, as it had been in her dream, but nine-thirty.

She read the next one. *Only 5 more days. Can't wait.* Darcy nodded her head and allowed a smile to lift her lips. She could almost feel Sam's excitement pulsating through her phone. If anyone was capable of helping her to break free of her dark thoughts, it was Samantha Palm.

She had never told Sam, or anybody else, about her moment of weakness in the dungeon beneath Ormiskos Castle last year. Nobody knew that Darcy had given in for the briefest of moments to the dark power that was Tselloch, so she didn't have anybody in whom to confide when it came to her nightmares and to her cold right hand. But Sam managed to be a comfort to her nonetheless.

That alone revealed the depth of Darcy's attitude change since the year before. A year ago Darcy would have said just about anything to get Sam to *stop* trying to be friends with her, but now Darcy clung to that friendship like the lifeline that it was. She had never had a real friend before Samantha.

And so she tried to reason as Sam would in her situation. *There's no use dwelling on it over and over again!* she chastised herself. *You can't change what you did.*

She texted Sam back. "Up," she muttered to herself as she worked the keypad. "Coming over?"

Her bedroom door banged open and Roger careened into the room. "Mom wants to know if you want french toast," he said.

Darcy hit send on her phone and looked up with a smile. "Absolutely."

CHAPTER 2

QUESTIONS WITHOUT ANSWERS

"I can't *believe* how much more excited I am to go to Cedar Cove this year than I've ever been before!" Sam waved her piece of bacon in the air for emphasis. "I didn't think it was possible for me to love it there any more than I already did, but I do. I *really* do!" She sat back against Darcy's footboard and shifted her plate of french toast and bacon to sit more comfortably on her crossed legs. "Good french toast, by the way. How does your mom make it?"

"Bacon fat," Darcy said, fixing her ponytail in the mirror above her dresser.

"Huh?"

"That's what she fries it in. She cooks the bacon first and then uses the grease to cook the toast."

"Oh. That seems a bit . . . fattening."

Darcy watched Sam's reflection in the mirror as the girl's round face fell and she regarded the piece of bacon in her hand as though it had betrayed her.

"It's a Southern secret. Everything tastes better when cooked in bacon fat." Darcy swung around and plopped down in her desk chair. "Come on, just eat it. It's french toast and bacon; it's not *supposed* to be good for you!"

"Yeah, I guess." Sam munched in thoughtful silence for a moment. "I *did* lose five pounds this year," she reminded Darcy with a full mouth.

"So you deserve a treat. Go hog wild. Get it? *Hog* wild. Bacon . . . hog . . ."

"Har har," Sam said, rolling her eyes.

"Darcy! Lewis is here!" Mrs. Pennington's voice sounded up the stairs.

"Just send him up!" Darcy hollered back.

A minute later Lewis Acres, who lived down the street and also traveled to Alitheia with them from Cedar Cove the year before, entered the room. Not much had changed about Lewis over the course of their eighth grade year other than the fact that he'd gotten new glasses. He was still rather short for his age, his mousy brown hair was cut in the same style, and he was still very introverted. One big change for him, however, was that he now had a friend in Darcy Pennington. A year ago he and Darcy had regarded each other with mutual dislike, he because he didn't like how Darcy treated Sam, and she because she did not want to be considered friends with the nerds at school, and Lewis and Sam were undeniably nerds.

Their year long sojourn in the alternate world, however, had forged Lewis and Darcy into tolerable acquaintances, and when they returned to their own world to relive their eighth grade year all over again, Darcy had determined that she didn't *care* if she was labeled a nerd at school; at least she finally had friends. Now the only real conflict between Darcy and Lewis was an ongoing quarrel over who was Sam's best friend.

"Hey, Lewis!" Sam chirped as he slid into the room and closed the door. He un-slung his backpack and went to sit on the edge of Darcy's bed.

"Only five more days, guys," he said, smiling.

"I know!" Sam squealed, bouncing. "Oh, by the way, that reminds me . . ." She put her plate down on Darcy's bedspread so she could fish her cell phone out of her pocket. "I heard from Amelia this morning. She is definitely not bringing Simon. Thank goodness. But she sent me a picture, look!"

Sam held up her phone so Darcy and Lewis could look at the tiny image of a boy on the screen. "Cute, huh?"

Darcy leaned forward to look at him. Simon was Amelia's seventeen-year-old boyfriend that she'd acquired as soon as she'd graduated from eighth grade. They had known each other for years through music classes, and he'd asked her out midyear. Her parents had agreed to let her date him on the provision that they waited until she was officially in high school. Amelia would be fifteen in August, so the difference in their age wasn't that great, but Darcy still thought it was weird. *Darcy's* parents would *never* let her date someone that old. But Amelia did act older than the rest of them, and she was very accomplished and mature; she already played five instruments—six including the lyre that she played in Alitheia—so maybe it was a good match.

The guy in the picture looked very thin and . . . artsy. He wore a fedora and had wavy hair that fell to his shoulders. A black vest over a tight V-neck T-shirt completed his look.

Darcy shrugged. "He's all right. I mean, if that's your type."

Lewis gave Sam a dry look as if to say, *"Why would I care what he looks like?"* Lewis had a talent for communicating without opening his mouth.

"I can't believe she was actually considering bringing him," Darcy said, sitting back. "I mean, what did she expect to do with him when we all went through the gateway? Lock him in her room?"

Lewis snorted, and Sam sighed. "Yeah, I don't know what she was thinking."

"She does realize, too, that she's going to be away from this guy for a year, right? A *year!* If I were her, I would have waited until after camp to get together with him."

"She's liked him for a long time, though," Sam said defensively. "I can't really blame her. Plus, *he* won't know she's been gone."

"Yeah, but she will. What if she doesn't like him anymore when we get back from Alitheia? That would be kinda awkward, wouldn't it?" Darcy chuckled as it struck her how nonsensical their conversation would sound to any outsider. All this talk of being gone for a year and reliving years over again was one of the more complicated side effects of their discovery of Alitheia the previous summer.

Cedar Cove, the summer camp that Darcy, Sam, Lewis, Amelia, and two other boys, Dean and Perry, attended with their families, had turned out to be far more special than any of them could ever have guessed. Nestled in the Upper Peninsula of Michigan, the camp contained a magical gateway to a world called Orodreos, of which Alitheia was just one kingdom—like America in relation to the rest of the world. Darcy, in her first week at Cedar Cove, had stumbled through the gateway and then returned to take the other teenagers back with her. The curious thing about the time difference, though, was that no matter how much time they spent in Alitheia, they always returned to camp at the exact same moment they left it.

"Hey, guys," Darcy said, "do you think the gateway is the only way to get to Alitheia?"

"What do you mean?" Sam asked, swallowing a bite of french toast.

"Well, you guys that have been going to Cedar Cove your whole lives kept saying last summer that you had always known there was something a little magical about the camp. And remember how the gnomes came to life at Gnome's Haven, in *our* world? How could there be any magic in our world at all if it had to come through the gateway? They told us in Alitheia that the gateway opened only for us and then closed again after we went through."

"Hmm . . ." Sam stuck out her bottom lip. "I guess I never really thought about it."

"It crossed my mind," Lewis murmured. He had pulled out one of his many notebooks from his backpack and was scribbling something intently, his nose just inches from the page.

"What made you think about it?" Sam asked, turning to him.

Lewis looked up and blinked once. "Colin," he replied.

Darcy nodded as Sam scowled. Colin Mackaby was the resident troublemaker during their week of camp. The same age as the rest of them, he was always in trouble for something at Cedar Cove, whether it was being accused of starting fires or just plain being creepy. He was far from being anybody's favorite person. To make matters worse, though, he had indicated that he knew they had traveled between worlds, and Darcy believed he might have been to Alitheia himself.

"*Colin*," Sam spat. Sam gave most everybody the benefit of the doubt, but she could never get over Colin's disrespect for the camp that was like a second home to her. "I obviously don't trust him, but he doesn't know anything. He was just trying to spook us."

Lewis's lips twitched downward in a disbelieving moue. Darcy agreed with him. Somehow, Colin Mackaby knew more than he should.

"Okay, but for the sake of argument," she said to Sam, "what if magical elements do get through from their world to our world without using the gateway? What does that mean for us? For the prophecy?"

The prophecy. Not only had Darcy led the other five teenagers into a new world, she had led them into a new destiny. Somehow, the six of them were supposed to work together to expel Tselloch and his minions from the land of Alitheia. They still didn't know exactly what that entailed but assumed they were supposed to find the gateways from Alitheia to Tselloch's world, lead him through one of them, and then destroy all the gateways behind him.

And then, when all of this was done, Darcy was supposed to marry the despicable boy prince Tellius, who would by then be the full and rightful king of Alitheia. It was a lot for a fourteen-year-old girl to process.

"I don't think it means anything for us or the prophecy," Lewis said.

"Really?" Darcy asked, sounding more sarcastic than she'd intended. "You don't think it's significant at all that magic can travel between the worlds without using the gateways? That possibly even *people* could?"

"We don't know that they can," he reminded her in a level tone. "If anything, I would say a few magical things here and there, maybe magical creatures, but people?" He shook his head.

"Why does it matter, anyway?" Sam asked Darcy.

Darcy sighed and closed her eyes. "I don't know. I was just thinking. I mean, what if they made a mistake and we're not even the ones the prophecy spoke of?"

Sam's jaw dropped. "Darcy! How can you even think that? We spent a whole year there. Our talents were revealed, our animals chose us, they—"

"Yeah, I know, I know. I'm sorry I said anything." Darcy waved her off. "I just don't want to—" She pursed her lips and looked at her nails.

"What?"

"You know . . . marry . . . Tellius," she mumbled.

Sam burst into giggles. "Is *that* what this is all about? You don't know that you're going to have to."

"It's in the prophecy, Sam."

"Yeah, but didn't Rubidius say something about Tellius having to 'declare you,' or something like that?"

Darcy shrugged. Rubidius, the master magician and alchemist in Alitheia, said a lot of strange things.

Sam looked at Lewis as if seeking help, but he was absorbed in his notebook, and it appeared that he wanted to stay that way.

They were all quiet for a moment.

Sam finally said, "I think we should just tell Rubidius that you're worried about people and things getting through without the gateway and see what he says about it. We certainly don't have any real answers of our own."

"You're right." Darcy looked up to find Sam watching her with worried eyes. She cracked a smile. "Lighten up, Sam. I'm not, like, second-guessing going to Cedar Cove this year. Just because I don't like *everything* about our time in Alitheia doesn't mean that I'm any less excited to go."

"Nah, of course I wasn't thinking that. You know . . ." Sam sat back and waved her hand, but she looked relieved.

"When everything really comes down to it," Darcy began seriously, and Lewis stopped writing to look up at her, "we are only fourteen years old, and we've already had more crazy experiences than most people have in their entire lives. How cool is that?"

Lewis nodded slowly, appreciatively, and Sam squealed, "I *know!* And there's only *five more days!*"

"Eeeeeeek!" Darcy let herself get drawn into Sam's girlish excitement. It was better that way.

CHAPTER 3

FINALLY THERE

Darcy's plaid suitcase was propped up beneath her window with her pillow and camera stacked on top of it. She shot a wry look at the camera. It would be great to take it to Alitheia, but she had an idea that it wouldn't work in the magical world.

She took one last look at the mirror above her dresser where she had a picture of herself and the other five teenagers taped in the upper corner. The picture was their group photo from last year, the first year that Darcy had attended Cedar Cove, and she still marveled at how much life had changed for her since then.

Her gaze traveled to her reflection. Straight, narrow nose, full lips, smattering of freckles, brown, wavy hair, and grey eyes. She looked a *little* older, she decided. Maybe Perry would notice her this year. She looked again at the photograph. Perry was on the end with his arm around Dean's shoulder. His head was tilted back as if he was trying to shake his blond hair out of his face, and he wore an easy smile. Darcy grinned just looking at him. But then she sobered. If Perry noticed *her* it would break Sam's heart.

It's not like she has dibs on him! she thought defiantly.

She turned away from the mirror to grab her stuff. It was early Saturday morning, and they had an eight-hour drive from their home in the suburbs of Chicago to the camp in upper Michigan. Her heart raced with anticipation as she took one last look around her bedroom. One week for her family, one year for her.

"Why, oh *why* did you eat that much for lunch, Roger?" Darcy groused at her brother. "What were you thinking?!"

Roger hung his head over the side of the road, his red curls hanging in listless strands as he emptied the contents of his stomach into the ditch. Sue Pennington, their mother, was hovering at his shoulder, and Allan, their father, was checking on some luggage that had shifted in the trunk of their van.

"He gonna be all right?" her dad called, shutting the hatch with a bang.

"He's fine," Darcy grumbled. "He's just carsick because he's an idiot and he ate three chili dogs for lunch!" They had stopped to eat at a fast food restaurant in Marinette, just on the border of Wisconsin and Michigan.

"Three *was* a bit much, Roger. I probably should have cut you off at two." Her dad put his hands on his hips.

"I was hungry!" Roger protested in a thin voice before another wave of sickness overcame him.

"Ugh, gross, Roger." Darcy huffed with impatience and climbed back in the van. They had been late getting out of the house that morning because Roger hadn't been fully packed, and now he was making them even later. Darcy checked her watch. What with all that, a long lunch break, and the time change, they would be lucky to make it to camp in time for dinner.

"We can stop in Logger's Head to get something for your stomach," her mom said, patting him on the back. "That's only about another half hour down the road."

"Mom, no!" Darcy whined, sticking her head out the door. "We're already so late!"

"Darcy, show a little sensitivity," her mom snapped at her. "How would you feel if it was you?"

"But it's not, because I'm not eleven years old and stupid," Darcy muttered, slouching back in her seat.

"What was that?" her mom called.

"Nothing!"

Darcy tried to focus on the serene shoreline of Lake Huron as she waited for Roger to get cleaned up. It was beautiful, and this year it was also *familiar*. She could see the deep gray of the water through breaks in the cedar growth, and wild daisies and black-eyed susans waved happily all along the highway. Sun-bleached rocks, patches of moss, and a dense grass that grew about two feet high completed the scene, with the occasional orange lily visible among the vegetation. Darcy couldn't wait to get out and dig her feet into the sand at Cedar Cove, to smell the air and laugh with Sam and the others about memories of the year before.

"Come *on*," Darcy muttered. She closed her eyes and leaned her head back against the seat.

After what felt like an eternity, movement on the seat next to her announced Roger's return. Darcy glared at him out of the corner of her eyes. At least he looked miserable; his myriad freckles stood stark against his pale skin.

"All set?" Her dad looked up from the map in the front seat as her mom buckled her seatbelt.

Yes, Darcy inwardly groaned, but she restricted herself to an outward eye roll.

"I'm good," Roger rasped.

Her dad started up the van and merged with ease back onto the highway. There wasn't much traffic in this neck of the woods.

"At least you didn't throw up in the car," Darcy grumped.

"*Bleh!*" Roger said, leaning over to pretend to throw up on her.

"Roger!" Darcy and her mom exclaimed simultaneously.

Roger bounced up and down and sat back, obviously starting to feel better.

As promised, they made a brief stop at the only general store in the tiny town of Logger's Head to purchase some pink bismuth tablets for Roger, but he didn't need them. Darcy glared at him. He was beginning to look as excited as Darcy was to get to camp. Although he did not have any otherworldly experiences from last year to make him more eager to be there, Darcy knew that he'd had a blast and had made some good friends. Regardless, it was already 6:15 p.m. Dinner had started fifteen minutes earlier, and it was all Roger's fault they weren't there yet.

Six miles down the road they finally broke even with the larger of the two bays at Cedar Cove. They had already passed the sign for the west side of camp, Mariner's Point, and the brown buildings and colorful sailboats were now visible about a mile out on the far edge of the arms of land that hugged the bay. That was the body of water they crossed in a ferry to visit Mariner's Point and hike some of the more remote trails, like the trail out to Whitetail Point . . . and to the gateway.

Darcy's face broke into a relieved smile at the sight; the sort that stretched from ear to ear and made her face feel a little goofy, but Darcy couldn't stop it. She felt new life coursing in her veins, as if she was returning, not to a place she had been to only once before, but to her real home . . . her heart's home.

"You look stupid," Roger said, poking her on the arm.

She punched him back, angry that he had interrupted her happy moment. "Shut *up*, Roger. You've done enough to screw things up today."

"Ow!" He yanked his arm out of her reach and sulked, his eyes to the floor.

A moment later gravel crunched beneath the tires of their van as their dad eased the vehicle onto the drive that led to the parking lot at Glorietta Bay, the east side of camp. They pulled into a parking space in the almost-full lot. Allan shut off the ignition and sat back with a sigh.

"We made it!" He turned around in his seat. "All right, kiddos, I want you to forget about unpacking for the moment. We're already late, so let's just get in for dinner."

He didn't have to tell Darcy twice. She was already halfway out of her seat by the time he turned off the car, and she slid open her side door and hopped down to the gravel the moment he finished speaking. She breathed deeply, taking in the smells of cedar and birch that reminded her both of the camp and of Alitheia, and she chuckled as she realized she was acting just like Sam had on their first day of camp the year before. She had thought that Sam was crazy then, but she understood now. "You were right, Sam," she murmured. "It's like no other smell on earth."

Darcy took two long strides toward the gray lodge building before she was stopped by her father's iron grasp on her arm. "You two go ahead," he called to his wife and Roger, "I want a quick word with Darcy."

Darcy turned shocked eyes on her father.

"Darcy," her dad began. He released her arm and looked down at her with stern eyes.

Darcy sighed deep in her chest. "What?"

"You need to be nicer to your brother."

"But he's so mean to *me!"* Darcy sputtered, indignant.

"You've had a very bad attitude with him today, and it's gotten him down. He looks up to you, and your treatment of him affects him very deeply, even if he doesn't show it."

Darcy rolled her eyes. "Dad—"

"I don't want to hear any excuses, Darcy." He held up his hands, palms out. "You're going into high school now and I expect a little more maturity out of you. I'm going to be watching this week to make sure that you treat him well, okay?"

"Fine." Darcy crossed her arms over her chest and avoided her dad's eyes, her mood plummeting.

"All right, then. Let's go eat." He put a hand on her shoulder and steered her toward the building. "Are you excited about this week?" he asked in an attempt at lightening the mood.

Darcy stared at him and he chuckled wryly. "Yeah, okay, stupid question. Just think, last year we dragged you here kicking and screaming, and this year . . ." He shook his head and regarded her with some bemusement.

Their feet made hollow echoing sounds on the planked wood as they crossed the walkway and entered the building. The lodge had its own wonderful sights and smells, enough to lift Darcy's spirits a little. She couldn't wait to get into the dining hall and see who they were sitting with.

Her dad stopped at the registration desk to make sure that his wife had checked them in, and Darcy left him behind. She quickened her pace as she crossed the sitting area outside the double doors to the dining hall. The doors were thrown open, and the happy sounds of chatting families and clinking cutlery wafted out.

Darcy tried not to skip as she crossed the tiled floor by the icemaker and drinking fountains. A few more steps brought her even with the kitchen and the potato bar. The room opened up before her, and she scanned the expanse for her friends.

About thirty families filled the heavy round tables interspersed around the room. The lake was visible beyond the porch through the wall of windows on the left side. Last year this sort of crowd would have made Darcy want to run and hide in a corner somewhere, but many of these people were no longer strangers; they were like family.

She grinned as she spotted Amelia, Dean, and finally Sam, whose family was at a table near the front. She waved at Sam when she caught her eye and then checked the chart pinned to a wooden post to find her family's table assignment. They were seated against the far wall.

"Where've you been?" Sam hissed at her when Darcy came near her chair.

Darcy rolled her eyes. "Don't ask. At least we made it!" She began to edge her way around Sam's chair, and Sam tried in vain to squish her chubby body in further. "I'll talk to you after dinner. I'm starving!"

A few people waved and greeted her on her way to her family's table, but she didn't see the one person that she *really* wanted to see: Perry. She thought with a rush that their families might be sitting together again, but her happy thought disintegrated when she reached her table.

Seated directly across from the open seat next to Roger was the one person she'd been dreading to see.

CHAPTER 4

DINNER WITH THE MACKABYS

Darcy thought Colin Mackaby would smirk at her or perhaps make some other sort of smart-alecky acknowledgement of her presence at the table, but he neither looked up nor spoke. He stared in sullen silence at his plate as he pushed around mashed potatoes with his fork. He'd added a streak of red to his dyed-black hair this year, she noticed. He still had the pale blue contact in his left eye, the skin around it bearing the green tinge of a bruise that had almost healed.

"What'd you do to your eye?" Darcy asked, annoyed that her curiosity got the better of her.

"What's it to you?" Colin spat, glaring at her.

She sat down very slowly, her defenses high, and jumped when her dad appeared next to her, his chair scraping as he pulled it out from the table.

"Hello!" he said with a bright smile, extending his hand to the well-dressed man next to Colin. "You must be the Mackabys. Lawrence, isn't it?"

"That's right," Colin's father shook hands with her dad.

"I don't think we had much chance to get to know each other last year," Mr. Pennington added. "This must be your wife . . ."

"Rebekah," Lawrence Mackaby spoke for her as she extended a thin hand first to Darcy's dad and then to her mom.

The contrast between Colin and his parents could not have been more striking. His father was powerfully built, tanned, and very blond, every hair on his head styled to perfection. He wore a button-down shirt and sport coat and an expensive-looking gold watch. When he opened his mouth to speak, Darcy could see that his teeth were perfectly white and straight.

Rebekah Mackaby seemed meek and tiny next to Lawrence. She was pretty, her dark brown hair pulled into a tight French twist, and she wore a white sundress with a blue cardigan knotted prep-style over her shoulders. A thick strand of pearls seemed to weigh down her thin neck.

The Mackabys tended to keep to themselves at camp, and Darcy didn't think that she'd seen his parents even once last year. Colin must have caught Darcy staring with incredulity at his parents because he snorted softly and shook his head.

"So, Lawrence, what do you do for a living?"

Darcy was aware that other words had been exchanged while she'd been observing them, but it wasn't surprising to her that this was one of the first questions out of her father's mouth. It seemed grown-up men always needed to know how other grown-up men made their money.

"I'm a real estate broker," Lawrence replied, pulling a card out of the inside pocket of his jacket and handing it across the table. "I mostly deal with high value property and land. In fact," he leaned forward and pasted on a smile, "there's some prime real estate up here that I'd love to get my hands on. Keeps me coming up here year after year, you know what I mean?"

"Oh? Is there a lot of money to be made on land up here?"

"Absolutely. That area of camp they call 'Paradise Cove?' I could make a fortune selling that off for condo development, but the camp won't sell."

"Hmm." Darcy's dad cleared his throat awkwardly, averting his eyes and focusing on his green beans.

"So what do you do?" Mr. Mackaby asked after a moment.

"I sell furniture," Allan said. "I own my own furniture surplus store. Actually, it's not all that different from what you do."

Mr. Mackaby forced a smile. "Oh, really?"

"Sure! You buy land off people to resell to others, and I buy surplus furniture off the big chain stores and resell it at a discounted price. You could say that I'm a broker of the furniture world!"

Allan Pennington looked amused at his own analogy, but Mr. Mackaby leaned back in his chair and appraised Darcy's father with narrowed eyes. Darcy's mom stared wide-eyed at her husband and made a noise in her throat as if she were about to laugh. Mrs. Mackaby just pursed her lips and stared at her plate.

Darcy dropped a dollop of potatoes on her plate and felt her ears grow warm with embarrassment. She wished somebody would change the subject, but nobody seemed to want to take the initiative. The silence at their table seemed to isolate them from the otherwise happy chatter in the dining hall. Darcy put a couple of slices of roast turkey and some gravy on her plate and decided to act like she didn't hear anything.

Mr. Pennington finally looked over at Colin and said, "That's quite a shiner you have there, son."

Colin nodded his head without lifting his gaze.

"Skateboarding, you know." Lawrence Mackaby seemed to come back to life. "I've tried to get him into more civilized sports, but you know teenagers."

Darcy shoveled food into her mouth, wanting to get out of there as quickly as possible and wishing now that her family had been just a little bit later and missed dinner entirely.

There was a faint buzzing and Mr. Mackaby reached down to his belt to pull out the newest touchpad phone on the market. "Ah," he said as he read the screen, "I've gotta take this. Please excuse me." He was slick and professional once again.

As Colin's dad walked out to the patio to take his call, Darcy's mom leaned forward to talk with Rebekah Mackaby, but from what Darcy could see, the woman said very little and played with her necklace the entire time. Once Mr. Mackaby was completely out of eyesight, Colin shoved away from the table and strode toward the back door of the dining room. He didn't even bother to clean off his plate before he left.

Mr. Pennington leaned over to Darcy and whispered, "Do you and your friends . . . spend much time with that Mackaby boy?"

Darcy snorted and green beans almost went up her nose. "Uh, not really, Dad," she whispered back, exasperated. She picked up her napkin and blew her nose.

"Mm-hmm. That might be best." His eyes followed Colin's black-clad form. "I don't know what sort of trouble he's into, but I don't want you anywhere near it."

"No problem!" Darcy assured him. She lowered her voice as far as it could go while keeping an eye on Mrs. Mackaby to make sure she was still engaged with her mom. "None of us like him, and he doesn't like us. We *never* hang out together."

"Fine . . . that's fine." Mr. Pennington returned to his plate. "Good turkey," he said.

Darcy tried to finish up quickly. People all over the dining hall were scraping off plates and finishing dessert bowls of chocolate cake, and Darcy's knot of excitement was returning to her stomach now that Colin and his father had left the table.

Sam appeared a few moments later and plopped down in Colin's vacated seat. Her face was flushed and her corn silk blond curls were mussed, but she still looked radiant to be at Cedar Cove.

"What took you so long? I expected you, like, an hour and a half ago!"

"Roger got carsick," Darcy answered, standing to scrape off her plate.

"Yuck!" Sam wrinkled her nose at Roger.

"*And* he wasn't ready to go this morning when everybody else was, and then we had a long lunch stop in Marinette. It was just . . . a crazy day."

"And then you got here and found out you had to sit with you-know-who," Sam said, lowering her voice.

Darcy sighed. "Tell me about it. I just keep thinking that at least we're here, and I'm not going to let one bad dinner ruin this experience." She finished cleaning her plate and looked around at her dad. "Can I have the car keys, Dad? I want to go get my stuff. Are we in the same room as last year?"

"Yep." Allan dug in his pocket and then handed her the keys. "Number six, across from the Palms." He winked at Sam.

"Darcy, be sure to get more than just your own suitcase," her mom said. "You can help with some of the other things."

"Yes, Mom," Darcy mumbled. She turned back to Sam. "Come on, walk with me."

As they edged out among the milling people, Darcy continued to look around for Perry. She still hadn't seen him. "Where's . . . everybody else?" she called to Sam over her shoulder. She didn't want to sound too interested in just Perry.

"I saw the boys leave about ten minutes ago. Lewis dropped by my table and said something about a new boat, so I bet they're out on the beach. And Amelia said that she would meet us in a few minutes; she had to run back to her cabin."

Amelia's family stayed not in the lodge, but in one of the more expensive cabins a little further in the woods, and Darcy wondered if Colin's family did, too.

They finally extricated themselves from the crowd and breathed a little easier as they crossed the sitting room and the lobby to get to the front doors. Sam kept shooting furtive happy looks at Darcy until Darcy laughed and asked, "What?"

"We're here!" Sam squealed.

Darcy laughed again. "Yeah, I know!"

"And in a few days we'll be *there*," Sam dropped her voice as they passed a couple with small children lugging in their belongings.

The knot in Darcy's stomach gave a lurch. "Yeah, I know," she breathed.

"Hey! Wait up!" Amelia's voice sounded behind them. "Sam! Darcy!" Her joyful smile illuminated her always-gorgeous face as she lithely jogged over to them and gave Darcy a quick hug around the shoulders.

"How are you?" She grinned at Darcy. "I can't believe how much I missed you this year. Did you see the picture of Simon that I sent? Oh, by the way, he says 'hi' and he's sorry that he couldn't come and meet everybody. Your hair's so long!"

Darcy laughed, unnerved by Amelia's greeting. Calm, collected, and usually aloof, Amelia was behaving more like Sam at the moment. "I'm good. What's up with you? *Your* hair looks great!"

Amelia's sandy blond hair was cut into a new, fashionable style with very heavy bangs. That, combined with her flawless skin, perfect teeth, and near six-foot height, made her appear more like a supermodel than ever. Darcy felt as though she and Sam must look like Tweedledee and Tweedledum next to Amelia.

"Oh, thanks," Amelia put a hand to her forehead. "It was kind of an impulsive decision."

She whispered the last few words as the family with the small children came back through for another trip to their car.

"Come on," Sam said, moving to follow the family. "Darcy and I were just on our way out to her car. Have you seen the guys?"

"Yeah, they're out at the dock looking at the new sailboat. Get this—" Amelia shot a knowing look at them. "It's called the *Cal Meridian*."

"The *Cal Meridian*?" Sam furrowed her brow. "But that sounds—"

"Alitheian, I know!" Amelia finished for her. "I wonder who named it."

"And how would they know?"

"Right, 'cause it would have to have a counterpart in Alitheia, too," Darcy added. "Wouldn't you think?"

"Definitely!" Sam bounced up and down as Darcy stopped and unlocked the doors of the van. "Oh guys, I'm *so* excited!"

"Here, take this." She handed Sam her suitcase and Amelia her mom's carrying case. She stacked her pillow on top of a bag of beach gear and shut and locked the van doors with a push of a button on the van's remote control.

"I wonder how many other things are like that around here that we've just never known about," Amelia mused, swinging the case back and forth as they returned to the lodge.

"We'll probably have more time to find out this year, since we won't have to be in hiding the whole time," Sam said.

"So we *think*," Darcy said, holding the door for them, "but we don't know that for sure. I mean, what's happened there since we left? They've had another year of their own!"

While earth time stood still when the six teenagers were in Alitheia, time continued to move forward in the magical land while the Six were away. So when they returned, their Alitheian friends would be one year older than when they'd left the year before, and anything could have happened during that year.

"We won a major victory last year, though. I can't imagine that Tselloch has regained his place in the castle. He's probably still hiding away in the forest somewhere with his tail between his legs," Amelia said, dismissing Darcy's concern.

Darcy was quiet. She disagreed with Amelia. The idea that Tselloch—the Shadow—could ever have his tail between his legs was absurd to her but, of course, she was the only one of the Six to have actually met him. She knew first-hand the strength of his charisma and his power. With a wave of his hand he had shown Darcy an alternate reality, and with a touch he had changed something physical in her that she didn't understand. He could take on many appearances, but in each one he was the embodiment of shadow, and he was anything but timid. The coldness in her right hand gave a sudden throb, and she shifted the weight of the bag she was carrying, her stomach feeling uneasy.

Together the three girls climbed the stairs in the lodge to the upper landing and turned down the hall to Darcy's room. Once there, they flipped on the light and dumped everything in the middle of the floor. The camp staff had left the two wood-side windows open, filling the room with the earthy scent of the forest.

Darcy inhaled, enjoying the familiar smells, and went to one of the windows to look out. It was just like the view from the room they'd had in the castle of Ormiskos in Alitheia, except instead of looking down on a castle courtyard, she saw a grassy field with picnic tables, a fire pit, and a dinner bell spread out below her. The trusty old camp swing-set abutted the tree line, and a movement near it drew her gaze.

She took a sharp breath. It was Colin Mackaby. He was standing facing the woods by a rear leg of the swing-set, gesturing with his hands and shaking his head. Darcy squinted, but she could make out only a dim form in the trees. It was someone very tall, but she couldn't quite make out his features because he must have been standing in a pocket of . . . shadow.

The man in the trees put a hand on Colin's shoulder, but it looked all wrong, like it was see-through. Darcy's heart gave a lurch of fear as her mind alighted on the impossible. But *he* didn't exist in their world; he *couldn't* exist in their world . . .

Her right hand had become so cold that it burned, and Darcy jerked and grabbed it with her left hand. Colin's head jerked up as though he had heard something, and he turned very deliberately and looked up at her window. Darcy gasped and dropped out of sight.

"Darcy?" Sam said. "Are you okay? What's wrong?" Her face registered alarm as she rushed to Darcy's side.

Amelia frowned. She turned away from the mirror where she had been playing with her hair and went to the window. "It's Colin," she muttered, staring down. "Idiot. What's he doing skulking around down there?"

"Is he alone?" Darcy asked.

Amelia shot her an odd look. "Yeah. Why?"

Darcy suddenly felt very foolish crouched on the floor beneath the window. Amelia didn't see anything unusual; Darcy's nerves must be getting to her, that's all. It hadn't been Tselloch in the woods; it couldn't have been. Colin had just found another camp friend as dark and creepy as he was. Good for him.

She stood up carefully, trying to act cool while her heart began to slow down. "Yeah, I . . . uh . . . was looking around down there and saw him staring at me. I just got startled, you know?" She laughed, but it sounded unconvincing in her ears.

"Sure," Sam said consolingly. "Was he a jerk to you at dinner?"

"No. He, um, actually didn't say anything to me at all." Darcy's hands were shaking, and she couldn't seem to make them stop. She jammed them into her pockets. "Are you sure he's alone down there?"

"Yeah. Well, he was." Amelia turned away from the window. "He's gone now."

Sam narrowed her eyes at Darcy. "Are you *sure* you're okay?"

"Yes." Darcy nodded and forced her lips into a smile. "I just got spooked, that's all. Colin creeps me out. Come on." She pulled her hands out of her pockets and held up the van keys. "Let's go give these back to my dad."

CHAPTER 5

THE TAIL

"So *that's* why they keep coming!" Amelia exclaimed with contempt, sitting back and hitting the pillows with her fist. "Colin's dad wants to get his grubby little paws on the land out at Paradise Cove!"

It was Sunday morning after breakfast, and the six of them had gathered in the library at the Stevenson Center, the recreation hall at camp. The library was a cozy loft above the Sticky Branch camp store and the game room on the main floor. Low bookshelves crammed with old books were built into the walls, and two alcoves with window seats overlooked the boardwalk. The rest of the room was filled with ratty wood-framed couches and chairs with faded royal blue cushions from the 1970s, and low tables with games spread out on them. The room was very warm and smelled of old paper and musty fabric.

Dean snorted. "Figures, really, Colin's a weasel; why wouldn't his dad be one, too?"

"You don't think that he will, though, do you?" Sam's anxious gaze flitted from one face to the next. "You don't think the camp will sell it to him."

"Nah." Perry leaned forward and twirled a piece of beach grass between his fingers. "All this land was purchased by the founders years and years ago. It *is* probably worth a fortune now, but they'll never sell."

Sam seemed a little mollified by his words. His family had been coming longer than the rest of theirs, since before he was even born, so she considered him something of an expert on the camp.

"What do you think would happen in Alitheia if they sold off that land and it got developed?" Darcy wondered aloud.

"Nothing." Perry looked up at her and her heart jumped. "I mean, it's a parallel world with Cedar Cove, but that doesn't mean that *everything* has to be exactly the same."

He sat back in his armchair, and Darcy stared at him for the umpteenth time that day. He had changed a lot since last summer. He was taller and broader in the chest and shoulders, and he'd cut his golden blond hair into a European-soccer-chic faux-hawk that made him look like a TV star. Even though the summer was still young, he was already tanned, as though he spent every day at the beach, and his blue eyes were piercing beneath his dark lashes. Darcy thought he was the best-looking guy she had ever known in real life. She tried to shake herself out of it as he raised a questioning eyebrow under her perusal.

Her ears burned red, and she continued with her thought. "Yeah, but a lot of the buildings are in the same place. You know, Ormiskos Castle is built right where the lodge is, and Kenidros Castle is built where the lodge is at Mariner's Point."

Perry shook his head. "I still don't think it would matter."

"Don't you *care* that he's trying to buy off that land?" Sam shot at him, sounding hurt.

"Of course I do!" he protested. "I just don't really want to talk about this right now. Why are we spending so much time on the Mackabys? Don't we have more important things to be discussing?" He raised his eyebrows at them.

"What's left to discuss?" Amelia said from the window seat. "We've already decided that we're not going to try to get through the gateway until this afternoon." They had, indeed, agreed it made the most sense to imitate their actions from the year before to get back through the gateway to Alitheia.

Now that their departure was imminent, Amelia's attitude had reverted to something closer to her normal self. As much as Darcy knew she was excited to return to Alitheia, it was undeniable that Amelia was a homebody and would probably suffer more homesickness than anybody else.

She seemed very pensive now, running the treble clef charm Simon had given her back and forth across her necklace chain. Darcy felt sorry for her, but she knew Amelia would snap out of it once they got to Alitheia and got settled in.

"I just wish we knew a little more about what we're supposed to do. They didn't exactly give us any instructions, did they?" Perry asked.

"We didn't ask, either," Dean said. He rubbed a hand over his army-style buzz cut. Like Perry he was taller and broader, but other than that, almost unchanged. He dropped his hand to rub at a spot on one of his army boots.

"It's him," Amelia said suddenly. She was looking out at the boardwalk.

"Who?" Sam asked.

"Colin," Amelia replied. "He looks like he's looking for somebody."

Perry sighed and went to the window. "Should I . . . you know . . ." He turned his backside to the glass and hooked his thumb into the waist of his shorts.

"No!" Darcy, Sam, and Amelia all cried at once.

Amelia scrambled to get away from him. "Gross! Why would you even suggest that?"

Dean howled with laughter as Perry looked over his shoulder and grinned. "I was just kidding!" He turned back to the window and rapped on it with his knuckles. "Oy! Up here!" His grin widened devilishly. "He's looking up," he said to his friends, then, "Oop! He's coming inside . . . I think he might be . . . yeah . . . Shoot!" He turned around and shot an apologetic look at all of them just as they heard the door to the stairs open and close.

"Why did you do that?" Amelia hissed at him.

"Why's he coming up here?" Sam whispered.

"He wouldn't be if Perry wasn't so stupid!" Amelia hissed back.

"Just act normal," Perry snipped.

They abruptly cut off their frantic, whispered conversation as Colin's head appeared at the top of the stairs. Like a spider stalking a wounded fly, he crept the rest of the way up and into the room.

For a long, uncomfortable moment they stared at him, and he at them. His gaze lingered especially long on Darcy, and she looked away, refusing to gratify him with her attention.

Finally, Perry asked, "What do you want?" His tone was cold.

"*You* invited me up here," Colin replied with a self-satisfied smirk.

"That wasn't an invitation. You're not wanted here, so why don't you leave?"

Colin was unfazed by Perry's rudeness. He gave a deep, fake sigh and began to move around the edges of the room. "My, my, what should I read?" he asked in the exaggerated tone of an actor on a stage, perusing the bookshelves as he went.

"How about *101 Ways to Make People Not Like You*?" Perry quipped, his gaze sweeping over Colin's head-to-toe black ensemble.

Dean sniggered behind his hand, but Darcy shifted, uncomfortable. She wished that Perry would just drop it and ignore him. Maybe he'd go away if nobody said anything else to him.

"Noooo . . ." Colin drew out the word and continued his walk around the room. "I think I'd rather read something *magical*, or *prophetic* even. You never know when a book like that could come in handy."

Sam squeaked and put her hand over her mouth, and Lewis's face went pale. Darcy stared at the carpet as her blood pounded in her ears. She tucked her right hand under her thigh.

Perry stood up, clenching his hands into fists, his mouth set in an angry line. There was nothing mocking in his demeanor any more. “Leave. Leave now, or I’ll make you leave.”

Dean stood next to Perry and crossed his arms over his chest, lending his unspoken support.

“All right, all right,” Colin said, holding his hands up in mock defeat. “No need to be so . . . *cold*.” He leaned over Darcy’s chair and breathed the last word in her face, his gaze boring into hers.

She instantly remembered what Colin had said the year before, just after the Six had returned through the gateway to Cedar Cove. *“I know what you did. You won't ever forget.”*

Perry made a move toward him, and he leapt back with a laugh. He skirted around the two boys and slinked down the stairs. They listened in silence as the door opened and closed.

“He’s gone,” Amelia announced. “Off into the woods.” She sat back from the window and looked at Darcy. “Don’t let him get to you so bad, Darcy! He’s just a creeper.”

“Yeah . . . just a creeper,” Sam said, biting her lip, a slight tremble in her voice.

Darcy touched a hand to her forehead; she was sweating. Everyone was staring at her now with mixed levels of concern on their faces.

“Hey, Darcy, I’m sorry!” Perry said. He came over and gave her a one-armed hug. “I didn’t mean for him to come up here. I wouldn’t have done it if I’d known how much he bothers you, honest.”

Entirely different emotions started charging through Darcy as Perry lingered with his arm around her. She glanced at Sam, who looked away, and she felt immediate guilt. She took a shaky breath. “It’s all right. I don’t know what his deal is with me.”

Lewis opened his mouth to speak, his eyebrows knit together and his face still white as a ghost, but Amelia cut him off.

“Let’s just shake it off and try to have fun,” Amelia said, standing and stretching. “It’s a gorgeous morning. We have a couple of hours left before lunch. Why don’t we hike out to the nature center? We should probably kick back a little before we, you know, travel to another world and all,” she finished wryly.

“That’s a good idea,” Perry agreed, and they all nodded.

They filed down the stairs, past the life jackets hanging in the stairwell, and out into the cool sunshine of upper Michigan.

They tried to relax and have fun, but it was in vain. Wherever they went, Colin Mackaby was close behind. He made his presence known while staying out of range of Perry and Dean's fists, and he seemed to enjoy his little game. *If it* is *a game*, Darcy thought and shivered.

"So, what?" Perry exclaimed when Colin followed them out to the rocky shoals. "Has he made it, like, his personal mission to make our lives miserable?" He skipped a rock out into the water and shot a dark look at Colin's form hovering at the edge of the lake about fifty yards away.

"I bet I could bean him in the head from here," Dean said, weighing a rock in his hand.

"At least we can lose him when we go to Alitheia," Lewis muttered.

"Yeah, well, that's going to be pretty difficult, isn't it, with him tailing us all day."

"We'll figure something out," Amelia said.

"All I can say is, if he tries to get creepy with Darcy again, I really *am* going to punch him in the face!" Perry growled.

Darcy hid her smile behind her hand. She didn't know why he was acting so chivalrous toward her, but she liked it. Sam, she noticed, was being much quieter than usual.

The sound of the lunch bell echoed out over the water, and the six teenagers headed in. Colin melted into the trees, and Darcy prayed that he would skip lunch.

He didn't. In fact, he spent the entire lunch hour staring right at Darcy, and she spent the same hour steadfastly ignoring him. When the camp administrator—a tall, kind-faced man with a bushy mustache—stood up to pitch some books that were for sale at the Sticky Branch, Darcy watched him with the rapt attention of an A-plus student on the first day of school. While Mr. Mackaby prattled on to her dad about the economy and stock market prices, she nodded along as though she were interested, and when Sam signaled her from across the room, she excused herself to go to the bathroom with a surge of relief.

Amelia and Sam pulled her into the small restroom and told her the plan in whispers.

"We decided how we're going to ditch Colin after lunch," Sam breathed.

"Okay . . . do the boys know?"

"It was Dean's idea," Amelia said.

Darcy laughed. "Yeah, that makes sense. I suppose he knows a thing or two about sneaking around. So what's the plan?"

"We're each going to leave at a different time." Sam looked at her watch. "Lewis should be on his way out now. He volunteered to go first. He's going to meet Dean in ten minutes at the ferry dock and take the first ferry over to the other side. You and I are going to go next and catch the 1:30 ferry, and then Amelia and Perry will come last on the 2:00 ferry."

"If we split up, we might confuse him," Amelia explained.

Darcy sincerely doubted that and figured Colin would follow her and Sam, but she decided to be optimistic and agreed to the plan.

Darcy returned to the dining room, sat back down at the table and smiled. Colin's seat was empty. Maybe he *would* leave them alone that afternoon. She was going to meet Sam at the rec hall at 1:15 and then hike down to the ferry. She glanced at the clock, scraped off her plate, and looked over at Sam's table. She looked just about ready to go.

"Dad," Darcy said loudly to catch his attention. "Me, Sam and the others are going to take the 1:30 ferry over to Mariner's Point to hike to Gnome's Haven. Is that all right?" she asked, knowing her dad would say yes.

"Gnome's Haven?" Roger interjected. "I want to go! Can I come, too?"

Darcy shot a withering look at her little brother. "No," she snapped.

"Darcy." Allan Pennington's eyes narrowed. "Remember what we talked about."

"But, Dad, it's just me and my friends! Nobody else is going to have their little brothers or sisters with them."

"But I really want to go!" Roger whined. "Please, Dad? Can I please?"

"Dad!" Darcy protested. He couldn't possibly say yes.

Mr. Pennington looked from Darcy to Roger as if weighing his options and then sighed. "Well, how about this: Roger and I *both* come along, and we'll stay far enough away from you not to cramp your style. How does that sound?"

Awful! Darcy stared at her dad with a pained look on her face, but he was undaunted.

"Come on, Roger. Let's get our hiking shoes on and meet Darcy and her friends at the dock." He took his son by the shoulder and steered him away from the table.

Roger looked back over his shoulder and stuck his tongue out at Darcy.

Now what are we going to do?

Darcy made her way very slowly down the boardwalk and into the Stevenson Center. She didn't even flinch when she saw Colin lurking in the far corner of the game room. Sam met her at the door and nodded in Colin's direction, her eyes grim.

"Yeah, I see him. It's worse, though," Darcy said. "My *dad* and *Roger* are coming."

Sam frowned. "Really? That's . . . that's . . ."—her eyes took on a strange, funny little gleam—"that's great!"

"Wait, what?"

Sam turned to her and grasped her arm. "Think about it! If your dad is with us, there's no way Colin's going to follow us all the way out to Whitetail Point. He's not *that* bold!"

"I guess so." Darcy didn't think that it was *that* great. Now they had to get through the gateway without her dad or Roger noticing, although . . . it was better than Colin. She had an inkling it would be a bad thing for Colin to find out where the gateway was.

Sam was so excited that she even looked at Colin and waved brightly, then she grasped Darcy's arm and spun her out the door. "Come on. If we hurry, we can get Amelia and Perry and all go out together." She broke into a jog. "They're hanging out at Amelia's cabin."

Ten minutes later they, along with Amelia, Perry, Mr. Pennington, and Roger, stepped onto the floating pontoon boat that was the camp ferry. Just before they pushed off from the dock, Colin Mackaby, too, stepped on board. Colin stayed in the far corner away from them, and Darcy noticed with satisfaction that he seemed put off by the presence of her father.

The breeze playing on their faces as they motored across the bay was cool, and Darcy enjoyed it with closed eyes.

"I'm gonna push him in the lake!" Perry muttered, snapping a twig between his fingers. Darcy opened her eyes and looked at him, but he was watching Colin.

"Don't do anything stupid," Amelia said out of the corner of her mouth. She glanced up at Mr. Pennington and smiled. She, too, felt it was *great* that he had come along.

"I'm really glad you're coming with us, Mr. Pennington," Sam said over the sound of the wind.

"Oh," he looked at her, surprised. "Well, thanks, Sam. Roger and I didn't get out to Gnome's Haven last year. We'll stay out of your way, though."

"Don't worry about that," Sam grinned at him, "really!"

She was talking so loud that Darcy's dad looked askance at her, but Darcy knew it was for the benefit of their tail. She snorted and shook her head. What if the gnomes wouldn't come to life while her dad and Roger were around? What if they couldn't get through unless they were alone? It wouldn't be so *great* to have them along then.

The ferry pulled up to the dock at Mariner's Point, and they all disembarked. Sam thanked the ferry driver, and they headed in toward the brown building that housed the rec hall on that side of camp. Dean and Lewis were sitting in two Adirondack chairs outside the building, and they frowned when they saw the large group that had gotten off the ferry.

"Hey, guys!" Sam said brightly. "Mr. Pennington and Roger are going to hike with us."

"Okay," Lewis said, his gaze questioning. He looked at Darcy, and she shrugged.

Dean stood and put his hands into the front pocket of his army sweatshirt. "Sounds good to me." His eyes traveled from Darcy's dad to Colin and back again. Understanding lit his face and he grinned. "It will be nice to have you along, sir," he said.

Colin scowled at them. He had remained a short distance away by the docks, and he hovered for a moment, poised in indecision.

Darcy's dad glanced at him over his shoulder, and Colin turned on his heel and took off walking toward the staff cabins that lined the inner bay.

"Well, I have to say," Darcy's dad said dryly as he looked at the six of them, "you all are very accommodating. Much more than Darcy, in fact." He put a hand on Roger's shoulder. "If you're ready, we'll follow you!"

Chapter 6

"Follow Me"

The forest was hushed. Hiking the trail out to Whitetail Point was like walking through a medieval cathedral during mass. Once they got through the body of camp and across the narrow isthmus that connected what would be an island to the shore, the trees closed in like ranks of soldiers, carpeting the path with fallen needles and causing the light that filtered through their high branches to be tinted green. All sounds, like the buzzing of insects, calls of birds, and occasional rustles in the underbrush seemed far away, as though muffled by the sanctity of the trail.

It *did* feel like a religious experience to Darcy, hiking back to find the gateway that would lead them into another world. She found that she couldn't even be too bothered by the presence of her father and brother, who walked about ten paces back from them on the trail. The atmosphere even served to hush Roger up. He was staring around him with his mouth agape as her dad pointed out various fauna and wildlife to him in near whispers.

None of the teenagers spoke. Amelia, walking at Darcy's side, looked deep in thought and kept stumbling over tree roots. Perry and Dean led the way with Lewis just a step behind, and Sam trailed a few feet behind Darcy. Darcy looked over her shoulder and tried to catch Sam's eye, but Sam was staring longingly at the back of Perry's head and didn't notice.

The silence could have been uncomfortable, but it wasn't. What could they say with Darcy's dad just behind them? And what was there *left* to say? Together the six teenagers had canvassed every Alitheian-related topic imaginable over the course of the year through phone calls, text messages, and Internet communications. All that was left for them to do was to get back to Alitheia and see what had changed while they were gone.

They reached the branch in the path where a sign with a little gnome painted on it pointed them down to the enormous boulder that housed Gnome's Haven. The six of them took to the new path without a word, but Mr. Pennington paused at the sign.

"Huh. That's cute," he said. "You see that, Roger?"

"Yeah, it's great, Dad. Come on, I want to keep up with Darcy!"

Darcy rolled her eyes as she heard her brother's tennis shoes thump up the trail toward her.

"You're supposed to be hiking with Dad," she reminded him without looking back.

"I *was* hiking with Dad. He's boring. I want to hike with you," Roger replied. "How come you guys are so quiet? How much further 'til Gnome's Haven?"

Darcy ignored the first question as they rounded a bend in the trail, and she stepped back to let her brother see. "We're there, look."

The boulder towered over their heads. Every nook and cranny was filled with rocks that college campers had painted over the years with the likenesses of little gnomes. A small sign near the rock advised to "Please leave the gnomes in their homes." Cedar trees grew from the top of the boulder, and the far side of it had sloughed off to form an area good for sitting after the long hike. The surf hitting the rocky shoals sounded from somewhere over to the right, where the trees broke to reveal that they were on an embankment about six feet above the rocky shoals and water line. An old cedar tree had fallen sometime between last year and this one, forming a sort of bridge between the sheared-off part of the rock and the beach beneath it. Someone brave enough to risk the scratches could shimmy down the trunk of the tree to the water below.

"Oh *cool!"* Roger exclaimed. He stared up open-mouthed at the boulder.

Darcy left him standing there and joined her friends by the fallen tree. "Okay," she whispered to them. "What now?" She shot a furtive look back at her brother.

"We need to distract them somehow," Perry said. "Do you think you can get your brother to climb the rock?"

Darcy snorted. "Are you kidding me? He'd love to; I'm just not sure about my dad . . ."

"I've got it, leave it to me," Perry said after a moment. "You guys start to look for gnomes that might, you know, come alive or something." He winked at them and strode over to her dad, who was perusing the rock with his hat pushed back on his head.

"You know, Mr. Pennington," Perry began in a smarmy voice, "there's a tradition out here."

"Oh, really? What's that?" Darcy could tell from her dad's tone that he was merely humoring him, but Perry either couldn't tell or didn't care, so he pushed on.

"The first time that you visit Gnome's Haven, you have to climb it."

"Is that so?" Mr. Pennington sounded amused.

"Ooh, really?" Roger bounced up and down on the balls of his feet. "Can I? Can I, Dad? Please?"

"And I suppose the camp approves of this activity?" Mr. Pennington continued, waving off his son.

Perry grinned. "Well, it's sort of off the record, you know."

"Ah, of course."

"Come on, guys," Sam hissed at the rest of them. "We're supposed to be looking for gnomes, remember?"

They scattered, each taking a different facet of the rock, searching for a gnome that looked more than painted on.

Darcy knew which gnome to check on: Brachos. But his spot was positioned right where her dad was standing. She made her way in that direction, trying hard not to look suspicious.

"All I'm saying is," Perry was continuing his argument undaunted, "if you want to be considered *true* Cedar Cove campers, you'll have to do it."

Darcy sidled up next to her dad and peeked behind him. The cleft where Brachos's rock usually sat was empty. She felt an electric jolt and straightened very carefully to find her dad looking down at her with a puzzled expression.

"Can I help you, Darcy?"

In her effort to see behind him, she'd gotten so close that her arm was almost brushing his. "Umm . . ." She gave him a goofy little smile. "Nah, it's nothing I just . . . I—I love you, Dad," she said with serious affection, leaning in and giving him an impulsive hug. "Just wanted to tell you that."

He didn't buy it. He patted her on the arm and pulled her off him. "What's up, Darcy?"

"Nothing. I was just *looking* for something, but it's *not there right now*," she raised her eyebrows at Perry as she tried to communicate her silent message.

A little crease appeared between Perry's eyebrows, and he gave his head a slight shake. He didn't get what she was trying to say.

Luckily for them, Roger had taken advantage of his father's lapse in attention to begin to scale the monumental boulder. He was already about five feet off the ground, and it wasn't until he dislodged a shower of dirt with his shoe that Mr. Pennington turned around to see him.

"Roger! Come on, now, I didn't say that you could do that."

"I promise I'll be careful," Roger said, moving his right hand up to another hold. "Perry said I could do it."

"Perry is not in a position to give you permission to do anything."

Roger continued his ascent. "It's not that steep!"

"Regardless, it's still dangerous."

"Come up with me, Dad. Unless you're too *old*—"

Mr. Pennington's chest swelled. "Hey—I am *not* too old. You're talking to a former baseball player here."

Darcy and Perry watched this interchange with bated breath. If Roger could just convince her dad to climb, they'd have the distraction that they needed. *Come on, Dad . . . you can do it!* Darcy urged him on in her mind.

Finally, Mr. Pennington sighed and took off his baseball cap, setting it down on a tree root and rolling up the sleeves of his flannel shirt. "All right, you two," he said, "I'm going to head up and make sure Roger doesn't hurt himself. Don't take off until we come back down." He looked hard at Darcy. "That would hurt Roger's feelings."

"Sure thing, Dad," Darcy said as a nervous, guilty knot twisted in her belly.

She and Perry watched her dad start to climb. They helped him find a few footholds and then stood in tense silence until he was just out of immediate earshot.

"Okay, what?" Perry said, turning to her just as she turned to him and said, "Brachos is gone!"

"Is that good or bad?" Perry said.

"It's good! It means that he's alive somewhere around here."

The other four teenagers joined them.

"We heard your dad say he was going to climb," Sam whispered. She looked up and called, "You're doing good, Mr. Pennington!"

He waved a distracted hand at her and didn't look down.

Darcy didn't waste any time in telling the others about Brachos. "And we've only got a few minutes before they finish looking around up there and start back down," she said. The top of Gnome's Haven was not very spacious, and her dad was just disappearing over the edge. "Come on, guys, think! Where would he be?"

"Let's listen for him," Lewis suggested.

They fell silent, straining their ears, but there were no sounds of madcap giggling, pattering feet, or rustling underbrush to be heard. They waited and waited. Nothing.

Amelia let out a huff. "We can't have come out here for nothing. Why won't he show himself? Should we head into the woods, closer to the gateway? Didn't we mark it last year?"

"No, remember? We tried, but we couldn't remember which two trees it was between." Darcy shook her head. The shimmer that had betrayed the existence of the gateway had been gone by the time they'd come back to mark it.

Perry kicked a rock with his toe. "This stinks," he muttered. He crossed his arms and looked up. "I think they're coming back down."

Darcy could hear her brother grunting as he swung his legs over the edge to begin his descent, but she didn't look up. She looked instead at the spot where Perry had kicked the rock. The ground looked strange there, as though he had made a hole in a pattern.

She took a step back and tilted her head to get a better angle. "Guys . . ." she breathed, trailing off. She took two more steps back and squinted. "I think there's a message here for us."

"Huh?" Sam looked at her and then down at the ground.

"There, see?" Darcy pointed. "Where that rock was that Perry kicked, there are a bunch of other rocks there. Doesn't that look like a capital 'F'?"

"There are a lot of rocks on the ground, Darcy. I think it's just a coincidence," Amelia said.

"No, Darcy's right!" Sam said. "I can see it now! There are letters. The rocks are lighter than the rest, you see? Each letter is about a foot long . . ."

"The next letter's an 'O,' " Lewis said. "They lead into the woods."

They moved as a group, huddled over the mysterious letters on the ground.

"Here's an 'L,' " Darcy exclaimed. "No—two 'L's!"

"And an 'O' again." Lewis looked around for the next one and took two steps further into the underbrush. "A 'W,'" he proclaimed, "and then an 'M' and an 'E.' I can see them from here."

" 'F-O-L-L-O-W-M-E,' " Sam spelled out. " '*Follow me.*' " Her face was flushed with excitement. "Follow me," she said again. "Follow who? I don't see any gnomes. Darcy?"

"I don't know!" Darcy looked around wildly; she took a few steps toward Lewis, staring at the second word, and then she saw it: a red squirrel. There were many red squirrels in the forests of upper Michigan, so it was not uncommon to see one, but it *was* odd for one to sit so still. And Darcy could swear that she'd seen this particular squirrel before, one year ago.

It was perched on one of the rocks in the "E" of "ME," and it was staring at her with rapt attention. It didn't move when Darcy hunkered down before it and peered into one of its beady eyes. "Are we supposed to follow you?" she asked.

The squirrel gave a slow, deliberate nod and twitched its tail. Darcy stood and grinned at the others. "It's the squirrel. We need to follow the squirrel!"

"Hey! Where are you guys going?" Roger shouted at them. He was nearly at the bottom of the rock, trying to find his last foothold while craning his neck to see them several feet off in the trees.

"Darcy?" Mr. Pennington's voice sounded from a little bit farther away.

"Go!" Darcy hissed at them, stepping back so she could head off her family. The other five darted into the trees after the squirrel, who took off with a bound. "Um, I'll be right back, Dad! I promise!" she shouted. He was nowhere near the bottom, but Roger's feet were firmly on the ground, and he started after her.

She had no choice. It was now or never. She took off after her friends, ferns slapping her legs, and she could hear her brother trying to keep up.

"Wait, Darcy!" Roger shouted, but she ignored him.

The red squirrel took a flying leap between two trees and disappeared. Darcy could see now the shimmering white strands between the two cedar trunks that looked almost like a spider's web. Her friends disappeared one after the other. Sam turned an anxious face in her direction to make sure she would make it and then plunged ahead.

Darcy was almost there. At the base of one of the two trees stood Brachos the gnome, ushering them through in his little brown trousers and blue jacket. He tipped his red pointed hat at her with a wink and gave her a salute. Darcy had no time to linger; she stepped through the gateway in a single stride.

Just as she left her world, she saw Brachos keel over and lie on the ground, just a gnome painted on a slab of rock once again.

Chapter 7

A Different Alitheia

It was like turning the dial on a radio. One second Darcy could hear her brother shouting and chasing her; the next second the sounds of his pursuit cut off and were replaced by the exultant exclamations of her friends. They had made it into Alitheia.

Sam was staring around the forest with happy tears in her eyes. As Darcy came toward her, Sam threw her arms around Darcy's shoulders in a bone-crushing hug.

They weren't the only ones in the clearing. Three individuals, each of unquestionable Alitheian origin, stood greeting those who had gone through the gateway first. One of them was the human Torrin, his dress and appearance showing his profession as scout and soldier. He had a very familiar face, as he'd been the first Alitheian Darcy had met last year. He was a little bit better groomed this year than last, however. His brown cloak was neither torn nor stained, and his once-shaggy brown hair was clean and slicked back from his face, rather than hanging in a ratty mess. His blue eyes shone clearly from his tanned skin, and the hand that held his bow was relaxed. Darcy assumed his stately appearance must be due to the princes that he served being no longer in hiding, but as they were now out in the open as the ruling power in the land, Torrin was also no longer a rebel.

The other two Alitheians were quite different indeed, marked with an air of otherness even as most of their features looked human. These were narks, sort of elf-like creatures in Alitheia. Darcy was thrilled to see her friend Yahto Veli in the clearing. She had gotten to know a great deal about narks from him the year before. Each nark body was inhabited by two beings, a night nark and a day nark, which was also why each nark had a double name. Day narks were fair skinned and blond, with light blue or grey eyes, and their names were the second of the two. At the moment the sun set each day, however, day narks went to sleep. In the brief lapse between waking and sleeping, day narks shared any necessary knowledge with their night nark counterparts who were just waking up, and then the body was inhabited by the night nark. Night narks were swarthy, with black or dark brown hair and dark brown or grey eyes. They were entirely different people from the day narks with whom they shared their bodies. The changing process repeated itself at sunrise.

Narks were also talented with swiftness, and with a twitch of his large, pointed ears, Yahto Veli was at Darcy's side, his blond hair settling around his shoulders in the wake of his movement. "Lady Darcy," he said with a sparkle in his eyes. "Welcome back." He bowed his head to her, and she grinned.

"Hello, Veli!" Yahto Veli had been with Torrin the day that Darcy had arrived through the gateway the year before, and she'd always felt a special bond with the cheerful day nark. His night nark persona, however, was a different story. "How's, um, Yahto?" She said his name very softly.

Veli flashed her a wry smile and shook his head a little. "He is, as always, not one to regard the world through a lens of positivity. But," he added, brightening, "I do think he has been looking forward to your arrival. Well," he swept his hand out, "all of you."

Darcy snorted in disbelief. While the two narks that shared each nark body typically shared similar personalities, likes, wants, and needs, Yahto Veli was an enigma in his own society. Yahto and Veli were as different as, well, night and day. While Veli was as bright and optimistic as his fair hair and twinkling eyes suggested, Yahto was glum and seemed almost disappointed if his nightly predictions of gloom and doom didn't come to pass. Besides the very different personalities, Yahto disliked Darcy as much as Veli regarded her with fondness and friendship.

"We've been waiting for you all day," the second nark—a female named Voitto Vesa—said, breezing up next to Sam and putting her hand on the girl's shoulder in greeting. "We are so pleased to see you. Rubidius was quite certain you would come back on the same day of the year as you arrived two years ago."

Two years ago? Darcy puzzled over Vesa's wording for a moment, trying to figure it through in her head. *A year ago we returned to our own world* after *spending a year in Alitheia. And then, of course, time continued on for them while we lived the same year over again. So, it* was *two years ago that we first arrived.*

Darcy must have looked a little cross-eyed, because Veli laughed at her. "Trying to figure out the timing?"

She nodded.

"Don't think about it too hard," he advised. "As you know, time does not stand still for us while you are away."

Darcy knew that, of course, but it didn't make the math any less confusing. "I know. It was just, that's the first time I've ever heard it said that it's been *two* years since we last arrived. Even though we did technically live two years in between then and now, it still feels like one to us because it was the same year lived over again—in two different places —"

"Oh, Darcy, stop, will you? You're giving me a headache!" Amelia interrupted her.

"Sorry."

"Is it just the three of you?" Sam asked, changing the subject. She scanned the trees as if looking for more people. Other than a few gnomes bobbing around in the rocks, chattering in their strange, earthy language, and fairies flitting from branches and flowers with quiet tinkling sounds, they appeared to be alone.

"Is it safe?" Lewis added, shoving his slipping glasses up his sweat-streaked nose.

"We have the protection we need," Torrin answered, stepping forward and slinging his bow across his shoulder. "It is a different Alitheia that you have come back to. We no longer have to hide from the Shadow."

"Just like that?" Perry frowned. "He's just . . . gone?"

Torrin gave a short bark of a laugh. "No, of course not, but the tables have turned. Tselloch is in hiding, as are most of his followers. We have, however, spent the better part of the past year securing the isthmus and the environs around the twin castles of Kenidros and Ormiskos. He will not bother us here." He spoke with confidence, but Darcy saw his knuckles whiten on the hilt of his sword, his eyes looking past her into the dark forest beyond.

"This place has always been somewhat protected for us, besides," Vesa intoned. "As you know, we used to hold secret councils out here. There are ancient enchantments that ward off evil on the isthmus, even if they do not protect it entirely."

"Why? Because of the gateway?" Darcy asked.

Vesa inclined her head. "That is most likely, but we have never known for certain."

"And that is a question better asked of Rubidius or Eleanor," Yahto Veli added, "who are both, by the way, quite anxious to see you." He held out his hand to indicate that they should follow Torrin, who began scouting a path back toward Gnome's Haven.

Dean fell in line behind Torrin. Being the prophesized "spy" of the group, and having always been into army stuff, it was no stretch for him to have come to idolize Torrin the year before.

The rest of them fell into step as well, and Darcy smiled at the fairies that were keeping pace with them. Tiny—their average size being only about three inches tall—winged, and colorful, the fairies were some of the magical creatures that made Alitheia glitter and gleam like Cedar Cove in high definition. Darcy had learned that it looked that way because of the magic that indwelt everything. Without the creatures, however—the fairies, gnomes, and nymphs—the magic faded and Alitheia looked as normal as their own world.

Part of the travesty of Tselloch and his shadow creatures, his tsellochim, was that they smothered whole areas of the forest, killing the magical creatures and leaving behind great swaths of oily darkness and choking weeds. Darcy could clearly remember traveling through the forest at night and seeing areas that were blacker than black, as if they sucked all blackness into themselves . . . She shuddered. Now was a time to be cheerful, optimistic. *Be like Veli*, she told herself, looking over her shoulder to smile at him.

They broke out of the trees at Gnome's Haven and found that the ground at the base of the rock had been cleared and a wooden causeway erected from there down to the water. In fact, it looked as if the causeway had been built in the exact spot where the tree had fallen down in their world.

Darcy raised her eyebrows. She turned to Sam to point it out, but Sam was giggling at the gnomes, hundreds of whom had come to the mouths of their nooks and crannies to peer at them and make rude-sounding noises.

"They think they are funny." Veli chuckled.

"They *are* funny," Sam said, wiggling her finger at a particularly chubby gnome who was puffing out his cheeks at her and crossing his eyes.

"My lord and ladies," Torrin interrupted them. He was standing at the causeway and had already ushered the rest of their company down the wooden planking to the water, where four wooden coracles bobbed in the shallow waves.

Sam took Darcy's arm and tugged her down. "Oh, wow!" she breathed as soon as they could see the water clearly. "Look, Darcy!"

Anchored out in the water was a large schooner, like one she'd seen on a sailing trip with her dad when she was eleven. She could not tell how long this one was, but it was large enough that the people on board looked no more than a few inches tall from where she was standing. It had two masts, the front one just shorter than the rear one, and each square sail was a deep navy blue, like the color of the sky just after the sun has disappeared. Emblazoned in gold on the foresail was the now familiar royal Alitheian crest: an eagle, wings outstretched and talons bared, with three four-point stars on its chest. The bowsprit, to which the forestays were attached, was also painted gold, but was otherwise unembellished. The gold ran along the railings of the vessel, but the rest of the wood was unpainted, its new cedar finish glowing under sprinkles of water.

"Wow," Darcy echoed Sam's sentiment.

"She's the *Cal Meridian*," Torrin said with a distinct note of pride in his voice. "She's brand new. Tullin commissioned her in honor of our victory over Tselloch last year. She's to be the flagship of the royal highnesses."

Darcy thought of the crown prince Tellius and his year-and-a-half younger brother Cadmus. "So, why did they send it for us?" she asked.

Torrin looked at her as if to determine whether she was joking. "You're to be queen," he said.

Oh yeah, I suppose there is that. Darcy looked sideways at Sam and Amelia. "The *Cal Meridian*, huh?"

Sam nodded, grinning from ear to ear. "Just like back at camp!"

They trundled down the walkway together and got into the last two of the four coracles, Torrin squeezing in with Lewis and Amelia. Their knees knocked together as Veli took up the two small oars and began to row them out to the waiting ship. The splash of the waves against the rocks, sounding like wet laundry being thrown onto concrete, receded as Veli's strong arms bore them swiftly away from shore. Gulls circled and cried in the air above them, and Darcy wondered if they were high creatures or low creatures, and whether she'd be able to talk to them.

The thought of her talent brought a new wave of excitement. In just a day or two she would begin training with Rubidius and learn more about her mysterious ability to talk with animals. All high animals in Alitheia could understand common speech, but no human could understand an animal's tongue. Darcy's ability to mind-speak with the wolf Lykos during their last visit to Alitheia had opened up a world of possibilities, but Darcy had had no chance to explore those possibilities outside of her interactions with Lykos. She hoped that this year Rubidius would change that.

Sam reached over and squeezed her hand. It wasn't often that Sam was without words, but at the moment she was happy to the point of being speechless. Darcy squeezed back and smiled at Sam's bright blue eyes.

Veli grinned at the two of them, the effort of rowing not even winding him. Narks were particularly adept at anything requiring physicality, and they had already left the other coracle that Torrin was rowing far behind. Yahto Veli was handsome in his own way, his face full of angles, planes, and depth that made his age impossible to guess. In fact, Darcy didn't even know how long narks lived.

A splash off the side of their boat caused her and Sam to turn their heads, and she disentangled her hand from Sam's so that she could put both on the edge to keep her balance as she peered over. Keeping pace with them were naiads, water nymphs. They often took the appearance of mermaids, but they could also just as easily dissolve into the water itself, or form legs and walk on dry land—but not for too long lest they dry out completely. They were petite beings, the size of children, and they had impish faces and very large eyes. Green, blue and grey hair ribboned behind them in the water as they waved and giggled.

Darcy and Sam waved back, and the naiads laughed louder and disappeared into the dark blue depths. They reappeared a moment later behind them at Torrin's boat, repeating their greeting.

"They're celebrating your arrival," Veli commented. "All of Alitheia welcomes you back."

"It feels a little weird," Sam said, hugging her arms around her chest against the breeze that got cooler the farther they traveled from shore. "Everybody waiting for us and being happy that we're here."

"What's strange about that?" Veli asked, his voice sounding musical in his curiosity.

Sam exchanged a look with Darcy, and they both snorted. "We're not the most popular people at our school," Darcy answered for Sam. They both, along with Lewis, had endured a fair amount of teasing the year before.

Veli gave a rare frown as though he didn't quite comprehend what they meant, but their conversation was cut short when the shadow of the large schooner's sails fell over them as they fetched up next to it.

Darcy looked up to see a man standing at the railing who shone as bright as the gold on the trim. He had bright golden curls and a deep tan. The chest hairs peeking out from between the fringes of his half-buttoned shirt were bleached white by the sun. He regarded them with a blue-eyed gaze that was piercing, but not unkind. At his word, a sailor scuttled down the rope ladder dangling over the side of the vessel and braced a foot on the edge of their coracle and offering a hand to Sam.

"My lady," the sailor said. "If you will," he nodded toward the rope.

Sam stood on shaking legs in the tiny vessel, a look of deep trepidation on her face. Yahto Veli helped steady her, and she muttered something about failing rope climbing in PhysEd as she took the sailor's hand in one of hers and put the other on a rung of the ladder.

"Use your legs to climb, don't try to pull all your weight with your arms," the sailor advised genially.

The boat rocked as Sam's weight left it, and she grunted as she hefted herself up the ladder with white-knuckled intensity. Veli stood balanced, completely at ease, despite the rocking of the coracle, and he offered his hand to Darcy as soon as Sam was halfway up.

Darcy stood with much more surety than Sam had. Years of horseback riding had given her a strong core and the ability to distribute her weight evenly. She stepped to the ladder and took the calloused hand of the sailor. He had bright red hair and a face so freckled that it looked tan; in fact, she realized with a shock, she knew him!

"Bayard, isn't that your name?" she asked hesitantly, looking him in the face.

He blushed under his freckles and nodded. He was a year older than the last time she had seen him, but he was definitely the youth that had been with them at Sanditha the year before.

"I didn't know you were a sailor," she continued, adjusting her hands on the rope.

"This is my first year," he admitted. "I'm apprenticing, but I hope to be a full crew member soon."

"It's good to see you again," Darcy said, feeling a bit awkward all of a sudden.

"And you, lady," he sounded embarrassed, but he helped her get her feet steady on the ladder and gave her a little boost.

It was more difficult to climb than Darcy had thought it would be. The rope was slick with seawater and it was tricky to get her fingers all the way around it as it hung taut against the side of the schooner. She managed to inch her way toward the golden railing and was impressed Sam had managed it at all, considering that she was still rather overweight.

When Darcy reached the top, a well-muscled, tanned arm appeared over the edge, its large hand grasping her forearm as it hauled her up and over. With a catch of her breath, she found herself in the grasp of the golden man, who set her on her feet and stepped back to regard her and her friends, all standing in a line. He studied them without speaking, and she was not surprised to see Yahto Veli pop up over the railing just a moment after her.

At last, the golden man unfolded his arms and said, "I am Boreas and this is my vessel. Welcome aboard the *Cal Meridian*."

CHAPTER 8

ON BOARD THE CAL MERIDIAN

"Children?" a soft voice questioned from above and behind them.

They all turned to find the one person who could call them children without offending them: Eleanor Stevenson.

She stood on the upper deck by the wheel of the ship, her silvery hair caught up in a knot at the back of her head. She had died in their world at the age of nineteen but had lived on in Alitheia for over fifty years now.

Eleanor came down a side staircase to greet them as Sam, Amelia, and Darcy rushed to meet her. As usual, Darcy stood aside feeling awkward as the other girls gave Eleanor warm hugs, but Eleanor, with a small knowing smile, pulled Darcy in for one as well.

"We didn't know you were on board!" Sam breathed. "It's so good to see you! Is Rubidius here, too? And the princes?"

Darcy stiffened and looked around. Was she to be faced with Tellius so soon? She hadn't even changed into proper Alitheian wear yet. She tugged self-consciously at the hem of her shorts.

Eleanor laughed. "No, no. I only got away because Tellius and Cadmus are absorbed in a special session with Rubidius this afternoon. They have a lot of studies to make up."

"What do you mean?" Amelia asked.

"Magic studies, that is," Eleanor clarified. "They had no chance to receive their customary magic training while they were in hiding for most of their lives, so I'm afraid that they are a bit behind other children their age. They are working hard, though, particularly Tellius. I think they should be caught up before too long."

"I thought you were their tutor," Sam said, wrinkling her brow.

"Yes, but I do not instruct in *magic*, and the boys' situation has always been unique—given who they are and the state in which we used to live. The nature of their upbringing has been irregular, at best."

The captain of the *Cal Meridian*, Boreas, cleared his throat behind the girls and they turned to face him. "Lady Eleanor, all the coracles are secured. With your permission I will begin to head back to Ormiskos."

"Oh yes," Eleanor smiled and nodded. "I'm so sorry to keep you waiting, Captain Boreas. Please carry on."

The captain turned smartly and barked orders to his crew. Darcy noticed the auburn-headed Bayard ducking around with the rest of them, and she smiled at the familiarity she felt, even on a strange vessel. The anchor was hauled in and the sails snapped above them as they caught the wind.

"If you will," Eleanor said to all of them, indicating a rounded doorway that led to a room beneath the top deck. "Now is not the time for stories. I have some things for you in the captain's quarters. We haven't much time before we reach the castle, and it would be nice for you to arrive in style."

Darcy twisted the heavy gold ring on her thumb and looked up and down the deck at her friends. They had exchanged their clothes for Alitheian garb: long white dresses with flowing sleeves for the girls and brown slacks with white linen shirts for the boys. They had fitted the jerkins that denoted their prophesied roles over the tops of their clothes and added to their ensembles the gifts that Rubidius had fashioned for each of them. Darcy thought they looked a bit too colorful, even against the golden railing of the ship. Each of the sailors wore practical, plain garb, and the six of them stuck out like fractured pieces of a rainbow. The only person on board who rivaled them for outstanding visual appearance was Captain Boreas who, with his golden curls and deep blue eyes, looked to Darcy like a Greek or Roman mosaic of the god Apollo.

Darcy's eyes continued to travel and eventually landed and lingered on Perry who stood laughing near the bowsprit with Dean and Bayard. He looked like a dashing prince out of a fantasy novel with the sun glinting off his hair and his unbeatable sword, hanging a few more inches off the ground this year, buckled at a jaunty angle around his waist. The red lion prowling on the chest of his yellow jerkin seemed entirely fitting. As if he felt her gaze upon him, Perry glanced over at Darcy and winked, grinning.

Darcy averted her eyes, her ears burning, and was glad when Sam, Lewis, and Amelia approached her.

"Fits a little better this year," Sam grunted, adjusting her blue jerkin across her chest.

Amelia looked perfect as always; her wind-whipped hair looked graceful and romantic, and her lavender jerkin fit her better than anybody else's. It was probably because she was so tall; the Alitheians had expected the Six to be adults, not children, when they arrived.

"Have you said hello to Bayard yet?" Sam asked Amelia with a mischievous gleam in her eye.

Amelia frowned down at her. "Bayard? The redhead? No. Why would I?"

"He had a crush on you last year."

Amelia's eyebrows rose. "I have a boyfriend, Sam, remember? Simon?" She grimaced and looked down at her hands intertwined on the railing.

Sam looked immediately contrite. "I'm sorry, Amelia. I wasn't thinking. I shouldn't have brought it up. I know you're going to miss him."

Amelia took a deep breath and then looked up. "Yeah, well, I suppose it comes with the turf, doesn't it? To be an inter-world traveler, sacrifices must be made." She smiled to let Sam know she was teasing, and Sam laughed.

Darcy was glad for the distraction, anything to keep her mind off her imminent meeting with Tellius. If it weren't for that tiny detail of her marrying him someday, Darcy thought she could fully enjoy her return to Alitheia. As it was, if she could just distract herself enough, she could ignore the growing knot in her stomach. She shot another wistful look up at Perry.

The late afternoon sun heated their backs as they rounded the point of the isthmus and sailed past the bay that cut between the two sides of camp, or rather, between Kenidros and Ormiskos. They had a strong wind, and the *Cal Meridian* skimmed over the swells.

A towering brown-stoned edifice rose up on their left. It was shaped like a wedding cake, with several tiers layered up to a single tower in the middle, from which a blue flag with the Alitheian crest flew in the breeze. A wall encased the fortress, but a large gate gave egress to the beach and harbor, and there were many outlying structures around it. In fact, it looked as if an entire city was laid out beneath it. Many construction projects appeared to be in the works, as the buildings were laced with ladders and scaffolding.

They had never been there before, but Darcy knew this must be the castle and city of Kenidros, where Tullin—first cousin once removed to Tellius and Cadmus—reigned as governor.

People high on the walls and on the scaffolding stopped and waved as they passed by, and Darcy lowered her gaze and glanced at Amelia and Sam. They both looked pleased, but a little embarrassed, too.

"I sure hope we don't let everybody down," Sam murmured after a moment.

Neither Darcy nor Amelia responded. Lewis made an indistinct noise in the back of his throat, something between a cough and a grunt. No one looked at each other as they just continued to stand at the railing, staring out. Before long they rounded another point into the next bay, and all but the peak of Kenidros tower disappeared from view.

Even though the afternoon sun was still bright and everything looked cheery and colorful, Darcy couldn't help but notice a dark haze on the horizon, far in the distance. It hovered over the trees like a bank of rain clouds, but unlike a cloud it didn't move across the sky. It seemed almost to be *breathing*, expanding and contracting ever so slightly. Darcy watched it, mesmerized, and then dropped her eyes with a shiver. A moment later, she glanced up to see Eleanor Stevenson standing at her side, peering at her with knowing eyes.

"It's not him, Darcy," she said so that only Darcy could hear. "We would know if Tselloch were that close."

"But he's still out there," Darcy whispered back.

"Yes, but he is not in that manifestation." She drummed her delicate fingers on the railing. "There are wards, enchantments, boundaries . . . all that have been set up to keep him out."

"Out of where? The castle?"

"And it's environs. We set a boundary three miles into the forest on all sides but the water. That is all Rubidius and the other magicians can maintain."

Darcy wrinkled her forehead. "So . . . he can't get through at all?"

Eleanor hesitated. "It is not foolproof, but will give us warning if he or any of his changed servants—tsellodrin or tsellochim—do manage to breach our defenses. That is why it will be so important for all of you to stay within the castle during your training this year. In the castle you will be safe."

Darcy recognized Eleanor's tone as the same Yahto Veli used earlier, as though she were trying to make herself believe her own words.

Darcy focused on the bay they were turning into and the light grey stone castle that was Ormiskos, the seat of the government in Alitheia. At least twice the size of the castle of Kenidros, Ormiskos was also structured in a more traditional manner. It had four turreted towers and a fifth taller tower set in the back wall of the castle proper. Another wall encased the entire castle grounds: the courtyard, stables, archery range, harbor, and several smaller buildings. This wall disappeared into the trees and only re-emerged to hug the bay. The ends of the wall sank to the seabed beneath the water, where guard towers stood with clusters of ships around them. A massive construction project was being conducted to extend the guard wall to encompass the bay. Darcy could see hinges where it looked as though a gate would be affixed to allow for sea traffic to come and go.

Darcy appreciated the view of the castle, one she'd only seen from this perspective in daylight once before, but she found her gaze drawn back to the dark mass on the horizon. She turned back to Eleanor. "Then what is *that?"*

Eleanor looked at it thoughtfully. "It is likely a manifestation of his tsellochim," she said.

"Can it see us? Does he know we're back?"

Eleanor sighed and dipped her head. "I'm certain he does."

CHAPTER 9

THE WEST WING

As soon as they passed into the bay, they were hailed by waving and clapping Alitheians aboard boats and ships of all shapes and sizes. The *Cal Meridian* was too large to weigh anchor at the docks, but instead of disembarking into the tiny coracles, this time they were handed down onto a large, flat barge bedecked with colorful festoonery.

Her ears rosy in a permanent blush, Darcy huddled close to Sam and Amelia as they were delivered to the dock with great fanfare. Never before in Alitheia had she seen so many people gathered together in one place. Now that Tselloch no longer held the castle, many people who had fled or lived in hiding were moving back to resume their old lives.

The next few minutes passed in a blur. The six of them were escorted by Veli, Vesa, Torrin, and Eleanor along the dock to the decorative gate that marked the entrance to the castle grounds. Guards in rich blue and gold stood at attention as they passed, and just inside the gate was another crowd of people, four of whom stood prominently in the foreground.

Darcy recognized Rubidius immediately, of course. His beard looked longer and was whiter around his mouth, but he was otherwise unchanged. The younger prince, Cadmus, was also easy to recognize with his mop of curly brown hair and impish brown eyes. He was standing to one side of the grey-bearded Tullin. The other youth—the one standing to Tullin's other side—couldn't *possibly* be Tellius; it just couldn't be, but it unmistakably was.

The last time Darcy had seen him, the difference in height between him and his brother had been but a few inches, and they'd both had the rounded look of childhood in their faces. This boy—this almost unrecognizable boy—held only a thin resemblance to the Tellius she'd known before. Other than his straight, freckled nose and brown eyes flecked with green, almost everything was different.

He looked . . . awkward, stretched—as though he was stuck in the middle of a painful growth transformation. He stood a full foot taller than his brother and an inch or two taller than her, but his hands and feet were much too large for him. His face was thin and covered with pimples and he was terribly skinny, as though he'd added height, but not weight. The disproportionateness of his form reminded Darcy of a Labrador puppy. Except, where a puppy was cute and endearing, there was nothing at all attractive about Tellius, particularly not when he was scowling at her like that.

Darcy scowled back, her gaze sweeping him up and down. They should be greeting each other; everybody else was clasping hands and exchanging pleasantries, but Tellius and Darcy stood facing each other in sullen silence. Finally Tullin cleared his throat and nudged Tellius toward her. Tellius looked up at him sharply, his eyes flashing with indignation. He set his shoulders back, and Darcy could again see the undeniable mark of royalty in his blood, even through his awkwardness.

"Welcome back, Lady Darcy," he grated out. He still had a little boy's voice.

Darcy realized that every eye was on the two of them, and so she put forth her best effort and managed a tight smile and a slight curtsy.

That seemed to satisfy the crowd, because conversation buzzed to life again around them, and Tellius turned on his heel and marched toward the castle, the crowd of people parting before him as though they were used to his stomping about.

"There now," Yahto Veli's bright voice sounded at her shoulder. "That wasn't so difficult, was it?"

Darcy rolled her eyes and didn't answer.

The feast was fabulous, and as long as Darcy didn't look at Tellius, who was seated at her right—somebody's idea of a cruel joke, she thought—she enjoyed the delicious spread of whole roasted chickens, cheeses, breads, fresh vegetable dishes, and watered-down wine. At the end of the meal there was even a dessert tray from which to choose, and Darcy ate chocolate mousse until her stomach felt ready to burst.

The great dining hall at Ormiskos was not in the same location as the dining hall in the lodge at Cedar Cove. That space in Alitheia was occupied by the receiving hall of the castle—the same hall in which Tselloch had tempted Darcy to betray her friends. The dining hall was above the receiving hall on the south side of the castle and, like the hall beneath it, also had floor to ceiling windows that overlooked the bay and the construction work being done on the sea wall. The décor was lavish, heavy with deep colors and flashes of gold, and Darcy wondered where they had gotten all the material to refit the castle after the long reign of Tselloch. When he had ruled here, she remembered, the walls and windows had been draped with black, and furniture was sparse. Perhaps the furnishings, like the people, were trickling back after long years of exile.

They dined for so long that the sun touched the water on the horizon, setting off streaks of red and orange before they were permitted to go to their rooms. Eleanor led them by way of a back staircase tucked into one of the towers that spiraled up several floors and onto a serene and comfortable landing. The narrow hallway that stretched beyond the landing and the warm colors in the carpet runner beneath her feet reminded Darcy of the lodge at camp. Evenly spaced ornate oak doors stood in the walls on both sides of the hallway, which terminated about thirty yards away into a banister and second staircase.

"This is the west wing," Eleanor told them. "It contains everything you need: your personal living quarters, a library and study, a weapons practice room, and even the entrance to Rubidius's cottage. My own quarters are just here," she put a hand on the first door to their left, "should you need anything from me. This wing of the castle has been sectioned off for your particular use; nobody who has not been invited can bother you here." She gave each of them a heavy brass key on a chain and showed them to their separate rooms.

The boys were on one side of the hall, and the girls on the other. Darcy was surprised to discover that they each got their own room this year. They had shared rooms last year, but she now realized that must have been only out of necessity. The three girls' rooms and the three boys' rooms were interconnected on the insides, with doors set in the connecting walls, and Darcy was glad for it. Knowing that Sam was just on the other side of her wall, and that Amelia was just beyond Sam's wall, was a relief. Even though she was a very solitary person, she still felt frightened to be alone in an unfamiliar room—really an apartment, as she had her own bathroom and sitting area—in an unfamiliar place. Sure, it was Alitheia, but it was so different from the Alitheia she'd known a year before. Darcy sat in a silk nightgown on the window seat in her room, gazing out at the sky turning indigo over the tree line. She remembered staring out her window at Cedar Cove just the night before and watching Colin Mackaby talk to a strange form in the trees, just over . . . there. Although much higher off the ground and facing west instead of north, she could still make out the spot in the trees where she'd seen the mysterious interaction.

All was silent in her room except for the occasional sputter of the oil lamps, and she wondered what the others were doing—if they, like her, were sitting awake with nerves stretched tight, adrenaline infused, or if they had collapsed onto their plush beds in exhaustion.

Darcy sighed and drew her cold feet up under the hem of her gown. Her brain was full of everything that had happened that day, and she knew that it was going to be a long time before she could fall asleep. Some thoughtful person had put her favorite book of Alitheian nursery rhymes on her bedside table, and she thought idly about retrieving it but abandoned the idea. She didn't think she could lose herself in a book that night.

A soft knock sounded at the door that connected her room to Sam's. Darcy hopped up and went to the door, remembering to unlock it with her key before she opened it wide. Sam and Amelia stood on the other side, both in their night clothes and clutching pillows and down comforters.

"Sleepover?" Sam asked, her face split into a grin.

Darcy let out a relieved laugh. "Definitely!" She opened the door wider, and the other two girls trundled through with their arms full.

"We felt lonely," Sam said, dumping her things in the middle of the floor. She regarded the bed with her hands on her hips. "I don't think we can all fit on there, even if the bed *is* huge. We should camp out on the floor!"

"Sounds like fun!" Darcy exclaimed, dragging the fittings off her bed and onto the floor.

They made a sort of nest on the enormous, circular rug in the middle of the room with their pillows in the center and flopped down with girly exclamations.

"Do you think the boys would ever do this?" Sam asked, propping herself up on her elbows.

Amelia and Darcy both laughed. "No way!"

Sam laughed, too. "Yeah, we know how to have so much more fun than they do. What do you think they talk about when we're not around?"

"Stupid boy stuff," Darcy shoved her hair over her shoulder. "You know, like how many cheese curls they can shove into their mouths, stuff like that."

"Simon's not like that," Amelia said, her gaze turning dreamy.

Sam turned to face Amelia with sparkling eyes. "Have you guys . . . you know . . . kissed yet?"

Amelia's narrowed her twinkling eyes and ducked her head to study her nails. "Maybe."

Sam squealed and chucked a throw pillow at her head.

"Hey!" Amelia said, throwing one back.

Darcy stayed out of the pillow fight and wondered, not for the first time, what it would be like to be kissed by a boy. She'd certainly not had any opportunities back home where her social circle was comprised of just her,

Sam, and Lewis. The idea of kissing Lewis made her want to laugh . . . but the idea of kissing *Perry* was much more pleasant. Unbidden, the image of Tellius greeting them that afternoon on the docks intruded on her pleasant, Perry-filled reverie. The thought of kissing *him* was just . . . nauseating.

"What are you thinking about, Darcy?" Sam demanded, throwing a pillow in her direction. "You're too quiet. This is a time for girl talk. No fair being all moody."

"Hey, I am *not* moody!"

"It's true," Amelia said seriously, "Darcy is a lot more unpleasant when she's moody."

Darcy could only nod in agreement.

They spent the rest of the evening discussing topics that had nothing whatsoever to do with Tselloch, evil shadow creatures, or anything unpleasant at all.

"You know," Sam said several hours later when the lamps were almost burned out and they were all lying with their heads on their pillows, "there is nobody else in the world that I would rather share this experience with than you two. *Nobody* else."

Thwump, thwump, thwump, thwump, thwump! "Sam? Are you up yet?" *Thwump, thwump, thwump!*

Darcy blearily cracked her eyes open and looked around. She squinted for her alarm clock and then remembered she was in Alitheia where digital alarm clocks didn't exist. A down comforter took up most of her vision, and she'd somehow managed to throw an arm over Sam's face in her sleep. She moved her arm, raised her head, and squinted at the window where morning sunshine was peeking in.

Thwump, thwump, thwump! "Sam, we're waiting for you guys! Rubidius is ready to start." Lewis's voice sounded strange and far away, and Darcy realized that he was pounding on *Sam's* door in the next room over, the sound drifting through the connecting door that was not quite shut.

Darcy groaned and shook Sam's shoulder. "Sam."

The other girl mumbled and rolled away from her hand.

"Sam!" Darcy prodded her harder. "It's Lewis. He says it's time to get up."

"Huh?" Sam's head popped up. "What?"

"*Lew-is*," Darcy said again. "Come on, get up. Go tell him that we heard and we'll be along as soon as we can."

"Ok*ay*." Sam's voice was very scratchy as she hauled herself ungracefully to her feet. She stumbled as she padded over to her room, and Darcy heard her speaking to Lewis in muffled tones a minute later.

Darcy stood, stretched, and took in the mess on the floor. She thought for a moment that Amelia must have already gotten up and left because there appeared to be no trace of her in the jumbled mass of comforters and pillows, but then she saw a chunk of straw-colored hair protruding from under a corner of blanket.

Lifting the corner very carefully, Darcy found Amelia's head. She was lying on her stomach with her head turned to one side, snoring. There was a strand of drool dangling from her open mouth. Darcy snickered and nudged her with her toe. "Time to get up!"

Amelia twitched and closed her mouth, slurping in her drool as she rolled on her back and passed a hand over her face. She opened her eyes and blinked up at Darcy. "Ugh," she rasped. "How late did we stay up?"

"I don't know. Too late." Darcy turned to the massive cedar wardrobe on the far wall.

"I was drooling, wasn't I?" Amelia asked from behind her, sounding embarrassed.

"Yep!" Darcy answered. "Very attractive."

"Ha ha," Amelia responded. "What are the maids going to think of this mess?"

"I don't know, but we don't have time to clean up now." Darcy had found several colorful, long dresses hanging in the wardrobe, along with under-things and a variety of footwear. She chose a green dress with gold trim along the collar and three-quarter-length sleeves and turned back to face Amelia. "Sam's in her room talking with Lewis. I think he said Rubidius is ready for us."

"Without breakfast?" Amelia scowled as she got to her feet. "It's the first morning; can't he give us a chance to settle in a little?"

"This *is* Rubidius we're talking about," Darcy said.

"Oh, right." Amelia shook her head and made for the door, intercepting Sam on the way.

"Lewis said they've been up for almost two hours already. Baran came up to give them a refresher course on morning forms, and then they ate breakfast in the kitchen with the servants. They've been exploring the weapons room and that's where Rubidius found them. They're all down in his cottage now. It's the last door on the right," Sam said in a rush. "I'm going to get dressed. Oh, and Lewis brought us some muffins. They're on the table by my bed, but I think we'd better hurry. They seem a little impatient." She ducked back into her room with Amelia on her heels.

Darcy got dressed as quick as she could, appreciating the soft cotton of the dress and musing that it didn't feel strange at all to dress as though she lived in the Middle Ages. She took the heavy gold ring from her bedside table and hesitated a moment before putting it on. It was elaborately engraved with swirling marks and set in the middle were three amber stones cut into four-point stars. She was the only one of the Six not to receive a magical gift. The ring was merely an Ecclektos family heirloom, something to bind her to Tellius in their supposed future marriage. Darcy sighed and slipped it on her thumb. Rubidius would be expecting her to wear it, she knew.

As ready for the day as she felt that she could be, she meandered over to Sam's room, which was identical to hers except in color. Sam's room was decorated in blues and yellows, while Darcy's room was red and cream.

"Are you ready?" she called to Sam, who was in her bathroom with the door cracked open.

"Almost," Sam called back. She emerged a moment later with her hands behind her head. "Can you tie my braid?"

Darcy put down the muffin she'd been examining and did as Sam asked. Then they nibbled on muffins together until Amelia finally appeared, looking put-together and certainly not like she'd spent the night on the floor.

Amelia took a muffin from the basket, and they exited Sam's room together, closing the door behind them. The hallway felt muffled and private. The ceiling was very high, making them feel very tiny. They passed a closed door and then one that was open, through which Darcy glimpsed rows upon rows of books. At last they came to the end of the long hall. Faint sounds echoed up the wide staircase, and Darcy felt the urge to look over the banister, but Sam was already raising her hand to knock on the last door.

"Come in!" Rubidius barked. "It's about time!"

Amelia rolled her eyes at them and turned the knob. Darcy knew what to expect, but it was still a shock to go from one of the highest floors in the castle to a quaint cottage tucked away somewhere in the forests of Alitheia. Rubidius would remind them that he hadn't *lost* his cottage, per se. He just couldn't remember where he left it the last time he magically relocated it. And besides, as long as he had the spell to conjure his front door, it didn't matter *where* the cottage was.

"We have wasted half the morning," Rubidius continued, sounding peeved. He snapped his door shut and glared at them, his eyes as fiery as the bottom portion of his beard, the portion that revealed he had at one time been a redhead.

Sam looked contrite, Darcy felt annoyed, but Amelia put her hands on her hips and said, "Well, it's the first morning. Plus, we were up late."

Rubidius's bushy eyebrows crept up to merge with his hairline, and he stared at Amelia until she lowered her arms and her gaze became contrite. "I mean, we're *sorry*," she revised.

Rubidius's eyes narrowed dangerously. "Sit."

Rubidius was not a bad sort, he was just prone to fits of emotion. He and Darcy had, in fact, had something approaching a heart-to-heart at the end of last year, and she had hoped he might reveal a little more of *that* side of his personality this year, but it didn't appear at this time as though that was to be. She supposed that, as the chief magician and alchemist in the kingdom of Alitheia, a key player in the rebellion against Tselloch, and a participant in the raising of the royal boys, he could afford to act however he pleased.

They hurried to take seats around his familiar, round, thick-planked table. Perry and Dean smirked at them, clearly enjoying their braiding-down.

Darcy noticed on her way around the table that a much smaller table had been pushed against the back door—which was unusable, anyway, unless they wanted to break the cloaking spell that Rubidius had placed on his cottage—and seated across from each other at the table were Tellius and Cadmus. She made a sort of strangled sound of surprise in the back of her throat, and the two boys looked up from the parchments they were studying.

"Focus!" Rubidius ordered them over her head, and they dropped their eyes back to their work. "By the end of the day I expect your essays on the elemental properties of objects of mixed composition and the recommended method of manipulation of said objects by individuals of your varying talents."

Darcy collapsed into her chair, her ears warming, wondering how on earth she was going to be able to focus on anything with *him* sitting in the back of the room.

"Why are you girls so tired?" Lewis whispered to her and Sam out of the corner of his mouth as Rubidius retrieved a stack of parchments and began handing them out. "We went to bed so early!"

"Never mind, Lewis," Sam said with a sigh.

They looked up as Rubidius loomed over them and placed several thick sheets in front of each of them. Darcy read the flowing script at the top of the page:

1. Please explain the properties of birch bark in potion making.

2. To set a fire that produces green smoke, what plants are most advantageous to burn?

3. Of the four elements, which is most commonly manipulated?

The questions went on for five pages.

"You're giving us a *quiz?"* Perry sputtered, looking up in disbelief.

"More like an exam," Dean muttered, thumbing through his pages.

"Of course!" Rubidius's chest expanded a little. "Did you think all of the instruction you received two years ago was for you to go off and forget? No!" He banged his fist against his open palm. "It was the basis of magical theory and survival. Of course I'm going to see what you can remember. Quills are in the center of the table," he pointed out. "You have until lunch to finish." And with that, he went to his rocking chair, sat down with his arms folded over his chest, and fell asleep.

CHAPTER 10

A COMPLETION

Rubidius sat across the table from her, regarding her with narrowed, intense eyes. "Focus," he murmured. "Focus."

Darcy held on for as long as she could and then released the quill. It fluttered to the table, and she sat back panting, a sheen of sweat on her forehead.

"Good!" he barked, handing her a glass of water and a rag to wipe her face. "Rest a moment and then we will begin again."

It was strange. The last year, when she had been "trained" by the traitor Lykos, she had been able to move whole objects with her magic and hardly break a sweat. She knew now, though, that there had been an external evil at play, some *other* force wanting her to think she required less training than she did. There had been the Shadow Stones, which she shuddered to recall. She would never forget Dean's illness—how she had almost killed him by stealing his magic without even realizing what she was doing. Now she could barely levitate a feather quill without requiring a nap.

She mopped at her face and took a deep drink of water. It was after lunch, and the other teenagers were off with Eleanor exploring the castle, but she was stuck here with Rubidius beginning her training.

"Rubidius," she said after a moment, hedging for more time before he made her start again.

"Hmm?" He had been looking over the shoulders of the two princes in the corner, checking their progress, but now he turned his attention back on her.

"Last time I was here, when I was . . . you know . . . working with Lykos on my talent—"

"Ah yes. Regrettable, that."

"Yeah, um, well, you told us that animals couldn't perform magic, not even the high animals, but he could. He . . . he made a blue fire appear."

Rubidius stuck out his lip with a thoughtful expression. "What Lykos did was not magic."

"But . . . it *looked* like magic."

"Did he begin with kindling or a small flame of any kind?"

Darcy frowned and thought back. "No, I guess not. He just made it appear out of nothing."

"And *there* is the giveaway!" Rubidius jabbed a finger at her to emphasize his point. "All performable magic in Alitheia is elemental. The only being who can create something out of nothing is Pateros, and that is not a gift that he shared with humanity when he brought them to Alitheia and gave them magic. What Lykos was doing was illusory."

"You mean the fire wasn't real?"

"No, it was not. Nor was it coming from him. He had already sold himself to Tselloch and was given the use of some of Tselloch's black arts. Tselloch is a master of illusion."

Darcy frowned as she absorbed what Rubidius was telling her. "So . . . whatever Lykos could do, it wasn't magic that he was born with."

"It was not magic at all."

Darcy sighed. "See, that's what's confusing for me. 'Cause, in my world the ability to make something appear out of midair like that, even if it is illusion, is still considered magic."

"That may be so, but we are not in your world, are we?"

Darcy was silent. Rubidius came back to the table and put a broad, shallow bowl on its surface. He placed the quill back in front of her. "This time, I would like you to place the quill in the bowl."

Darcy nodded and sat up straighter in her chair. She focused her eyes very intently on the quill, taking in every detail of it as Rubidius had told her to do, mentally noting the complexities in the colors and the curvature and design. She imagined taking hold of the object, but not like grabbing it with her hands. Rubidius had told her it was easiest to move an object by dispersing her grasp on it to the smallest denominator, like moving it on an atomic level, and so she focused on the downy fuzz between the strands of the feather, grasping them and lifting with her mind.

It felt like lifting a waterlogged shoe out of a lake by its shoelaces, particularly after all the practice she had already put in that afternoon, but Darcy held on with tenacity. She twined her fingers together to keep from reaching out with her hand and physically grabbing the quill; this was supposed to be a magic exercise, after all.

She managed to get it about six inches off the table but, try as she might, she could not move it sideways over to the bowl. She strained at it and knew that she must look ridiculous sitting there with a red face and puffed out cheeks, but she tried not to let that bother her. At least there was nobody in the room she was trying to impress.

She was just about to give it up and let it drop when she felt a breeze on the back of her neck. The window wasn't open—that was impossible because of the cloaking spell on the cottage—but she heard the flutter of parchment and realized that one of the princes was fanning himself in the warmth of the room.

Darcy became hyper-aware of the breeze and, tuned in as she was to her magical abilities, she felt as though she could see the shimmery, translucent particles of air floating past her face. She watched the bluish, silvery specks and knew that, if she wanted to, she could grasp onto them and bid them to do her will.

With her last remaining reserves of energy, she raised her hand and took a handful of the wind particles. Flicking her wrist, she shoved them toward the floating quill. With a jolt the quill spun head over heels past the bowl, overshooting it by a good three feet, and tumbled to the floor beyond the other side of the table.

Darcy released her hold on her power with a huff and sat back, spent. She shot a weary glance at Rubidius, but he was staring at the quill on the floor and stroking his whiskers.

She sat in silence, afraid to be the first one to speak. What had she done?

Finally, the old alchemist turned his gaze on her. "Interesting," was all he said. He paced to his cupboards, muttered to himself for a moment, turned back to her and said, "I hadn't thought . . ." He shook his head and paced back to the table. "Of course, it *would* make sense." His gaze went to Tellius.

He wasn't talking to Darcy, but she paid attention as though he were. "What would make sense?" she finally blurted. "What did I just do?"

He blinked owlishly at her, as if suddenly remembering that she was present. "Air magic, of course. I would have thought that was obvious."

"Air magic. I . . . I didn't know I could do that."

"Neither did I; I thought you were solely earth. I overlooked it, somehow." He went back to his cabinets and rooted around. "It also means," he continued, his voice muffled behind a cabinet door, "that you have inverse talents."

"*What* talents?"

He didn't answer right away but approached her with a large dusty scroll clutched in his hands, which he unrolled onto the table and then turned to face her. "Inverse," he said again.

The image on the scroll looked very old, like an illustration out of an old copy of Beowulf Darcy had purchased for summer reading, but there was no script on it. Instead it was covered in what looked like runes, with four prominent runes at the corners of a central square.

"Earth." Rubidius pointed to the rune at the top left corner. "Fire." He pointed to the top right. "Water." He pointed to the rune beneath earth. "And air," he finished, pointing to the rune beneath fire. "The four elements, naturally, laid out as Pateros designed them. Those in opposite corners," he put a finger each on earth and air, and then on fire and water, "are considered inverses of each other." He sat down and laced his fingers together, piercing Darcy with a startlingly intense gaze. "There are several unusual magical combinations in practical elemental magic. For one, most Alitheians are born with earth magic, many of them with *only* earth magic, so it is strange to find somebody who can control other elements but cannot control not earth."

"But that doesn't apply to me, does it?" Darcy frowned. "I mean, I wasn't born here, but I *can* perform earth magic."

"No, it does not apply to you, but it does apply to the point I want to make if you will let me finish."

Darcy shrank back. "Sorry."

"Moving on. Secondly, it is very unusual for an Alitheian to have inverse magical talents, and because most are born with earth magic and air is its inverse, air magic rarely manifests. Thirdly, it is also very unusual for an Alitheian to be able to manipulate *three* of the elements, which logically follows my last point, because in order to control three, two of those make an inverse."

"So it's weird that I can do earth and air magic. What does that mean for me?"

"It means that you have the potential to become a powerful magician if you work hard to master your talents. Complementary magic—the possession of, say, earth and fire or earth and water talents—enhances the practitioner because there is an inherent friendship or cooperation, if you will, between the elements. But there is a potential for even *greater* enhancement in the use of inverse talents because of the natural opposition between the elements. If you can harness that aggression and channel it into a unity of power, force them to work together and play one off the other as a cohesive unit, you can achieve greater control over each independent element, as well."

Maybe I should have been writing this down, Darcy thought, her mind spinning. There were a lot of big words in that explanation and she wasn't sure that she completely understood what Rubidius was saying. As far as she could make out, she had a combination of magic talents that rarely appeared together, and she had the potential to become very powerful because of them.

"Have you ever heard somebody say that they would 'move heaven and earth' to get something done?" Rubidius asked unexpectedly.

"Yes," Darcy said, giving him an odd look. "That's a saying in my world."

"Ah!" Rubidius looked pleased. "Further proof that some things get through," he added. "Have you ever wondered what it means?"

"Honestly, no. I never really gave it much thought. I mean," she continued, "I know that it means a person will do whatever it takes to get something done, but I never wondered where it came from."

"It's elemental, and it refers to this particular inverse magic. It is so rare to find people who *can* move heaven and earth—or who possess both air and earth elemental magic—that it became a saying that means exactly what it means in your own world. A person who says that they would move heaven and earth is someone who will do the near impossible. Does that help you to appreciate how rare your combination of talents is?"

Darcy's eyes got very wide and she nodded.

"So," he clapped his hands together, "to return to my original point, it is also rare, remember, for anyone to be born without earth magic or some combination including earth."

Darcy nodded. "Right."

Rubidius squinted at her but spoke across the room. "Tellius, have you been paying attention?"

"Yes, sir," Tellius said.

Darcy jumped. She had forgotten the boys were there.

"Come to the table, please."

She heard a rustle of papers and a chair scraping across the rough floor before Tellius appeared at her side and sat down without looking at her.

"Please tell Lady Darcy what two elements you can control."

Darcy looked at Tellius and noticed that his ears were flaming red. *We could start a "we blush with our ears" club*, she thought ruefully. He looked as uncomfortable as she was.

"Fire and water," he said shortly.

Rubidius was quiet, looking at Darcy as though he was waiting for her to figure something out. She stared at the side of Tellius's face for a moment and then looked back at the element chart on the table before her. She traced the lines on it with a finger and then said, "So he also has inverse talents."

Rubidius gave her a slow, deliberate nod, but still didn't talk.

"And . . . they're the opposite of mine," she added, looking up at him.

"Have you learned yet about how marriage works in Alitheia?" Rubidius asked.

Marriage? "Ummm . . ." Darcy wracked her brain and remembered something Tselloch had told her. "Tselloch said that when two people get married, the more magical of the two becomes less powerful, or something," she paused, and now she was blushing, too. "He said that if I married Tellius my magic would diminish because he wasn't as strong as me."

Tellius made a tisking sound in his nose, but Rubidius didn't seem surprised. "A typical lie in its perversion of the truth—in fact, it is the opposite of that. Marriage enhances magical abilities, and spouses take on some of each other's abilities. Marriage is, I hope you know, much more than just a physical union; it is a binding of mind, body, and soul. Magic is only diminished in marriage if one forsakes a spouse. When Alitheians get divorced, it severs the magical tie between the two, and they find themselves weaker magically than before they got married."

Rubidius reached out and traced the gold thread that made the square on the page, connecting all four elements. "It has been so many years," he ruminated, and Darcy inwardly rolled her eyes.

What *has been so many years?* she wanted to yell. Why couldn't he just get to the point already?

He finished tracing the square and tapped his finger on an elaborate rune in the center of the page that was speared down the middle with a line of three four-point stars. "It's called a Completion," he said at last. "When two people marry with opposite inverse talents, it's called a Completion."

"What does that mean?" Darcy asked.

A flash of impatience crossed Rubidius's eyes, and his voice lost some of its ethereal quality. "It means that if the two of you do indeed marry, you each will be able to control aspects of all four elements; you will be the most powerful magicians in recent Alitheian history, perhaps in *all* of Alitheian history. This also makes it of the utmost importance, of course, for you to discipline yourselves to train in your abilities."

Both Darcy and Tellius flinched away from each other.

"But, that's not, like, *necessary*, is it? We don't *need* to make a Completion to defeat Tselloch, do we? I mean, even the prophecy doesn't state that we *have* to get married to get the job done, does it?" Darcy could hear the desperation in her voice and thought that, for once, Tellius probably was in agreement with her.

"No, it's not necessary," Rubidius sounded peevish. "Think of it as a reward."

A *reward?* Darcy choked back her indignation. There was nothing rewarding in the expectation that she was to marry Tellius; it was more like a death sentence. She zoned out as Rubidius intoned something about "the beauty of Pateros's plan." Darcy felt like she was going to be sick.

Rubidius finally stopped talking and stood, rolling up the parchment with the elemental runes on it. Tellius, too, stood abruptly and went back to the corner table. Cadmus leaned forward and sniggered something at him, in reply to which Tellius kicked him hard under the table.

Darcy sat shell-shocked, waiting for Rubidius to give her something else to do. She was happy she had more magic than they'd originally thought, but thinking about Completions was just too disturbing. *It doesn't have to turn out that way*, she told herself.

Rubidius returned from putting the chart away and told her she was finished for the day. "We will explore your talents with air tomorrow," he said, as if the intermediary conversation had never taken place. "And your *other* talent, as well," he seemed to be collecting his own thoughts as he spoke. "It is high time you had some *proper* training in animal communications. You may rejoin your companions for the evening meal."

CHAPTER 11

TELLIUS'S PROPOSAL

"A whatsit?" Sam wrinkled her nose at Darcy over her dinner plate.

"A Completion," Darcy whispered again.

"And that means, like, you and Tellius will be super master magicians if you get married?"

"Something like that." Darcy scowled and stabbed her salad as though it had offended her. "What I don't get," she burst out, "is why the whole deal about us getting married is even *in* the prophecy. I mean, what I told Rubidius is true: from the wording, it doesn't sound like the marriage is a prerequisite for defeating Tselloch, it just states that it will happen. And Rubidius had the nerve to tell me that the marriage, and the Completion that comes with it, is a *reward*," she spat. "It's so backward. It's like . . . arranged marriage! And all that nonsense he spouts: 'It doesn't mean you have to get married, but you will.' It's just garbage. It's the same as saying 'you don't have to, but you do.' Where's the choice in that? It doesn't make any sense at all. And nobody's ever been able to explain to me how I can marry somebody in Alitheia when I go home to our world at the end of every year—"

"Darcy, keep your voice down," Amelia muttered. They were eating in the spacious kitchen with assorted castle personnel and servants, and people at other tables were starting to shoot her concerned looks.

"Great, I can't even talk to you guys about how I feel," Darcy lowered her voice to an angry whisper.

"You *can*, but you should wait until we are alone in our rooms," Amelia replied.

Sam stared at her with a concerned look on her face. "Well . . . that's really cool about your air magic, though. Don't you think?" She was clearly trying to find the positive in the situation.

"Yeah, whatever," Darcy said and pushed her plate away. "I'm not hungry anymore. I'll see you guys upstairs."

Darcy took the spiraling stairs two at a time and almost ran headlong into Tellius on his way down. "Oh!" she exclaimed, pin-wheeling her arms as she struggled to regain her balance.

Tellius shot out his arms and grabbed her shoulders to steady her so she didn't go careening back down the stairs.

"Thanks," she muttered begrudgingly once she was stable and he'd removed his hands. She tried to dodge around him at the same time that he went the same way to try to get around her and they almost collided again. "Sorry," Darcy said as they both then feigned the other direction. "Here," she said, "you go this way, and I'll go that way."

The plan agreed upon, they managed to successfully pass each other, and Darcy was almost out of his sight when she heard him blurt out, "The prophecy might not be entirely accurate, you know."

Darcy froze and turned around. "What do you mean? About what?"

He stood several stairs down, worrying his fingers with a calculating look on his face. "About us. That is, getting married and all."

Darcy felt the floor go out beneath her, and she clutched the banister. "What do you mean?" she asked again, except this time in a whisper.

"Well, I've been doing some research, and . . . I think I found something interesting." He took a step up, toward her. "Do you want to see?"

"Yes!"

"Okay, come on." He jogged up to her and led the way up the rest of the stairs, all the way up to the west wing. At the top he took out a key like hers and opened the door. "I've been spending a lot of time in the library up here. It's the one place Cadmus won't bother me," he said by way of explanation.

They counted doors down the hallway until they reached the library on the right hand side, and Tellius pushed open the door. "They put all the really old books up here when they redid this wing. I guess they figured you six would find them useful in your training."

Tellius stood back so that Darcy could see inside the room for the first time. She stood gaping in the doorway for a full minute at least; the room was like something out of her wildest dreams. The library was circular with floor to ceiling shelves. Ladders on casters reached all the way up to the ceiling. It was shaped like a donut with a ring of shelves in the center of the room, as well. Darcy could do a circle around it and have books on both sides at all times. The only interruptions to the bookshelves were two enormous windows on the far wall and six evenly spaced alcoves, each with two armchairs and a small writing table. The wood finish looked like a deep, polished oak, and it reflected starbursts from a brilliant gas chandelier that hung from the twenty-foot ceiling directly over the center circular shelf, which was only half as high as the outer walls of the room. A narrow doorway led to the inside of the center circle where Darcy could just make out a large round table with chairs all around it.

"Oh, wow!" Darcy exclaimed, stepping in and craning her neck to look up at the ceiling. It was painted gold and engraved with flowers and runes. About twelve feet above the door through which she'd just entered there was a balcony that was accessed by double oak doors. A very narrow staircase followed the curvature of the wall down from it.

Tellius hurried off around the room with hardly a glance at the staircase. "That leads to my quarters," he said as he breezed past it. "Cadmus and I live one floor up on the top floor of the west wing."

Darcy hurried to keep up with him, appreciating the bright colors on the spines of the books and inhaling the smell of old leather and paper. Once deeper inside the room, she noticed that the walls were not curved, but rather faceted, with vertical wood creases every two feet or so, allowing the books to sit in straight lines. She couldn't help but think that the room must be a masterpiece of architectural design.

She came around to the far side of the wall to find Tellius halfway up one of the ladders right next to the thick windowsill. As he searched, she peered out the window, down into a small internal courtyard she'd never seen before. The people beneath her looked like tiny figurines bustling about their chores. Looking out over the castle wall, she could see all the way to the horizon from this vantage point, and there, just like on the night they'd arrived, was the black haze.

"Here it is." Tellius hopped down next to her. He straightened up, and Darcy thought again that it was strange to look up at him rather than down. "Come on."

She followed him to one of the alcoves, and they drew the two armchairs together beneath a sputtering oil lamp. "What sort of book is this?" she asked. It was very thick, and the mahogany leather cover was flaking around the edges. The pages were splotched with dark stains in places.

"It's a history book, of course."

Darcy noted with a touch of irritation that Tellius had picked up Rubidius's habit of saying "of course" in a superior manner, as if she should have already known the answer. She wanted to make a snarky comment back at him but refrained; she was too interested in what he had found to antagonize him. "It looks old," was all she said.

He looked at her incredulously. “Old?” His dark hair had fallen forward into his eyes, obscuring his vision, and he shook it out before going on. “You could say that. This book was written over four hundred years ago.”

That's older than the United States of America, Darcy thought, impressed, but she tried not to show it.

“Okay, here's the section. It's about the translation of the prophecy from Old Alitheian to Common Alitheian. Here,” he put his finger on the cramped script in the center of the page and read aloud: “‘Of the many curious and problematic sections in the Old Alitheian translation, the usage of the word “intended” is the most puzzling. During the original translation work, there was no mention made at all to the king marrying any particular individual. The word used for “intended” could have just as easily been translated as “one who is made for a specific purpose,” but for the sake of preserving the poetic nature of the prophecy, accuracy has been sacrificed for suitability to the rhyme scheme. The Old Alitheian word is more commonly found, if one will take the time to cross-reference other sources from the same era, in a sacrificial sense. If “intended” is, however, in reference to a marital engagement, then who is the king in question? Is he an earthly king or a metaphysical one? Is the phrase meant to be understood literally or symbolically? The imposition of the phrase “to the king you'll be wed” insinuates that the intended is thus female. A strange imposition indeed, for why should the pivotal role go to a woman, rather than a man? My research has uncovered the existence of earlier renditions of the poem that do not contain the twenty-first or twenty-second lines at all. It is my opinion that these lines were added at a later date based on a misguided assumption that the word translated as “intended” carries a marital obligation. The elongating of this title to “King's Intended,” therefore, is a misnomer and should be stricken from all official records.’”

Tellius stopped reading and scanned the page before looking up. “It goes on from there, but that's the most important part.”

Darcy felt like she could hardly breathe. “So . . . we *don't* have to get married? It wasn't even in the original prophecy?”

Tellius looked uncomfortable, and he closed the book slowly, tapping his fingers on the worn cover. “Well, at least, not according to this historian. There're a lot of different historians out there who say different things. I found more than one book suggesting those lines were missing from the original prophecy, but this fellow seemed more opinionated than the others.”

“So, some historians say the part about us getting married is in the original prophecy, and others say it isn't. How do we know who is telling the truth?”

“I don't know.” The corner of Tellius's mouth quirked to the side. “But I do know that we have reason enough to second-guess what we've been told.”

Darcy had stood without meaning to and was pacing back and forth across the carpet outside their alcove. She stopped and faced Tellius, who was still seated. "How did you find that book?"

"Oh, well," he scratched the back of his head, "I've been looking for information on the prophecy all year, actually."

"Yeah, but why do you care so much? It's not like you're one of the Six."

"Why do I care?" he snorted. "Seriously? All my life I've been told that I *might* have to marry a stranger someday. I've been trained to believe, even while we were in hiding, that it was my *duty* to stay unmarried as long as I could, just so that if the Six came in my lifetime, I would be available to marry the mysterious Intended. I've never had a choice in my future, or even who I can like. Last year—" he stopped and blushed, lowering his voice, "last year I liked this girl here in the palace. She was pretty and nice, and . . . and Eleanor told me that I had no business liking any girl but you. She told Rubidius and they made me tell her that we couldn't even be friends." His hands curled into fists. "And then they had her family relocated to a different city, I think, because I haven't seen her since. I could have gotten to know her if it wasn't for—" He froze before he finished his sentence, but Darcy knew what he'd been about to say.

Darcy felt simultaneous guilt and empathy. They were both in the same boat, weren't they? She wondered what Eleanor would say if she could hear her thoughts about Perry.

Tellius seemed to collect himself, and then he went on. "It hasn't just been me, you know."

"What do you mean?"

"Well, we never knew when the Six were going to show up, did we? So every male heir in the line of Ecclektos since the time of Baskania has waited until late in life to get married."

"Really?"

"Of course! Think about it. Take my father, for example. Have you ever wondered why Tullin is so old, even though he was only my dad's cousin? He's old enough to be our grandfather, but he was only two years older than father, who was forced to wait until he was fifty to marry our mother. She was young, only twenty-two when they got married. I remember her better than I remember him."

Gross, Darcy thought, but then she noticed the look on Tellius's face and knew that he was thinking back to the night his parents were murdered by tsellodrin. "Well, did they love each other, at least?"

"I don't know. Either he never told me or I don't remember. I *do* know that he talked to me about it one time, though—this 'special duty' that the Ecclektos men have to bear. He told me it would be difficult, and I think he really meant it. He said there had been another girl, before my mother, who he hadn't been allowed to marry. I think she ended up marrying somebody else."

"That's really sad," Darcy said. It was strange to be having a conversation like this with Tellius, she thought; last year he had been so aloof, even though he was only a little kid. Of course, he'd always born heavier burdens than a young child should have to.

"It's not fair," he said bitterly. "I don't want to be rude, but I don't *want* to marry you."

"I don't want to marry you, either," Darcy assured him.

"Okay, so . . . so we agree."

"Yeah."

"It's not that I don't think you're a nice person!" Tellius added in a rush. "I mean, I was really upset when you got hurt in the dungeon last year. That was awful!"

"Thanks, I know that you came to see me in the sick ward. I appreciated that."

"So . . . maybe now that we know that we're each nice people—" Darcy nodded in encouragement—"and neither of us wants to marry the other—"

"Not even a little bit!" Darcy actually laughed.

"Then maybe we can work together to get Rubidius and Eleanor to look at this." He tapped the book again.

Darcy felt excited, but a little apprehensive at the prospect. "Sure, we can do that."

"But maybe we should talk to them about it first, before we show them the book."

Darcy nodded her agreement.

"I'll leave this here." He went back to the shelf and started up the ladder. "It's the sixth shelf up, five books from the window, okay? In case you want to look at it later."

Darcy heard somebody calling her name in the hall, and she turned toward the door. "I should go. I don't want them to wonder where I am."

Tellius stood next to her and slapped a hand to his forehead. "I almost forgot; there's one more thing."

"What's that?" Darcy asked impatiently. The voices were getting closer.

"If Rubidius doesn't believe us, there *is* another option that we can use to figure out the truth. I read about it in one of the chapters in this book, but I'll have to show you later."

"Darcy? Where are you?" She could hear a muffled knocking on her door down the hall.

"Okay, sounds good," Darcy said. She stuck her head out the library door to see Sam and Amelia standing in front of her door, their arms akimbo. "I'm down here, guys," she called to them.

Tellius squeezed out past her and raised his hand in farewell. Before he walked away, he whispered, "It's called the Oracle."

CHAPTER 12

THE ARGUMENT

"Hey, Darcy. Oh . . . hello, Tellius." Sam's eyebrows retreated up her forehead as she watched Tellius go by, and Amelia's jaw dropped so far that she looked as though she were trying to catch flies with her mouth. She turned a full circle to watch the crown prince walk to the stairwell and then turned back to Darcy with accusing eyes, but Sam got to her first.

"Do you want to explain what *that* was all about?" Sam asked, her voice full of incredulity.

"Seriously," Amelia couldn't seem to restrain herself, "you left dinner all ticked off about Tellius, and then we find you up here cozying up with him in the library!"

"Was it really just the two of you in there?" Sam hissed, sticking her head into the room as though looking for more people.

"Okay, hold on." Darcy raised her hands, trying to sound amused and innocent, but she could feel her ears heating up. "We were *not* cozying up. We were just talking."

"I thought you couldn't stand the sight of him, that you were humiliated at the thought of having to marry him someday, that—"

"I get the idea, Amelia," Darcy cut her off. "It just so turns out that Tellius feels pretty much the same way as I do about the whole thing and, well, he found some stuff that he wanted to show me."

"Stuff like what?" Sam pointed a finger in her face. "Whatever it is, you should really have me look at it, what with, you know, my talent and all."

"It was a book, Sam. And your talent only works with people. You can't tell if a *book* is trustworthy or not."

"It works with high animals, too," Sam reminded her. "I never trusted Lykos, remember?"

"Don't remind me."

"Sorry. But, a book?" She frowned. "I don't know. I bet Rubidius could help me figure that out."

"Right, Rubidius, that's just what we were thinking—"

"What, you and Tellius?" Amelia cocked an eyebrow.

"*Yes*, and you don't have to say it like that. It's not like we're best friends now, or anything. We just have something in common."

"What's that?" Amelia asked.

"Trying to convince Rubidius and Eleanor that the prophecy might not actually say that we have to get married."

Both Sam and Amelia were quiet for a moment before Sam said, "But it does. We all heard it. It says just that. How can it mean anything different?"

"Look, it's not that simple, and I can't really explain it without showing you the book, but just trust me, okay? I think we're onto something. And Sam, you reminded me only a week ago that I might not have to marry him —that Rubidius said he has to 'declare' me, so what the heck?"

"That's not the same thing, Darcy," Sam retorted. "I wasn't questioning the accuracy of the prophecy. I mean, it says what it says. I think Rubidius just meant there's still some free will involved."

"Free will?" Darcy squeaked. "Yeah, right."

Sam and Amelia continued to stare at her until she finally got annoyed. "Come on, guys, be happy for me! I might not have to marry Tellius!" She raised her fists in the air in a mock cheer and opened her eyes wide, mouthing *yay!*

"I don't know, Darcy," Sam said. "It's not really about just questioning whether it means you have to get married, you know."

"What do you mean?" Darcy lowered her fists and frowned at Sam.

"Sam's right," Amelia continued. "If the prophecy is wrong about that part, how can we trust the rest of it? And so far the rest of it has turned out to be pretty accurate, right? I mean, we're here and we fit the roles set out for us, so wouldn't you think that the marriage part is correct, too?"

"No, it's not like that, you don't understand." Darcy struggled. "This historian believes the prophecy was translated or copied wrong and that the word 'intended' doesn't even mean—"

"What are you guys doing?" Perry interrupted them. "Why are you huddling outside the library? You look like you're having a secret meeting."

The three boys were standing just behind them, having come up the hall while they were arguing.

"Nothing. We're doing nothing, just talking." Darcy shot a silencing look at Sam.

"Well, do you want to go down to the grounds? Yahto Veli, Cadmus, and a few others have promised to teach us some Alitheian games."

"Sure!" Darcy said, too brightly. "That's a great idea. I haven't really had a chance to talk to Yahto Veli since we got back."

"We're not dressed for running around, though." Amelia unfolded her arms and looked down at herself.

"That's okay. I think they have some version of horseshoes that you can play just fine in a dress," Perry said. "And you girls do look *fine* in your dresses!"

He smirked, and Dean gave him a fist bump. "Nice!"

Darcy might have been imagining that his gaze rested a fraction of a second longer on her than on the others, but Sam blushed as though Perry had complimented only her and sputtered, "That's—great—okay—fun—now . . ."

"Oh, and also," Perry continued as though he hadn't single-handedly shattered the composition of two of the three girls in the hall, "our animals will be outside to meet us."

"Just forget I said anything about it, Sam," Darcy muttered on their way downstairs.

"I just think it's unlikely that the prophecy is wrong; that's all I'm saying," Sam persisted.

"I get that, and if that's the case, then okay. But I don't want to talk about it anymore. I'm sorry I told you guys in the first place."

Sam sputtered a little but Darcy held up a hand, "Really. Tellius and I will work on what we need to do and you won't ever have to worry about it again, okay?"

They emerged at the bottom of the stairs into a back hallway by the servants' quarters. At last Sam nodded reluctantly. "Okay."

Darcy sighed. She hadn't known it was going to be such a drama production to tell the other girls her news. She resolved to put the whole argument out of her mind as she followed the boys through the winding halls to a small door that looked like it was for putting out the garbage.

It was still light when they stepped outside into the early evening air, but the sun was beginning its track down to the horizon, and Darcy figured they probably had less than an hour to enjoy being outside. She could see Yahto Veli's figure silhouetted across the stretch of grass against a copse of trees inside the castle grounds, and she picked up her pace.

"Veli!" She waved as she came up next to him.

He opened his mouth to greet her but was caught off-guard by a massive yawn that stretched his mouth toward his large pointed ears. "Great

Gloria," he exclaimed. "So sorry. It's getting on toward my bedtime, you know."

Darcy giggled. His hair was already a deep chestnut brown, and his eyes and skin were starting to darken. "I think it's funny how you narks say 'bedtime,' but you, your bodies, that is, don't ever really lay in a bed, do they."

He grinned at her. "True. It's a saying we have picked up from the humans, no doubt."

"At least I have a little time with you before Yahto wakes up."

He squinted his eyes. "Hmmm. Indeed." And then, "How did you find your first day back? Are you satisfied with your accommodations?"

"Yeah! They're great. *Much* better than staying in a cave underground."

"The castle staff worked hard all year to prepare that wing for you. It has everything you need."

"Yeah, that's . . . exactly what Eleanor said, actually," Darcy replied, pausing for a moment. It sure seemed important that the Six know how *complete* a living unit the west wing was. Were they not going to be allowed anywhere else?

Maybe, another portion of her brain pointed out, *they want to make sure you don't go running off again like you did last time*. Darcy pushed that thought aside with a guilty lurch. What she had done last year was in the past; she wasn't about to repeat her mistake.

Darcy opted to change the subject. "Perry said our animals would be here. Are they around? I'd love to say hello to Hippondus."

"Oh, yes! They should be on their way, in fact—"

Just then, as if in answer to her query, Hippondus trotted into the field, followed by the great shaggy lion Liontari, Ptino the songbird, Koukoubagia the owl, Alepo the fox, and lastly, hurrying on stumpy little legs to keep up, Pinello the badger.

Sam gave a happy cry and ran to bury her face in Pinello's fur while the others met their animals with similar happy exclamations.

Darcy took a few hesitant steps toward Hippondus, suddenly shy. She knew all of these animals were high animals, that is, they were of the same intelligence and nature as humans, narks, and nymphs. It struck her that she could, if she wanted to, attempt to talk with Hippondus using the talent she had discovered with Lykos.

She reached her stallion and stroked the side of his face, letting him bump her with his nose. "Hello there," she whispered, but she didn't yet try to activate the link with her mind that would allow him to communicate back to her. She was afraid to try. Would Rubidius be upset with her for trying before they'd had a chance to experiment with it in session? Hadn't she gotten into such trouble last year by doing something just like that—communicating with a high animal without seeking direction and training first? But this was not Lykos, it was Hippondus, and he was unfailingly loyal to her and to their cause.

But then another fear assailed her: what if she could no longer perform her talent? What if touching the nose of Tselloch the panther last year had killed her talent? Or what if Pateros had taken it away from her because she had so totally abused it?

She still didn't fully understand the Alitheian concept of Pateros: the mysterious bear eagle stag creature that had created all of Orodreos, brought humans from her world to this world, and gifted all of humanity with hereditary magic; the character who had created the first gateways, giving humans the ability to create them but forbidding them to do so; the being who was apparently in control of all of their destinies. The Alitheians regarded him as some sort of god, she knew, and of course he must be if he could do all that, but she still didn't quite know what to think of him herself. He was good, she knew that; he had saved her life last year, after all, but why was he so distant from them? Her life sure would be a whole lot easier if he would just appear once and let them ask him a few questions. But Rubidius and Eleanor had insinuated several times last year that that wasn't the way Pateros operated.

Hippondus bumped her cheek again, and she laughed. "I'm sorry, boy, I was just thinking." She stared into his liquid black eyes, her heart thumping unnaturally loud in her chest. Should she try it? *Oh, why not? What do I have to lose?*

She reached out with her mind for the horse's consciousness. Performing this special talent was unlike trying to perform elemental magic; talking with Lykos last year had never made her as tired as practicing moving objects around. This was more natural to her, like something she could just *do*. She felt Hippondus's closeness in her mind, just as she could feel Yahto Veli's proximity without even looking at him, and she made the connection, knowing at that moment that it was going to work. *Hippondus, can you hear me?*

Hippondus snorted and tossed his head in surprise. *Lady Darcy? How can you speak to me in this manner—in the manner of other equines?*

Her face split into a grin. *It's my special talent, as one of the Six.*

It is remarkable! But more remarkable still that you can hear and understand me in return. Never in all the history of our world has a human been able to do what you are doing now.

His voice was rich and inhuman and, just as Lykos had sounded distinctly like a wolf when he spoke in her brain, so did Hippondus sound like a horse. *I mean, he doesn't sound like Mr. Ed, or anything*, she thought to herself. She had learned last year that her private thoughts were still her own; Hippondus could only hear words that she directed specifically to him.

Cool, huh? she replied.

Cool? He sounded puzzled and turned his head to peer at her with one eye. *Is this revelation of a low temperature?*

No, no! Darcy laughed out loud, and the other teenagers looked askance at her, but she ignored them. *It's a saying we have in my world. Something is 'cool' if it's really awesome. You understand what I mean by 'awesome,' right?*

Yes, Lady, I do understand that.

Good. I should let you know that I think this only works one way, okay? If you want to talk to me, you'll have to nudge me to let me know. I have to make the connection between us, you see?

I understand, he said.

Cool.

Cool, he said, and even though he was a horse, Darcy could tell he was smiling.

"Hey, Darcy—" Amelia began, but she was interrupted by a thin scream echoing through the air, getting louder and louder. It was coming from above them. Darcy looked up and her stomach lurched.

Quick as a flash, Veli herded them into a tight group and shouted, "Don't look!"

But Darcy couldn't close her eyes quickly enough. The man hit the ground just ten feet from where they stood, with a sound like a sack of grain and wooden sticks that snapped upon impact. His scream cut off abruptly, and he lay on his stomach like a discarded doll with his face turned toward them. Bright red blood began to dribble from his still-parted lips.

CHAPTER 13

THE MESSAGE

Everyone screamed, even the boys. They all had seen men die in Alitheia, in their battle last year; but for it to happen like this, in a place that was supposed to be safe and protected—they'd never seen anything like this before.

Darcy possessed a vague awareness of frenetic movement all around them, of the two princes passing by surrounded by ranks of bodyguards, of people shouting and somebody trying to force them to get inside. Veli was squatting next to the body. He'd closed the man's eyes, at least, and was checking him, lifting hands and feet as though looking for something. He looked too grim; he looked like Yahto.

Veli turned the man over onto his back. The dull roar that filled Darcy's ears began to subside as Veli lifted the hem of the man's shirt and froze. Carved into the unfortunate soul's chest were words, words that were red with his own blood: *FOLLOW ME*.

Sam's screaming abruptly turned into hyperventilating whimpers as she read the words over Darcy's shoulder.

"Follow me? How could they know? *How?*" She screamed the last word, and Amelia pulled her into a bracing hug to silence her.

"It's not possible," Perry was shouting. "Veli, what does this mean?"

Veli looked up sharply, as if he'd forgotten they were still there. "Inside," he barked. "Come."

As he stood, five other men rushed to tend to the fallen man and Torrin escorted them with Veli back to the castle. "It was one of Ulfred's men," he said in a low voice to the nark. "He will need to be notified."

"Ulfred?" Perry asked. "I know him. I stayed with him last year, the first night we were here."

"Never mind about Ulfred," Torrin snapped.

"What's this about? Please tell us!" Sam begged tearfully.

Neither answered until they reached the side entrance they had emerged from less than a half hour before. At the door, Veli turned to them with a sigh and, despite a warning look from Torrin, began to speak.

"Tselloch has sent us a message," he said quietly.

"What message?" Darcy asked at the same time Dean said, "By dropping somebody out of the sky?"

Veli held up his hands. "He wanted us to know *he* knows you are back. He did it this way to frighten us. To get our attention."

"I thought you said the castle grounds were protected, that none of Tselloch's followers can get in!"

Torrin answered this time. "They didn't get in; they got over. The wards act like a bubble. They flew over the top and dropped him in."

"Who did?" Amelia asked in a whisper. "Tsellochim?"

"More likely it was Tselloch's crows. A large number of them could have carried a full-grown man."

"But those *words*," Sam persisted. "The squirrel in our world, he spelled those words out on the ground to lead us to the gateway."

Veli looked troubled by Sam's remark, and he exchanged a deep look with Torrin before throwing up his hands in frustration. Darcy had never seen Veli frustrated before.

"I don't know how he could have known those words," he admitted.

"Do you think it was a coincidence?" Lewis spoke for the first time. He was very white around his glasses and kept taking them off to clean them.

Torrin answered, "Tselloch knows exactly what he is doing."

"It could have a double meaning," Amelia added, her tone ominous.

They all turned to look at her.

"He . . . he could intend for us to know that he knows we're here, and how we got here, but he *did* write the words on a dead man's chest, or at least, somebody who *would be* dead by the time we read the words."

"What are you getting at?" Perry frowned at her, but Veli seemed to understand.

" 'Follow me,' from a dead man means 'follow me into death,' " he finished Amelia's thought.

Sam squeaked and put her hands over her mouth. "Oh, Amelia! How could you even—why would you—"

"Don't lose it again, Sam," Darcy commanded even as she put a hand on her friend's shoulder to comfort her. "It's no secret Tselloch wants us dead."

"I know, but to put it like *that*—"

"Okay, that's enough for tonight," Torrin said. "Veli, can you see them up to their rooms? I want guards on all their doors tonight and patrols on the grounds the entire night, three-hour shifts. You six," he pierced them with his gaze, "are not to leave the west wing under any circumstances tonight, understand? Oh, and Veli, please check with the princes as well. Make sure they understand the gravity of the situation."

"It will have to be Yahto," Veli said, his eyes on the horizon where the sun was just kissing the trees. "I'll make sure he is fully informed."

A sharp knock on Darcy's door the next morning woke the three of them from their troubled dreams. They were once again in a pile in the middle of her floor, but they had not stayed awake this time with girly conversation; in fact, they hadn't talked at all. In unspoken agreement they had reformed their nest, drawn the curtains tight across the windows, and nestled much closer together. Sam had cried herself to sleep, and Darcy had lain awake for hours until she finally slept amid dreams of the man hitting the ground again, and again, and again. It was a relief to be woken up.

Rubidius was at the door, looking weary as though he, too, had spent the night with disturbing dreams. On the contrary, he informed her at the door, he had not slept at all but had been up all night in council with Tullin and the other castle leadership.

"We will have group session this afternoon," he said in a gravelly voice. "I must sleep until then."

It was the first time Darcy had ever known the old alchemist to admit anything close to physical weakness, and it made her feel even more insecure herself. When she turned away from the door, Amelia and Sam were dragging themselves off to their own rooms.

Eleanor came to see them later that morning, bringing with her a tray of breakfast biscuits, thick creamy cheese and tea, but the girls were too distracted to eat. The boys, however, made quick work of the food.

They sat together in a common room down the hall on the left—close to where Rubidius stayed—which was stocked with board games, chairs, large cushions, and several round tables. Absorbed in their own thoughts and activities, they counted off the time until lunch. Even Eleanor was quiet. Darcy thought she might even be asleep as she sat in a rocking chair in the corner with her head down and her fingers intertwined in her lap.

Lewis had brought in his gift—the phoenix feather quill with which he was able to exercise his talent—and he settled himself into a chair with several fresh pieces of parchment and began to write.

Sam had also brought along her gift, the empty leather pouch that filled itself with objects deeply needed by those she called her companions. She kept checking it, as though expecting it to fill itself with something that could make right what had happened the night before.

Perry and Dean absorbed themselves in a card game they had learned last year in Alitheia, but Darcy got the impression they were only playing it to keep their hands busy. Neither of them was smiling, and they kept pausing for long lulls while one or both of them seemed to lose track of what he was doing.

Amelia paced back and forth from the door to a window, fingering the pendant necklace that Simon had given her, and every now and then she muttered something to herself.

Darcy watched them with a detached interest. She couldn't seem to make herself do anything at all. Yesterday she had been so absorbed with her own problems, and now she felt guilty about her preoccupation with them. What did it matter if the prophecy did or didn't say she was to marry Tellius, in light of Tselloch's evil plans for Alitheia? If he succeeded, none of them would be left alive to worry about marriage at all.

Finally Eleanor raised her head. She hadn't been sleeping, it was now apparent, as she looked as sharp as ever, her face lined with concern. "Your year was not supposed to start out like this," she said. "I am sorry you have had to witness such an event so soon."

"How about *at all*," Amelia spat, stopping her pacing to stare at the old woman. "I'd hoped to not see anybody die *at all* this year. I thought things were going better!"

Eleanor sighed. "Things are, of course, better than the last time you were here. We've retaken the castles and are rebuilding the cities that once surrounded them. Families that have long been in hiding are returning to the ancient lands of their fathers and there is a general spirit of optimism. But through it all Tselloch has been gaining strength, and without you here to help us fight him, our forces have lost ground."

Amelia sat down very slowly and the boys looked up. "What do you mean?" Perry asked.

"We send out regular patrols," she explained, "but only about half their number come back. That haze on the horizon," her eyes flitted to Darcy's, "grows ever bigger. We do not know if it is some gross manifestation of his tsellochim or something worse. Tselloch himself has not been seen since we stormed the castle at the end of last year, and we know that he is not nearby, but he has somehow managed to project himself, or his will, into the proximity of the castle grounds. I could not tell you, Darcy, how bad it truly is." Eleanor's eyes begged her forgiveness. "When we spoke on board the *Cal Meridian*, I wanted you to feel safe. I thought we could get you acclimated to being back before you had to face the harsh reality."

"The prophecy says we will defeat Tselloch," Sam said, "but how can we be of that much use to you in fighting against him? You said you lose ground when we're not here, but that seems . . . I don't know . . . kind of sad! I mean, we're just kids!"

"And therein lies another problem," Eleanor said, nodding her head. "We need you; we need your *abilities*, but you are still so young, and you have so much training left to undergo! How can we ask you to put your lives in danger when we would never ask the same of *our* children or grandchildren?"

"You have kids?" Perry asked.

Eleanor looked at him askance. "Figuratively speaking, dear." She shook her head. "The longer we take to train you, the more ground Tselloch gains back, and the more people lose faith in our cause. The kingdom is crumbling from without and within."

"But I thought you agreed with Rubidius that we need the training before we can be of any more help," Amelia said.

"I do, but I also have seen what you already can do. And . . . and I'm afraid for this land." She twisted her fingers in her lap. "If we do not find and close the gateways soon, I am afraid that all will be lost."

Darcy stared bleakly at Eleanor. The older woman had always seemed indefatigable in her faith in Pateros's plan and the workings of the prophecy, and now, when it seemed that they had already won back so much from Tselloch, she was questioning what needed to be done.

"What should we do?" Lewis asked from the corner, his quill still poised over his parchment.

Eleanor seemed to shake herself, and she looked around at them with new eyes. "I'm sorry, that was not a burden I should have shared with you. Rubidius, of course, has his plans laid out for your training. Pateros will see us through. And you *are* back! That is encouragement enough for most Alitheians. Please pay no heed to my words; my mind has been much affected since the events of last night."

When they at last finished lunch and made their way to Rubidius's cottage, they all felt as though they needed naps just to sleep off the gloom of the day. They hadn't been allowed to leave the west wing even for the meal, and they were beginning to feel a little penned up in the single hallway.

Rubidius did not immediately answer the knock on his door, so they knocked again, louder, and finally heard him grumbling his way over to let them in. He wore a long dressing gown, and his hair was mussed on one side as though he had just gotten out of bed. They sat at their spots around the table while he poured himself a steaming cup of tea and yawned before he began.

"What I need to know from you," he said, his voice very scratchy, "is whether any of you told anybody here about the words spelled out for you on the ground that led you to the gateway."

Darcy cast a blank look around at her companions, and they stared back just as blankly. Darcy certainly had not told anybody in Alitheia about it—leastwise, not before the man fell from the sky. Until that moment, she'd hardly given it a second thought since she arrived.

They each answered a solemn 'no' to the old alchemist. He sighed and sat down with them. "That is as I feared," he said. He wrapped his long fingers around his mug, and Darcy noticed that they bore many shiny scars. *Probably from throwing his cauldron when he gets upset*, she thought, smug.

"It means that one of two things has happened," Rubidius continued. "Have you ever heard of the veil between the worlds?"

They all shook their heads no, but Darcy thought she knew where this was going. "We might know what you're talking about," she said. "We were just talking last week about how magic seems to leak through from Alitheia to our world. It seems like this might happen close to the gateway, but without coming *through* it."

Rubidius nodded, pleased she had made the connection. "We learned of it because of Baskania's original gateway. Do you remember Eleanor telling you that people eventually moved away from Tselloch's gateway because they felt haunted by phantom noises and an evil presence?"

Darcy nodded.

"We came to discover that the veil between the worlds becomes very thin over time in the vicinity of an *active* gateway. The gateway to your world is active but not always open, but the gateways to Tselloch's world remain open."

"So magic *is* getting through," Lewis said.

Rubidius nodded. "In very small doses. But the longer the gateway is active, the more magic will leak through."

"What about people?" Darcy asked.

"Darcy," Sam protested. "I don't think—"

"People?" Rubidius seemed very cautious. "People are not able to enter Alitheia without going through a gateway, no . . ." he drifted off and shook his head. "Rather, Tselloch may have devised a means of communicating with someone in your world, someone who might be willing to cooperate with him. Is there anybody you can think of?"

"Yes," Darcy, Perry, and Amelia said all at once. "Colin Mackaby," Darcy finished.

Darcy knew now was the right time to come clean about what she had seen her first night at Cedar Cove. "Saturday night I looked out my window at camp and saw Colin talking to somebody in the woods. It looked like . . . like him, like Tselloch. But I couldn't be sure," she added quickly as Sam squeaked and covered her mouth. "Whatever it was, it was almost transparent, like it wasn't quite there."

"Darcy, you didn't tell us that part!" Sam said, uncovering her mouth.

"I didn't want to scare you," Darcy said.

"Is this Colin Mackaby the type to be easily swayed by someone of Tselloch's charisma?" Rubidius pressed on.

"I don't know," Darcy said, "I haven't known him for that long. The others have known him a lot longer."

Perry sat forward with intense eyes. "He's always been a creeper," he said, "interested in the dark arts and black magic and stuff. I wouldn't be surprised *at all* to find out he's been communicating with Tselloch."

"And he was following us all day Sunday," Amelia reminded them. "I bet he *did* follow us all the way out to Whitetail Point. He probably stayed back far enough so your dad wouldn't notice him, Darcy."

She shuddered. "Yeah."

"Wait, wait, wait. There's a big problem with this theory," Dean said, also leaning forward. "Time stops in our world while we're here, right? So Colin wouldn't have time to read the "follow me" message and tell Tselloch about it, would he? We'll be back before he even gets to it."

They looked to Rubidius. "This is all hypothetical," he said after a thoughtful moment. "This time difference is unique to your experience, and I can only think Pateros allows it because you are children and your parents would worry if you disappeared for a year."

Darcy snorted. *You think?*

"Perhaps Tselloch has made a way for this Colin to slip into the time continuum in the infinitesimal period that you are gone from your world. Perhaps time does not actually *stop* while you are gone, but slows to a minute crawl. We must consider the possibility this boy has the power to move at regular speed while the rest of his world—your world—is frozen."

"This is too weird," Lewis said.

"What's the other option?" Sam asked. "You said that one of two things might have happened; what's the other one?"

"Well, relating also to the thin veil between the worlds, sometimes beings in our world can see into yours, and vice versa."

"So, last summer, when that squirrel nodded at me, maybe it wasn't actually in our world, but looking at me from Alitheia?"

Rubidius looked bemused. "I do not know to which squirrel you are referring, but what you are saying sounds logical. In this case, then, perhaps a servant of Tselloch was able to see the words from our world through the veil, but this is very troubling as well."

"More troubling than Colin Mackaby being a servant of Tselloch?" Amelia snorted.

"It would mean," Rubidius continued, ignoring Amelia's comment, "that Tselloch has found a way to penetrate the old wards around the peninsula, in which case we are in much more imminent danger than we thought."

Oh, Darcy thought, and Amelia wilted.

"In either case," Rubidius said, "we have some things to consider. But," he clapped his hands and made his now-empty teacup float over to the sink and deposit itself inside with a gentle clatter, "this was not meant to take up all our time today. In all honesty, I spent most of the night discussing the message from Tselloch, and I'm ready to move on, aren't you?"

And just like that, as though he hadn't just suggested some of the most radical ideas they had ever heard since coming to Alitheia, he began to go over their exams from the day before.

Chapter 14

The Invocation

Rubidius fed them supper that evening and then dismissed them with instructions to come back the following morning. "I'll work with Darcy alone in the afternoon," he said as they filed out his door. "She and I have some important training to continue, but that does not mean I want the rest of you to be idle. Practice your talents in whatever ways you can think of until I have the chance to meet with each of you individually."

The instructions given, they stood in the hall, aimless and wondering what to do next with their time. Guards stood at either end of the hallway, and the six felt as though they were on display until they separated to different tasks. Amelia declared she wanted to take a bath and go to bed early, and she left for her room. The three boys went to the common room to check out some of the games, and Sam and Darcy stood in indecision.

"Darcy?" Sam finally said, but she was watching Perry disappear into the common room. "Do you want to go play a game with Pe—I mean, with the guys?"

The corner of Darcy's mouth turned up into a smile. "I think I'm too tired, Sam, but you go ahead."

Sam hovered in indecision. Darcy could tell that she really wanted to be with Perry, but she also didn't want to abandon Darcy. "Are you sure? What are you going to do?"

"Probably start getting ready for bed, like Amelia. I didn't sleep great last night."

"Yeah, I know what you mean. I guess we're sleeping in our own beds tonight, then?"

"It's probably about time," Darcy laughed. "I mean, we're grown people, right? We don't need to share a room."

Sam laughed, too, but it was tinged with nervousness. "Okay then, I'll go hang out with the boys. Come join us if you can't sleep, okay?"

"Okay. G'night." She turned to walk down to her room.

"And Darcy?"

Darcy looked over her shoulder. "Yeah?"

"If you have bad dreams again tonight, just come on over. I'll leave the door unlocked on my side."

Darcy gulped. She hoped her dreams would not be frightening again tonight. "Thanks, Sam."

Sam waved and skipped off to the common room. Now that Darcy was alone, she didn't feel like going to bed. She was worried she'd just lie there thinking about the fallen man, and Colin, and Tselloch, and . . . There was no way she was going to fall asleep. She came up next to the library and paused, peering into the dimly lit room and thinking she needed a distraction.

She stepped through the door and looked up at the balcony to Tellius's room, but he wasn't there. The door was shut tight, and she could hear no noises coming from inside. She wondered if he and Cadmus were being kept under even tighter lock and key than the rest of them.

She squinted in the dim light, wondering how anybody could read in that sort of gloom, and noticed a large key protruding from the wall by the door. Curious, she reached out and turned it; the chandelier overhead flared brighter. *That's better,* she thought.

Now that she could see properly, Darcy took off around the deserted room until she came to the first of the two windows on the far wall. The ladder was still where Tellius had left it, so she had only to climb up to the sixth shelf to retrieve the history book he had read to her the night before. She came back down with the heavy book under her arm and sat gingerly on the narrow window seat.

Without Tellius present, she was able to examine it with more liberty, and she turned it over curiously in her hands. There was no title on the front or back, but on the spine there were faded gold letters that read, *Batsal's Histories*. She turned open the cover and found that there was no table of contents. As she flipped through the pages, she saw hand-drawn illustrations and chapter headings, but there was nothing else to guide a reader through the text; there weren't even any page numbers.

Darcy felt a stab of annoyance as she realized she was going to have to search to find the section that Tellius had read to her; he hadn't marked it with anything. She shifted on the hard wooden bench and tried to draw her skirt up around her knees, but she couldn't quite make it work. "Well," she muttered to herself, "Tellius never said not to take the book out of the library. I'll bring it back when I'm done." She stood to leave, turning the chandelier back down to low on her way out.

She paused in the hallway, clutching the book to her chest and thinking about Sam's insistence upon seeing the book to verify its trustworthiness. Competing desires began to war within her. While she knew that Sam only wanted to help, and that she should do all she could *not* to repeat her stupidity of the year before, she was also afraid that Sam's talent *would* work on the book. Not just work, but reveal that the source was untrustworthy. *And then I would have to accept that the prophecy might be accurate after all*, she thought glumly.

She took two steps toward her room, then turned around and took two steps back. Thinking she'd made up her mind, she again headed toward her room before changing her mind and turning around a second time. She thought she must look ridiculous to the guards at the end of the hall and finally settled on at least showing the book to Sam. *Try to be wise, Darcy,* she told herself.

She marched down the hall to the common room door and stopped outside it when she heard laughter.

"No, I'm serious!" Dean quipped. "No piece of paper can be folded in half more than seven times!"

"What?" Sam remarked incredulously. "Even if it's really thin?"

"I don't believe you," Perry said.

Darcy heard a shuffle of paper.

"Go ahead, try!" Dean sounded smug. "You won't make it past seven, I promise."

Darcy listened with amusement to the concentrated silence that followed Dean's statement, and then she heard Perry exclaim, "Dang. Seven. Okay . . . let's find a thinner piece."

Sam laughed, and it sounded like they began to search the room for scraps of paper. They hadn't seen Darcy, and Sam sounded so happy and distracted. *I don't want to worry her again*, Darcy reasoned, meandering back to her room.

"You know what we *really* need?" Perry's loud voice wafted down the hall as she reached her door. "*Toilet* paper!" They howled with laughter.

Darcy sat in the comfort of her room with the lights turned up high and her pillows stacked around her. She was sitting in bed, her favorite place to read when she was at home, and she had the large book propped open on her knees. One after another she turned the rigid parchment pages of the book, some of them sticking together and yielding only to her fingernails. The script was handwritten, but it looked as though the author Batsal had taken very good care in forming the letters because Darcy could read it without any trouble. There were some archaic words and references she didn't understand, but she found most of it legible.

Most of it was also very boring. She passed over chapters with such titles as, *"The Sociopolitical Underpinnings of Narkian Aesthetics,"* and *"Dryads and their Trees: An Essay on the Classification of Tree Nymphs, Sea Nymphs, and Land Nymphs."* She almost flipped right past a chapter entitled simply *"The Oracle,"* when she paused.

The Oracle. Wasn't that what Tellius had whispered to her last night, as an option for deciphering the prophecy's true meaning? She began to page with interest through the chapter, pausing here and there to examine a page. The chapter was very long, and she knew that there was no way she could read it all that night, but it could serve as a good distraction for a while. She went back to the beginning and began to read:

> The existence of the Oracle in Alitheia has long been contested by various groups, but the Oracle is undoubtedly real, based on the testimony of many of the finest wilderness explorers this land has ever seen.

Darcy skipped over the several pages in which he digressed into long accounts of those he had interviewed.

> One must have a pressing query of significant importance to one's life and wellbeing to even invoke the Oracle. As I have never wanted for anything in my life, likewise I have not been to see or been able to invoke the Oracle. I do, however, have it on the good authority of these explorers and scholars that the Oracle is present in our land, timeless and active.
>
> The nature of the Oracle bewilders many, as our kind cannot easily comprehend a being who is neither god nor person, who is amoral, and who knows and tells the truth always. Is the Oracle, as some have suggested, a member of an extinct race Pateros cursed to such a basic existence? Or is it simply a sentient accumulation of magic itself?

And off he went again for several pages discussing things Darcy didn't feel like reading. She was beginning to think there was nothing of importance for her to read in this chapter when her eyes happened to light upon her own title.

> Regarding the role of the Intended in the prophecy of the Six (see chapter entitled the same), it is my

> opinion that the meaning of lines twenty-one and twenty-two can be divined by querying the Oracle. An invocation of the Oracle will fail, however, for all except that person most affected by the answer.
> I have recorded the process of invocation as follows, as dictated by those scholars who have extensive experience in invocation.

Near the bottom of the page were his written instructions. Darcy felt a thrill in her stomach as she traced the swirling letters with her finger. What would happen if she followed these directions? Was asking a question of this Oracle thing really as easy as just speaking the words at the bottom of the page as he instructed? *She* was the person most affected by that portion of the prophecy, so her question *should* go through, according to Batsal. And it *was* a matter of life or death. *To me, at least.*

Darcy bit her lip and studied the words; they were just ink on parchment. If nothing happened, she would never even have to tell anybody about it. She released her bottom lip and perused the instructions again very carefully.

> A petition to the Oracle must be presented in the form of a spoken invocation. The petitioner must speak the words below while holding firm in his mind the question he intends to present. If the question is of great enough import to the petitioner, the Oracle will accept the invocation. The petitioner will know that his invocation has been successful by the appearance of a mark on the body. The petitioner will also find that the words of the invocation will fade from the page of any enchanted text such as this one, thereby forming a magical bridge between petitioner and Oracle. The words return only for the next petitioner. Potential petitioners must be wary, however. One question and one question only may they present to the Oracle. It is recommended that the question be solid in mind before attempting the invocation.

Darcy felt a thrill of excitement. *I can do this!* she thought. *It's no big deal. All I have to do is figure out exactly how I want to phrase my question.* She sat deep in thought for some time. She didn't want the question to be too narrow or too vague. She didn't want to simply ask if she and Tellius had to get married someday; she wanted to know the exact meaning of the term "Intended" in the prophecy.

After several minutes of contemplation, she thought she had a good grasp of what she wanted to ask. *What is the role of the Intended in regard to the prophecy of the Six, and is this role tied to marriage with the king?* She worded the question in her mind as officially as she could, and she focused on the words of invocation, written in large full caps on the following page. Holding the question very firmly in her mind, she whispered the words aloud: "Oracle of the sacred stone, I invoke thee. I present to you my petition. Please grant me with an audience and the answer that I seek."

She felt foolish and looked around self-consciously. She expected a voice to speak to her out of the air, answering her question, but her room was as quiet as a grave. She looked back at the page and studied the letters of the invocation. They hadn't faded. She checked her body, but she didn't feel any different and she wasn't marked in any way that she could tell.

Oh yeah, she remembered. Batsal had mentioned going to *see* the Oracle. *I bet you're supposed to do the invocation once you've found it, stupid.* She fought the hard lump of disappointment in her throat. Against all logic, she had really hoped she'd been close to knowing the truth.

A soft knock sounded on her door and Darcy jumped, feeling guilty. With deft fingers, she pulled the ribbon out of her hair and marked the page with the invocation on it before she snapped the book shut and shoved it under a pillow.

The knock sounded again and she scrambled off the bed and over to the door.

She cracked it open. It was Sam.

"Hey," Sam whispered. Her cheeks were flushed and she looked happy. "I'm heading to bed, and I saw that your light was still on. I just wanted to say goodnight again."

"Oh, okay. Goodnight." Darcy still held her door only ajar, feeling as if she had done something wrong and had to hide the interior of her room from Sam's prying eyes. "I'll see you in the morning."

"Bye!" Sam grinned and turned off to her room.

Darcy waited at least fifteen minutes to make sure that Sam was definitely in her room before she retrieved the book from under her pillow and tiptoed to the door with it. Sticking her head out into the hallway, she found it dim and deserted except for the guards. Putting on as innocent an air as she could, she strolled to the library with the book tucked under her arm.

She turned the chandelier up with the key when she stepped into the room and flinched when she felt a slight pinch in the middle of her left palm as she did so. She looked at her hand and noticed a tiny, purplish sore in the center of her palm, kind of like a zit. It itched a little, and Darcy wondered if she had been burned by the key. *It's warm, but not that hot*, she thought.

Darcy went to the far wall and replaced the book on the shelf. Then, not wanting anybody to know she and Tellius had been in that section, she rolled the ladder as far as it would go. She turned the light down and scratched idly at the sore on her hand as she hurried back to bed.

CHAPTER 15

WHAT WAS LOST

"It's out of the question!" Rubidius's growl echoed out his door and down the hall to where they were leaning along the wall, waiting to be called in. It was time for morning session, but when they'd arrived at Rubidius's cottage, the door had been open a sliver, and they'd heard him talking with somebody.

"You do realize," he continued, "that one of them would actually have to *go* to find the answer, don't you? It's frivolous. Ridiculous."

The other person's reply was too soft for them to hear. The six of them crept closer.

"No, it could *not* be just anybody. The Oracle has very specific rules. It is too dangerous and not worth the risk."

"But it always speaks truth!" Tellius's voice finally became audible. "Isn't that worth the risk? I would go!" He sounded agitated.

Rubidius was silent for a long time, and the six exchanged glances.

After this moment of silence, he answered gravely, "It may always speak truth, but that truth is often misconstrued. It speaks in riddles, riddles maddening enough to obsess a person for the rest of his life over their meaning. You're too young to understand. You cannot go, and if one of *them* goes, it may end in disaster. The Oracle never gives a clear answer."

Perry stepped forward, clearly tired of being left out of the loop, and poked his head through the doorway. "If one of us goes where?"

Darcy sucked in her breath, expecting an angry explosion from the old alchemist.

"You heard that, did you? All right. Come in, all of you, and don't think you are getting away without a session this morning!" he barked as they filed in. "And stop looking so pleased with yourself," he snapped at Perry, who was giving the rest of them a double thumbs up.

They took their usual seats around the large round table and gazed up with expectant faces, waiting for Rubidius to tell them something enlightening, but instead all he said was, "Forget what you just heard. It is of no consequence to you."

"Of no consequence?" Perry sputtered. "It sounded pretty important to me!"

"Were you talking about the Oracle?" Darcy felt a shiver, remembering her attempt to invoke it the night before. She looked at Tellius. He hadn't told her he was going to take it up with Rubidius already.

"It is a fool's errand," Rubidius snapped. "Do not think on it."

Darcy was surprised at how vehemently opposed to the Oracle Rubidius seemed. "Tellius mentioned the Oracle to me earlier this week."

Rubidius gazed piercingly at her, as though trying to guess her true motivations. "He did, did he?" Rubidius turned to glare at the young prince. "He hasn't yet mentioned where *he* found out about it."

Darcy shrank back a little. All her friends were staring at her with some surprise. "In a book," she said. "He was looking up the prophecy." She looked at Tellius, trying to gauge his reaction.

Rubidius straightened and looked imperiously down at Tellius. "Please bring the book to me."

Darcy felt guilty; she hadn't intended to get Tellius in trouble.

"The rest of you," he turned back to them as Tellius slinked out of the room, "take out a piece of parchment paper and label it 'non-magical means of opposing a magical opponent.'"

"We're still going to take notes?" Perry whined, but when Rubidius speared him with a furious gaze, he lowered his head. "Never mind."

Rubidius talked, and the six took notes, their quills scratching furiously to keep up with his clipped pace, but Darcy was only forming letters. Her mind was on the mysterious Oracle and the book that Tellius was going to retrieve. He seemed to be taking an eternity. He only had to go down to the library and take it from the sixth shelf by the window!

And then, at long last, the door creaked open and Tellius reentered, clutching the large mahogany book to his chest, followed by Eleanor. He shot an accusatory look at Darcy before he faced Rubidius.

Rubidius finished his sentence and then turned to Tellius, holding out his hand for the book and snatching it out of Tellius's grip when the boy extended it to him. He turned it over to inspect the spine and a sneer lit his face. "Ah. Batsal," he spit out the name. "I should have known. One of the most discredited authorities on Alitheian history I have ever read." He looked up at the prince. "Where did you find this?"

Tellius straightened his shoulders. "In the library."

"And you were looking for information simply because, in your narrow-mindedness, you cannot imagine ever falling in love with the Intended and choosing to marry her?" His voice was very dry and both Darcy and Tellius blushed at his words.

"You don't have to be so hard on him," Darcy blurted out. "I wanted to know, too. You don't understand what it's like having your future decided for you!"

Rubidius's gaze on her was very cool. "Don't I?"

The room was dead silent. It seemed like they all were holding their breath. Nobody knew what to say.

Finally, Rubidius continued as though teaching a lesson. "And what did you find?"

Darcy and Tellius exchanged silent encouragement before Tellius said, "Batsal says the marriage wasn't in the original prophecy. He . . . he says there are a lot of problems with the idea that we have to get married."

"He does, does he?"

Darcy got the impression Rubidius already knew exactly what Batsal had written about the prophecy. Eleanor did, too, it appeared as she stood pursing her lips.

"And what did Batsal have to say about the Oracle?" Rubidius continued in a deadly soft tone. Darcy almost wanted to shout for Tellius to stop speaking, but it was too late.

"He said you can ask any question of the Oracle, and it is bound to tell you a true answer in response." Tellius looked down at his fingers.

"Hmmm . . ." Rubidius paced to his window and stared out, very still. All of their eyes were glued on him. "Hence why you petitioned me to let you go and ask the Oracle about the marriage obligation. Because to you, right now, even with everything else going on, it is the most pressing problem on your young minds."

It sounded so selfish when Rubidius phrased it like that, and Darcy cringed. Sam looked at her with sympathy, and Amelia crossed her arms over her chest. Darcy couldn't tell if she was annoyed with her or indignant on her behalf.

"What Batsal does not say is that the *majority* of historians *agree* on the reliability of the prophecy as it stands today rather than disagree." Rubidius went into lecture mode and turned from the window to look at them.

Tellius hung his head. "Batsal's not the only one—" he began.

"Oh, I *know* he's not the only historian to disagree with parts of the prophecy. But he *is* the most vocal." Rubidius exchanged looks with Eleanor. "And I suspect he was glowing in his recommendation of using the Oracle, am I correct?"

"Yes."

"But he never went to see the Oracle himself, so he wouldn't know, now would he?"

Tellius hesitated. "No. I guess not." His voice was almost a whisper.

"Sit down, Tellius," Rubidius ordered, and Eleanor dragged a chair to the table for the prince. Rubidius took his customary spot and looked around at them with tired eyes. "All criticisms tend to contain a grain of truth," he admitted. "While I disagree whole-heartedly with Batsal's conclusions, he was not working from completely inaccurate information. Let me explain.

"What I said about the prophecy is true; most historians, both ancient and modern, agree that the prophecy as we interpret it today is both complete and as accurate as can be expected under the circumstances. What most historians don't mention, however, is that the last four lines of the prophecy are a reconstruction."

"They're a what?" Sam wrinkled her nose and frowned.

"A reconstruction," Rubidius said again. "They were lost."

Darcy felt this revelation like a punch to her stomach. Those were the lines that talked about her and Tellius getting married.

"I don't even remember the last four lines of the prophecy," Sam said. "What are they?"

Eleanor spoke the words in a murmur. "*At the end of all things to the king you'll be wed, Marked by a ring and the deepest color: red. Now comings and goings will lead to the end, To vanquish the Shadow, Alitheia to mend.*"

Rubidius let her finish before starting again. "The prophecy was passed down orally for many years before it was ever written down. And when it was written down, several hundred years ago, it was determined that the official master copy would always be kept here, in the castle of Ormiskos, in a special box under lock and key. There were copies made, of course, but as they proliferated throughout the kingdom, minor changes appeared between the various copies. But the master copy remained intact."

"What happened to it?" Amelia asked.

"There was a fire. The box was recovered, but it had been burned through, and the final lines of the prophecy were illegible."

"So Batsal was right, wasn't he? How can we make any guess at all of what it said?" Darcy squeaked, feeling betrayed that this information had never been shared with her.

"An effort was made to collect copies of the prophecy throughout the kingdom, and the most reliable sources were brought together to fashion what we have today. Batsal's ridiculous suggestion that the lines regarding your marriage be cut are not based on the most reliable copies of the prophecy, as agreed upon by the most reliable historians."

"But . . . that doesn't mean anything!" Darcy protested.

"Of course it does," Rubidius snapped. "Do you think great care wasn't taken in reconstructing the material? Furthermore, do you think Pateros would continue to let us operate under false assumptions if the lines about your marriage were inaccurate?"

Maybe! Darcy thought but didn't reply.

"So, what's the truth about the Oracle?" Lewis brought them back to the second point of contention. "In our world oracles existed a long time ago, but they were just fakes. I mean, the only oracle I remember hearing about was the Oracle at Delphi, and she only comes up in stories. I mean, she existed in real life, but there's no way she could have actually foretold the future."

"This Oracle is not a person," Rubidius said. "It is a being, neither male nor female, that has existed since the birth of Alitheia. While it always speaks truth, it is self-seeking and harsh. Those who seek the Oracle do so only under compulsion; many would seek to turn back from their journeys and find that they cannot. To seek out knowledge in this manner is not in line with Pateros's order. He alone is meant to know the future before it happens. When he reveals aspects of the future to us in prophetic form, it is a *gift*. Questioning his word through a being such as the Oracle, which is *not* of him, is worse than foolishness; it is idiocy. It is a journey that would result in compunction."

"Comp—what now?" Dean asked.

"Regret," Eleanor said softly. She had her back turned to them and was staring out the window.

Rubidius nodded and continued. "As I said, the Oracle never gives a straight answer. In other words, you can ask for the original four lines of the prophecy, but that is not the answer you will get. You can ask plainly if you have to marry each other, but it will not provide a simple yes or no. The Oracle is more likely to give you a new riddle to ponder, that if you can decipher it, *might* help you to discern a deeper meaning of the last four lines, but it could take you a lifetime to figure it out.

"Secondly," and at this he looked even graver, "the Oracle can only be queried by the person most affected by the outcome. In the case of the last four lines of the original prophecy, that would be—"

"Me," Darcy said. "So, I would have to go. Or Tellius, I suppose."

Rubidius shook his head. "Not Tellius. You, Darcy. The prophecy is about the Six, and you are one of the Six. While Tellius is affected by the prophecy, he is not the subject of it. You are the only one who could go, and that is *entirely* out of the question. It is too frivolous a reason to go even if it wasn't extremely dangerous."

"But . . ." Darcy tried to reason it out in her mind. This seemed to her another one of those situations where Pateros created something and then forbade its use, and that just seemed wrong. "It's not frivolous to *us*. It affects the rest of our lives!"

Rubidius held up two hands to stop her. "I'm not suggesting that marriage is insignificant. I understand the lure of the Oracle, particularly at your age. You young people want everything at once; you do not appreciate the sacrifice of waiting. And in the case of the Oracle, you do not understand what you are asking us to let you do."

"How do you *know* the Oracle is so bad, anyway? Isn't everything in Alitheia created by Pateros?" Darcy pressed.

"Correction, everything in Alitheia is part of his created universe, but that does not mean he directly created the Oracle."

"Then who did?" Perry asked.

Rubidius hesitated. "Nobody knows how it came to be."

Darcy remembered Batsal's book saying the same thing and she smirked inwardly. *Well, at least he got something right.*

"It is a common trend, however, to take something created by Pateros as good for mankind and twist it against Pateros to become a bane. It is possible that the Oracle was created as a sort of mock prophet, an antithesis to his revealed truth."

"I thought you said it always speaks truth."

"Exactly!" Rubidius smacked his fist to his palm. "That is *precisely* what makes it so tempting. It will tell you the truth, but you will find in the end that knowing the truth was not worth the cost you paid to get it."

They all were silent for a long time, thinking to themselves. Darcy kept going over her failed invocation in her head, thinking she should feel relieved that it didn't work, in light of what Rubidius had told them, but she couldn't quite muster those feelings. There was a deeper, more desperate part of her soul that still wanted to know the answer.

"You speak as though you went to see it yourself," Tellius said after several moments.

Rubidius looked at him, and his face was an unreadable mask. "I did," he said.

His admission hung heavily in the room as the seven young people stared at him. Eleanor nodded sadly, as if she had already known. Darcy, indignant, finally sputtered, "Then how can you lecture *us* about not going? *You* went and it turned out fine."

"You do not know what you are saying."

"What did you ask it?" Tellius narrowed his eyes in curiosity.

"Now is not the time. I will not indulge this foolishness any longer!" His voice rose to a shout, and they fell silent.

He regarded them with heavy-lidded eyes and then looked back down at Batsal's book. He stood from the table and brought it to his cupboards. "I will keep this book here to prevent you from further attempts to satisfy your curiosity. That is my final word."

As he put it away, Darcy noticed that he hesitated a moment, shoulders tensed. He fingered the ribbon she had used to mark the chapter on the Oracle. With deft fingers he flipped the book open and gasped. "The words of the invocation; they are missing." He spun around, and Darcy was terrified of him.

They're not missing! They were there when I put the book away last night.

"Your hand," he said to Darcy. "Show me your hand!" He marched over to her and held out his hand for hers, and for a brief, terrifying moment she thought he somehow knew about her cold right hand and how she had reached for Tselloch in the dungeon.

She clutched her right hand to her chest, but he was not concerned with it. Instead he grasped her left hand and turned it over to look at her palm. There, right in the center, was the tiny sore she'd had since the night before. It still itched, and Darcy thought it looked a little bit bigger than when she'd first noticed it.

Rubidius stared silently at it before he let her hand drop. "Did you speak the words of invocation?"

"I—" She didn't see a point in denying it now that he seemed to know anyway. "Yes, but nothing happened." She reached over absently with her right hand and scratched at the sore.

Rubidius closed his eyes and took a very deep breath as Eleanor inhaled sharply across the room.

"What's wrong?" Sam asked, looking around at their grave faces. "So, Darcy spoke some words. What's the big deal? Like she said, nothing happened."

"Something did happen," Rubidius said without opening his eyes. "She invoked the Oracle."

"It didn't work," Darcy said again. "You don't have to worry about it."

"Of course it worked," Rubidius snapped, sounding at once much more like himself. "That sore on your hand is evidence enough. It will only grow larger until you satisfy the invocation. The longing will become greater. It will haunt your waking hours and your dreams at night until you respond to the call. Eventually you won't be able to eat or sleep; all your focus will be on it."

"What does that mean?" Darcy asked in a tremulous voice.

"It means," Rubidius continued in his furious tone, closing his eyes and pausing for a deep breath. "It means that you now have no choice. You *must* go to the Oracle, or you will die."

Chapter 16

Rubidius's Story

"*What?*" Sam cried. "That can't be right! What about the prophecy? Darcy can't die!"

"Not all prophecies are unconditional," Rubidius answered cryptically. "She created a magical tie between herself and the Oracle when she spoke the invocation. The words themselves are a spell, a powerful enchantment. It cannot be broken; she must go."

"But, Rubidius," Eleanor said, "she doesn't have the magical discipline to work that kind of spell! How can it have worked?"

"And I thought you said all magic in Alitheia is elemental," Amelia added.

"It *is* elemental, and the worker of the magic is the Oracle itself, not Darcy, which is why it is called an *invocation*. Darcy invoked the magic of the Oracle; it lies dormant until awakened by the invocation. It now has a physical—or earthly—elemental hold on Darcy. It will draw her to itself, and like I already said, if Darcy does not go, the draw will eventually kill her."

"But the words!" Darcy protested weakly. "They were supposed to disappear from the page, but they didn't. I checked!"

Rubidius handed the book to her, his finger holding it open to the page of invocation so that she could see. The page on which the words had been written was now blank parchment with only a shadow of the words; they had faded almost completely from sight.

"But—" Darcy said again. She could feel her heart sinking down to her toes.

"This sort of magic takes time," Rubidius said, drawing the book back from her. "It's a slow fade; you would not have noticed it right away. It is the same with that sore on your hand. It will only grow bigger and more troublesome until you go."

"Oh, Rubidius!" Eleanor was standing with her hands over her mouth. "Is there nothing we can *do?* She can't go!"

"I would say that we can delay her a week, maybe two, before the pull becomes too strong. We can use that time to prepare her, both physically and magically. That is all we can do."

"Tullin will never allow it," Eleanor continued.

"He will have no choice!" Rubidius snapped. "He may be king regent until Tellius is of age, but this falls outside of his control. The call of the Oracle supersedes all human authority. The most he can do is prepare a good escort for her. A strong escort." He went to Eleanor, as though his next words were for her ears alone. "Not a force too large, we do not want to draw attention, but a well balanced one. Narks, two or three, and the same number of human soldiers. A nymph if we can find one who is willing, and a magician . . . I will think on a recommendation. Of these six," he turned back to the teenagers at the table, "the spy, the warrior . . . that is all."

Eleanor gave a quick nod of understanding and left the cottage, on a mission to fulfill Rubidius's requirements.

"Wait," Sam cried as the door snapped to behind Eleanor. "Are you deciding who goes with Darcy? I want to go, too!"

"No," the alchemist said.

"What about us?" Amelia pointed to herself and Lewis. "Aren't we important enough to go? Shouldn't we all stick together?"

Rubidius sighed. "You are each powerful in your own way, but those whose talents will be most valuable on a journey such as this are Perry and Dean. Tullin will never allow all six of you to go, and rightly so. This was not our plan for you this year—"

"Then what was?" Perry demanded. "Hang around the castle and practice while Tselloch gets stronger and stronger? At least this way we can be out there *doing* something. You know, like possibly *finding gateways* instead of sitting here talking about it?"

Rubidius shook his head at Perry. "That is not the purpose of this journey." But he seemed too tired to fight with the young man. "Amelia, Lewis, and Samantha will stay here with me and Eleanor. We will work on perfecting their talents, and if they have any revelations that concern your journey, we will get them to you through Dean."

Dean sat up. "Huh?"

"You will take your bow and arrow, of course. I will expect you to send us regular updates on your progress, and we can send any needed messages back."

"Oh, yeah, of course." Dean looked a little embarrassed that he hadn't thought to suggest it himself.

"But enough of this talk for right now," Rubidius snapped. "I need you to go, all of you, except Darcy. There are some important things she needs to know that do not concern the rest of you. Dean and Perry, I want you to seek out Baran. Eleanor will have gotten a message to him. Go. Make good use of the rest of your time today."

The other six teenagers shot Darcy frightened looks as Rubidius shooed them toward the door, but the only person Rubidius stopped was Tellius. "*You*," he said waspishly, "will go to your quarters and wait there. I expect your cousin will want to have a word with you!"

Tellius hung his head. He looked very white, a few blemishes sticking out like red beacons on his bent face. Darcy couldn't help but feel sorry for him even as her stomach knotted in fear for herself. What had they done?

"Rubidius," she whispered as the door closed out her friends, "I'm so sorry! I didn't know what I was doing . . ."

"That is clear," he said, returning to the table and sitting beside her. "But now is not the time to wallow in regret. What's done is done. We have very little time to prepare you, and I refuse to send you to the Oracle without offering you all the help I can. We must work on your magic, both earth and air, and on your other talent. Tell me, what did you learn under Lykos last year?"

Darcy was a little taken aback. She didn't like to reminisce on her time with the wolf-prince, but she had, at least, gotten to know quite a bit about her ability to mind-speak with animals, and she pulled on those memories now. She told Rubidius about how she had to initiate the contact, how it was similar to speaking out loud in that she had to shout in her mind if the subject was far away, how the link stayed open as long as she focused on it, how she could locate an animal that she was speaking to, even if she couldn't see it, by following the link, and how her own thoughts remained private even when the link was open. "I think that's everything," she finished. "I practiced with him almost every day."

He sighed and leaned back in his chair. "Well, at least *some* good came of it." He was silent for a moment. "And you said you never spoke with any animal other than Lykos?"

Darcy shook her head. "No, but I . . . I did try it on Hippondus the other day, and it worked. I hope that's okay," she added in a small voice. She was feeling very guilty about the Oracle. Her chest ached for want of a good cry, and she was determined to be as open and helpful as possible now that she'd screwed everything up. *Again*, she thought miserably.

Rubidius nodded as though that didn't surprise him. "So the equines know, and the wolves know."

"Is that bad?" she asked. There was a faint buzzing in her ear, and she twitched her head to get rid of it.

"No," he said. "While most of the wolves betrayed Alitheia, some have remained loyal. Tselloch has known of your talent ever since Lykos betrayed you, and he's made no move yet to capitalize on that. Just be wary and do not trust any animals that are not known and trusted by others. What I am most concerned with right now, is broadening the scope of your talent. We must discover how many animals you can talk with at a time, whether you can determine the high or low status of animals just by sense, and whether you can act as an intermediary to link other humans to high animals, or two high animals of different species."

"Are we going to work on that right now?" Darcy asked. She scratched at the sore on her palm. The buzzing in her ear hadn't stopped.

Rubidius considered and then shook his head. "No, I do not want to take the time to seek out high animals to practice on at the moment. Right now, since I have you here, I would like to continue working on your magic."

Darcy nodded in understanding, but she felt disappointed. Her legs felt restless, and she adjusted her position. She really wanted to get out of the cottage and go find some animals to distract her from the buzzing in her ear.

Rubidius stood and retrieved a mug, a pitcher of water, and some herbs hanging from his ceiling. Waving a hand over the pitcher, he muttered a few words and crushed some of the herbs into the pitcher. Darcy knew she should recognize them from sessions last year, but she didn't. She was having a difficult time focusing on anything but her itchy palm, buzzing ears, and restless legs. She shifted to her knees as Rubidius gave the pitcher a quick swirl and poured some of the liquid into the mug. "Drink this," he said. "It will help."

She reached over and took the drink, gulping some of it down and making a face at Rubidius. It was bitter and left her mouth feeling dry and sandpapery.

"Finish all of it," he insisted.

Darcy wanted to ask why, but she noticed the buzzing in her ears had quieted. *Oh!* She held her nose with one hand and swigged the rest of it down. It was awful, but the more she drank, the better she felt. By the time she finished the mug, the buzzing had completely gone away and she could sit still in her seat, her restlessness gone as well.

"Can I have a glass of water?" she croaked, running her tongue over her dry lips.

"No," he said shortly. He poured the rest of the contents of the pitcher into a ceramic decanter and sealed it with a stopper. He then used a hand pump to refill the pitcher in his sink, adding different herbs and speaking a new spell over it. "Drinking water within an hour following this potion thins it out and destroys its effects. What you *can* have is this," he poured the new potion into her mug. "This one is to give you strength."

She wanted to ask if it would taste as bad as the potion she had just consumed, but she didn't want to cause trouble, so she tilted the mug to her lips. She was relieved to find that this one was sweet and tasted like honeysuckle mixed with lavender. It wasn't thirst-quenching, and she still longed for a cold drink of water when she was done, but it made the hard edge from the first potion go away, at least. She felt bolstered and light, as if she could do anything she put her mind to.

"Strength to help me through the lessons," she said. "Why didn't you give it to me before?"

"It is better to struggle through the strengthening process on your own," he replied. "Without aid, you would be stronger in the long run. But I can already see the mark of the Oracle on you—oh, not just that," he said, for Darcy had looked down at her palm. "Your restlessness has begun, and I could tell your focus was becoming impaired. That's why I gave you the other potion; I invented it to use on my own journey to the Oracle. At first it will take away all your symptoms for several hours at a time, but the call will come stronger and stronger. Soon, even the potion will not fully alleviate your discomfort. I will give you the strength potion until you leave to help you practice your magic as much as you can in the little time we have left.

"Now, I would like to begin with air," he said. "Air magic is much easier to *begin*, as you may have noticed. Did you have any difficulty taking hold of that air current in our first lesson together?"

Darcy shook her head no.

"Air magic is like the nature of air itself: flighty, unpredictable, volatile, and difficult to control. Thus, while it is easy to initiate contact with it, it is a much more difficult branch of elemental magic to perfect."

"Can I call up winds?" Darcy wondered aloud.

"Not without an air current to call upon. Like all elemental magic, you cannot create something out of nothing. Because you have air magic, however, you should be able to sense air currents that are not detectable to the rest of us. I would like you to close your eyes and try."

Darcy did as he instructed, squeezing her eyes shut and sending out little tendrils with her mind. It was, like he said, very easy to initiate, and she felt as though she could sift through the atomic particles of air like a mouse sifting through rice. She searched for particles that were moving, and suddenly she found some. Once she had them, they became visible to her as she opened her eyes to look. They were silvery and shimmering, slipping out the tiny crack beneath his door. "I have some," she murmured to Rubidius, not taking her eyes off them.

"Okay, good. Now I want you to try to make them move faster. Don't forget that you can channel your magic through your hands for a better degree of control."

Darcy's focus increased as she took hold of the particles and willed them to move faster. Raising her hands, she began to move them in slow revolutions and, as she did so, she created a new breeze with her hands that she could add to the existing current. She revolved them faster still, and a distinct breeze began to ruffle Rubidius's beard.

"Good!" he cried, sounding genuinely pleased.

Darcy grinned for the first time that morning and pushed harder, but many of the particles began escaping her grasp. She had let it get out of control. Without warning the breeze became a gust and slammed against the door, rattling the hinges. It swept back around the room, tearing herbs from the ceiling and sending pieces of parchment scattering from their various cubbies. She gasped and abruptly dropped her arms, covering her head as it whooshed past her face before dissipating.

Darcy peeked over her arm at the destruction of Rubidius's cottage. "Sorry!" she gasped.

Rubidius didn't look angry, however. He stood to collect his things, directing some back to their homes via levitation and picking up others by hand. She scurried to help him, but he waved her off. "Sit down, please. You have done well."

"Well?" she squeaked. "I destroyed your cottage!"

"Oh no, no, no," he chuckled and shook his head. "I once blew up an entire cauldron full of quicksilver. Now *that* was a mess. No, no—you *have* done well. How do you feel?"

"I'm fine." Darcy frowned, noticing she hardly felt tired at all. "A little winded, perhaps. No pun intended," she joked, and Rubidius's face lit up in appreciation. She wasn't anywhere near as tired as she'd been the last time she'd practiced her magic. "The strength potion?" she guessed.

He nodded. "You would never have been able to accomplish even that much control over that current without tiring if I had not given you the potion. I am pleased with what you have done." He finished putting the last stack of parchment away and sat back down at the table. "The potion will not, however, prevent you from feeling the effects of your practice, the same as if you exercised for several hours. You will be sore this evening."

"Great," Darcy muttered.

"Now," he folded his hands on the table, every inch a teacher, "I want to hear your observations, and then we will try again."

Darcy practiced with Rubidius as the morning wore away into the afternoon until they took a short break for lunch. While Darcy ate cold meat, cheese, and nuts, Rubidius lectured her on the proper use of air and earth magic. Shortly after lunch the buzzing once again took up in her ears, and she began to pace restless circles around the room, so he gave her another draft of the bitter potion to counter the effects.

Finally, around late afternoon, the strength potion began to wear off as well, and Darcy slumped in her chair, sweaty-faced and exhausted after successfully channeling an air current into a miniature dust devil on the floor. Her first few attempts had resulted in dust being flung all over Rubidius's belongings. It wasn't until he suggested she simultaneously control the dust particles, using her earth magic, with the air particles, using her air magic, that she finally gained control of the entire thing. She worked on letting it go carefully so that it didn't explode or bounce erratically around the room, until it became smaller and smaller before disappearing, the dust settling into a nice little pile on the floor.

"I . . . don't think . . . I can go . . . again," she breathed. Her muscles were beginning to ache as though she'd done hours of aerobics, just as Rubidius said they would, and a headache lingered in the area of her temples.

Rubidius seemed about to protest, but changed his mind and handed her a glass of water instead. "It's been long enough since your last draft," he said. "I want to tell you one more thing before I let you go for the night." He sounded very serious.

Darcy sat forward with great effort. "Yes?"

"The Oracle . . . it will require payment."

Darcy's stomach fell. *Payment?* "I don't have anything to give it, I mean, how—"

He held up a hand. "It is nothing you can predict or prepare for. What it asks of each petitioner is different, but it is always something that you would be loath to give up."

"Like, money, or . . . or something else?"

"The Oracle has never taken money. It is . . ." he struggled for the right words, "a collector of sorts. Rare or valuable items, or creatures even, and if you have no physical object to give, it will accept promises as payment."

"Promises?" Darcy wrinkled her nose. "What good does that do? How would it know if I broke my promise, anyway?"

"It feeds off misery, I believe. A promise that will make the petitioner miserable is acceptable payment for a query. A petitioner who pays with a promise is henceforward bound by an oath. The Oracle binds him or her with the oath so that if it is ever broken, the petitioner will suffer an immediate, and terribly painful, death."

Darcy felt weak at his words. "Will I at least be able to determine what I give in payment?"

"All payment must be made willingly, but ultimately the Oracle will determine what it will accept. You have one chance to pay, and if you refuse, you will never leave its lair. You yourself become the payment, you see?"

This is getting worse, Darcy thought, feeling miserable. She was achy in mind, body, and spirit and beginning to wish she had not come back to Alitheia. But, of course, that wasn't really up to her in the first place; nothing was. She felt like her life had been laid out for her, and any time she tried to regain some measure of control over it, she ended up in trouble. She wanted to cry again, but she didn't want Rubidius to see.

"Rubidius," she murmured after a long moment. He seemed lost in his own thoughts. "What did you ask the Oracle?"

He turned tortured eyes on her, and she could see his humanity shining through his magician's exterior. "What do all alchemists want?" he asked wearily.

"To turn lead to gold, right? Is that the same thing as making a philosopher's stone?" She had read up on alchemy since her last visit to Alitheia, interested because of Rubidius's unending quest.

He didn't acknowledge her question but turned his gaze inward, closing his eyes as he said, "I asked the Oracle how I could achieve the alchemical Great Work. It was selfish of me, but I was very young. I had just achieved master-magician status and made the solemn vows that granted me the title of alchemist, and I wanted all the glory for myself. *I* wanted to be the first to create a philosopher's stone, to do what nobody else has ever done . . . and so I invoked the Oracle. My mentor disowned me because of it."

Darcy blanched. "Are . . . are you going to disown me, too?"

He opened his eyes and almost smiled at her. "No, Darcy."

"Oh, okay. Good. So what did the Oracle tell you? Are you ever going to be able to do it?"

Rubidius closed his eyes again and chanted as though he had repeated the lines over and over again:

"To achieve your work of Magnitude
You have one sacrifice to make
A mentored friend will give a life
Whose blood is yours to take
When the Red Lion prowls between the bones
Once living, ancient, forsaken
Your prima materia ready at hand
Chrysopoeia, of the sacrifice taken."

Darcy held her breath, wanting to ask what it meant, but she knew that Rubidius himself didn't know, and he looked so sad that she found she didn't want to pry. She noticed with a lurch of embarrassment that crystal tears were glittering on his cheeks, and she cleared her throat. She was terrible at consoling people; she never knew whether she should give them a hug, pat their back, or just give them space.

Rubidius didn't seem embarrassed by his show of emotion, however, as he opened his eyes and gazed at her. "I have given over a lifetime to the pursuit of this goal, and I could not turn back now even if I wanted to."

"Why not?" Darcy whispered.

"Because the Oracle elicited a promise from me in payment for my answer; I promised never to rest until I had completed the alchemical Great Work. I am sure you see my double curse."

"Umm." Darcy felt a little silly because she didn't fully understand what he was getting at.

"I cannot rest until I achieve the alchemical Great Work, but the achievement of that goal will cost me the life of a friend, someone I have mentored. So you see, I will have no joy either way. And that is fitting punishment, I think, for my act of selfishness in going to the Oracle in the first place." He looked down at his hands, knotted and gnarled with age. "I pray that your payment will not be so harsh and your answer not so puzzling, but I know the ways of the Oracle, and I am afraid for you."

Darcy's stomach rumbled in the quiet of his room, sounding crass and inappropriate in the mood of their conversation. Darcy blushed and put a hand on it. Rubidius chuckled and stood to retrieve the decanter full of the bitter potion.

"The demands of the flesh," he said, "will not be ignored for long, I am afraid." He handed her the vessel. "Take this whenever you feel the need, and do not forget to forsake drinking water for at least an hour following each draft. I will prepare more for you tomorrow."

He placed an uncharacteristically kind hand under her elbow and helped her to stand. She felt wobbly with pain and discomfort from the long hours of practice. "I'm certain that you will find your companions in the kitchen. It is about the dinner hour."

He walked her to the door and as she stepped into the high-ceilinged hall, it suddenly seemed like a foreign land. After Rubidius shut the door, she stood and stared at it for several minutes before limping off to her room.

Chapter 17

The Call of the Oracle

Darcy dropped the potion off in her chamber, not wanting to have to explain it to Sam and the others just then. She stared at her wan reflection in the gilt mirror above her sink for a full minute. She was paler than usual; every freckle stood out sharply against the bridge of her nose, and her grey eyes, usually tinted with blue, looked colorless and washed out. Sweat stood out on her upper lip, and her hands shook where they gripped the edges of the basin.

She worked the hand pump to fill the basin with cool water and dipped her hands in to splash her face. The water eased the itchiness in her palm, a symptom not remedied by the potion, but that only served to remind her of the colossal mess she had made of things again. She gasped as all the pent up emotion from the day overcame her, and she let the sobs come—deep, wracking sobs that shook her thin frame and caused her aching muscles to protest.

Her grandmother had always said that you could start fresh after a good cry, but that was not going to be the case here. *Because I can't start over; I have to see this thing through to the end.*

It took some time, but Darcy at long last felt she was all cried out. She washed her face again and pressed cool, dripping fingers to the puffiness under her eyes, willing them to go down. *I'm not going to go downstairs looking like I just had a cry-fest*, she told herself. She didn't want the pitiful looks and well-meaning but uncomfortable questions, so she still worked at her face to make it look normal. She was starting to feel wiggly again, and the buzz was coming back, so she retrieved the decanter from her bedside table with a sigh and poured herself another drink.

After choking down the potion and feeling as prepared as she was going to get, she let herself out of her room and locked the door behind her. She went down the winding staircase tucked away in the tower and was rather embarrassed when the guard insisted on escorting her all the way down to the kitchen.

Her five friends were indeed there, as Rubidius had suggested, in various stages of finishing their meals. They turned as one to stare at her when she came through the arched door. She offered them a wobbly half-smile that didn't quite reach her eyes and stumbled over to plop down next to Sam.

"We made you a plate," Sam said carefully, pushing a plate piled with food toward her.

There was a leg, thigh, and half a breast of some sort of bird, a cake of what looked like granola, and fresh fruit. "What is it?" Darcy asked, trying to sound light and unconcerned.

"Quail. I don't know what the cake is called, but it's really good. Asa Rhea is still the cook, and you know she can turn out some tasty food." Sam was doing her best to sound normal, and Darcy appreciated the effort—and the restraint—that she was showing.

She took a tentative bite of the granola cake; it had a buttery-sweet flavor, like honeyed biscuit with chopped nuts, and it flaked in her mouth. She chewed slowly with her eyes on her plate and then looked up. She swallowed hard and asked, "Are you guys just going to stare at me the whole time? 'Cause if you are, I'm just going to take my food upstairs."

"Darcy . . . you don't have to pretend—"

"We know you're not okay," Amelia picked up Sam's thought.

"And that's okay!" Sam took it back from Amelia, shooting her a furtive look. "We just want you to know that we're here for you, whatever you need."

The others nodded their heads solemnly, and Darcy felt her bottom lip start to tremble. *I will* not *cry in front of the boys!* She took another bite of the granola cake to give her mouth something to do and forestall bursting into tears.

"And we don't have to talk about it ever again if you don't want to," Sam added. "We just don't want you to feel like you're in this alone."

Darcy swallowed and nodded until she felt she could trust herself to speak. "Did you guys practice that?" She attempted to be playful.

"Heck yeah!" Perry said. He leaned forward, his eyes narrowed in jest. "How'd we do?"

"Pretty decent." She looked at Amelia and Sam. "A little shaky there on the delivery at first, but you pulled it off in the end."

Sam stared at Perry with a horrified look on her face, and she turned back to Darcy with her mouth gaping like a fish. "I—"

"Sam," Darcy tilted her head toward her, "I'm kidding."

Sam deflated in relief. "Oh, good, okay."

"Seriously, though, I appreciate it. And I . . . I don't mind talking about it." And it was the truth. She had so much swimming around in her head that it might be good to get some of it out. "But why don't you guys tell me what *you* did today first."

Perry and Dean exchanged looks, and it was then Darcy noticed they both were a little sweaty. In fact, she could smell them from across the table. They winced as they adjusted themselves in their seats.

"We basically went to boot camp today," Dean supplied. "It was not awesome; it was the *opposite* of awesome."

"Ah, come on. It wasn't *that* bad," Perry countered. He stretched his hands back behind his chair.

Dean snorted. "Easy for you to say, you're in sports back home. I haven't done anything athletic like that since the last time we were here."

"Don't you mountain bike?" Perry asked, pointing a quail leg at him.

"That's a *totally* different workout—"

"Yeah, but it's not like you're completely out of shape."

"Maybe you guys should have continued doing morning forms all year," Amelia interrupted them testily. "Then you would have been better prepared to come back this year."

Perry grimaced. "Yeah, I think Baran expected that," he said, referring to the weapons and combat master. "He was less than *pleased* to find out we weren't in very good shape."

Dean put a hand over his ribs and said, "I have felt the wrath of his stick, and I have learned!"

Amelia snorted and speared a chunk of melon with her fork. "Serves you right."

"So," Darcy interjected, trying to get everything clear, "are they, like, trying to get you guys back in shape in case we have to fight out there?"

"Yeah, something like that," Perry answered. "We get specialized attention from Baran until we're ready to leave."

"Yippee," Dean added, his voice morose.

"What about you guys?" Darcy waved her fork at Lewis, Sam, and Amelia.

"We didn't really do anything today," Amelia said. "But Eleanor came to see us just before dinner and told us we'd continue lessons and training as usual once you guys are gone. We'll just be meeting with her, and not Rubidius, until you guys leave."

Sam sighed and folded her arms. "This stinks, guys! I wish they'd let us all go."

"Yeah, but I can understand why they're not," Lewis said. "It makes sense."

"Lewis has been trying to work on writing something for you," Sam said, changing direction. "But nothing's coming to him."

He shrugged. "I can't force it. The last time, when we found that trail out of Paradeisos, I had been writing about it for ages before realizing what I was writing about. Hopefully we can figure it out quicker this time, that is, if any message is sent to me."

"And you can always send it along through Dean," Sam said.

"I wonder what you're going to wear," Amelia said, gazing with unfocused eyes at the table.

"What? Why would you think of *that*?" Perry asked incredulously.

"Well, think about it: she can't go hiking through the woods in a *dress!*"

"True," Darcy said, "although I did last year when I went off with Lykos. But that was for only one night, and it was a pain! It kept getting snagged on everything."

"But I've never seen an Alitheian woman in anything *but* a dress," Sam insisted.

"Voitto Vesa doesn't always wear a dress. She wears a kind of knee-length jerkin with pants underneath sometimes," Darcy said.

"You guys are ridiculous." Dean sat back and muttered, "I can't believe you're talking about *clothes* at a time like this!"

"Oh, hush," Sam waved him off and turned back to Darcy. "Voitto Vesa is not a woman, she's a female nark. Don't you think the rules are different for her?"

"I don't know," Darcy admitted, "but I'll tell you one thing. If they expect me to wear long skirts for the entire journey, I will sneak into Lewis's room and steal some pants before I go!"

Sam laughed. It felt good to hear someone laugh.

"There will be no need for any pilfering of pants, I'm sure," a high, musical voice interrupted them, and they turned in surprise.

"Voitto!" Sam exclaimed, "We were just talking about you."

"I'm still Vesa for a little while longer," the nark reminded her, eyes twinkling.

"Oh, yeah, sorry," Sam said. "Are you here for us?"

"Not for all of you, I'm afraid. Just for Darcy."

Darcy lowered her knife and fork. "Me?" She ached more with every passing minute from the magic practice she had done, and she'd thought she was finished with her training for the day, but Vesa looked as though she meant business. She was clutching two short bows and had a quiver of arrows slung across her shoulder and a sheathed knife in her other hand.

Vesa inclined her head at Darcy and said, "When you have supped, meet me in the rear courtyard. We have work to do." She dropped a wrapped bundle beside Darcy's chair and breezed away.

Perry snickered after she was gone.

"What?" Amelia snapped at him.

"After you've *supped*," he laughed again, and Dean snorted into his food.

"Really?" Amelia snipped. "You're *really* going to make fun of how she talks?"

"Wha's *sup,* man?" Dean said in falsetto.

Perry lost his composure entirely and howled in laughter; even Lewis had to hide a smile.

"Boys!" Amelia exclaimed with a roll of her eyes. "Honestly."

"Lucky!" Sam hissed at her under her breath. "I wanted to learn to shoot a bow and arrow the last time we were here!" She, Amelia, and Darcy were walking through the door to the back courtyard, the area where they'd had their end-of-year feast the year before.

"You guys aren't going to stay and watch, are you?" Darcy adjusted her new clothes, uncomfortable. The bundle Vesa had left her was full of boots, woolen slacks with leather thigh and calf guards, a long-sleeved linen shirt, and a short leather jerkin to go over it all. It felt strange to wear pants again after several days in skirts.

"You don't want us to?" Sam pouted and stared across the narrow courtyard at Voitto Vesa, who appeared to be arguing with Yahto Veli.

"Well, I don't know." Darcy stopped and put her hands on her hips. "I think I'll feel weird if you two are staring at me the whole time. Do you mind leaving?"

"It's okay, Darcy," Amelia stepped in. "Come on, Sam. We'll see you later, Darcy."

"Sorry, Sam," Darcy called at the girls' retreating backs, but she really did feel much more comfortable once they disappeared into the castle. If she had to make a fool out of herself, she'd rather not do it in front of an audience.

Twilight was falling, but the courtyard was lit with multiple bracketed torches along the low walls. Voitto Vesa and Yahto Veli stood silhouetted next to one of the torches, clearly deep in tense conversation. She wondered if they were arguing about her, but she couldn't imagine why, so she shook it off.

Finally, Vesa looked up and noticed Darcy. She waved her over and dismissed Veli with a sharp shake of her head. "It's just not our way," Darcy overheard her say as Veli turned to go.

He ignored Vesa's comment and put a hand on Darcy's shoulder in passing. "I know you are tired," he murmured, "but pay good attention. You are learning from the most talented female combatant Alitheia has seen in many years."

"But—I'm not a nark," Darcy protested. "I can't move like her!"

He smiled, his eyes crinkling at their corners. "Don't worry. She will not ask you to do anything beyond your reach."

"Lady Darcy!" Vesa called. "We are losing time."

"And I'm keeping you from it," Veli said, straightening up. "I will see you later." He gave her a fond pat and was gone.

"I'm most concerned about three things," Vesa said without preamble as Darcy approached her cautiously. "Hand-to-hand combat, knife defense, and archery. Hopefully I can teach you enough in these three disciplines to help you survive your journey."

"Vesa," Darcy said weakly, "I don't mean to be difficult, but Rubidius worked me all day. I can hardly stand up straight, let alone learn how to fight right now."

"Oh, yes." Vesa went to a bundle she had left on the ground and drew out a leather flask. "From Rubidius." She tossed it to Darcy.

Darcy fumbled to catch it and it fell to the ground through her aching fingers. She bent over to retrieve it, wincing all the way, and finally drew it up, uncorked it, and tipped it to her lips. Sweet, honeyed flavor flowed into her mouth, and she felt herself rejuvenated.

Darcy swallowed and wiped her mouth on the back of her arm. "Strength potion," she gasped. She took another swig and then replaced the cork in the flask. The cool energy spread through her muscles, and she straightened her back and stretched experimentally. "Okay," she said, "I'm ready."

When the sun went down, Vesa closed her eyes and went to sleep, trading places with Voitto, her night nark counterpart with raven black hair and steely grey eyes. She took an abnormally long time with her eyes closed, and Darcy figured Vesa was being a little more thorough than usual in communicating through images and flashes all that had transpired that day.

Voitto opened her eyes and focused on Darcy with a pitying expression.

"Oh dear," she breathed at her. "We *do* have a lot to do!"

Together they continued with basic self-defense techniques until Voitto moved on to archery. Darcy stretched and grimaced, not expecting her strength potion to have already begun wearing off.

"Keep your arm straight," Voitto instructed. "Your hand should be even with your ear. Good! Elbow up!"

Darcy was sighting down the feathered arrow at the straw practice target fifty yards away. Her arms shook with fatigue, but she finally managed to loose an arrow that struck the target, even if it was on the edge.

"Good!" Voitto declared again. She ran to the target and was back with the arrow in less than five seconds, her speed creating a soft breeze that tickled Darcy's face. "Did you feel what you did differently that time?"

Darcy nodded, but she was too tired to speak. She dropped the bow down to her thigh and tugged at the collar of her shirt, loosening the ties to let the cool night breeze play on her collarbone.

She must have looked desperately tired, because at last Voitto said, "All right, that's good for tonight. I might have Vesa steal you tomorrow afternoon. I bet we could combine your earth and wind talents with archery practice."

"You know about that?" Darcy asked. "My magic, I mean."

Voitto laughed as she took the bow from Darcy's cramped grasp. "Of course! News of inverse magic travels quickly. It's very unusual, you know."

"So Rubidius told me."

"Even more so because our prince has the opposite inverse talents," Voitto continued, her ears twitching with glee.

Darcy narrowed her eyes and changed the subject. "Do you really think this is necessary—all this training? I mean, do you really think I'm going to have to fight? Aren't soldiers going with me?"

Voitto sobered. "Alitheian wilderness is a dangerous place. You have never left the relative safety of the castle environs and the enchanted locations around them. What you could encounter out in the wild is much less predictable." She gathered the scattered practice arrows and stuffed them into her quiver until it was full. "Out there, you will have much more to contend with than tsellodrin and tsellochim," she murmured. "Alitheia was not a perfect place, even before Tselloch came here, you know. Evil exists in many forms."

"What sorts of forms?" Darcy shivered and pulled the strings at her neck closed again.

Voitto shrugged. "All sorts. Creatures and beasts such as the great lizards —"

"Dragons?" Darcy interrupted. "You have dragons in Alitheia?"

Voitto nodded. "Dragons, griffins, giants, centaurs, sprites, goblins . . . And not all high animals are friendly, either."

"I know. The wolves, I mean."

"Yes, the wolves, among others. And the spies of Tselloch are everywhere." She placed a hand on Darcy's shoulder and steered her toward the castle.

Small orbs of light flickered and faded all around them. Darcy assumed they were lightning bugs until she got right up next to one and saw that it was actually a tiny fairy holding a little ball of light. The fairy giggled and zipped off as soon as she saw Darcy looking at her, and Darcy smiled in spite of herself.

"I don't mean to frighten you," Voitto said, stopping her under the lantern at the door, "but I think you should be prepared." She opened the door for her, and Darcy found the guard waiting to escort her back up to the west wing.

"Thanks, Voitto," Darcy sighed. She stepped into the warmth of the castle, the buzzing in her ears getting louder as soon as the door was closed.

Darcy took a drink of the bitter draft just before falling into bed fully clothed. She drew the covers over herself and fell asleep almost at once. Her tiredness went beyond exhaustion, and she figured she'd have no trouble sleeping through the night. She was wrong.

In the middle of the night, Darcy woke up shaking and sweating in her bed. Her ears were buzzing so loudly she thought they must be making her head vibrate; her legs were twitching with a mind of their own. She'd been dreaming about an inhuman voice calling her name over and over again from a dark tunnel, compelling her to get out of bed and go to it.

Darcy gasped and flailed out of her covers. The impulse to leave the castle was so strong she wasn't sure she could resist it on her own. She sat up, her head reeling, and reached for the decanter on her bedside table. Her motions were jerky, uncontrollable, and in her reach she swept it off the table and onto the floor where it smashed into tiny shattered pieces, the precious potion soaking into the edge of the carpet.

"No!" Darcy cried, rolling clumsily out of bed and falling to her knees next to it. She pressed her fingers into the wet carpet and tried to suck the liquid off them, but it wasn't enough. She looked crazily around the room. "Sam!" she gasped. She swayed to her feet and stumbled toward their adjoining door, but her legs wanted to pull her to the hallway instead. She wrenched herself toward Sam's room, crying out in pain as her body protested, and finally fell to hands and knees, clawing her way across the carpet to the thick oak door.

"Sam!" she cried again, pounding a fist on the door. "Sam, please!"

"Darcy?" Sam's voice sounded muffled and remote through the thick wood, but it was only a moment before Sam flung open the door. She was in her nightdress, her blond curls falling around her frightened face. "Darcy, what's wrong?" She fell to her knees beside her.

"Get—Rubidius," Darcy gasped. "I need—Rubidius. Please, Sam!" Darcy cried out again as her body lurched toward her other door, and she clung to Sam to keep herself steady.

"I can't leave you like this!" Sam cried. She looked frantically over her shoulder. "Amelia! Amelia, get up!"

"Sam?" Amelia opened her door and peered through. "Darcy? What's going on? I'm trying to sleep!"

"Amelia, something's wrong with Darcy! Go get Rubidius—please! She's asking for Rubidius. Hurry!"

Amelia's face betrayed her shock. She nodded once and dashed past them and out Darcy's door, leaving it open as she ran down the hall.

Two guards from the hall shouldered their way into Darcy's room, but she didn't have the energy to feel embarrassed. All her focus was on trying to stay while her body fought to leave. She ground her teeth together as another convulsion hit her, and then the two guards were over her. They each took an arm and held her down.

"What's going on in here?" a familiar sleepy voice called. Perry, Dean, and Lewis rushed into the room, stopping to stare in shock.

Darcy felt a shriek escape her throat, and she arched her back off the floor, her strength surprising, but not enough to shake the burly men that held her down. "Don't let go of me!" she panted when the convulsion had passed. "Please don't let me go!"

"Sam, what's wrong with her?" Perry asked, horrified.

"I don't know, I don't *know!*" Sam was wringing her hands and dancing from foot to foot, starting to cry. "Hold on, Darcy!"

Perry slipped a comforting arm around Sam's shoulder, and Dean and Lewis exchanged stunned glances.

"Sam, your bag. Go check your bag!" Lewis said.

Sam gasped and pulled away from Perry, darting to her chamber and back in a matter of seconds. Frantically, she tugged open the strings of the bag and tipped its contents into her waiting hand.

"Well, what is it?" Lewis asked, eyes wide.

"It's . . . *it's an alarm clock!*" Sam shrieked, dissolving into hysterics, clutching the alarm clock with trembling fingers.

"A *what?* How is an alarm clock supposed to help Darcy, Sam?" Perry asked accusingly.

"I don't know!" she shouted. "I didn't choose it; I don't know what it's supposed to—"

Just then, Rubidius burst into the room. His robes billowed around him and his eyes blazed. In one hand he held a pitcher of potion, and Amelia cringed behind him. His eyes swept the room, and he glanced at the broken decanter on the floor.

"Move!" he commanded them, and Perry, Dean, and Lewis quickly scooted out of the way. He strode to where Darcy lay and tilted her chin back.

Darcy opened her mouth, and Rubidius poured the bitter potion down her throat. She choked and spluttered, but he ordered her to keep swallowing.

Finally, he eased the pitcher away from her mouth. Her shaking had subsided to a shiver, and the unnatural compulsion to fling herself toward the door was fading, too. With a deep, throaty sigh she relaxed against the floor and felt calm overtake her as the buzzing quieted. At last she lay still, and the guards let go of her arms.

She sat up, dazed, and blinked at her audience. Tears began to spill down her cheeks and she put her head in her hands. "It was so strong," she whispered. "I couldn't stop myself."

Rubidius stared grimly at her and then went to her bedside. With a wave of his hand, her decanter repaired itself and refilled with the potion, which Rubidius topped off. He muttered a few more words and then replaced it next to her bed. "I've put an unbreakable charm on it," he said. "Help her up," he told the guards, and they each took an elbow and helped her to her feet. She felt wobbly and dizzy and let them steer her firmly back to the bed.

Rubidius knelt beside her. "The call of the Oracle has become strong for you, faster than I have ever seen before. You must take the potion every three hours, no exceptions, to forestall this sort of episode."

"How can I take it every three hours in the middle of the night?" Darcy sniffed. "I'll be sleeping!"

"Darcy?" Sam's quiet voice echoed from across the room. She gave them a watery smile and held up her hand. "It came out of my bag." She walked forward and tipped the object into Darcy's hands.

Darcy half-laughed, half-sobbed when she saw the old-fashioned windup clock with little alarm bells on top. "Thanks, Sam," she whispered, letting her head fall back on her pillow and closing her eyes.

CHAPTER 18

THE TWELVE COMPANIONS

Darcy's hands shook as she turned the pages of the old volume, and she absentmindedly reached for a glass of her potion. She swallowed it down without even tasting the bitterness, having become so used to it. It was a full week since she had invoked the Oracle, and its pull on her was now so strong she was forced to take the potion every hour just to stay sane. Rubidius said they could delay their journey only another day, or two, at most.

Rubidius was away at the moment, acquiring something for her journey, and he had given her an hour in the library to read up on inverse magic. She was supposed to be looking for information to help her find a better balance between air and earth, but the words were all blurring together, so she put her head back on the upholstery of the chair, wishing she could take a nap. Getting up every hour in the middle of the night to take the potion had drained her to the point of near-constant exhaustion, and even Rubidius's strength potion barely helped her get through her daily magic and fighting lessons anymore.

Just as she felt her eyes drifting closed, the sore on her left palm, now the size of a large walnut, gave a particular jab of itchiness. She jerked her eyes open with a deep grumble and scratched at the skin around the sore with her other hand; it was now much too painful to scratch the sore itself, and she'd taken to wrapping the palm of her hand in strips of linen to hide the ugly suppurating wound. It gave off a sour smell now, too, like milk that had just gone bad. Darcy wanted to cry with frustration, but tears would be of no help to her.

She tried to focus on the book again, but it was no use. With a disgusted sigh, she tossed it unceremoniously onto the table beside her.

"Psssttt! *Darcy!*"

She sat up and looked around, but the library was still empty.

"Darcy!" The hiss came a little louder. "Up here."

It sounded like Tellius, but she hadn't seen him since the day after she'd said the invocation. She turned and looked up at the balcony. Sure enough, she spotted Tellius's dark head of hair sticking out over the railing, as he looked down at her with anxious eyes.

"What are you doing?" she croaked at him, wondering when her voice had become so harsh. "Are you supposed to be out here?"

Tellius grimaced and gingerly closed the door to his chamber before tiptoeing to the staircase. "Not really," he said very quietly as he trotted down the stairs. "You could say I'm under house arrest—or, chamber arrest, I guess."

"So how—"

"My guard went to the kitchen for some food. He thought I was sleeping, but I wasn't." He jumped over the banister five steps from the bottom and ran over to her alcove, plopping down in the seat across from her and wrinkling his nose. "What smells?"

Darcy said nothing and held up her wrapped left hand.

"Oh, right. Sorry." He averted his gaze and picked at a zit on his nose.

"How can *you* be under house arrest?" Darcy asked, lowering her hand to scratch at it some more. "Aren't you the king?"

"I *will be* the king—when I'm seventeen. Tullin is regent, and he's really, *really* angry with me." He sighed and pushed back his hair with hands that looked disproportionately large for his skinny arms. "He reckons this is all my fault."

Well, it is! Darcy wanted to shout at him, but she couldn't do that. He hadn't *forced* her to go back for the book and invoke the Oracle. On the other hand, she wouldn't have known about it in the first place if he hadn't shown it to her. She settled on stony silence.

"Anyway, I wanted to see you before you left," he continued rather quickly, as though he were afraid he wouldn't get the words out, "and let you know I'm very sorry. I didn't mean for this to happen. And I definitely didn't want you to get hurt!"

"I know," Darcy mumbled. "It's not all your fault," she added reluctantly. "I'm just as much to blame."

"Still, I feel really bad."

Darcy bit back the urge to tell him he *should* feel bad and instead nudged the book she had been reading toward him. "Rubidius has me reading up on this inverse magic stuff."

"Oh, yes? Have you been able to learn a lot more about how to use your magic this week?"

"You could say that. It's been something of a crash course." At his puzzled expression, she added, "That is, I've had to learn a lot in a very short amount of time." Her mind catalogued all she had worked on that week: earth magic, air magic, combination earth *and* air magic, hand-to-hand fighting, knife fighting, archery, and using her magic with those fighting techniques. On top of that, she'd practiced talking with high animals and opening links between animals and other species. She yawned.

"When are you leaving?" Tellius interrupted her thoughts.

"Tomorrow or the next day."

"Do you know who's going with you?"

Darcy shook her head. "Rubidius had Eleanor put together a team, but I haven't met any of them, other than Dean and Perry, of course."

"Are your animals going, too?" Tellius asked.

"No. Rubidius said we didn't need them, whatever that means." Darcy yawned again and covered her mouth. "I guess he thinks they ought to stay close to the castle," she added.

Tellius bit his lip as he thought for a moment. "I bet they'll send Tokala and Daylan; they're the best human fighters we have."

"Who—" Darcy started to ask, but Tellius froze and held up a hand. The doorknob on the balcony door creaked, and he reached toward the chandelier. With a swift downward motion of his hand, he snuffed out the flames, bathing the room in darkness. *Fire magic,* Darcy thought, and she felt a little impressed despite herself.

The door squeaked open and the chandelier blazed to life again. They blinked up at the guard, his hand on the wall key for the chandelier. "Nice try, Highness," the man said dryly. "Now, will you come back up yourself, or do I have to call for help?"

Tellius slumped in his chair and made a face. "I'm coming," he muttered. He turned morose eyes to her, and Darcy could see genuine sorrow in them. "I really am sorry, Darcy. I wish I could go instead of you, but I can't."

He stood and walked toward the stairs with as much dignity as he could muster with the guard standing at the top like a chiding babysitter. He turned back once he reached the balcony to raise a hand in farewell, and then his guard nudged him back into his room, the door closing and locking behind them. Darcy sighed and sat back with her eyes closed. She could still catch a few minutes' nap if she tried.

Darcy had a pack full of extra clothes, canteens of both the bitter potion and the strength potion, several knives, and her grandmother's mirror compact, which Sam had pulled out of her satchel for Darcy the year before. Just last night Sam had reminded her to take it. "If I can't go with you to use my talent, at least take the mirror; it kind of acts in the same way, you know, showing people as they really are on the inside. Maybe you can use it on someone to find out if they're trustworthy or not," she suggested, and Darcy had thought it was a good idea.

The food and cooking supplies were in a separate pack, carried by a large, burly man named Tormod. He had long yellow-blond hair styled into three Viking-like braids. He was beardless, but he had a long drooping mustache that Sam had giggled at when she'd first seen him.

As the company bustled about taking care of arrangements, Sam walked back and forth, taking the time to introduce herself to everybody as Rubidius watched her reactions.

Sam's talent was discerning people's trustworthiness, and she was putting it to work as best she could. She squinted at each member of the group as they exchanged pleasantries, and at each stop she seemed satisfied. It was only when she reached Yahto Veli at the very end of the line that she frowned.

Yahto Veli chuckled, his blue eyes twinkling, and chucked her lightly under the chin. "What's the matter, Sam, you don't think I am trustworthy?"

Sam smiled weakly, "Of course I do, it's just . . ." she trailed off and shrugged. "I don't know, honestly. I feel different."

Voitto Vesa stood next to Rubidius, ready to see them off. She frowned at Veli with her arms crossed over her chest. Sam shrugged at Veli, smiling and brushing off her concern as she said goodbye to him and walked over to Rubidius. She nodded silently and he dipped his head in acknowledgement and thanks. Lewis and Amelia stood by, silent and solemn in the early morning air. Darcy appreciated how well each of them was taking it, especially considering that Sam had cried all through breakfast.

Three human soldiers, three narks, a human magician, an oread nymph, and a wolf were to accompany Darcy, Perry, and Dean. Many of them had family and loved ones who came to the castle to see them off.

Darcy practiced the names of each person in her head as she watched them all say their goodbyes. Tormod was the human soldier with the long yellow hair and twin battle axes strapped across his pack. Tokala was the young human soldier with reddish-brown hair and dark brown eyes, who was good-looking enough to be a fashion model. Daylan was the third human soldier—middle-aged with salt and pepper hair and a scruffy beard covering a deeply cragged face. Wal Wyn and Borna Fero, were the two male narks she'd never met. Wal Wyn—just Wyn at the moment—was the fairest day nark Darcy had ever seen. His eyes were so pale they were almost clear, and his hair was not just blond, but white-blond. Fero, by contrast, was much darker as a day nark. His hair was light brown, and he was unusually thick and stocky. He wore his hair in tiny braids, and his face wore a crazed expression. He stood swinging a large knife between his hands, and when he'd introduced himself to Darcy that morning, he had told her he'd been raised by bears.

"Nobody knows if it is true," Veli had whispered in her ear after he'd seen her shocked expression, "but he enjoys telling the story; it adds to his mystique. He does fight like a bear, wild-like, you see? I think he's missing the part of the brain that experiences fear—that might be where the story came from. Do trust me; you'll be happy to have him along."

"I'm surprised Yahto let *you* come," Darcy had whispered back. "He's still not very fond of me, you know."

Veli had hesitated for a moment and then said, "It's not that he doesn't like you, Darcy." He was silent after that.

The wolf had been another story. When he'd breezed into the courtyard that morning, Darcy had shrieked and flung a knife at him. She was so terrified she didn't even feel pleased with her aim when the knife stuck point-in to a cedar tree next to him. And she was certainly too scared to feel relieved that she had missed him.

"Darcy!" Rubidius had admonished her. "This is Lupidor. He is on our side. He betrayed his own kind to save your life last year, and he has volunteered to escort you; you can trust him."

Darcy had nodded and apologized, but she didn't feel ready to let another wolf into her mind. She kept her thoughts to herself.

Darcy noted now what a handsome animal he was, sitting at attention with his head cocked to one side. He looked nothing at all like Lykos. He was a dark charcoal gray with white around his muzzle, and he had beautiful, stunning blue eyes. She remembered him now, how he had joined her and Lykos for a few of their covert sessions. Lykos had trusted him, but he hadn't been loyal to Lykos. He had been loyal to her.

The oread was the only other female member of their party, and Darcy wondered if they had asked her along just so Darcy wouldn't be alone with a bunch of men. Her name was Terra and, although she had a womanly figure, she was only as tall as Darcy's armpit. She had wild hair that hung in tight curls around her face, which looked sometimes short and sometimes long, depending on the angle. Her coloring changed, too, depending on where she was. Her hair, eyes, and clothing became grey-mottled-white as she sat on a rock, and if she stayed still long enough, even her skin began to look like the rock.

The only person left for Darcy to remember was the magician. His name was Badru, and Darcy guessed him to be in his mid-twenties. He was very thin with dirty-blond hair and light brown eyes hidden behind tiny square-lensed spectacles, and he reminded Darcy of the mathletes at her school back home. He had the same nerdy, bookish air about him, and he tended to mutter to himself and twitch without warning. He looked as though a stiff wind could blow him over—Darcy was tempted to try, but she restrained herself. She supposed Rubidius must have had a good reason for choosing him. He was already a registered alchemist and a master magician with earth and water magic, and Rubidius had said he was "one of my finest pupils." *Whatever you say, Rubidius*, Darcy thought again, studying the young magician with a critical eye.

Rubidius gave Darcy a nod, and she knew it was time to go. She took a quick swig of her bitter potion, impressed it had tided her over for ten whole days since the invocation.

Darcy stood with her five friends and they stared at each other, at a loss for words. Finally Amelia said, "Be careful, you guys." She stepped forward and gave Perry, Dean, and Darcy each a hug. When she pulled away from Darcy, tears glistened in her eyes.

Lewis stepped forward and handed Darcy a single sheet of parchment. "Take this," he said. "I don't know if it means anything, but it's a poem I wrote this week. It just sort of came to me. So maybe that means something, right?"

Darcy gave him a thin smile and took the parchment from him. She wanted to read the poem right then but felt awkward about it—like opening a birthday present in front of the person who's just given it—so she stashed it away in her pack. Neither she nor Lewis was big on touching, so they nodded appreciatively at each other instead of hugging.

Lewis said goodbye to Dean and Perry, and Darcy thought she detected longing on his face. Did he wish he were a fighter, too, and that he could come along?

Sam crushed Darcy in a very squashy hug and did the same to Dean and Perry. She let go of Perry after only a brief embrace, looking embarrassed. She seemed to want to say something, but she cleared her throat awkwardly instead.

"Oh!" Sam clapped her hand to her little leather pouch, which was always attached to her belt. She tipped it upside down and out fell a small whistle, ivory colored, flat, and about the length of Darcy's index finger. It had no finger holes and was slightly curved, tapering at one end. It was attached to a long leather thong.

Darcy held out her hand, but Sam clenched the whistle in her fist. "No," she said almost dreamily, "it's for Perry." She held it out to him, and he took it in bewilderment.

"For me?" he questioned, holding it up to look at it.

"Yes, definitely," Sam nodded. "I don't know how I know, but I do."

"What is it?"

"It's a whistle, obviously," Amelia said.

"Yeah, but what's it made out of?" He turned it over in his fingers.

"Bone," Amelia said. She took it from Perry and looked at it closely. "Yep, definitely bone." She handed it back to him.

"How do you know that?" he asked, sounding a little annoyed.

"My orchestra director has a whistle made out of bone," Amelia retorted, "but it's got finger holes so he can play notes on it. This looks just like it, except for the shape. And lack of holes, of course."

"Okaaay," Perry drew out the last syllable and tossed the leather thong around his neck. The whistle hung to mid-chest, and he grabbed it, putting it to his lips and blowing hard.

No sound came out, but the three narks winced and covered their ears. Lupidor whined and ran to the opposite end of the courtyard.

"Stop, Perry!" Sam cried, looking after Lupidor.

He dropped the whistle. "Sorry. So it's made of bone and gives off a super high-pitched note. It's like a dog whistle! Why would I need a dog whistle?"

Sam shook her head. "I have no idea, but I would keep it."

"Of course I'm going to keep it," he snipped. "It came out of your pouch, didn't it? I'm not stupid."

Sam looked like she might burst into tears at his callousness, and Amelia punched Perry hard on the arm, glaring at him.

"Whoa!" Dean sniggered, drawing their attention. "Look at *that!* Do you think he's going to miss her?"

They looked over to where Dean was pointing and saw Tokala planting a passionate kiss on a tall, slim, beautiful girl with long black hair.

"Oh my," Amelia smirked. "I wouldn't mind kissing him like that."

"Amelia!" Sam chided her. "What about Simon?"

"I'm just talking, Sam, I'm not going to *do* it. And look at him, he's gorgeous!"

"I don't know, he's not really my type," Sam said, looking at Perry.

Amelia rolled her eyes and mouthed "give me a break" to Darcy, who hid her laugh behind her hand.

"I'm going to have to talk to him about sharing his moves with me," Dean said pensively while Perry laughed. Lewis only looked queasy.

One of the other soldiers, Daylan, was also kissing a woman goodbye. She was rather plump and had a pretty face, and four little girls hung onto his legs and her skirts. He said goodbye to each of them in turn, and Darcy felt sick knowing that if he died on this journey, he would leave his daughters fatherless and his wife a widow, and it would be all her fault.

She rubbed nervously at her palm, but it wasn't as itchy as usual. In fact, she felt better this morning than she had all week. Rubidius said it was because the Oracle knew she was about to be on her way. "The symptoms will decrease as you close the distance between it and yourself."

Rubidius raised his hands to gather everybody's attention, and the six of them perked up. "If I may have the twelve travelers gather before me please."

They separated themselves from the well-wishers and stood before the old alchemist. "All of you either were chosen for this or volunteered of your own accord because you desire to protect the Intended." Darcy blushed, but he continued. "You are the very best companions I could have hoped for." Badru sniffed and smiled unctuously. Rubidius raised his hands over them. "May Pateros bless you on your journey and bring each of you home safe in the end."

The massive gates hinged to two cedar trees set into the castle wall began to creak open as if on cue, and Darcy felt the Oracle's pull toward the opening. The members of her company turned to look at her, not knowing which way to go.

She followed the pull in her chest, and at the gate's opening she turned back once to look at those she was leaving behind. Vesa, Eleanor, Rubidius, Sam, Lewis, and Amelia stared remorsefully after her. She nodded at them, shoving down the rising lump in her throat, and stepped through the gate.

CHAPTER 19

THE UNWILLING PARTICIPANT

The view outside the castle gates could not have been more different from what Darcy had seen the last time she'd been in Alitheia. If she hadn't known where she was, she wouldn't have believed it was the same place. The dark, oily vines were gone, and the undergrowth had been slashed to reveal the old highway as it was: smooth, paved with white stones, and sloped toward gutters on each side so the driving surface was slightly convex. Construction was underway in the trees across from them, and shirtless, sweaty men stopped their work clearing underbrush and dead trees to stare at them as they exited the castle. A few mules trundled by, pulling carts on the road, their drivers also staring curiously.

Darcy felt Veli move up beside her, and she glanced at him. "Do they know who I am?" she whispered out of the corner of her mouth.

Veli shook his head. "No, of course not. I doubt any of them know what you look like, and we did not trumpet about where you are going."

"So, nobody else knows we're going to see the Oracle?" she confirmed, surprised and relieved.

The corner of Veli's mouth twitched into a smile. "As far as most Alitheians are concerned, you and your companions are safe behind the castle walls, deep in training. The only people who know of your quest are the royal family, those who saw us off at the gate, a few people at the castle, and these who are with you."

"What if people wonder who we are and what we're doing? What will we say?"

"We'll tell them the truth, of course, with a few omissions. We are travelers—simple." He put a hand on her shoulder. "People do not ask many questions these days. There are many unfamiliar faces streaming through Alitheia as people return from far-flung lands. You do not need to worry about sticking out."

"Are we there already?" a deep voice growled from behind them, and Darcy and Veli turned. It was the yellow-haired Tormod, and he looked fierce.

"N—no," Darcy stammered.

"Then what are we waiting for?"

Darcy swallowed hard. "Nothing. Nothing at all. We're going this way," she turned to her right and marched up the street. The pull in her chest told her to head northeast.

Once out of the view of the men working in the trees, the oread nymph Terra jumped out of the earth and landed in front of Darcy, who took a step back, startled.

"Don't let him bother you," Terra said without preamble. She had to skip a little to keep up because of her short legs, but it didn't seem to faze her.

"Who?" Darcy asked after she recovered from her surprise.

"The big yellow one, Tormod. He doesn't like females, but he is a good man, an earthy man." She twirled a lock of curly hair around her finger and squinted back over her shoulder.

"Oh . . . okay," Darcy said.

"Oh! Gotta go!" And Terra dove, literally, into the road, disappearing from view.

"Wha—" Darcy looked around at Veli, and he laughed out loud.

"Nymphs are rather like that, in whatever form they come."

"Why did she say she had to go? Isn't she coming with us to the Oracle?"

"Oh yes, certainly, but we're coming up on the city, and she didn't want to be seen traveling with us." He pointed up the road ahead of them, and Darcy could see they were about to pass through a wall being reconstructed, beyond which was a bustling cityscape.

"Why not?" she asked, distracted by the city. She remembered seeing evidence of it from the bay their first night, but it still startled to her to see this many people in Alitheia.

"Nymphs do not usually travel with humans; it would seem odd to the city folk." Veli raised his hand to the men working on the wall as they passed beneath the arch of the gate. They nodded and called greetings.

"And she can just . . . swim through the earth to meet us on the other side?"

Veli smiled at her. "Something like that, yes."

Darcy looked over her shoulder at the rest of her party. They stretched out behind her and Veli like a line of ducklings. Perry and Dean were studying the city around them like children in a museum, and when Perry looked her way, he gave her a thumbs up. Lupidor stayed close to Tokala's legs, Darcy noticed, and she wondered if he were trying to look like a pet dog. She supposed the residents of Ormiskos would know the wolves were betrayers, and Lupidor likely wanted to make it clear he belonged with them.

Darcy faced forward as they came into the main flow of traffic on the old highway through the city. People were everywhere, hawking their wares, directing wagons full of hay and fish, and simply traveling from one place to another. Darcy had her shoulder jostled several times, but nobody paid them much attention. She continued leading them straight ahead through the city center, as the pull in her chest had not changed direction.

"So, where was all of this when Tse—" she began in a loud voice, and then thought better of shouting his name in the crowd of people. "When Tselloch was ruling," she finished in a whisper.

Veli replied, "Oh, the city was here, but it was overrun by his servants."

"Tsellodrin?" Darcy said it quietly, but a few people glanced at her nonetheless.

"Yes, it was a place for them, but also for his other servants: the shadow creatures and those who are unchanged."

"Who?" Darcy asked, waiting as a large cart full of rocks rumbled past on a crossroad.

"The unchanged, as we call them. He had many servants, like Lykos, who were neither tsellodrin nor tsellochim, who swore fealty to him without becoming part of his essence."

Darcy remembered the man who had taken her away from the dungeon the last night of her captivity. "Why would he let people do that? Wouldn't it make more sense for him to just make them tsellodrin? Then he wouldn't have to worry about them changing their minds, right?"

Veli shook his head. "Think about it, Darcy. The tsellodrin are mindless; they cannot make independent decisions. And, although they are fierce fighters and unfailingly loyal, they are also easily identifiable. His tsellochim are not mindless, but they cannot take true corporeal form, like he can, so they also are no good at infiltration. But a *human*, or a *wolf*," he added with a sidelong glance, "who swears loyalty to him without becoming a tsellodrin can be a powerful tool. They can become spies, and they are dangerous in a way his tsellodrin and tsellochim can never be. They can make you think they are on your side."

Darcy laughed hollowly. "I suppose I should know all this already. I guess that was kind of a stupid question."

Veli put a fatherly hand on her shoulder and squeezed. "It is not stupid to thirst for knowledge."

"You sound like a teacher."

He tilted his head with a puzzled look.

"Never mind." She gazed around some more. "So this is Ormiskos City —"

"Ormiskos Prime," he corrected her. "It is the city of Ormiskos, but we call it Ormiskos Prime."

"Oh, why?"

"Because it was the first of the two cities."

Darcy pointed to where the sea was just visible at the end of a side street. "You mean it was built before Kenidros?"

"Yes. They were both considered part of Ormiskos at one time, thus this city became Ormiskos *Prime*."

"When was the other part renamed Kenidros?"

"When the twin castle was built. Originally it was just a watchtower, but several hundred years ago, a king had twin sons and wanted each of them to inherit a castle. He separated the part of the city across the bay into its own province, renovated the watchtower into a castle, named it Kenidros, and gave it to the younger of his twin sons as his inheritance."

"Was he an Ecclektos king?"

Veli nodded. "Yes, and the royal family has governed Kenidros ever since."

"Who's the current governor?"

"Lord Tullin Ecclektos."

"But, isn't he king regent?"

Veli nodded. "Yes, but no others remain in the family. Tullin, Tellius, and Cadmus are the last of the Ecclektos line."

Darcy felt a stab of pity for Tellius. "So, when Tellius turns seventeen and takes the throne as king," she reasoned, "Tullin will go back to being governor of Kenidros?"

"Yes, and when Tullin dies—"

"Cadmus will be governor."

"Exactly."

"How did Tullin govern over Kenidros all this time with Tselloch on the throne?" Darcy asked.

As they ventured through the city, Veli told her how Tullin had sworn a false oath to Tselloch so he could remain as governor, all the while passing information to the rebellion. Tellius and Cadmus had hidden at Kenidros Castle as servants. "Tselloch, in his own hubris, never thought to look for them among the ranks of the poor," Veli told her with amusement. "They were right under his nose the entire time."

Darcy gained respect for Tullin and the princes as she listened to Veli's tale, and by the time he finished his story, they were nearly to the opposite end of the city.

They came upon a great crowd of people, and Veli stopped. "We're almost to the wharf," he said, peering over the crowd. "It's fish market day; that's why all these people are here. Do we need to cross the inlet?"

Darcy closed her eyes. The pull on her told her still to go forward, so she nodded.

"Okay. We will catch a ferry on the other side of this multitude." He looked over his shoulder. "Stay together everybody. We're going through." He began to cut a path through the crowd.

Conversation became impossible as they jostled through the masses of fishy-smelling people, and it wasn't until they emerged from the crowd on the other side that Darcy had a clear view of the inlet they were to cross. They passed through a narrow gate in the wall of the city, bypassing the main wharf facing into the castle bay, and found themselves on a deserted dock. A wooden wharf with stone pillars stretched out into the water, eerily still and quiet after the bustle of the crowd. The dock, outside the bounds of the sea wall that encased the castle harbor, looked lonely and forsaken. Very few boats were moored to the pillars, and Darcy got the idea that not many people crossed from here to the other side, even though it was only about two hundred yards away. The land opposite was covered in trees and rocks shrouded in mist.

"Okay," Perry's voice sounded, and she jumped. "In our world that over there would be . . . Canada?"

"It looks like the end of the world," Dean said, coming up beside them.

She glanced at him. "Don't be dramatic," she said, trying not to agree with him.

A large raft served as the ferry and an ancient man clung to a long, gnarled pole as though it was an extension of his arm. He stared at them, one eye completely obscured by cataracts. *He looks like Charon the ferryman of the dead,* Darcy thought with a shiver. She hoped she wasn't being prophetic.

Yahto Veli approached the old ferryman and handed him a few coins. "You can take us to the other side, yes?"

The ferryman looked down at the coins and back up at their party. He nodded slowly, but added in a voice as rough as his skin. "It's unprotected land over there, you know. The wards, they don't exist on that side."

"I'm one of the magicians who put up the wards," Badru said, stepping forward. "We're not afraid of the dangers of the wild."

The old man stared Badru down and then snorted. "As you wish, master magician." He gestured for them to board his raft, and they moved as one to comply.

Darcy stuck close to Perry and Dean, feeling bolstered by their familiarity and confidence as they cracked jokes and poked lightheartedly at each other. She was suddenly very glad to have them along because she was shaking in her boots. They were about to leave the protection of the wards, and she couldn't help but remember all the evils Voitto had warned her about.

Water lapped at the sides of the raft as the ferryman pushed off from shore and began to pole laboriously toward the other side. There were no seats on the vessel, and Darcy wobbled to keep her balance. She reached out impulsively and grabbed Perry's sleeve but snatched her hand away again as soon as she felt sure on her feet. "Sorry," she muttered.

"It's okay. You can hold on to me if you need to," Perry said. He held out his arm for her to hold.

"Thanks," she said, putting her hand on his sleeve again. She looked up to see Tormod's stony eyes on her, and she looked down again, her skin crawling.

They rode in silence the rest of the way, the sounds of Ormiskos Prime fading as they entered the mist. Darcy thought it strange that the far bank was shrouded in mist; it was late in the morning, after all. But the mist was still there, dampening their clothes and making their hair stick to their faces in wisps as they sailed into it.

The raft lurched and Darcy, Perry, and Dean all tumbled to the planked wood.

"Oof! Sorry!" Darcy said, struggling to push herself off Perry with her heavy pack weighing her down.

She felt herself being lifted bodily and placed on her feet and looked up into the friendly face of Wal Wyn the nark. "Perhaps next time you should hold on to somebody more sure-footed," he suggested.

"I'm sure-footed," Perry grumbled, struggling to his feet on the gently rocking vessel. They had reached the dock on the far side.

"No offense intended, Master Perry," the nark said, bowing.

"Man, I can't see a thing!" Dean exclaimed, getting to his feet with assistance from Tokala. "What *is* this?"

"It is a magic mist," Badru said, taking off his glasses to wipe them on his cloak. "It's part of the wards, and it is bothersome to the tsellochim."

"And to the tsellodrin?" Darcy said.

"It is not pleasant for them, either." Badru gave her a wan smile.

They filed off the craft one at a time, Veli giving each of the humans a hand. When they were all soundly on the dock, the ferryman started back without a word.

"Okay, that was creepy," Perry muttered to her out of the corner of his mouth.

"Let's get to where we can see each other properly," Daylan said, and they followed him several feet up the dock until they broke through the mist into clear air.

The ancient weathered dock ended in a patch of beach grass, beyond which was an area of loose gravel that might at one time have been the end of a road, but now it led to nowhere. The forest encroached just beyond the gravel. They truly were entering the wilderness, no trace now of the bustling city that was just on the other side of the inlet.

"I suppose this was once a road, right?" she asked Veli, looking up.

"A long, long time ago," he murmured, "when the Shadow was not yet here."

Terra appeared out of the ground then, looking around in a pleased sort of way. "Good, you made it through."

"Now that we're all here, let's get our bearings," Daylan said. "Lady Darcy, which way next?" Daylan seemed to want to take leadership, and he looked capable, but Darcy still looked to Veli for approval. He nodded.

"We need to go north from here," she said. "It's calling me north."

"It's calling you, eh?" Borna Fero shook his head. "Outrageous business, this." He pointed to the dense forest to the north. "Isn't there any better way of finding the Oracle? Couldn't someone have given us directions?"

"No." Darcy felt emboldened by the knowledge she'd gained after a week working with Rubidius. "The Oracle moves around; it's never in the same location twice, and it can be found only by the one who has invoked it."

Fero shook his heavy mane of braids again. "Insanity."

"Let us have a quick sup, and then we can be off again and get some distance behind us," Daylan interceded.

Perry snorted and whispered to Dean, "Wha's *sup*, man?" Darcy rolled her eyes.

She found a large, water-pocked rock to sit on and munched on a piece of the granola cake that Asa Rhea had made. It kept very well and was sustaining for travel, so they'd brought several wrapped loaves of it along with them. Darcy tried a bit of transformation magic on her handful of nuts to see if she could give them a salty coating, but she found that sort of earth magic still beyond her reach. The nuts remained plain and dry. She considered asking Badru to do it for her, but she barely knew him and didn't want to bother him with something so trivial.

"You don't remember me, do you?" Tokala's voice sounded in her ear, and she turned to face him. He was just as handsome up close as he was at a distance.

"I think I would remember you," she answered under her breath. But to him she only blushed and shook her head no.

"I was at Paradeisos with you two years ago. My hair was long then," he said, tugging his sleek locks back from his face as if pulling them into a ponytail. "Eh?" he asked. "Look familiar at all?"

Darcy tried to place his face but couldn't. "No, sorry. There were so many soldiers there," she offered by way of apology.

"Ah, oh well." He smiled, and she noticed two deep dimples in his cheeks. "Everybody knew who you were, of course. We were all sworn to protect you."

"Guess I kind of screwed that up when I ran off with Lykos," Darcy muttered, looking down.

He shrugged with casual ease. "Maybe you wouldn't have been able to run off if we had all done our jobs properly. I don't blame you; you just wanted to get out there and fight, right?"

Darcy laughed nervously. "Something like that."

"All I know is I couldn't turn this job down when old Rubidius asked me to come. I felt I had failed you once before, and I wanted to do the job right this time."

"Why *did* he ask you?" Perry asked from Darcy's other side.

"Because I'm the best!" Tokala cocked a flashy grin at them. Other than slightly longer canine teeth, his smile was perfect, as well.

"Better than Daylan, or Tormod, or the narks?" Perry asked pointedly.

"The narks—they're in their own league. No sense comparing myself to them. Daylan is a respectable fighter, and at one time I would have called him the best, but he's starting to get old. Tormod . . . well, I don't know much about him other than he's surly and a good man in a fight. But there's no way he's better than me," he finished with absolute confidence.

Perry snorted and bit into his granola, but Dean looked at Tokala with glassy-eyed admiration.

"All right, let's pack it up," Daylan said, clapping his hands. "Tokala, I want you up front with Veli and Lady Darcy. I want the young sirs in the middle with Badru, and I will bring up the rear with Tormod. Terra and Lupidor, you cover the outlying forest; be our eyes and ears. I want Wal Wyn and Borna Fero on our flanks. Hold to those positions and keep your wits about you. Weapons at the ready at all times," he growled.

Northward, ever northward; the call of the Oracle had not wavered. Darcy didn't know what to expect of the land outside the environs of Ormiskos. Eleanor had told them last year that the topography was only similar to upper Michigan in the vicinity of the gateway. Once outside that area, everything changed. So far, the forest around them still seemed familiar. The trees were thick, but not impassible, and moss-covered boulders loomed about them like sleeping giants. Ferns were dense in the undergrowth, and the knotted roots of cedar and birch trees intertwined to form a treacherous network under their feet. Several times Darcy had slipped on, or tripped over, a root and needed to be helped upright again by Veli.

But Veli would not be Veli for much longer. The shadows were increasing under the forest canopy, and the fairies that had been keeping progress with them were beginning to disappear to their tiny, leafy beds. Darcy would miss their company. Their very presence assured her of safety, as surely they wouldn't show themselves in the presence of evil when the passage of tsellochim would killed them.

She shot a glance up at Veli. He had been very quiet, and sweat was beading on his forehead. She didn't like it when Veli looked nervous.

They broke into a boulder-strewn clearing, and Tokala held up his hand. "Daylan," he called back. "What do you think of this for a campsite?"

Daylan came up behind them, his feet making almost no noise in the spongy moss and pliable ferns. "It's a good spot," he confirmed. "Let's pitch camp while we still have some light." Terra and Lupidor appeared in the clearing, but Daylan instructed them to continue keeping watch, so they disappeared back into the trees.

In a matter of minutes the narks had the tents spread out and pegged to the ground. She offered to help, but they shooed her away. "Rest," said Wyn. Even though it was late for him, he looked as fair as Veli did in the middle of the day.

She sat wearily on a fallen log, thankful they wouldn't let her help. With shaking hands she pulled out her potions and took a long draft of the bitter one even though she didn't feel like she needed it—not now that they were on their way. Still, she wanted to be safe, and Rubidius had advised taking it whenever they stopped for any length of time. She was tempted to drink some strength potion, too, but she figured her exhaustion would help her sleep.

She unwrapped the linen binding on her hand, wrinkling her nose at the smell, and looked down at the large purple sore. A faint smile crossed her face as she noticed it was a little bit smaller. She changed the linen and rewrapped it with a sigh.

Tormod was busy building a fire in the center of the clearing, and every now and then Lupidor would breeze into the circle like a ghost and deposit a dead rabbit. *I guess that's dinner,* Darcy thought as Tormod began skinning and cleaning them. Darcy looked away, nauseated.

Badru walked a circuit around the edge of camp, and Darcy thought he was muttering to himself until she saw him gesturing and realized he must be performing some sort of magic.

The smell of cooking rabbit began to fill the clearing, and Darcy sat near the fire. Even in the summer in Alitheia, the temperature could dip close to freezing at night, and she noticed that a small one-person tent had been set up very close to the flames. *I hope that's for me,* she thought with a shiver.

She kept a close watch on Veli now, as the light in the clearing diminished. In a matter of moments he would go to sleep, along with Wyn and Fero, to be replaced by their night nark counterparts. Veli kept glancing at her as though he had something on his mind, but he never said a word.

When the last of the sun's light faded, the narks eerily closed their eyes as one, their physical appearances making the final transition. Wal Wyn's hair turned brown, Borna Fero took on a dark-chocolate-brown appearance, and Yahto Veli's hair darkened to its familiar raven black. With a snap he opened his eyes before either of the other two and jerked his head about in surprise, processing his situation. He turned to see Darcy staring at him, and his eyes flashed frighteningly in the firelight.

"No," he said, the one word imbued with contempt.

Chapter 20

A Meeting of Old Friends

Yahto turned on his heel and began to walk out of the clearing. Darcy leapt from her spot by the fire. "Yahto, wait! What's wrong?"

He turned back to her, his eyes full of blazing anger. "Never in all our years—*never* has any nark dared to do what Veli has done!"

Darcy came up short; her suspicions of Veli seeming to be true. "He . . . he didn't ask you?" she whispered.

Yahto's voice was low and cool, barely controlled. "Ask me? No, he didn't ask me. He didn't even *tell me*!" he roared. Darcy took a startled step backward.

"You don't understand," he continued, seething, "you *can't* understand! It is against our law to act expressly against the wishes of our nark counterpart. It is *forbidden* to conceal information of this import unless one has no choice. I would say he had a choice, wouldn't you?"

Darcy gulped. "I didn't know, Yahto. I would have told him not to do it, I swear!"

"It's too late for that," Yahto said coldly. With a snap of his cloak, he was gone.

Darcy spun around to the stunned faces of the rest of the company. "Do something!" she cried to the other two narks, but they shook their heads.

"This is unheard of," Wal said.

"Veli has grossly violated our code of ethics," Borna added. "Yahto must be allowed to make his own choices."

"We will not go after him," Wal finished.

Darcy turned desperate eyes on the men, but they shook their heads. No human could catch a fleeing nark, let alone one that did not want to be found. Yahto was gone.

Darcy sobbed, collapsing to her knees with her hands over her face, feeling as though everything she touched went to pieces. "It doesn't make any sense!" she moaned, wondering what would possess Veli to start a journey without seeking Yahto's permission first, why he would break the most ancient code of the narks just for *her.*

"Lady Darcy," Terra's hands were on her shoulders, shaking her. She had returned from lookout duty to comfort her, as Darcy supposed none of the men wanted the job. "This is not your fault. Put it from your mind."

"How can I?" Darcy cried, looking into Terra's eyes. The oread's brown hair was very short at the moment and her eyes were dark brown mottled with green, like the moss beneath her feet. "Veli's my friend, but Yahto's always hated me! What is Yahto going to *do* to him?"

"Nothing," Terra said firmly. "He cannot hurt Veli without hurting himself."

Darcy groaned and tugged on her hair, wondering if she would ever see Veli again.

"My lady," Terra tried again, "you must eat something."

"I don't want to," Darcy spat. "I'm not hungry."

"It's orders, Lady," Terra said. "You cannot march on an empty stomach, no matter how much strength potion you have."

"Fine," Darcy snapped. She sat back on her heels and choked down a chunk of rabbit meat, but she couldn't drink any water because she had just taken her potion. Grumbling, she wiped her greasy hands on her slacks. "Is that enough?" she asked waspishly.

"Have some bread."

Darcy sighed. There was almost nothing more unappealing on a dry tongue than starch, but she knew she would not have any peace from the nymph if she didn't accept it.

When she finished the bread, Terra finally let her go to her tent. "Sleep fully clothed," she instructed. "We must be ready to move at a moment's notice."

With a despondent nod, Darcy let her tent flap fall.

Loud bird calls woke Darcy long before she was ready to be up, and an insect buzzed loudly in her ears. She rolled over and buried her face in the pack she was using as a pillow, her back protesting the night on the hard, knotty ground, and the buzzing persisting in her ears. She rolled over again, restless, and sat up. Grumbling, she dug in her pack for her potion; the Oracle must want her to get moving.

She was tempted to go back to sleep after she had finished her drink, but the events of the night before came swarming back to her in a rush, and she groaned aloud. *Oh, Veli.* She sat with her head in her hands before gathering herself to leave the tent. Several loops had escaped her long braid in her sleep, and she re-braided it easily. Her hair was already starting to feel greasy, and she shuddered to think how gross she would be by the end of her journey. *However long that may be.*

She stood stiffly, bent over in the low tent, and reached for the flap. The cool breeze outside hit her almost as strongly as the sharp morning sunshine, and she exhaled her breath in white puffs.

Dean and Perry were already up, tousle-headed and stiff-looking as they worked their way through their morning forms. Darcy eyed Perry appreciatively while he wasn't looking.

They turned in a slow circle with their arms outstretched, but stopped abruptly as soon as they saw her. "Darcy—" Perry said, stepping toward her. He shot a furtive glance toward the fire circle and then back at her.

She followed his gaze and gave a start. "Veli!" she cried. Seated on a log by the cold embers of the fire was indeed Veli, his eyes morose. She went to sit with him, but he only offered her a weak smile.

"I'm sorry," he said in a penitent tone. "I should have told you."

"*Me?*" Darcy gaped at him. "You should have told *him*."

"Perhaps."

"*Perhaps?* How can you say that? Do you have any idea how he reacted?"

"I do. He told me everything."

"Then—"

"He came back on his own, you know," Veli interrupted her, "in the middle of the night."

She gaped at him. "So?"

"It means I was right. At least about his desire to help you."

"Then why didn't you just tell him in the first place?"

Veli sighed and twined his fingers together. "Yahto is a realist and, as you know, he tends to look on the darker side of things. I knew he was—pardon me for saying so—disgusted with your invocation of the Oracle. He would have refused to come on the journey because it would have been, in his opinion, a fool's mission. I also knew, though, that as time passed and his disgust abated, he would regret not going with you, not trying to protect you. I told you the truth yesterday: Yahto does not hate you; he has . . . less patience for your human foibles."

"I don't understand what you're saying. You mean Yahto would not have wanted to come right away, but he would have wanted to once some time had passed?"

"Yes. But by that time it would have been too late to find you. Despite what he may have told you, he did not *expressly* forbid us to come on this journey, if only because he didn't know I had any plans to take us on it."

"So you forced his hand," Perry's voice sounded, and they looked up.

Veli nodded. "Yes. I forced his hand."

Perry seemed impressed. "Bold move."

Veli's ears twitched. "You could say that."

"But why was it so important for *you* to come that you would risk destroying your reputation as a nark?" Darcy pressed.

"Why, you, my friend."

"Oh, *please* don't put it like that," Darcy mumbled. So many people were putting their lives on the line for her, and she couldn't stand the thought that Yahto was now also sacrificing his own desires to be with her.

"I could not bear the thought of you facing this peril without me here to watch over you. We are friends; it is only natural that I come."

"Okay," Darcy said. "Just don't do anything stupid, okay? Like die, for instance."

Veli laughed.

"Yahto's really okay with it now?"

"He will be. For now he is accepting the direction in which I take him."

"And he won't make another big scene tonight?"

"No more big scenes; I promise."

Yahto had been true to Veli's word. That night after the transformation, he'd sat down by the fire without a word of protest and finished the dinner Veli had started. In fact, he hadn't just refrained from protesting, he'd refrained from talking at all. He hadn't looked at or acknowledged Darcy in any way and had answered only direct questions from the other narks.

As the days wore on, his attitude had not improved. In fact, he'd been the one dark spot on an otherwise pleasant journey.

About a week in, Darcy'd thought perhaps everybody had been mistaken about the dangerous Alitheian wilderness, because so far they hadn't been challenged by any unfriendly forces. Fairies and the occasional gnomes had remained their constant companions, and conversation had been light among the party of travelers. They'd continued ever northward, the Oracle never wavering in its call. Darcy's only concern had simply become how far it would take her and when would they return to Ormiskos Castle.

They'd sent regular dispatches to the castle using Dean's enchanted bow and arrow, which he kept strapped across the back of his pack, carefully separated from his other set. Rubidius had sent notes of encouragement and guidance in return, and Sam had sometimes written personal notes to

Darcy, usually accompanied by funny little sketches. Darcy enjoyed the feeling that they were simply in school, passing notes as they always did.

The topography of the land had begun to slowly change. They were still traveling through deep forest, but the ground beneath them had started to become less flat and more unpredictable. A couple of times they'd come up against narrow ravines, at the bottom of which flowed trickling streams. They'd been able to jump over the ravines easily enough, but once or twice Terra had had to find them a safe place to cross.

Darcy had practiced her mind-speaking talent with animals to pass the time. She had found with Rubidius that she could throw out a kind of open net and connect with any high animals in the area. She liked practicing as she hiked through the wilderness—it was so startling to the animals she encountered, as they had never met a human who could hear their voices in her head, let alone speak back telepathically in return. Once she'd so startled a poor raccoon it had fallen right out of its tree, landing on Tormod's head. He had cursed the animal soundly, and only Darcy had been privy to the raccoon's exasperated response, which had been almost as colorful as Tormod's.

Two weeks wore into three weeks, then four, but Darcy felt great. Her symptoms had almost completely abated, and she was constantly befriending new forest animals. It now seemed as though the animals were seeking her out. Even low animals, those with whom she could not communicate, seemed to follow her with their eyes.

Terra, too, had been a welcome companion. She'd been easy to befriend and she never made Darcy feel uncomfortable. She always had something interesting to talk about, and she'd told Darcy all about the soil and rock layers beneath them in a way much more interesting than Darcy's earth science teacher had back in school. Terra knew the history of the earth—Orodreos, to her—and how the earth's layers had been placed upon each other by a great cataclysm long before Pateros had brought humans to their world.

Not to mention, Terra had been invaluable as the only other female on the trip, because there were some things Darcy just couldn't do in the company of boys or men, but Daylan required a "buddy system" for everything. And he did mean *everything*.

Late one afternoon, almost five weeks out from Ormiskos, their company had come upon a deep ravine bordered with steep cliffs and a fast rushing river at the bottom. The men had decided, instead of immediately rigging a crossing or finding a way around, they would make camp and tackle it in the morning. Darcy hadn't been thrilled about that, as longer stops required her to wake up in the middle of the night, needing her bitter potion, but she did see the logic in staying the night; it really had been too late in the day to plan a ravine crossing.

"Oof," Darcy mumbled as she tripped over a fallen branch. She'd gone off with Terra and a bucket of water from one of many tiny waterfalls trickling over the edge of the ravine, to find a private place to bathe for the first time in days. It wouldn't be a true bath, what with only one bucket of water, but at least she could sponge off a little.

She and Terra walked until they could no longer hear the voices from camp and found a suitable place in a small clearing that abutted the ravine and was sheltered by two large boulders.

"As long as you don't fall over the edge," Terra said, looking down over the drop, "you should be perfectly fine. I'll be right over there." She pointed to the other side of one of the boulders. "Have fun!" she called as she skipped away.

Darcy set down the bucket, being very careful not to slosh too much water out, and rubbed her arms. No matter how many times she did it, it always felt strange to strip down in the middle of the forest. She was very thankful, though, that it was a particularly hot August day, because the water in her bucket was very cold. She could have asked Badru to heat it up for her, but he had been busy putting up the wards around the campsite, and he didn't like to be interrupted.

Darcy first removed the quiver of arrows and the bow she kept slung over her shoulder, and then she unbuckled her belt with its knife sheath. Now weaponless, she shrugged the leather jerkin over her stiff limbs.

As she bent to undo the ties on her boots, the hairs on the back of her neck prickled and she looked up, afraid. The forest had gone very still. *Too still,* Darcy thought. She remained in her half-bent posture as the blood started to pound in her ears—the only sound she heard in the silent forest, until a nearby bird chirped. Darcy relaxed, closing her eyes and exhaling.

She finished removing her boots and stockings, but just as she was reaching up to undo her hair, she heard it: a low, menacing growl. She whirled to face the sound and cried out. In her startled recognition, she opened the link. *Lykos!*

The former wolf prince of Sanditha looked much the worse for wear. He was skinny, his grey fur bedraggled and a large chunk was missing from one ear. His peering yellow eyes, though, were unmistakable. She knew it was him beyond a shadow of a doubt.

Hello, old friend, he replied through the link. *Have you missed me?* His lips pulled back from his fangs in an awful grimace, his expression deadly enough to kill.

Darcy's mouth gaped uselessly and she cast her eyes to her weapons, lying feet from her on the ground. *How did you find me?*

I've been hearing rumors, you see. He was circling her now, getting closer and closer. *Rumors of a girl who can speak inside an animal's mind; of a powerful enchantress who understands the language of the high animals. You've been careless to reveal your talent so readily. Didn't I tell you it was best kept a secret?*

"You told me a lot of things," Darcy ground out in a loud voice, hoping Terra would hear her.

I knew it could be no one but you, for you are, indeed, unique, Darcy Pennington.

"What do you want with me?" Darcy tried to make her voice carry.

The oread won't be bothering us, Darcy, Lykos said smoothly. *I have already seen to her.*

"So, *what then?*" Darcy screamed, desperate for somebody to hear her at the camp. "What do you *want?*"

I want what I have wanted since the day you escaped Tselloch and ruined my life. I want you dead!

He launched himself at her.

Darcy shrieked and covered her head with her arms, expecting to feel claws tearing her skin, but they did not come. Instead a dark blur shot from the forest and collided with Lykos in mid-air, knocking him in another direction. The two wolves rolled together, a snarling, wriggling mass of fur, claws, and teeth. They ripped at each other, separating and circling, snapping and foaming at the mouth.

Darcy had seen a dog fight before, but this was more terrifying by far. Lupidor's fur stood up in a rigid line along his back. His ears were flat on his head, his shoulders hunched, showing his dominance over Lykos, who slunk lower to the ground. Both wolves looked ready to tear the other's throat out, and Darcy didn't doubt they could do it.

Another old friend! Lykos's voice sounded in her ear. *I knew you were the betrayer.*

Lupidor answered with a low growl and launched himself at Lykos again, but Lykos's concern was Darcy. He danced backward out of Lupidor's reach and scrabbled up the side of a large boulder in the clearing, Lupidor snapping at his heels.

Lykos paced back and forth atop the boulder, his yellow eyes staring menacingly down at them. From the ground beneath him, Lupidor followed his every motion, but he wouldn't climb the rock and leave Darcy exposed. Darcy backed up until she reached the edge of the ravine.

Lykos gave a terrible howl and launched himself from the boulder toward Darcy, but Lupidor sprang from the ground like a cat and caught Lykos's leg in his mouth, slamming him to the ground with a bone-jarring crunch. Darcy still within his reach, Lykos lunged for her, his jaws gnashing.

"No!" Terra cried, appearing between them out of the earth. She grabbed Darcy around the middle and pulled her down with her, into the ground and out of Lykos's reach.

Darcy's lungs immediately began to burn. She couldn't see or hear anything, and the weight of the earth pressed down on her, squeezing the air from her lungs. She could feel Terra pulling her, like a rescue diver pulling an unconscious person through rough waters, but she couldn't do anything to help her.

She felt herself propelled back up through the surface, and she gasped in precious air, finding herself several feet inland from the ravine. She heard snarls and yips but couldn't see the wolves anywhere. Holding her pounding head in shaking hands, she turned a full circle. "Where are they? Where's Lupidor?" she gasped.

A piercing yelp ripped through the air, and a splash of water followed. "I'll be right back!" Terra cried, diving back into the ground.

Feet pounded behind Darcy, and she spun around to find Veli and Fero charging into the clearing, weapons drawn, Tokala and Tormod not far behind.

"What's happened?" Tormod demanded as Veli sped to her side.

"Wolves!" Darcy sputtered. "It was him—Lykos—"

"Lykos?" Veli's alarmed eyes met hers.

"I have him!" Terra shouted, and Darcy saw the slight nymph struggling to help Lupidor scramble up over the edge of the cliff. "He was—caught—in a tree," she huffed.

Fero and Tormod hurried to help them. Darcy feared Lupidor was injured, but once he had all four feet soundly on the ground, he shook off his companions and paced back and forth along the edge of the ravine, his fur still on end and a deep rumble echoing in his chest.

She ran to Lupidor and tried to keep pace next to him, opening their link for the first time. *Lupidor, where is he?*

He looked at her, a deep red gash, oozing blood, running between his fierce blue eyes. He returned his gaze to the river below them. *He fell into the river, but he's not dead. I saw him climb out downriver on the far side.* Lupidor's voice was deep and wolfish, but pleasant for all that. It lacked the oily, unctuous tone that Lykos had.

Darcy looked back over her shoulder. "He said Lykos fell into the ravine and crawled out downriver," she called.

The four warriors rushed to the edge and peered down. Fero notched an arrow in his bow.

He's gone now, it's no use, Lupidor said. He finally ceased his pacing and the rumble left his chest. He sat and hung his head.

Chapter 21

The Pursuit

"He said he's gone," Darcy repeated to the others, but they continued to scan the trees downriver. She could have attempted to link their minds with Lupidor's, as she and Rubidius had discovered she could do, but that took focus and energy she didn't have at the moment.

She sat back on her heels and dug her fingers into her messed-up braid. She thought about Lykos's beat up appearance and the desperation he betrayed.

Lupidor, what happened to him?

Lupidor raised his head. *He was dethroned by his pack after Tselloch fled Ormiskos. His challenger should have fought him to the death but he didn't finish the job. Lykos has been without a pack ever since, wandering the wilderness. I'm not sure if Tselloch even has any use for him anymore. Rumor among my people was that he blamed you for everything. He became obsessed with finding you.*

Darcy shivered and placed a cautious hand on Lupidor's neck, noticing the matted blood. *Lupidor?*

Yes? He swung his great grey head around.

I'm sorry I haven't talked to you before now. You know . . . with Lykos it had been—

It's okay, Lady Darcy. I understand.

Darcy bit her lip and nodded. *Thank you for saving my life.*

That's why I'm here. I'm only sorry I couldn't eliminate Lykos as a threat once and for all. He swung away from her and trotted over to join the others at the edge of the ravine. *Tell them, please, that Lykos will most likely go to Tselloch with his information.*

His information?

About you. Tselloch will soon know not only that you are no longer in Ormiskos, but your approximate location.

Darcy's skin went cold. Why hadn't she thought of that? She repeated his words to the others with a shaking voice, but they didn't seem surprised.

"I guessed as much," Veli said grimly.

"Let them come," Fero said with the crazy glint in his eyes. "I welcome the chance to kill some of those shadow-swine!"

Tell them also that he's wounded, Lupidor interjected, and she repeated it.

"That gives us some time, at least," Tormod growled.

"But not much," Fero added.

"Darcy, come, let's get back to camp," Veli said, and he helped her gather her scattered belongings.

"Are you okay?" Terra asked with an anxious gaze, popping up to trot beside her.

Darcy nodded but felt shaky as she took a deep breath. "Thanks to you and Lupidor, I guess."

"No, I mean, how's your chest . . . your breathing? Is everything all right?"

"I guess I still feel a little tight, but otherwise okay." Darcy frowned at her. "Why?"

"It's very risky to take a non-earth entity into the ground; that's why I did not keep you under for long. Some people can be crushed or suffocate from the experience. But I felt I had no choice; I had to save you!"

"You did the right thing," Darcy reassured her. "Lykos would have killed me for sure if you hadn't done it. I'm not saying I want to repeat the experience anytime soon," she said, grimacing, "but I'm glad you did it."

"Good!" Terra sighed.

They ducked under a broken-down tree together, and Darcy looked sideways at her. On either side of the nymph's neck were scabs that ran in fanning V's to the front of her throat, some deeper pocks scattered over her neck, and Darcy realized with a jolt that they were teeth marks. "Terra!" she exclaimed. "Your neck; you're hurt!"

Terra put a hand to the scabs. "I *was* hurt. I'll be all right. I'm almost healed now."

"*How?*" Darcy sputtered.

"He snuck up on me while I had my back turned, the coward," she spat. "He must have followed us and waited until just the right moment to attack. He tore at my throat before I could even cry out to warn you."

"But how—" Darcy started again, bewildered.

"I returned to my element before I bled out," the oread said matter-of-factly.

"You returned to your element*?*"

They rounded a bend and stepped back into camp, and Terra turned to smile at her. "I'm only flesh and blood while I am topside, Darcy. As long as I return to the earth before my heart stops beating, I can regenerate." She touched her neck again. "With an injury like this, however, it takes some time. That's why I was not able to help you sooner."

Her grin deepened at Darcy's astonished expression, and she stepped aside as Perry and Dean hurried forward.

"What happened?" Dean demanded.

"Are you guys okay? Darcy?" Perry put his hands on her shoulders.

"Veli mentioned Lykos; was it really him?" Dean continued.

Darcy stepped back out of Perry's reach and held up her hands. "One question at a time, guys. It's a long story. Yes, I'm okay, and yes, it was Lykos."

"Dean," Daylan barked, coming up to draw the boy aside. "Prepare your bow. We must send a dispatch to Rubidius. And Perry," Daylan turned his powerful gaze on him, "try to recall how it was that you killed the tsellochim in the last battle of Ormiskos. We're going to need your skills before too long."

"What's going on?" Perry whispered fiercely to Darcy as Dean went off with Daylan. "Are they expecting us to be attacked by tsellochim?"

Darcy sighed and explained about Lykos and how they thought that he would go to Tselloch.

"So, obviously he's going to send some after us, right?"

"Yeah, that makes sense." Perry looked nervous as he fingered the hilt of his sword. "The thing is, Darcy," he leaned forward to whisper to her, "I don't *know* how I killed the tsellochim; it just happened!"

"Then I'm sure it will happen again," Darcy replied. "Besides, we have Badru, and . . . well . . . I'm sure he knows what he's doing."

They looked over at the young magician who appeared to be arguing with himself. He kept changing positions jerkily, shaking his head and muttering.

"Right. That makes me feel so much better."

Darcy wanted to say something clever, but the words died on her lips as Veli approached them. He drew her aside with an apologetic remark and put his arm around her shoulders. "Do you want to tell me how Lykos was able to find you?" he murmured as they faced the dark canopy of trees.

"I've been practicing my talent," Darcy admitted, casting a glance up to judge his reaction. "I didn't think it would harm anything!"

Veli sighed, more sad than angry. "I *thought* we had an abnormally large following of animals. I only wish you had told me; I could have warned you of the danger."

"But, I thought the animals didn't speak each others' languages. How could he have heard from the animals I was talking to?" Darcy frowned. "He said he'd heard rumors."

"Many animal dialects are similar to each other, and over the ages they have found ways of communicating amongst themselves. Who knows? He could have been following us all along." He gave her shoulder a squeeze. "No more using your talent unless directed to do so, agreed?"

"Yes," Darcy nodded. "You're not going to tell Daylan, are you?" she added. She was a little intimidated by him.

"No, but . . ." he hesitated. "I am going to tell Yahto. He's a little . . . *testy* . . . about me keeping secrets from him at the moment."

"Gee, I can't imagine why," Darcy said dryly.

"Yes . . . well, that's that, then," Veli nodded and yawned behind his hand.

"You did *what?"* Yahto threw back Darcy's tent flaps and grabbed her arm. Hauling her to her feet, he dragged her from her tent to the edge of camp. It was just after nightfall, and Darcy had been getting ready to go to sleep early. The rest of the company were either hunched around the fire deep in conversation or off in the woods on perimeter watch. They didn't look up when Yahto confronted her.

"Ouch!" Darcy complained. "Let go, Yahto." He let her wrench her arm free, and she rubbed at it, glaring at him.

"You *foolish, infernal* girl!" he spat. "Have you no brain in your head at all?" His charcoal grey eyes glinted like iron.

"I—that's—that's not very nice—" she swallowed hard against the hot sting of tears. Yahto had not said a word to her on the journey until this point, and *this* was how he chose to open communication.

"You're going to cry now, are you?" He rolled his eyes. "You humans, you are like *infants*. You blunder about making thoughtless decisions and then weep when confronted."

"Do I really disgust you that much, Yahto?" Darcy choked out. "Or do you just enjoy tormenting me?"

"You still think this is all about *you,* don't you?" he retorted. "It's always been about you—who *you* have to marry, what *your* future looks like, what makes *you* happy. You're so absorbed with yourself you don't even think before trumpeting your talent about to the entire animal kingdom! Didn't Rubidius teach you *anything?"*

"Rubidius never said I couldn't practice my talent on our journey!" Darcy fired up. "Don't you think he would have mentioned it if he'd thought it was important?"

"I suppose it never crossed your mind that Rubidius is not omniscient."

"Huh?"

"You don't think he *possibly* could have forgotten to mention it with *everything else* he had to do to prepare for this ridiculous journey? That maybe, just maybe, he was distracted with the task of trying to keep you and everyone with you *alive*?"

"I . . . he did tell me to be careful with it—"

"And were you? *No!* You spoke with any animal within hearing range!"

Darcy sniffed and folded her arms belligerently. "I know you don't want to be here, Yahto, but you don't have to take it out on me."

"Oh? And who else is to blame?"

"Veli—"

"Oh, now this is very interesting! You're going to sacrifice him to your cause, are you?"

"No! I just meant he was the one who didn't tell you he was coming!"

"My fool of a counterpart did only what he thought was necessary to keep *your* skin in one piece. If I didn't have such respect for him, I would never have come back. And I am *seriously* reconsidering that choice right now."

"*Go, then!* I don't *care!*" Darcy shouted. She'd had enough of him, and at the moment she didn't even care how it would hurt Veli.

His upper lip curled into a sneer. He looked nothing like her dear friend Veli.

A throat cleared behind them, and they turned. It was Daylan. "Lady Darcy, you should get some rest," he said, his eyes boring into hers. "We will start early in the morning. We must get far away from this location to throw off anything Tselloch should send after us."

"Fine." She tossed her head and stalked off to her tent.

It was still dark when Terra woke Darcy in the morning. "Come on, my lady, we must go," she whispered. "Quickly!"

The urgency in the nymph's voice woke Darcy like a splash of cold water, and she hurried to shove her feet into her boots and reassemble her bag and weapons. The moment she exited the tent, Wal Wyn and Borna Fero made quick work of tearing it down. Yahto Veli, she noted with surprise, was still there. His hair was turning chestnut brown in the early morning, but the sun had not broken the horizon yet. He remained Yahto. Darcy ignored him as studiously as he ignored her.

Lupidor stood at attention with his nose in the air and his bushy tail held out stiffly behind him. Daylan looked down at him, his expression grim.

Lupidor? Darcy opened the link and knelt down next to his great shaggy body with her hand on his back.

Lupidor looked from her to Daylan, and Darcy understood what he wanted her to do. With an effort, she extended the link to cover Daylan and searched inside it for his human awareness. Once she found it, she brought it into her link with Lupidor. *Okay*, she said to both of them, and Daylan looked down at her in surprise.

You can mind-speak with humans, too?

Only if an animal is connected; the link won't activate with a human alone. Lupidor, what did you want to tell him?

They are close, Lupidor said. *Four, maybe five miles away.*

How do you know this? Daylan asked sharply.

Because they are my own kind and I can hear their thoughts. I was wrong; Lykos did not go to Tselloch first. He found another pack and challenged their leader. He killed him and took control. He has sent envoys to Tselloch, but he is leading his new pack here, to us. He wants the glory of killing the Intended himself.

You said he was injured! Darcy protested.

Never underestimate the power of hatred, Lupidor replied with a grim growl.

Then we must make haste, Daylan said. *We've no time to lose.*

Yes, Lupidor agreed, *but we must be prepared. They will overtake us; we cannot possibly get away.*

Daylan squinted. *Then we will find a place to make a stand!* "Let's go!" he shouted to the rest of the camp. "Wolves are coming, and unless you want to be dog food, you will be ready to leave in two minutes!"

That got everyone moving. Tormod and Tokala busied themselves at the edge of the ravine where Darcy noticed they had already rigged together some sort of rope crossing. There was one rope at foot level and another at chest level; they would have to cross by inching along the lower rope while clinging to the upper.

Will this slow the wolves down? she asked Lupidor uneasily.

They will not come this way; Lykos will have found a better crossing for them, he replied.

Great.

The rest of her grim-faced companions gathered along the edge with her. Tokala went first. He made it look easy with the lithe grace of an athlete. He grinned at them once he was across and motioned for the next person.

"I'll go," Dean said. He clearly idolized the young soldier and wanted to make a good impression on him.

Darcy watched with bated breath. Dean swayed and bobbed his way along the rope, almost falling several times. When he reached the other side, he collapsed to the ground and lay still. Darcy wondered if he was crying.

Perry gritted his teeth and took to the rope next. His legs shook, causing the whole rigging to quiver, but he took it slower than Dean had and managed to make it across without looking like too much of a bungling idiot.

"Lady Darcy, you're next," Daylan's voice sounded in her ear.

She took a deep breath and gazed fearfully at the fifty-foot drop to the river, when a voice of reason awoke in the back of her mind. *This is exactly the sort of thing Rubidius would expect you to do well on, you know,* it said. *Why not use your magic?* Darcy caught her lip between her teeth. Sure, why not?

She grasped the top rope and focused on it until she could make out every fiber. *Be like a magnet,* she thought. *Stick to it, slide along it.* She put one foot on the rope, and then the next. She could feel the magic expending her, but it only encouraged her that it was working. She shimmied her feet sideways, and they moved like oiled casters in a track, without slipping. A grin lit her face and she closed her eyes, both for focus and to keep from looking down at the void beneath her.

She shimmied more quickly, her hands and feet practically gliding along the rope, and before long she was on the other side. Tokala caught her arm and hauled her off the rope, looking impressed.

"How did you *do* that?" Perry asked, awed. Darcy noticed his hands were still shaking from the effort of hauling himself across.

"She used her magic, I expect," Badru answered for her, stepping from the rope. He clearly had used a similar technique because he barely looked ruffled at all by the crossing.

"Really?"

Darcy shrugged and nodded.

"That's . . . awesome!" Perry said.

"Yeah, totally cool, Darcy," Dean agreed. He was sitting up now, but his face still looked white.

The other two men and the three narks joined them, and Terra cut off the ropes so they could pull them back before she slid into the ground.

"What about Lupidor?" Darcy exclaimed as they headed north. *Lupidor!* She called for him, but he was already too far away, the link severed.

"He went around to find a crossing," Terra said, appearing next to her. "Don't worry, he'll catch up."

A wolf's howl echoed somewhere far behind them, and they paused to listen.

"They've caught our scent!" Borna growled.

"Come along!" Daylan urged them, and they followed after him as he beat a path through the brush.

The narks slipped off into the woods to lay false trails, and Badru worked at erasing their scent behind them whenever they stopped, but the following wolves always seemed to pick up on it again. Every time they heard a howl, it sounded a little bit closer.

"We *can't* go a different direction to throw them off. We cannot go backwards or around in circles," Yahto insisted that night when they stopped to rest. It was long after dark, but they'd kept on in hopes of putting more distance between themselves and their pursuers.

"Why not?" Tormod snapped. "They've figured out by now that we are moving in a straight line. Why not throw them off, for just a day or two, and then resume our course?"

"Because if we do that," Darcy answered for Yahto, "I can't say what will happen to me. If I turn back from my journey, my symptoms will come back. I could become . . . unmanageable. I'm not even sure how much the potion would help me at this point, since it's been so long since I invoked the Oracle."

"I still maintain we need to find a spot to take a stand," Daylan said. "Lupidor was right; we can't outrun them."

"Where *is* Lupidor?" Perry asked.

"He's out scouting a possible course for us," Darcy said.

"So, we're just going to keep running all night?" Dean asked incredulously. "When are we going to sleep?"

"We'll sleep when we no longer have wolves breathing down our necks," Daylan growled at him.

"You've got to be *kidding* me," Dean muttered under his breath.

Soon Lupidor returned and relayed the lay of the land to the others through Darcy, and they gathered themselves for another long haul. Darcy slipped Dean a drink from her flask of strength potion. "Here," she whispered. "I don't have much left, but it will help. Give some to Perry, too."

"Wow!" Dean said after he drank. "That stuff's amazing. Rubidius sure knows his potions."

"Yes, he does," Darcy agreed.

They set off together after the rest of the party, and Darcy hoped desperately that the wolves would stop to sleep and give them some margin of safety. Lupidor had informed them that the land sloped down gradually from their location to a bowl-shaped valley. He'd scouted to the edge of the trees and been able to see that the other side of the valley rose up in sharp foothills. They were approaching a mountain range.

"If we can find a spot to dig in against the foothills of the mountains," Daylan had advised them, "we might be able to hold them off."

They charged forward. The night was dark as pitch, but they dared not light a torch to give away their position. Terra and Lupidor led the way, and the narks brought up the rear, all of them needing less light by which to travel.

Darcy was tempted to curse every time she tripped and stumbled as she clawed her way through the forest growth, but she refrained, foolishly fearing Yahto might take up her mother's promise to wash Darcy's mouth out with soap. She was contemplating a more intelligent way of expressing herself when, without warning, her feet fell away beneath her. She cried out as she slipped down the side of a moss-covered embankment.

"Whoa, I've got ya!" Tokala said. He'd caught her arm just before she'd fallen all the way down. He made as if to set her on her feet, but a howl issued behind them, not far away at all. "On second thought," he muttered, putting his shoulder into her middle and hoisting her up. "Come on, everybody, let's move!" he called insistently, jarring her as he jumped down the embankment.

Lupidor! she called. *How close are they?*

Close, he answered. *But . . . they have been distracted by something! I don't know what it is, I—*

His voice cut off as coldness descended around them like a fog, and Darcy felt a jolt of terror rip through her stomach. Something much worse than wolves, she feared, was upon them.

CHAPTER 22

THE DARK PLACE

The forest went silent, and then they heard it: hundreds of wolves crying out with painful, terrified howls that echoed around them like ghosts.

Darcy grunted as Tokala slung her roughly to the ground.

"I cannot fight an enemy I cannot see!" he cried, and he put steel to flint to light his torch.

Tokala's torch sputtered to life, revealing darkness, utter and tangible, surrounding them like a cage. They could hear the wolves, but they still couldn't see them. Black fog curled around their feet, lapping against their skin and chilling them like ice water. The fog above was held only momentarily at bay by the flickering of Tokala's light.

"What—is—this?" Dean chattered. "It's—so—cold!"

Darcy shivered, more from fright than from the cold. An unnatural terror had invaded her bones, and she wanted to simultaneously dig a hole to hide in and run for her life. It took all her willpower to stand up and cast out her link, seeking to touch the minds of the wolves, not to talk to them but to locate them.

"The wolves," she breathed, balling her hands into fists to keep them from shaking. "They've stopped. They're . . . terrified!"

"No kidding?" Perry sounded as though he was trying to joke with her, but the hollowness in his tone belied his true mental state. He was just as afraid as she was.

The torchlight wavered. Tokala's hand was shaking, and he stared at it in horrified wonder, as if he had never seen himself react that way before. The darkness above them continued to descend.

"What *is* this?" Tokala echoed Perry. His handsome face was pale as a ghost's in the wan light. "Is it tsellochim?"

"No," Yahto's voice sounded out of the darkness. "It is something worse. No tsellochim has an aura this strong."

"Then . . . what? Tselloch himself?"

"I don't know," Yahto responded with a slight tremor in his voice.

With a hissing sputter, Tokala's torch went out and darkness fell. The fog touched her head, and Darcy took a deep breath.

She was screaming. Screaming for days. Her voice was going hoarse with the effort, and the unearthly disembodied call of the Oracle started up again, louder, in her ears.

Come. Come to me. To me! Come, come, come!

Over and over it pounded a relentless pattern in her skull. Her feet were moving without her willing them to do so. *Not without my friends!* Darcy resisted, grinding her heels into the ground. *I can't go without them!* But her body kept moving of its own accord, and Darcy couldn't stop it. She flung her arms out, grabbing for trees, rocks, anything she could, but she felt nothing until finally, *smack!* She walked right into the back of another person.

Her body spun, and Darcy grasped and held tight to the figure's woolen cloak, coarse and scratchy beneath her fingertips. "Come with me," she tried to say aloud, but the words came out only as a whisper. The figure grunted as she tugged on him, but he moved with her. They trudged with agonizing slowness, and Darcy's fingernails almost ripped off with the effort of clinging to him. Eventually they moved faster, and faster, until they were moving together at a brisk jog. Darcy didn't know where the rest of her companions were, but she couldn't stop to go back for them; she had almost no control over her own body.

The sky grew lighter, and Darcy almost cried with relief, but no tears would come. "The sun is rising!" she croaked.

"No . . ." the figure whispered hoarsely. "Not rising. We're coming out of it."

Together they burst out of the darkness into late afternoon sunlight, and Darcy turned to find that her companion was Perry. He ground to a stop to look back, but Darcy kept going. She couldn't help it. The terror had left her mind, but the buzzing in her ears was unbearably loud.

"Perry!" she cried in her rasping voice, "I—can't—*stop!*"

"Darcy, what—" Perry began, bewildered.

Her feet kept propelling her forward, and she clawed at the pack on her shoulders, hoping Perry would understand what she was trying to do. She needed her bitter potion; if she didn't get it soon, she would not be able to stop at all.

Perry stared dazedly after her and then seemed to come fully awake. He set his mouth in a grim line and ran after her. "Here!" he panted, yanking her pack from her. He rummaged around for what felt like an eternity, running beside her the entire time, before he came up with a flask of the potion. Darcy held out eager hands, and he placed it in them, uncorked.

She tipped it back and gulped greedily; swallow after swallow, until she finally felt herself regain control of her body. She slowed to a jog, a walk, and then she tumbled to her knees, dropping her face into her hands. She let loose a dry sob as Perry skidded to a halt beside her, dropping to put his arms around her shoulders in an embrace that would have thrilled her were it not for the bizarre situation in which they found themselves.

"Why can't I *cry?"* she wheezed. "What's happened? I don't understand . . ."

Perry shook his head, hopeless and defeated. "I don't know!" he croaked.

Darcy looked up at him, seeing him for the first time since emerging from the dark place. His lips were cracked and caked white like he'd been wandering in the desert. Salty tear tracks lined both cheeks, and his eyes looked almost swollen shut with redness.

"Perry!" she exclaimed, her voice breaking. She reached out quivering fingers to touch his cheek and then felt her own. It, too, was dry and grainy feeling; she was sure she looked the same way he did.

"Do you—remember—anything?" he managed, catching her hand and holding onto it like a lifeline.

"No," Darcy said, but images began coming back to her like half-remembered dreams. "Wait . . ." she closed her eyes. It had been fear. She'd been trapped—trapped inside a nightmare of all the things that frightened her the most. She'd witnessed horrible things: her parents' deaths, Roger's death, and her friends . . . dead, dying over and over again in horrible ways. Her travelling companions, all dead because of her foolishness . . . There'd been voices in her head that didn't belong, whispering for her to do terrible things. Voices of despair and loneliness, of violence and greed . . .

Her eyes snapped open, and she saw the hollow remembrance on Perry's face. She covered her mouth with her hands. She couldn't cry; she had used up all her tears. She couldn't talk; her voice was gone from all the screaming. She remembered the wolves; they must have blundered into it, too. That must have been why they hadn't attacked yet.

"How long do you think we were in there?" she whispered. "It felt like days."

Perry looked up at the sky and then back down at her. "I don't know. I think it was."

"What do we do? About the others?" Darcy wheezed. "We have to get them out!"

Perry looked ashamed and dismayed. "I can't go back in there. I only got out because of you; how did you—"

"The Oracle. The call took over." Her palm itched fiercely, and Darcy unwound her hand to find the sore open and suppurating. She grimaced and rewrapped it. "We have to do something," she ground out.

Perry nodded with a grimace and helped her to her feet. He pulled his sword as they turned to face the line of trees they had just broken free of. "I don't think I can fight fear with a sword," he rasped sheepishly, "but it makes me feel better to hold it."

Darcy nodded in understanding.

Perry squared his shoulders and took the lead, Darcy clinging to his cloak. The sunlight dimmed as they re-entered the trees; rocks and fallen logs loomed out of the shadows. Darcy's breath came in frightened little gasps, and Perry was noticeably trembling beneath his cloak, but he kept on. They'd run farther from the fog than they'd thought, and it took them over ten minutes until they could see the veil from a distance. Together they froze. Only then could they hear the voices, the screams and cries of terror that reached their ears as if from over a great distance, even though their companions must be no more than fifty yards away.

"Come on," Darcy took the lead now; Perry seemed stuck in a trance. She tugged him closer, until they felt a cool breeze as the curtain of darkness reached out toward them, as if seeking to suck them back in. Darcy backpedaled. "We can't be caught again!" she rasped.

The deep growl of wolves sounded close behind them. Darcy and Perry turned as one to face a small group ten, but Lykos was not among them. They hadn't been caught in the net of dark fear, and they had been waiting.

"What do we do? " she squeaked.

Perry seemed to gain strength as he faced the wolves. Here, it seemed, was a foe he could challenge; not some nameless, bodiless spell of fear. He brandished his sword and boldly put himself between her and the beasts. He seemed to grow in size before her as he raised his sword to a ready stance and flung his cloak from his shoulders.

The wolves charged. Perry caught the first one across the chest with a swipe of his sword, and it fell to the ground, gushing blood. The second bounded over its fallen peer and lunged for Perry's face, fangs bared, but Perry impaled it on the blade. Darcy scrabbled for her bow and arrow, but her hands were unsteady with exhaustion and fear. She settled on her knife instead, but it seemed pitifully small against the beasts facing them. A black monster of a wolf lunged at her, and she swiped crazily, missing, but scaring it into lurching backwards and circling for another go.

"Come on!" Perry called as loudly as he was able, and he yanked her by the arm to the side of a car-sized boulder nearby. "Put your back to it," he cried, but the boulder was close to the darkness and, as though sensing their nearness, it expanded, trying to snare them. Perry yelled in frustration, but they stayed where they were. The wolves closed in, advancing now in a cautious semicircle. Perry had killed four, but six more had appeared out of the wilderness to replace them.

The wolves' growling was rhythmic and hypnotizing. Darcy's desperate eyes met Perry's, and she knew they were thinking the same thing: *This is how it ends.* She dropped her eyes to his throat, where his pulse beat rapidly beneath the leather thong around his neck. She reached out to touch it, and her touch startled him. She yanked at the cord and the bone whistle slid from beneath his tunic.

As if drugged, Perry stared stupidly at the whistle, and then his eyes widened with hope. He dropped his sword arm and grasped the whistle. The wolves lunged as he blew on it with his last deep breath.

It was like they hit an electric fence. With horrible, keening yelps, they jerked away. A few of them bolted immediately, while the rest shook their heads, beat at their ears with their paws, and rubbed their muzzles on the ground, turning in spastic circles before they could stand it no longer and fled.

Perry blew and blew, and Darcy could hear it this time. But it wasn't unpleasant at all; rather, it was sweet and piercing, like a song at the end of a tear-jerking movie. The resonance was painful but tolerable because it sounded familiar, like the call of a long-forgotten friend.

The veil of darkness began to retreat on itself. Darcy's eyes widened and she gripped Perry's arm. Perry gulped in more air and blew harder, as he and Darcy advanced on the retreating curtain. The pained yowls of the wolves trapped in the darkness became even more frantic. They, too, would flee before the sound of the bone whistle.

They walked until they found an embankment covered in moss. Darcy gave a cry of recognition and hurried to follow the mound around several trees and boulders to where four men, three narks, an oread nymph, a teenage boy, and a wolf cowered in miserable silence. Lupidor had his nose pressed to the ground with his paws over his ears, but he remained where he was.

Perry kept blowing, gesturing to the companions to haul themselves to their feet. Terra sank into the ground, and Darcy ran to help Dean, grunting as she slung his tall form against her shoulder. She managed to half-drag him along with Perry's help, and together they brought up the rear, keeping the darkness at bay until they broke free of the trees into the sweeping field of grass that Perry and Darcy had reached before.

Perry finally stopped blowing the whistle, and the sound dissipated along the valley, echoing back at them from the jagged foothills across the basin.

"Great Gloria," Veli rasped when the sound was gone.

"The whistle?" Darcy asked.

"No . . . no," he whispered. "That was loud, but it—it called me back from—" He cut off and swallowed hard.

"Even *I* couldn't get away," Terra emerged much more slowly than usual from the ground at their feet. "It had me . . . *paralyzed*."

"How did we escape?" Tormod asked. His voice was not as hoarse as the others, but his eyes were bloodshot and almost swollen shut.

"The Oracle," Darcy answered, "and the whistle, but I . . . I can't explain right now." She collapsed to the ground in an exhausted heap. "I have to . . . sleep." Her eyes drifted closed. She could hear the others settling around her and water being passed, but she couldn't dilute her potion. All she wanted was a full night's rest. Explanations would wait until the morning.

CHAPTER 23

THE VILLAGE

Darcy couldn't make it through to the morning. She didn't know if it was her burning thirst or the call of the Oracle that awoke her, because both were insistent when she cracked open her eyes. She stared bitterly at the two flasks, wanting the water, but needing the potion, and started when Yahto's voice sounded out of the darkness.

"Take your potion and stay up for an hour, then take a drink of water and go back to sleep," he said rather irritably. He was right, though, so she did as he said; the sandpapery feeling from the potion in her mouth almost unbearable in her state of thirst.

She cleared her throat experimentally, testing to see if she had gotten any of her voice back. It still felt raw and painful. She settled back against her pack and squinted in the darkness. A faint glow surrounded their impromptu campsite, and Darcy puzzled over it until she spotted the orb-carrying fairies resting in a rough circle around them. Darcy breathed out a relieved sigh. They must be safe.

"I called them here," Wal remarked in a soft whisper, "the orb fairies. They do not usually inhabit this valley because of the darkness, but they were willing to come and keep watch over three of the Six."

"That's . . . very nice," Darcy rasped. "You can talk with them? I didn't think they spoke loud enough for us to hear."

"I have a special affinity with them, yes. They are nocturnal, after all."

Darcy observed the three narks as they kept guard. Wal didn't seem to expect any further conversation out of her, as he was now gazing skyward at the expanse of stars stretched above them. Borna and Yahto were at opposite ends of the group, their eyes bright in the gleam from the fairies' orbs.

The rest of her companions were sprawled about on the ground in various postures of collapse. No tents had been erected, no fire prepared, and nobody had bothered to remove cloaks or shoes. Darcy would be surprised if they even woke with the sun the next day.

She looked back at the narks and noted how patiently they waited. "Do you ever get bored?" she whispered to none of them in particular. "Is it terribly boring watching over us all night as we sleep?"

No one answered for a moment, and Darcy worried she had offended them before Wal turned to her and smiled, his white teeth glinting in the soft glow. "Night narks are naturally more contemplative than day narks. We are quite able to occupy ourselves with our own thoughts."

"And you don't get bored at all?"

"No," Wal answered.

"Speak for yourself," Yahto muttered.

"Ah, pay no attention to him," Borna growled. "The old grump."

Darcy's eyes darted to Yahto, but he turned his back and said nothing.

The narks fell silent again. She could feel her eyes wanting to close, but her throat ached with thirst, so she stood and stretched, hoping walking around a bit would keep her awake. As she walked a circuit around her sleeping companions, she noticed a very distant haze of light farther down the valley. She frowned and squinted, but she couldn't make out anything distinct.

"Is that—" she started.

"A village, yes." Borna appeared beside her, looking the same direction. "We noticed it just after we awoke. It's due north of us."

Darcy stared out at the distant lights. To keep on their northward path, they would have to either pass through it or pass very close, but maybe that was not a bad thing. There was no reason to think the villagers would know who she was, and their company certainly was low on supplies after several weeks of journeying. It would be strange, though, to enter civilization after so long in the wilderness. She wondered how the people there could stand to live so close to the fearsome darkness.

"What's past the mountains?" she asked the burly nark after several minutes of contemplative silence.

"Mayim," he answered.

She looked at him. "Your what?"

"No, no," he chuckled. "*Mayim.* It is a country to the north of Alitheia from which Tormod hails."

"Oh? He's not an Alitheian? I didn't know that." Darcy turned to look at the sleeping bulk of the yellow-headed warrior.

"He's half," Borna replied. "His mother is from Mayim, his father from Alitheia. His father brought him south into his country when he was ten, but his mother refused to leave her home. He's been bitter ever since."

"Is that why he doesn't like females?" Darcy asked.

Borna grunted in assent. "He thinks they are all faithless, like his mother, he says." He put a heavy hand on her shoulder. "I, on the other hand, grew up without *either* of my parents. They were killed in a tsellodrin raid when I was only a babe, and I was raised by a family of bears!"

"Oh, don't start in on that ridiculous story again," Yahto grated from behind them.

"Is it *true*?" Darcy hissed at Borna Fero.

He grinned broadly in return and raised his eyebrows. He certainly *looked* a little bear-like, compared to other narks.

"I've always wondered," Darcy continued, "how narks even get married at all. How does it work, you know, with two narks sharing one body?" She blushed, realizing her question might be inappropriate, but the darkness hid the reddening of her ears.

"It is a long process," Wal answered, coming to stand with them. He turned his abnormally light eyes from the stars onto her. "It usually takes many years."

"Because you *both* have to be in love with *each* nark, right? If you love a particular night nark, Wyn has to love that same nark's day counterpart, right?" Darcy said.

"Something like that," Wal said. "Although we narks do not value being *in love* as highly as you humans do. To us, compatibility of mind and spirit are most important, and they are the building blocks of true love. Once married, narks remain together until one—or both—dies; there is no divorce and no remarriage after a death."

"Wow! That's . . . crazy."

He chuckled. "Well, to your mind, I suppose. But too much is at stake for a nark couple to separate or remarry. The joint marriage of day narks and night narks strengthens the bond, and the raising of children is of tantamount importance, as well."

"Children," Darcy mused, not having considered the possibility before. "How does that work?"

"A female nark's womb opens only twice in her life: once during the day, and once during the night. Thus only two children will be born to any nark couple. The children—or narklings, as we call them—conceived at night are born at night, and those conceived during the day are born during the day."

"But the nark is pregnant the whole time, right? Both at night and during the day?"

He laughed out loud, "Yes, of course. Each child belongs equally to both nark counterparts, but each female experiences being awake when a narkling is brought into the world."

Darcy shook her head. “This is kinda hard for me to wrap my brain around.” Given the difficulty and the time it took for narks to find the right partner, she was beginning to understand why Yahto considered *her* question for the Oracle trivial and frivolous.

“We live long, so it does not seem a burdensome wait to us,” Wal said.

“How long *do* you live?”

“Between one hundred and fifty and two hundred years,” Borna answered, “is a natural lifespan for us.”

“Darcy,” Yahto interrupted them. He breezed to her side and handed her a canteen of water. “It’s been one hour.”

“Thanks,” she rasped with relief. Talking had made her throat even rawer, but she was thankful. She took a long, gulping drink.

“You should go back to sleep,” he added.

She tipped the canteen back down and wiped her chin on the back of her hand. “Yeah . . . I think I will. What time is it?”

“There are five hours until sunrise,” Wal said.

Darcy took another long drink, and then Yahto took the canteen from her. She wondered at how kind he was being to her, but he quickly turned his back and retreated to the far side of camp. With a wave to the other two narks, she stumbled over to her pack, careful not to step on anybody. She lay on her side, making her arms into a pillow, and fell almost immediately asleep.

Darcy awoke in the morning to find somebody had covered her with a wool blanket from her pack. It was indeed cool that morning; she hadn’t noticed it in the middle of the night. Her sleep had been mercifully dreamless, as though her mind could conceive no further horrors after their time in the dark place. The sun was already climbing in the sky, and as Darcy took a drink of her potion, she saw that several of the others hadn’t even stirred yet.

“Hey,” Perry’s voice sounded from her right, and she looked around. “You all right?” he asked. His voice sounded a little rough, but better after the long rest.

“Yeah. You?”

“Sure. I’m fine. I lost my cloak, though.”

“Oh, right. You took it off to fight the wolves.”

He squinted at the tree line. “Well, I’m sure not going back for it. I’m not going anywhere near that place ever again.” He turned the bone whistle over in his fingers. “She saved all our lives,” he mumbled, looking down at it. “Sam did. We have to remember to tell her.”

His expression softened at the mention of Sam's name, and Darcy's chest constricted. "We can send a message through Dean today," she said. "The last arrow came back sometime while we were on the move these last few days."

"Yeah," Perry said, tucking the whistle beneath his shirt.

"Maybe you can get a new cloak today, too," Darcy kept on.

His smile turned bemused. "How? Do you have a cloak factory hidden away in your pack?"

Darcy rolled her eyes. "*No*, smarty pants. There's a village just north of us. I think we're going to stop there."

He looked in the direction she indicated but couldn't see anything just yet. "A village, really? Kind of an odd place for a village, isn't it? I mean, there aren't any roads around here at all."

"Not that *we* know of," Darcy pointed out. "And who knows? All sorts of Alitheians have been hiding from Tselloch for so many years. Maybe this is, like, a refugee camp, or something."

"What's a refugee camp?"

Darcy pulled a face at him. "Don't you ever pay attention in history class or current affairs?"

"Nope." Perry stood and stretched, offering a hand to help her up. They walked together and joined Dean, who still lay sprawled on his back with his mouth open, deep snores issuing from his throat. His army-short buzz cut was getting long after all their weeks in the wilderness, and it stuck up oddly on one side of his head. Perry gave him a well-aimed kick in the ribs, and he jolted awake with a snort.

"Huh—wha—*hey*!" He grabbed Perry's foot and yanked, Perry hopping like a one-legged bird before falling over.

Darcy rolled her eyes and abandoned the boys to their furious wrestling, joining Veli instead, who handed her a bar of the granola cake. She bit into it appreciatively, her stomach rumbling, and tried to listen in on what the grown-ups were saying.

"We can restock there," Daylan was saying. "They don't need to know anything about us other than that we are on our way north."

"It is not a usual trading route," Tormod replied. "I don't know of any easy pass through the mountains into Mayim from here."

"We wouldn't know one," Tokala said. He rubbed a hand along his stubbly chin. "It *would* be nice to spend even one night in a bed, for a change."

"If they have any inns," Tormod growled. "They can't have many visitors, being where they are."

"We're living just fine off the land; why must we stop?" Fero asked with crossed arms.

"Because it would look strange," Daylan said, "for us to pass by the village without stopping. I worry it would cast suspicion on us."

"So we'll go around," Veli said, "along the edge of the basin."

“How many days will that take?” Tokala asked. “We still risk running into villagers, or the wolves, if they decide to come back. We also risk getting stuck in the darkness again. We don’t know how far it stretches, after all.”

“Perry needs a new cloak,” Darcy chimed in.

“*And* Master Perry needs a new cloak,” Tokala repeated with a small smile and a wink at Darcy. She blushed and looked down.

Tormod grumbled under his breath but nodded. “I don’t like it, but I will follow you wherever you lead.”

Daylan chewed the side of his cheek thoughtfully, caught in indecision, but he finally nodded. “One night in the village, then.” He called for all to pack up and prepare to move out.

The valley in the basin was bone-achingly beautiful in full sunlight. Ringed by forest, most of the valley itself was smooth, sloping grassland, with the odd boulder and clump of trees slung here and there. Happy looking daisies and black-eyed susans bobbed in the morning breeze, adding color to the beige and green grasses. On the far side of the valley—the north side—slate-grey foothills rose up like jagged broken rib bones sticking out of the earth. Beyond them the land continued in a steep incline, joining layers of mountains on the horizon. A white-frothed waterfall, shrouded in mist, cascaded out of the foothills into a small river that meandered toward the village.

Despite the beautiful scenery, Darcy couldn’t shake the uneasy feeling of being followed. She suspected she was nervous from the dark place, which was still too close behind them, and she kept looking over her shoulder. The presence of very few visible fairies added to her unease, but she knew they must be present because the valley retained all the brilliance of color that the rest of Alitheia had. Still, they almost never saw one. Those she did glimpse were flitting hurriedly from plant to plant, and many disappeared into the flowers or blades of grass at the appearance of their company.

She walked in the middle of the group, letting Perry tell Daylan about how the bone whistle had saved them. She didn’t feel she had the energy to relive it, although she felt much better now that they were moving purposefully toward the Oracle again.

“It’s a curious object, this bone whistle,” Veli said, dropping back to walk with her.

“It came out of Sam’s bag,” Darcy said.

“So Perry said,” Veli skirted around a boulder and ended up back at her side.

"It hurts your ears, doesn't it?" Darcy asked, looking at his large, almost conical ears.

"Only because it is so loud for us, but it wasn't unpleasant. It was like . . ." he trailed off and frowned. Then he chuckled, "Well, I don't really know *what* to say it was like because I've never heard anything quite like it before, and yet—"

"You have," Darcy provided, nodding. "I felt the same way. I could barely hear it, but it seemed almost familiar." She paused, thoughtful. "What do you think about this village we're going to?" she asked, stepping over a large tussock of grass with his assistance.

"It is just a village," he answered after he'd released her arm.

She tilted her head quizzically. "That's not really an answer, Veli. It seemed like you didn't want to go there."

"I was merely weighing all our options, but I think that, ultimately, Daylan and Tokala are correct. It makes the most sense and casts the least suspicion for us to stop there, even just to resupply."

"You don't think there's anything to be afraid of, do you?" Darcy asked with a nervous shiver.

He smiled down at her. "We have no reason yet to feel fear. Why not just take things one step at a time?"

Despite her line of questioning, Darcy was looking forward to stopping in a real village. If they got to spend the night in beds, all the better.

It took them the better part of the day to get within range of the village, which was a rather sad sight. No fence or wall of any sort protected the residents; it was just a sprawl of farmsteads and houses, getting gradually denser as they came together and met in the center.

"See you on the other side," Terra said once they'd passed a few farmhouses, and she dove into the earth. Lupidor, likewise, indicated he would travel around the village through the forest. He took off with Darcy's cry of *Be careful!* echoing between their minds.

They hadn't seen any people, although there was plenty of evidence of civilized life around them. Fenced in cows and goats munched their cud, watching the visitors pass, and every now and then they passed a hen house or an abandoned plow. Veli reminded Darcy in a low tone not to engage with any of the animals lest she draw attention to herself, and Darcy was only too happy to comply. These animals looked malnourished and sad despite their lush surroundings.

They clambered across a trickling creek that joined with the running river. A millhouse was in the rapids with its wheel turning, and a covered bridge ran from the mill across the river to the other side where a group of three men with cloaked faces stood upon it. They turned to observe the newcomers, and one of them stepped forward to the railing and lowered his cowl. His face was gaunt, as though his skin was stretched too tightly over his bones, but he wore a broad smile on his face.

"Welcome to Fobos," he called. He muttered to his companions, and they hurried from the bridge, down the far embankment and out of sight.

CHAPTER 24

BOITHEIA

The man who greeted them disappeared into the millhouse and reappeared on their side, hurrying down the sloping bank to welcome them. His head dipped with each step, the breeze causing his scant hairs to stick up oddly on his otherwise bald crown.

Daylan stepped forward to meet him, letting his hand rest lightly on the hilt of his sword. The narks, too, seemed hyper-alert; their ears twitched toward the newcomer. But their caution appeared unwarranted, for aside from his rather vulture-like appearance, the man seemed genuinely hospitable.

"Visitors!" he exclaimed in breathless excitement, going straight to Daylan and grasping his forearm. "We don't get many outsiders our way. Tell me, how did you come to be here? Our valley is so well-protected that we see *very* few travelers."

Daylan regarded the man with curiosity, pulling his forearm free from the man's grasp but not loosening his own grip on the sword hilt. "We came from the south, through the woods," he answered. "We found your . . . *protection* . . . to be quite ominous."

The man bobbed his head, looking even more like a vulture. "Yes, yes, the fear spell. I am surprised you made it through at all! Most travelers are deflected around it by the natural aversion it produces."

"I guess we just blundered through," Daylan replied, careful not to reveal too much about their struggles through the fog. "Tell me, if you are so pleased to have visitors, why not lift the spell?"

The vulture-man gave a short laugh that did not quite convey amusement. "We would if we could, now that Tselloch has been driven back, but it has been too long in place. An old magician conjured it to protect this valley over a hundred years ago. He is, of course, long dead, and nobody now knows how to lift it."

Badru shifted beside her, frowning. He opened his mouth as if to protest but then pursed his lips instead. She, too, wondered why the villagers would fight the Shadow with a spell of fear, if darkness and fear *fed* the tsellochim.

"Well, now that you are here, I hope you will let us show you some hospitality." His grin widened to reveal several gaps where teeth should be. "And then you can continue on to . . ." he raised his eyebrows in question.

"Mayim," Tormod volunteered, stepping forward. He let a slightly different, northern accent creep into his voice. "I am taking them to my village. We had hoped to open a new trade route through this way, but I'm afraid the fear spell will cause some difficulties."

"Indeed. Well, perhaps we can find a new magician who can lift the spell."

Badru did not volunteer his services.

"Perhaps," Daylan said.

"Please, come with me." The vulture-man began to retreat toward the mill. "We do not have an inn, but we can offer you warm food and supplies. The ten of you could sleep quite comfortably in one of the community stables. We could, I am sure, find a bed for the lady in one of the residents' houses—"

"No! No, I—I'd rather just stay with my friends, if that's all right," Darcy protested.

He inclined his head. "Whatever you wish, of course." He placed two spindly hands on his thin chest. "My name is Grypas; I run the mill."

"And your friends?" Daylan queried, following Grypas up the hillside.

The other two cloaked men who had been on the bridge were long gone, but Darcy remembered how they had stared on their arrival.

Grypas's boots echoed on the planking at the mill's entrance. "They went ahead to notify the village of our visitors. It is, as I said, quite an event."

"So it would seem," Daylan said. He exchanged looks with the other adults and Darcy felt a shiver of apprehension.

Despite vulture-man's insinuations that the people of Fobos would be pleased to see visitors, the more villagers they passed on their way to the center of town, the less comfortable Darcy felt. Most of them did not even uncloak their faces, and those that did gave them suspicious stares. Every face she saw had the same gaunt look as Grypas's, even though they passed several blacksmiths and carpenters and market stalls full of everything from fruit to fresh fish. Children played in side streets and house gardens were abundant, yet the village felt strangely subdued.

Other than the green gardens, everything in the village proper was brown. Mud-brick structures crowded the packed-dirt streets, and nobody seemed to own any clothing that wasn't brown, grey, or beige. The entire place seemed like a blight on the otherwise beautiful valley, and Darcy wondered if the villagers saw themselves as drab, or if they just didn't care, having nobody to impress.

Grypas led them to where several buildings clustered around a square, the sort of grounds that would hold a fair or an art exhibition. He pointed to a large structure on their right. "A community stable," he said. "My friends will have prepared it for you with fresh straw. You will be comfortable enough." Next, he pointed to a building in front of them with tall, narrow windows. "This is Center Tavern. I am sure you all must be famished. Here we can offer you our best fare."

"Thank you," Daylan answered for all of them. "That sounds excellent. Could you also help us locate the supplies we need? We have money, of course . . ." Daylan drew Grypas aside to give him a list of what they required. He handed him some coins out of a pouch at his belt, and Grypas's eyes lit up. He promised to return in an hour with everything they needed.

With a nod, Grypas disappeared down the street, and Daylan pulled them all into a tight huddle. "I'm afraid we may have made a mistake coming here," he said in a brisk whisper.

"They are hiding something," Veli agreed.

"Do you think they mean us ill?" Wyn asked. "They can't possibly know who we are."

"They could," Daylan replied grimly, shooting a look at Darcy. "If Lykos's messengers got through to Tselloch and if Tselloch has contacts here—"

"So soon?" Tokala asked. "Tselloch cannot communicate over great distances any faster than we can."

"Who says that he's far away?" Perry chimed in, and the men looked at him in surprise. "I mean, you guys don't know *where* he's hiding, do you?"

They were silent. Daylan finally sighed and said, "Like it or not, we're committed to at least a meal and a rest. If we try to leave now, they will become suspicious."

"Maybe they're just a little strange," Darcy contributed. "You know, 'cause they've been isolated here all these years." She rubbed at her cold and throbbing right hand.

"Let's hope that's all it is," Fero said.

"People are starting to stare," Tokala said out of the corner of his mouth.

He was right; villagers had begun gathering at the edges of the square, watching them from beneath their hooded cloaks. Some held themselves like rigid statues, while others whispered to each other behind their hands. Tokala straightened and gave a group of women his most winning smile.

I bet that usually works for him, Darcy thought, but on these women it seemed to have no effect.

"Okay," Daylan muttered, "let's just get inside the tavern and eat our meal. We haven't been threatened, so there's no need to overreact."

They nodded in greeting at the villagers they passed on their way into the tavern, and when they stepped through the narrow doorway into the smoky dining hall beyond, the world began to feel a little more normal. More cloaked villagers were within the tavern, but many more were uncloaked, eating and talking like regular people. They did turn to look at the entering visitors, the room growing quiet briefly, but they went back to their conversations with much less interest than the people outside had shown.

Daylan released a small, pent-up breath of air, and Darcy joined him in feeling some relief. Something about food and drink brought out the normalcy in people.

A round-faced man with red cheeks—in fact, the only man that Darcy had seen who appeared to be well fed—bustled over and told them he'd been expecting them. "Take a seat over there," he jerked his thumb toward a long wooden table against the far wall. "Boitheia will be with you in a moment."

They sat where he indicated, laying aside their packs on the floor. Darcy kept her knife sheathed at her side, and the others likewise kept their weapons readily accessible.

After only a minute or two, a very petite girl, sallow-faced like most everybody else in the town, approached their table with a stack of empty bowls and cups. She looked to be about a year or two younger than Darcy, and she gazed at them with large, liquid brown eyes that seemed to swallow up the rest of her face. An enormous mass of dark brown hair weighed down her head and hung around her thin neck. Darcy thought Amelia would say she had musician's fingers.

Her hands shook as she passed out the eating vessels under their watchful eyes. Darcy wanted to say something to make her feel comfortable, but her old shyness was kicking in, and all she could manage was a tight smile. Continuing to place bowls in front of Darcy, Dean, and Perry, the girl glanced up at them and started, almost dropping her armload of utensils.

"Boitheia!" The tavern proprietor's voice echoed from the kitchens, and the girl jumped and ran to him.

Darcy watched her with concern. Veli, too, stared after her, a worried crease between his eyes. He met Darcy's gaze, and Darcy offered a small smile, feeling a surge of affection for his constant sensitivity to the needs of those around him. *Yahto could take a page or two out of his book.*

Boitheia reappeared after several minutes with a platter of whole, roasted chickens. She set down the platter without a word and took up a knife to carve them. Veli placed a gentle hand on her wrist and she flinched in surprise. "We can manage that," he said softly, "if you have other duties to attend to."

She nodded and gave Veli the knife, hurrying back to the kitchen as Veli cut the chickens into eatable portions. She was back next with fresh, boiled vegetables, and after that with what Darcy had been most looking forward to: fresh bread. The final addition to their meal was strong wine. After she had served everything, Boitheia hovered in a corner near their table with her hands folded, ready to jump at their beck and call.

Daylan looked at her and then to the kitchens where the proprietor stood in the doorway, glaring at the girl. Daylan caught Veli's eye and looked meaningfully between Boitheia and the proprietor. They were not to have a private meal, it seemed.

Darcy's mouth watered and she paid no further attention to the silent communications going on at the table. She bit eagerly into the bread; even without butter it was delicious. The chicken, on the other hand, tasted of bitter herbs, and the unseasoned vegetables were cooked to mush. Darcy ate it all, though. On the road, she'd learned that without food her energy didn't last half the day. She smiled inwardly thinking of how her dad told her the same thing countless times, but the thought of him made her feel homesick, and she swallowed hard around an unexpected lump.

The door to the tavern opened and closed, letting in more cloaked patrons. Darcy's right hand gave a stab of pain, and she winced, dropping her fork. Veli looked up at her before shooting a glance at the men who had just entered, but they simply ordered a few drinks and moved off to a corner table.

Boitheia hadn't made a sound the entire meal. She'd cleared their plates when they were through and had disappeared into the kitchens when Grypas entered the tavern.

"Ah, excellent, excellent!" he exclaimed, clasping his bony fingers together. "I trust the meal was to your liking?"

"Everything was quite satisfactory, thank you," Daylan said. He stood and began to gather up his pack, indicating the others should do likewise. "Is our lodging prepared?"

"Yes, the stable is ready for you. I took the liberty of dropping off your supplies there; I hope you don't mind. If you'll follow me . . ."

They trooped out after him, the tavern once again going quiet as the patrons watched them leave. Darcy craned her neck to see Boitheia, but the girl was nowhere to be seen.

Grypas led them across the square to the stable and opened one of the large doors to let them in. Daylan hesitated, turning on a calculated smile. "We must leave before sunrise, and I would hate to inconvenience anybody at that hour. Can you point me to the quickest way north out of town?"

Grypas smiled broadly, showing the many gaps in his teeth. "Oh, it would be of no inconvenience for me to guide you north in the morning. The mill runs itself."

"Really, I insist," Daylan answered smoothly. "You have been so hospitable, and I feel certain our early departure would only be a burden on you."

Grypas seemed to consider Daylan's words before finally pointing a long finger down the street toward the mountains, now cast in a reddish evening glow. "As you wish," he said. "This road will take you to the end of town. From there you will look for a narrow dirt path that will take you up into the foothills. It may be difficult for you to spot, as only our hunters use it. An ancient cedar tree standing taller than the others will be your marker; the path begins there. Beyond the foothills, I cannot help you." He lifted his hands and shrugged his shoulders. "We do not travel the mountains. There are . . . beasts you should be wary of."

Great, Darcy thought, but Daylan smiled and shook Grypas's hand.

Grypas directed them into the stable. Lanterns hung on every other post cast circles of light on the packed dirt at their feet, and curious horses poked their noses out of their stalls as they passed by. The ceiling stretched up far above them, the rafters deep in shadow. He walked them to the rear of the building to an open space with a loft high above. There were no windows or doors, but the space looked comfortable enough. Fresh straw had been laid out for them, and the lanterns cast a warm glow. Several wrapped packages lay against the wall.

Darcy slung her pack to the floor and stretched her back, watching as Grypas bid the men goodnight and took his leave.

The moment the large door closed behind Grypas, Daylan, the narks, and the men spread out along the walls, listening at the wood planking. Darcy shot a questioning look at the boys, but only Dean paid close attention. Perry had gone immediately to the packages to ferret around. He found what he was looking for, his new cloak, and held it up for inspection.

"Ugh," he muttered, turning his face away. "Smells like goat." He glanced up and noticed the men spaced out along the walls. "What the—" He turned to Darcy and Dean, who shrugged their shoulders in unison.

Daylan called them all together in the middle of the room and they huddled in a group. "They know who we are," he growled. "They must. Unless they have a habit of imprisoning *all* visitors to their village."

"Imprisoning!" Darcy squeaked. "How do you—"

"Shhhh . . ." Veli held a finger to his lips. "They are listening." He pointed to the walls.

"How do you know? What gave them away?" Perry asked.

"If they have been isolated in this valley for over a hundred years, they're likely to never have seen narks before. And yet, they didn't look twice at any of us," Veli said.

"No one asked for one word of news from the outside world. Do you not think they would be curious?" Daylan said. "They are not as isolated as they pretend to be. Somebody, or some*thing,* communicates with them."

"The serving girl," Tormod continued.

"Boitheia?" Darcy asked incredulously.

"She was placed at our table to eavesdrop," Tokala said. "It was obvious. I'm only surprised they did not work harder at their deception."

"But Grypas told you the way out of town," Dean reasoned.

"Indeed, and I doubt he was lying to us; his directions were too specific. It is more likely he told us the truth, which is even more frightening," Daylan said, fingering his beard.

"Why is that more frightening?" Darcy whispered.

"Because it means he was confident we cannot escape," Daylan answered.

A rustling in the corner cut off their hushed discussion, and the men spun around. Daylan's sword appeared in his hand as though it were an extension of his arm, and he brought it to rest beneath the chin of the serving girl, Boitheia.

"You have been listening," he growled at her.

She trembled in the dim light and held up an armload of blankets. "They sent me in with these . . . for you," she whispered.

"And to spy on us, yes?" Daylan pressed. He did not lower the sword.

Her eyes darted around the room like a trapped bird. "Yes," she answered tremulously.

"Drop the blankets," he said with deadly calm.

She complied and began to wring her hands once she was burdenless.

"So, what do we do with you now?" Daylan continued. "What do they expect of you tonight?"

"To—to stay here." Her eyelids fluttered and tears appeared. She licked her lips. "I was to hide in a stall and listen. There's a door—hidden—I was to escape once I confirmed who you are. But I didn't want—"

"Do not bother to explain yourself; we will not trust you. What I want are answers, and quickly. Your life depends on them."

"Daylan," Veli stepped forward, but stopped under Daylan's furious gaze.

Daylan continued. "Who is it, exactly, you are supposed to confirm we are?"

"They believe you are traveling with three of the prophesied Six," she answered in a small voice. "They received warning that . . . that the Intended, the Warrior, and the Spy might come this way with a company your size." She lowered her eyes. "But it doesn't matter who you are," she added. "They'll kill you anyway. You've seen too much."

"How did they come by this information?"

"They work for him."

"Tselloch?"

She gave a small nod. "Yes. They have ways of . . . communicating with him, but I don't know how."

"Why not kill us outright?" Fero interjected, taking a stand next to Daylan. "Why the song and dance?"

"They're waiting for reinforcements."

"What sort of reinforcements?" Daylan demanded.

"Tsellochim, a huge force of them. Tselloch can transport great numbers of the shadow beasts here in very little time."

"How little?" Fero pressed her.

"Three, maybe four hours . . . But I can help you escape," she whispered.

"Fero," Daylan said, lowering his sword, "bind her hands."

The nark was at her side in a second, tieing her wrists in front of her.

"Come on!" Darcy interjected. "She's trying to help us!"

Daylan shot her a look. "Don't be naïve," he said, before narrowing his eyes on Boitheia. "Do you know, Darcy, who betrayed Prince Tellius's parents to Tselloch?" he asked.

"Um . . . no."

"An eleven-year-old boy," Daylan continued, his voice soft. "He delivered their milk every morning, and they trusted him. Youth is not synonymous with innocence. I will not make the same mistake."

"Is it true, then?" Boitheia breathed. "You are who they think you are?" Tears welled over in her eyes. "I prayed it would be true."

"Whoever you may think we are, your association with us will be very short, I assure you," Daylan said, unmoving. "We will let you live, but you will not leave this stable until we are gone."

"Please," Boitheia begged. "You must understand. I prayed it would be you so I could be *rescued*. I want to help you escape, and I want to *go with you!*"

Daylan snorted and shook his head.

Darcy smacked her hand against her forehead. "There is a way we can know if she's trustworthy," she said, wide-eyed. She dropped to her knees and began rummaging through her pack. Her fingers closed on the small metal square and she pulled it out: her grandmother's compact.

She held it up for all to see. "It came out of Sam's pouch, the magic one Rubidius gave her."

"And?" Daylan sounded impatient.

"And it acts in basically the same manner as Sam's talent; it shows one's inner reflection. If Boitheia is trustworthy, it will show her reflection as beautiful. If she's in league with Tselloch," Darcy shrugged, "it will show her as really ugly, you see?"

Daylan frowned and opened his mouth to argue, but Veli stepped in.

"If it came out of Lady Samantha's bag, it will steer us true," the nark said. "Let us see what it shows us. If she is telling the truth, she could be invaluable to our escape."

Daylan deflated and waved Darcy forward. "All right," he agreed. "But it must be absolutely clear. If the mirror cannot tell us definitively, then she will not help us."

Boitheia looked eager as Darcy approached, holding up the mirror. "Hold still," Darcy said. She walked around behind the girl and stretched out her arm, positioning the mirror so she could see both of their reflections.

In the polished metal, Boitheia was radiant. Her face was smooth and her cheeks rosy, no sign of the sallow emaciation she showed in the flesh. Her hair and eyes gleamed with vitality, and she gasped and touched the reflection with delicate fingers.

Darcy grinned. "She's good," she said.

Daylan insisted on checking for himself, and reluctantly ordered Fero to unbind her wrists. "If you steer us false, girl, I will kill you myself."

Boitheia rubbed her wrists and nodded, her face shining. "You'll take me with you?" she breathed.

Daylan snorted. "We cannot promise that, but we will allow you to help us escape."

"But—" Boitheia looked to Darcy for assistance.

"How can we not take her with us?" Darcy hissed. "They'll kill her!"

Daylan scratched his beard. "Where're your parents, girl? I'll not be accused of kidnapping."

"They're . . ." Boitheia's face crumpled, "dead. I belong to the village. There are others like me—"

"Oh no," Daylan held up his hands. "We're not rescuing half the village orphans when we're not even sure we can get our own party out of here in one piece."

"That is where I can help you . . . if you let me," Boitheia whispered urgently. "But you must take me with you!"

"It is not an easy road we're taking," Wyn interrupted. "You could die."

"I *will* die if you leave me here. Please!"

Daylan held up a hand. "Fine. Okay. But we have very little time. How can you help us?"

Chapter 25

Magician and Mayhem

"The tsellodrin are watching you," Boitheia said, careful to keep her voice low.

Darcy started. "Tsellodrin? Here?"

The girl's enormous brown eyes met hers. "Half the villagers are tsellodrin," she said matter-of-factly. "The rest have sworn loyalty to Tselloch in their own ways. There are some, like myself, who stand against him, but they are secret and few."

"How many tsellodrin?" Daylan asked.

"Twenty just outside, but there are more watching the route out of town."

"And how many men?"

"At least as many, but they are not the watchers. Grypas won't risk men where tsellodrin can do his dirty work."

"He doesn't run the mill, does he?" Tokala said, no hint of a question in his voice.

"No. He is . . . our leader, but everybody knows he is only a puppet for Tselloch."

"Are there tsellochim here in the village?" Daylan continued.

"Not right now. There were three, but they left two days ago to scour the wilderness for you. Nobody expected you to make it through the fear spell."

"Magicians?" Badru asked. "Grypas insinuated your village doesn't have a strong magician."

"He was telling the truth. Some villagers have learned enough magic to place certain spells, but nobody approaches magician or master-magician status. Tselloch does not encourage it."

"I imagine he doesn't," Badru said, smiling and narrowing his eyes.

"They sealed the stable with a force spell. It's meant to make the walls too strong to break through," Boitheia continued.

"I can take care of that." Badru waved a dismissive hand.

"You will not have to. That is, I can take you out the secret door; they will not expect it." Her eyes gleamed.

"Darcy!" Veli said, turning to her. "Can you reach Lupidor?"

"Maybe, it depends on how far away he is," she said uncertainly. She squeezed her eyes shut and focused, searching for the spark of life she would recognize as the wolf. She was careful to exclude other animals from her search, not knowing if she could trust the horses in the stable.

She found his position in the woods just north of the village. "It's a long way," she murmured, "but I'll try."

"Tell him what's happened and ask him to notify Terra."

Darcy nodded. *Lupidor!* her mind cried as loudly as she could. She felt the link take hold, flickering weakly. *We've been captured. Tell Terra. Attempting to escape.*

Silence answered her on the other end of the link, until she heard a very faint response, cutting in and out like a radio with bad reception.

Need—help?

Darcy gasped, blinking open her eyes, and said, "He wants to know if we need his help." She was sweating and wiped her forehead.

Veli looked to Daylan for direction.

"Tell him to wait until he hears the commotion," Daylan said. "We won't get out of here without a fight. Tell him our rendezvous is the game trail by the tallest cedar tree north of town." He turned to Boitheia. "That *is* where the trail begins, is it not?"

Boitheia nodded in confirmation.

"Okay." Darcy took a breath, preparing to expend her magical energy to talk with Lupidor over such a great distance. *Wait until you hear the fight. Meet at largest cedar tree after.*

She hoped it was enough to make him understand.

At—tree—now. Lupidor's choppy reply came back. *Trail—north. Will—help.*

Darcy dropped the link, too tired to hold on any longer. She looked up at the others. "He's at the tree right now, and he confirmed there is a trail leading north from there out of town. He said he'll help." She sat down to regain her breath.

"Good, that's good," Daylan paced the length of the room and back. "What else can you tell us, girl?"

"I—I think that is everything," Boitheia replied. "I will lead you out the door and out of town. But there may be more watchers out there now than when they sent me in."

Daylan came to a stop and put his hands on his hips. "I don't think there is any way to escape without being seen. We are surrounded and outnumbered. Still, we will wait for the cover of night."

"But, isn't night *their* time?" Perry protested. "We don't want to give them that advantage, do we?"

"Night is the when the tsellodrin are strongest, true, but it is also when *we* will be sharpest," Fero said, stepping forward. He and the other two narks were fading to their darker colors, but the sun had not yet set. "We are tired now, but in thirty minutes we will be strong. Narks are never more alert than the moment they awake."

"It would be . . . bad . . . for us to change in the middle of a fight. Sometimes it is unavoidable, of course, but if we have a choice . . ." Wyn drifted off and yawned.

"If we have three or four hours until the tsellochim reinforcements arrive, we still have a small window to wait for the best time to fight," Tormod said. "Striking out and attacking *them* will lend us the element of surprise."

"If we fight through to the mountains, we will be safe, at least from the tsellodrin and the men," Boitheia said. "I cannot speak for the tsellochim . . . They never appear to be afraid of anything."

"They're afraid of me," Perry said with a wicked gleam in his eyes.

"And we have a master magician; they do not." Daylan grinned at Badru. "Can you concoct some trouble for these shadow-lovers?"

Badru smirked back. "It would be my pleasure."

"What about Dean?" Darcy asked, recovering from her mind-speaking. "He can use his talent, too." She turned to him eagerly. "Can you throw your camouflage over several of us at a time?"

"I—" Dean hesitated, looking uncomfortable. "I don't think I can. I can't hold onto it for very long before getting beat-out tired. It's been a long time since I practiced. I can use it on myself, and maybe . . . maybe one other person, but—"

"That will be plenty of help, indeed." Veli put a hand on Dean's shoulder. "We know your talents are not yet fully mature, and we do not expect more of you than that."

Dean frowned, his forehead creased, and Darcy felt guilty for having brought it up.

The next half hour passed with irritating slowness. Darcy, Dean, and Perry shared sips of the strength potion just to be safe. Darcy gnawed her fingernails, wanting to talk with Boitheia but too nervous about the imminent fighting. The adults continued to plan in low voices, and Darcy imagined the tsellodrin all around them, trying to hear through the thick walls. The narks looked more restless than usual, and Veli paced the floor.

It was almost changing time for him; he was as dark as he would get before Yahto awoke.

"Veli," Darcy whispered as he came to sit with her. "Is it hard going to sleep and knowing that you might not wake up? You could be killed, you know, because of some decision Yahto makes, or because of how he fights!"

Veli sat with his forearms resting on his bent knees, and he smiled. "No. It is not hard," he said.

"You aren't even the least bit concerned?" Darcy sputtered.

He turned his eyes on her, and she saw the otherworldly wisdom of an elf, not a human. His ways were not always explainable by human standards.

"I have absolute trust in Yahto, it is part of what makes us a nark. So, no, I do not worry about the decisions he will make because I know he makes them wisely. Our lives, quite literally, rest in each other's hands."

"And that's why your coming on this trip without telling him was such a betrayal," Darcy murmured, finally understanding.

"Yes," Veli said, a deep sadness in his voice, even as she knew he didn't regret his decision. He went very still and his eyelids drooped closed, his eyes moving beneath them as the only sign anything was going on in his brain, and his physical transformation completed itself.

Yahto opened his eyes and looked at Darcy, for once with no animosity in his gaze, only a deep, probing awareness. They exchanged a long look before he stood and joined the others.

"It is a good plan," he said without preamble. "As good as it's going to get, at least."

Daylan exchanged nods with Yahto and the other night narks and then turned once again to Boitheia. She had spent the last half hour whispering details of the village's layout to them.

"Only two of us will use the secret door," Daylan said.

Boitheia furrowed her brow in question.

"Dean," Daylan said, turning to him. "Can you cover both yourself and Boitheia, at least long enough to get out of town with the bulk of the supplies?"

Dean looked uncertain, but then he squared his shoulders and nodded. "If I'm not expending energy fighting, I should be able to hold on to it for that long."

"Good. I'm sending you on ahead with Boitheia." He turned back to the girl. "Take him out the secret door and go to the game trail. They will not be able to see you. Take a different route from the direct one the rest of us will take. I don't want you in the fighting at all. We need you two to carry as many of our supplies as you can manage to free us up for battle."

Dean and Boitheia obediently began to gather together various packs, consolidating as much as they could and leaving behind what they could not. To his credit, Dean didn't ask the question Darcy saw in his eyes: What would they do if everybody else were killed? Instead, they made ready very quickly, finally standing at attention under the weight of multiple packs.

"Okay, Dean," Daylan said. "Show us what you can do."

Dean grasped Boitheia's hand, blushing a little, his face showing deep concentration. The two of them flickered twice and disappeared, taking on the appearance of the objects around them. Darcy squinted but could only make out a faint outline of their bodies.

Dean and Boitheia flashed back into sight. "How was that?" he asked, somewhat out of breath.

"It was excellent." Daylan placed his hands on Dean and Boitheia's shoulders like a proud father appraising his children. "You know what you must do. We'll see you at the trail."

Boitheia nodded and tugged Dean toward the line of stalls. Lumbering awkwardly under all the extra weight, they disappeared into an empty stall. Darcy held her breath, knowing that in a moment they would be outside—in danger.

Nobody moved or spoke until Daylan let out a sigh and said, "We can only assume they have made it safely through. Our turn."

They armed themselves, each of the adult males carrying an assortment of knives and swords. Tormod had his two double-edged battleaxes; Tokala tucked a weapon into his sleeve for easy access, and each nark strapped double blades across his back. Darcy felt foolish with her small bow, arrows, and her knife, and she wondered why Voitto Vesa had even bothered teaching her to fight.

"What I need is a sword," she muttered to herself.

"No," Yahto said, appearing at her side. "What you need is to keep your nose out of the fight."

"Yahto's right," Daylan chimed in. "Stay behind Badru at all times, no matter what happens. Perry, you stay with her."

Perry nodded his understanding, swinging his sword in front of him, limbering up for the fight.

Badru stood along the wall that faced across the square and down the road they needed to travel. He carried no weapons but pushed back his drooping sleeves to above his elbows, his eyes glinting behind his square spectacles.

"Are you ready?" he called over his shoulder.

"Almost." Daylan prodded Darcy to take her place behind the young master magician. "Keep that handy," he whispered, nodding at the bow she gripped with white knuckles. He positioned Perry just beside her and Yahto just behind. The rest took up positions in a half circle around them.

"Remember, our goal is to escape, not to engage too long in a fight we cannot win," Daylan said to all of them. "When we're through, we will get to the northern path as quickly as possible—no detours, and no heroics." He met Badru's eyes. "Whenever you are ready."

Darcy glanced bemusedly at the wooden wall against which Badru stood. He lifted his hands very slowly with his palms toward the wall, and she felt a chill. With a great, wrenching crack, the entire side of the stable tore up from the ground.

Dust and shingles rained down as the blast of chilly night air hit Darcy in the face. She ducked instinctively, cringing beneath the slab of wall now hovering above them where Badru held it up without physically touching it. He made a great throwing motion with his arms, and the wall hurtled through the air, landing with a crash on top of a group of watching tsellodrin and crushing several of them.

The men gave a loud battle cry, rushing out the gaping hole in the side of the barn, and Darcy was swept along with them. The few torches lighting the streets made it difficult to see, but Darcy could hear quite clearly the animalistic snarls of the tsellodrin. Her right hand throbbed with cold energy, pulling her to join the servants of the Shadow, but she resisted. *I will not become one of them!*

She hurried along behind Badru, stumbling in the darkness and trying to keep her bearings even as she heard her companions engaging the enemy on all sides. She could smell metallic blood in the air and hear the inarticulate grunts, shouts, and screams of people and tsellodrin fighting around her. She was horrified that she could be losing her friends.

Shadowy figures lurched into her periphery and Badru threw up his arms and a pillar of rocky earth shot up at his call, separating them from their assailants. He continued to throw up pillar after pillar on either side, forming a corridor through which they ran.

The whistles of arrows began to sound and several imbedded themselves in Badru's pillars. A moment later Badru grunted in pain as an arrow shaft stuck out of one arm. His next pillar came slower and the next even more so, with large gaps forming between them, rendering their company exposed.

Darcy heard Lupidor's howl; turning to watch as he shot past her, a charcoal shadow that tore at the throat of a tsellodrin in the dim light. She inwardly cheered even as her stomach churned with disgust.

Perry shouted next to her, and she swung around to see him clutching at Badru. The magician's face had gone grey and another arrow stuck out of his shoulder. "I—can't—" he wheezed. He stumbled against them, but Yahto appeared as if out of nowhere and supported his weight.

"Come on!" Yahto growled. With the strength only a nark could possess, he bodily lifted the magician and ran. But the extra weight of the full-grown man slowed him, and Darcy saw the tsellodrin closing in on him fast. They moved like hunting tigers, their heads slung low over their shoulders and their black eyes intense. Beyond them, Darcy glimpsed a rooftop, with men stationed there with their arrows trained on Yahto.

"No!" she cried as five arrows were released at once. Without thinking, she dropped her bow and grabbed hold of a passing gust of wind. With all her might she slung the wind at the arrows, knocking them off course and sweeping the archers off their feet. Two of them plummeted to the ground with sickening thuds.

I just killed two people! Darcy halted in her tracks.

"Come *on*, Darcy! We can't stop!" Perry yelled as he swung his sword upward into the belly of a tsellodrin that lunged from the door of a building. Black blood splashed their legs as Perry yanked his sword free. He took her hand with his free one and they dashed further down the street.

"Look!" Perry pointed ahead with his sword.

Through the fog of battle, Darcy saw men and tsellodrin all down the street with half of their bodies sticking out of the ground, some almost fully embedded. She watched as yet another tsellodrin sank into the earth as it issued a deep, bellowing snarl.

"It's Terra!" Darcy half-laughed, half-sobbed, "she's . . . pulling them in!"

Tormod ran by wielding his battleaxes and yelling like a wild man. He was sweeping his axes in great arcs that toppled men and tsellodrin as they emerged from buildings on either side of them. Another form lunged at Darcy and Perry shoved her behind him, raising his sword to fend off the attacker. Cold hands grasped her shoulders and she was swung around by a leering tsellodrin.

She fumbled for her knife, knowing she would be too late even as the tsellodrin hesitated, nostrils expanding like he was sniffing her.

He lurched against her, black blood dribbling from his lips. She extricated herself from his grip, horrified, as he slumped lifeless to the ground, a throwing star embedded in the back of his skull.

"You all right?" Tokala cried, skidding to a halt beside her and wrenching his star out of the head of the dead tsellodrin.

She swallowed a mouthful of bile and nodded.

"We're almost there," Tokala added. "I can see the edge of town, hurry!"

"Perry—" Darcy said weakly, resisting.

"He's right beside us."

"I'm here, Darcy," Perry said, again grabbing hold of her hand and tugging her forward.

The buildings thinned on either side of them, and Darcy could just make out an ancient cedar tree whose topmost branches pierced the sky ahead of them. She didn't know which of her friends were there already and which of them were still fighting, but she kept moving as the snarls and clashes of metal and wood continued to ring out behind her.

Darcy and Perry skidded around the last outlying house and found Yahto waiting for them with Badru. Tormod and Daylan engaged four enemies nearby, and the other two narks sped up behind them like breaths of wind. Lupidor leapt over a hedge by the house and launched himself into the battle, but Terra was nowhere to be seen.

Just past the house, at the very edge of town, stood a line of boulders through which a single opening gave egress. The cedar tree stood next to the opening, partially obscuring it. “We’re almost there,” Darcy cried, eyeing the opening. “We just need . . . to . . .”

Through the gap in the boulders poured forth a great force of tsellodrin, fifty at least, and Grypas was with them, smiling wickedly. Darcy gasped and stumbled back. Daylan, Tormod, and Lupidor finished dispatching their four assailants and turned to face the new horde as still more forces came up behind them from the village. Darcy felt a surge of anger; they couldn’t all die here! She wouldn’t let them perish just because she had invoked the Oracle.

She raised her face to the sky, feeling the wind on her face, her senses becoming hyper-aware. She could see every particle of wind like a symphony of color, could feel every rock in the wall of boulders. With a primal cry, she leapt toward the advancing horde of tsellodrin and swept her arms in a great circle, gathering the wind and directing it. The gust, at her command, slammed into the line of shadow servants and flattened them beneath it. She wrenched at the boulders and watched in near-disbelief as they groaned, rolling into the mass of bodies, crushing and pinning them.

An eerie silence settled over the scene in the wake of her magic, and she felt as if her skull were splitting in two. Distant shouts rose from their pursuers in the village, and then everything went black.

Chapter 26

The Apparition

Darcy could sense their height above the valley even with her eyes closed. It was as if she could read the wind currents that swept up from beneath them. Heavy breathing sounded beneath her ear, and pain gnawed in her midriff. Her cheek was raw where it rubbed against a woolen cloak, and her head kept banging against a muscular back. She realized that she had come to hanging upside down over someone's shoulder as they climbed a steep path.

She lifted her eyelids groggily, but everything was blurry. She closed them and waited for her head to clear before opening them again. This time she could dimly see rocks and dirt passing beneath her. She turned her head and then wished she hadn't as they rounded a bend and her head swung out over an empty void, her body dangling over the tiny pin-pricks of fire lighting the village of Fobos a thousand feet below.

She gasped and stiffened, her arms coming alive and grasping at the back of the person who carried her. "Be still!" Yahto snapped. She tried her best to comply, but she couldn't relax her stiffness now that she'd regained her awareness.

They continued upward with Darcy bouncing along uncomfortably on Yahto's shoulder. Eventually they came to a halt, and he slung her to the ground with her back against the trail's rocky embankment. "Stay here," he ordered her, and he went to speak with Daylan.

As if I have a choice, she thought. Her head spun from the time spent upside down and also, she suspected, from the elevation. They had stopped just above a switchback, and she could just make out the grey form of the mountainside slipping away beneath her into darkness. She closed her eyes and leaned her head back, wondering how long she'd been out.

She heard shifting pebbles and the crunch of someone sitting down next to her. She peeked to see Perry and Dean settling in at her side.

"They're saying they've given up the pursuit," Perry said. "That's why we've stopped."

She nodded, feeling weary. "How long . . . ?"

"Over an hour, maybe even two; I don't know," Perry said, wiping at the sheen of sweat on his forehead. "I've never climbed so fast in my life!"

Darcy put a shaky hand on Dean's arm. "You—Boitheia?"

"We made it okay. We saw the ambush they set for you, but there wasn't anything we could do about it! We climbed over the rocks and waited up the trail."

"Terra?"

"She's fine; she couldn't meet us at the trailhead because she was in the ground healing from a wound, but she caught up to us a little later." Perry gazed at Darcy. "By the way, that was . . . really cool, what you did down there. You saved all our lives, you know."

Darcy shook her head. None of them would have been in that situation at all if it hadn't been for her.

"Badru was impressed," Perry continued. "I think he felt bad about being shot."

"How's his—"

"Arm?" Perry supplied. "He'll be okay. They're more worried about the arrow in his shoulder. We haven't even had time to stop and clean his wounds, but Tormod did break off the shafts for him. Borna had to carry him all the way up here so we could keep up the pace."

As if on cue, Badru gave a sudden cry of pain, and they looked over to see Tormod standing over him holding a bloody arrow shaft. He bent down to remove the second one as Tokala wrapped Badru's arm in strips of linen. Darcy looked away, her stomach unsettled.

"Whoa," Perry said as a dim glow issued from his scabbard. He reached over and pulled the sword from its sheath; the blade was unmistakably glowing. The weak light flickered once or twice before diminishing and starting up again. Perry raised his eyes to Dean's, a look of grim understanding passing between them.

"What?" Darcy struggled to sit up straighter. "What is it?"

Perry jumped to his feet. "I'm letting them know," he said and hurried up the trail.

"Dean, what's going on?" Darcy asked.

Dean released a long, slow breath. "It happened once before."

"What happened? His sword . . . ?"

"When we were fighting in the battle at Ormiskos Castle."

"What does it mean?" she pressed.

"It lit up when he was fighting the tsellochim. The light seemed to burn them. But it's glowing now . . . maybe as, like, a beacon, warning us that they're near."

The adults peered intently down into the valley. "Help me up," Darcy muttered to Dean. He did as she asked, and they dragged themselves over to the others. The lights of the village flickered erratically as dark creatures passed in front of them. The reinforcements had arrived.

The narks could see best, and they dictated to the rest of them what was happening below. "They're swarming the streets," Wal said. "There are too many to count; I can't distinguish them from each other."

"They're phasing in and out of shadow form," Borna growled.

"They'll climb the mountain in spider form," Yahto added. "They move fastest that way."

Darcy shivered, remembering well those great, globular bodies slung between four hideous legs, almost physical, yet mostly menacing shadow.

"They don't need the trail," Wal said. "They can climb over anything."

Borna looked at him. "They will take it, though, to keep track of our scent."

"How long do we have?" Daylan asked.

"It's difficult to say," Yahto said. "They can't go on forever. If we can evade them until morning, we should get ahead of them during the day."

"You don't think they'll sleep with this sort of quarry in their sights, do you?" Tormod jerked his head at Darcy and the boys.

"They'll need to rest, and they can't move well in full sunlight. Even if they continue the pursuit during the day, they will be very slow. There aren't many trees for them to hide under up here," Yahto said. "We have a couple hours on them; I think we can make it."

Darcy glanced at Yahto, surprised at his optimism.

"All right," Daylan said with finality. "Everyone needs to have some water. We'll move out in five minutes."

Darcy felt stronger with each passing minute and was ready to use her own two feet, as long as they weren't going to start running again. She guessed they would take it easier, as Yahto did not offer her any further assistance and Badru stood on his own, cradling his arm to his chest.

Boitheia, small and pale in the moonlight, came up to Darcy's side. "I can help you, if you need it," she said as she put her hand on Darcy's shoulder. "I'm stronger than I look."

"Thanks," Darcy said sincerely.

The climb was not too steep, but the path was narrow, allowing for only one or two people to walk abreast. It reminded Darcy of hiking in the mountains of Denver, which she had done on vacation with her family one spring break. It had the same switchback feel and in the darkness Darcy couldn't tell how far above them it stretched.

"Where does this *lead?"* she asked Boitheia finally, huffing to catch her breath.

"I don't know," Boitheia responded, sounding very tired. "Nobody from the village ever comes up this far."

"Oh—right—because of the monsters," Darcy recalled.

"So they say," Boitheia said, tripping over a protruding rock. Darcy caught her arm, and they continued on in silence.

The sky finally began lightening to grey as they looked for a place to rest. Darcy was trudging by that point, keeping herself going only by imagining the story she'd tell Sam when they got back—when they were through with this.

They passed several dank-smelling holes in the mountainside, each one reminding Darcy of a horrible beast. They stopped now at the mouth of a larger one, and the narks went in to investigate, returning before a minute had passed.

"It's not as deep as I would like, but it is dry," Yahto said.

"And abandoned," Borna added. "Whatever used to live here is long gone."

"Good," Daylan said, ushering everybody inside.

Once Darcy's eyes adjusted to the dim light, she saw that the cave was like a large, squashed sphere, with the rear wall only about twenty-five feet back. It smelled nauseatingly of sulfur and old animal droppings, but as long as she got to lie down and rest for a couple hours, she couldn't care less.

"They are still far behind us," Wal muttered. He gazed down the mountain the way they had come. "And the cave is east-facing. They won't risk the morning sunlight after a full night of travel."

"I agree," Borna said. "We can rest for a few hours, at least."

That was all Darcy needed to hear. She dumped her pack on the floor next to Perry and Dean and sat down next to it, preparing to make herself comfortable.

"I'm surprised it's glowing at all, since they're so far away," Perry mumbled to Dean, studying his flickering sword.

"Maybe it knows we're being hunted by them," Dean reasoned.

" '*It knows*,' " Perry snorted. "Dean, it's a sword; it can't *know* anything."

"It's a *magic* sword," Dean pointed out.

"I agree with Dean." Darcy lent her support, wiggling down to prop her head and upper back against her pack.

The boys fell silent, shuffling around to find comfortable sleeping positions like Darcy, but sleep evaded her after all the excitement they'd gone through. She lay very still with her eyes closed, forcing herself to relax, but it just wasn't working.

She heard some faint sniffles and glanced over to see Boitheia curled up near the mouth of the cave with her arms around her knees, staring out into the rising sun. She shook with suppressed sobs, and Darcy felt a stab of pity. She stood and padded between the sleeping bodies to Boitheia's side. She sat down next to her and said nothing for several moments. Boitheia didn't look at her.

Finally Darcy whispered, "Your parents aren't really dead, are they?"

Boitheia's chest heaved, and she dropped her head as her tears came faster. "N—no," she stammered, sniffling. "But they're as good as."

"They're tsellodrin, aren't they?" Darcy asked, almost too softly to hear.

Boitheia turned frightened eyes on her. "Please don't tell anybody!" she begged. "Especially not Daylan; he'd leave me behind!"

Darcy gave her a small smile. "Nah, he wouldn't. He has four daughters of his own, you know. And the oldest isn't even as old as you are."

Boitheia looked terrified that someone else might find out, and she continued to weep in silence. Darcy, still awkward about comforting people —especially people she barely knew—simply stayed at her side as long as she could before sleep finally started to intrude. Even the warm sun curling in through the mouth of the cave and washing over her face couldn't keep her awake. She stretched out on her side and slept.

Darcy awoke several hours later, feeling as though her head had been doused in ice water. The sunlight no longer shone into the cave; instead it warmed the rocks outside from directly overhead. She sat up, wondering what woke her, as everybody else was still sleeping. The three narks stood silent guard outside with their backs to the cave, and Boitheia was snoring a gentle pattern at her side.

Darcy looked around the cave, and there in the back she saw him, smiling like he'd been waiting for her to notice his presence. Colin Mackaby, as real as any of them, with his hands behind his back and a wicked gleam in his eyes. He raised one hand and beckoned to her.

Darcy scrambled to her feet and went to him. He looked different than he had the last time she'd seen him at camp, though he wore the same clothes he'd had on the day they left Cedar Cove. She remembered Rubidius had theorized he continued on at regular pace while the rest of his world slowed down. She felt mesmerized looking at him, incapable of speaking out loud.

But he didn't speak, either. He regarded her with his sharp gaze and then looked around the cave in amusement. His eyes met hers again and he mouthed, "*I know where you're going.*" He raised his left hand very slowly and showed her his palm. There was a strange puckered oval of a scar in the center of it, and Darcy grabbed at her own left hand. He lowered his hand just as slowly as he'd raised it, seeming pleased with himself. But he was not actually there. Darcy could now see through his form as though he were a projection on a wall. That was why he didn't say anything aloud; he *couldn't*.

He stepped around her and walked unconcernedly toward the entrance of the cave.

"Wait," she hissed, jerking to life. "How are you—" She stumbled after him.

But he was already gone, evaporated into the sunlight like the apparition that he was. Darcy stared in silent bafflement at the spot where he'd disappeared. Heart pounding and eyes darting wildly, her brain tried to make sense of what she'd just seen. Colin was involved with Alitheia—that much was confirmed, but . . . She looked down at her left palm where the sore itched beneath its wrappings. "How?" she murmured aloud. She squeezed her left hand into a fist until the sore stung in protest. Groaning in frustration, she dropped it to her side.

From the mouth of the cave, Veli's ears twitched toward her before he turned his face, his blue eyes clear and piercing.

She picked her way forward to meet him. "Hey," she muttered.

"Something is bothering you," he said. He extended his arm and pulled her into a side hug, and her confusion and frustration immediately lessened. She felt deliciously safe and secure for a blessed moment as she closed her eyes and breathed in his scent, always pleasant as was the nature of his kind.

She opened her eyes and looked down from the dizzying heights into the valley below. The village was laid out like a distant patchwork, and halfway up the mountain a dark haze obscured the trail. Had Darcy not known better, she would have thought it was a rain cloud. But she knew what it was.

"That's where they are, isn't it?" she asked, pointing down.

"Yes. We think they must fashion a covering for themselves when they rest during the day, to shield them from the sun."

"I've seen it before . . . the first day, when we came in on the *Cal Meridian*. Eleanor said it had something to do with the tsellochim."

"Eleanor was right," Veli said.

"And they can't hold the covering over them while they move?"

"They don't seem to be able to."

Darcy sighed. "Well, that's something, I suppose."

"What did you need, Darcy?" Veli asked after a moment. "You awoke rather suddenly, and I don't believe you are fully rested."

Darcy looked at the ground and thought about how to proceed. "Um . . . well . . . I saw something—that is—some*one*, rather . . . in the cave."

A crease appeared between Veli's brows. "Oh? In a dream?"

"No. I was awake. But I don't think he was actually there, either, if that makes sense."

"Not really," Fero said. He and Wyn had come up beside them without her noticing. "What is it you want to tell us, Lady Darcy?"

"Okay . . . here's the thing . . ." Darcy told them about Colin Mackaby at camp and how they suspected he was getting into Alitheia somehow, or at least seeing Alitheia from the other side. She added that she was afraid he was in league with Tselloch and that he had appeared just then in the back of the cave as an apparition. "And he showed me something . . . a scar . . . on his hand," she added.

"And he didn't say anything at all to you?" Wyn confirmed.

"No—well—he did *mouth* something."

"What was it?" Fero said.

"He said 'I know where you're going.' " Darcy looked from nark to nark, but their faces were unreadable.

"We must go," Fero finally said. "Now."

CHAPTER 27

THE WATCHER OF THE VALLEY

"You think Colin will tell the tsellochim?" Darcy called after Fero, who had ducked into the cave to wake the others. "Veli?"

"We must not take any chances. Perhaps we have let you sleep too long as it is."

Veli walked briskly back into the cave and stooped to rouse the boys. He handed Darcy her pack and said, "However that boy is involved, he does not have your best interests at heart."

They gathered outside the cave, everyone munching on whatever they could eat on the go. Darcy was tempted to take her last swallow of strength potion, but she decided it was best to save it.

In the daylight, the path looked pitifully narrow and almost impossible to follow. In some places she felt sure they had lost it entirely, but then they would round a bend and find it once again by cutting through a bramble or slide of rocks.

"How did we follow this last night?" Darcy muttered to herself as her feet slid on the loose gravel for the umpteenth time that afternoon. She picked herself up wearily with Boitheia's help, her knees dribbling blood from her many trips and stumbles.

"The nark creatures helped guide us," Boitheia said. "They are more wonderful than I ever imagined."

Darcy looked at her sideways. "You really had never seen a nark before?"

The girl shook her head. "I'd only heard stories. We saw some magical creatures in the valley, but never narks."

"These monsters that are supposed to live up here—what are they like?" Darcy asked.

"I don't know." Boitheia shrugged. "Sometimes I wondered if there were any monsters here at all, or if it were just an old story."

"One of my favorite teachers always says that all myths are based on a grain of truth."

A shower of pebbles rained down on their heads, and Darcy threw up her arms to shield herself. Sulfuric air blasted them, and then everything fell still again.

They froze on the path, Lupidor growling deep in his throat, all the fur on his back standing up.

What is it? Darcy asked him, but he didn't answer.

Terra sank into the path, her eyes intent on the ridge above them. "I'll go up and check it out," she whispered and was gone.

Veli positioned himself between Darcy and Boitheia, his ears turning to and fro like satellite dishes. His double blades were out and ready as the other adults un-strapped weapons and got themselves into position. They huddled up as well as they could on the narrow path and searched around and above them, but no further sound was heard.

Out of the silence, a creature bellowed horribly and there came a great wrenching and crumbling sound, like a boulder splitting in two.

"Run!" Terra's scream cut the air as she catapulted off the ridge above them, snapping jaws and a sinewy neck just inches behind her. The creature drew back and blasted her with fire, singeing her feet mid-dive. She cried out and closed her eyes, sinking into the path as she hit it. Darcy grabbed for her knife, the only weapon she had since she'd dropped her bow in Fobos.

The dragon had a chest that was fully five feet across. Its front legs sported plate-sized, iron-clawed feet that gripped the edge of the ridge where it gouged chunks out of the rock. The creature had three horrible heads set on six-foot-long necks that sprouted out of its body like mutated fingers.

The dragon turned and prowled the ridge, growling like a jackhammer and revealing three legs on either side of its body. It shook one of its rear legs, encased in rock as though Terra had tried to trap it in the ground, but it had pulled itself free. It was dull brown, like the ugly carapace of a spider or scorpion, and its scales clicked together unnervingly as it moved. It unfurled its wings to their twenty-five-foot span and raised itself on its rear legs, its chest expanding.

Shields! The thought exploded in Darcy's mind a moment before the dragon spewed flame from its three mouths. She squeezed her eyes shut and heard a violent sizzle. She gasped and looked up to see a shimmering force field between them and the dragon on which the flames sputtered and died. Badru focused intently, his hands raised and his water canteen open on the ground next to him. He'd fashioned the water into a shield and multiplied it, making it stronger. Darcy laughed, relieved.

The dragon stopped, and Badru let the shield fall, sprinkling them all with hot, wet drops. They eyed each other as two of the dragon's heads lunged impatiently, its third head regarding them intelligently. It hissed and leapt into the sky.

The sulfurous downdraft from its wings flattened all but the narks against the mountainside. The men muttered instructions to each other as the dragon winged above them, preparing to dive.

"Stay together; don't scatter until it is almost upon us," Daylan growled.

"Give me a clear shot with my axes, and I'll take its heads off," Tormod added.

"We can take its wings," Fero said, looking excited.

Veli pushed Darcy and Boitheia back to the ground. "Stay down," he ordered.

"Ready?" Daylan shouted. "Here it comes!"

The dragon tucked its wings and plummeted, and Tokala pierced it in the side with one of his arrows before the sky went dark. Something huge had descended. *Tsellochim,* Darcy thought, horrified, even as she knew it didn't make any sense.

It was a second dragon.

This one was silvery grey and much larger than the one already attacking them. It had only one head—the size of a small sedan—with jaws that opened up to snatch the three-headed dragon right out of the air. Sunlight glinted off its scales as it circled once and swooped down, the smaller brown dragon shrieking pitifully in its jaws. The whole mountain shook as the beast landed, causing the others to stumble and Perry and Dean to fall over.

The huge dragon gave a tremendous *chomp* as multiple snaps signaled the breaking of the smaller dragon's bones. Its quarry now limp, the silver dragon tossed it into the air with a flip of its head and caught it again in its mouth where the small dragon disappeared down its gullet with a single swallow.

Darcy gulped and looked to the others, but nobody seemed to know what to do. Lupidor had his tail between his legs, and the men and narks gaped at the monstrosity in silence. It looked like a cross between a brontosaurus and a t-rex, but with wings.

Its meal finished, the beast turned its milky-white reptilian gaze upon them. Instead of a leathery membrane around its head, it had feathers, at odds with its otherwise tough looking exterior. A low thrum of a growl began deep in its chest, and Darcy knew that, from this proximity, there was nothing even Badru could do to save them from its fire.

The silvery dragon advanced, each footfall causing the ground to shudder, its wing tips gripping the side of the mountain as it pulled itself forward. Step by step their party backed away, helpless against its advancing power.

But it didn't attack. Instead it seemed to be regarding them, a long, thin tongue slithering in and out of its mouth, tasting the air like a snake. *It's thinking,* Darcy thought, *it's a high animal!*

She gasped, unable to catch her breath, and stood, reaching out tentatively with her link. She brushed the dragon's consciousness, confirming it was, indeed, a high animal. It recoiled physically from the mental touch, snorting in surprise and raising its head to strike.

Veli gave a strangled cry and grabbed Darcy's arm while Tormod raised his battleaxe.

"Wait!" Darcy cried, throwing up her hands. "Just wait, please!" She was talking both to them and to the dragon, and they all stopped to listen. Veli let go of her arm.

Please! She connected fully with the great beast before them. Their link pulsed with magical energy, and Darcy could feel that this animal was ancient. *We thank you for killing the other dragon! Please do not kill us!*

The dragon shook its massive head as though to clear it. *I have never,* he answered back in an unmistakably male tone, *heard the voice of a human in my mind. How came you to possess this ability?*

Darcy hesitated, remembering Rubidius had told her not to trust any strange animals, but wanting to be honest. *I . . . was born this way,* she answered as truthfully as she was able. *What do you want from us?*

You cannot pass. I do not permit men from the valley to cross the mountains, he answered. *I must kill you if you try.*

Why didn't you let the other dragon kill us?

His growl intensified. *I prefer to avoid human bloodshed. And that beast was a wicked beast who had plagued my territory long enough. But you . . . you must turn back now.*

But we're not from the valley. We escaped *from the valley. If you don't let us pass, we will have to go back and be killed!*

You are lying. Nobody comes through the valley but the servants of the Shadow.

Darcy struggled to find the right words to persuade him. *We came from the south. We got caught in a dark spell, and then the villagers tried to kill us. We are enemies of the Shadow; that's why we must get through. His tsellochim are chasing us.*

The dragon stayed very still. At last he said, *I have seen the haze on the mountain. If it comes through, I will not be able to stop it. What do you hope to accomplish by running from it? You cannot evade it forever. It would be kinder to send you back.*

Please! Darcy took a chance and walked closer to him, close enough so she stood just beneath his snout. She placed a hand on the side of his face. *I have to see the Oracle, and all of them,* she gestured behind her, *are here to protect me. I have to make sure they survive. Their lives are on me. Do you know of Pateros?*

He snorted, almost knocking Darcy over with the hot blast. *Of course I know of Pateros. It was he who charged me with watching this valley and protecting this pass.*

Then you must know that he would not want you to send us back to be killed by the tsellochim.

But how can I know you are telling me the truth? If I let you pass, and you are from the valley, then I will have failed in my duty.

Darcy threw caution to the wind. She turned around. "Perry, Dean!"

The two boys looked at her with incredulity but obediently stepped to her side. "Show him, Dean, what you can do. Perry, show him your sword."

Dean phased out, becoming like the mountainside behind him, and Perry pulled his weapon to show its light to the dragon.

You see? Darcy said. *I can speak with animals, Dean can disappear, and Perry is a great warrior; his sword is glowing to show us the tsellochim are near. We are three of the Six that the prophecy speaks of; we are the ones who will destroy Tselloch!*

Prophecy? I do not know of any prophecy.

But, Darcy sputtered, *how can you know of Pateros and Tselloch but not of the prophecy? You have even met Pateros!*

Many, many years ago, human girl, he rumbled. *He did not tell me of any prophecy.*

Darcy wanted to cry and stamp her feet in frustration. She turned desperate eyes on Dean and Perry, but they just shrugged, uncomprehending. Perry sheathed his sword and started to back up, stepping awkwardly on a wobbly rock and falling forward onto one hand to catch himself. His shirt fell open where his ties had come unfastened and the bone whistle swung out on its leather thong.

The dragon gave a startled snort and raised its head in alarm. *Where did you get that?* he cried in Darcy's head.

The bone whistle? She looked at Perry and then back at the dragon. *It came out of . . . No, I mean . . . it was a gift.*

That I have not seen in . . . His voice drifted off and he shook his head. *If you are in possession of the bone whistle, then of course you may pass.*

He hadn't finished his thought, but Darcy didn't care. She breathed a sigh of relief at the little whistle's usefulness so far and picked herself up off the rocks.

The dragon reversed and began to lumber up the path ahead of them. *Come,* he said, *I have a safe place where you can rest.*

Darcy gestured to her party and turned to jog in the silver dragon's wake. *Wait up,* she called. *What's your name?*

Archaios, he rumbled back. *My name is Archaios.*

CHAPTER 28

RAIN ON THE MOUNTAIN

Archaios led them up the mountainside with measured steps, but they still had to hurry to keep up with him, following at a safe distance as his twenty-foot tail swung with every step he took. Darcy relayed her conversation with the dragon to the others as they went. She kept the link open, but Archaios didn't talk much, and she didn't press him. They were approaching the peak of the mountain, where a dark cave opening looked closer than it was on first inspection. It looked small from far away, but when they stumbled to the summit in the late afternoon, it was big enough to allow Archaios to comfortably pass through.

Darcy stepped just inside the entrance to the cave, put her hands on her hips, and breathed a shallow sigh of relief. Her lungs were burning more than usual, her limbs shaking, making her feel as she had during their first week of travel when her body was just getting used to the physical activity. The air on the mountain was very cold and thin, and she focused on slowing her breathing.

"Is this . . . your home?" she wheezed at Archaios. She was too tired to mind-speak through the link—just keeping it open was work enough.

Yes, he answered. *Ever since my youth.*

"You've got a nice view." Darcy gestured outside his cave. The entire valley was visible from where they stood, like a deep, dark bowl with a forest around it.

This is where I watch them, he said. *They can sense my presence.*

Darcy uncorked her water canteen and took a deep drink.

"You said Pateros told you to keep Tselloch's servants from passing through the mountains, right? When was that?" Darcy asked him.

When the Shadow first came to this land.

Darcy squinted at him. "But that was over five hundred years ago!" she protested.

Yes, he rumbled deep in his chest.

"How old *are* you?"

I am over three thousand years old.

"Wow. That's . . . old!"

His rumble deepened.

"I mean no offense!" she added quickly.

I do not take offense. I am indeed old, and tired. If it is as you say, and you are to destroy this shadow, then my job soon will be complete. I will be able to rest at last.

"You mean you'll die?"

I am ready. Don't you think you would be, too, after three thousand years? He chuckled and the sound filled the cave.

"Yeah, I guess so.

You may tell them to go inside.

"Huh?"

Your protectors. They may enter my home. It is not a dwelling designed for your kind, but it is dry and warm if they go further in. There is a spring far in the back where you can refresh yourselves.

He swung his head around, and Darcy followed his gaze. All twelve of her companions were hovering near the entrance to the cave, looking uncertain and watching her converse with the old dragon.

"Go on in, guys," Darcy said. "He says to make yourselves comfortable. There's water in the back."

Darcy turned immediately back to Archaios, much too interested to go and rest.

"Why do you need to keep the people and tsellodrin from crossing over the mountains? What's on the other side of these mountains that's so important?"

Pateros was deeply disappointed when Baskania of Alitheia opened his gateway and allowed this particular evil to enter the land. The world of the tsellochim is a dark one, and Pateros did not want other lands to suffer for what the Alitheians had invited upon themselves. So he separated Alitheia from the land of Mayim, which lies just over these mountains. It is my duty to keep the servants of Tselloch from passing through as well as I am able. It is a small role to play . . . he trailed off.

"It seems pretty big to me," Darcy said.

No, no. I am just one player in one episode of history. Tell me of your part . . . of this prophecy. He trained a milky eye on her, the black slit of his pupil narrowed in expectation. Unnerved, Darcy looked out over the valley and watched the shadows lengthen.

"Pateros foretold the coming of my five friends and me to Alitheia to take out Tselloch. They say we're to close all the gateways, too, which will make everything right again."

You are to close all the gateways? Something tells me you will not accomplish this on your own.

"Well—no—not just *me*. I mean, the rest of the Six will have to help."

That is not what I meant, he rumbled.

Darcy crossed her arms and looked at him sideways. "I thought you said you weren't familiar with the prophecy."

He didn't answer for a long time. Finally, he said, *This is not the first time evil has entered Orodreos through a gateway. I have lived long enough to see it happen before.*

Darcy dropped her guard a little. "When?"

Have you not learned our history? Pateros opened gateways to many worlds, of which yours was only one.

"Our tutor, Eleanor, taught us your history, but she didn't mention the evil coming through."

Archaios dipped his head. *And yet, evil did come. Pateros knew it was a risk to create the gateways, but he also knew Orodreos would flourish because of them.*

"But . . . Pateros closed those gateways, didn't he? Didn't that destroy the evil coming through them?"

Pateros destroyed what he had created, that is true. And he did it in such a way that any evil creatures who had come through the gateways were destroyed, as well—banished back to the lands from whence they had come. He made possible the sort of banishment that you *must attempt. But evil exists in all worlds, and it was only a matter of time before Baskania acted on his wicked nature and invited more evil to Alitheia.*

"Why don't you believe we'll be able to do it on our own? The prophecy seems pretty clear."

I witnessed Pateros's destruction of the first gateways. No mortal can achieve such destruction.

Darcy grew excited. "You were *there?* You saw what he did?"

Archaios shifted. *The first time, it took only a single act to close them all.*

"*What* single act?" Darcy pressed him.

I do not believe I should share it with you. Perhaps Pateros will make it known to you when he is ready, or perhaps you must discover it on your own.

Darcy stared in stunned disbelief at the immense silvery dragon. Here was someone who knew how to close the gateways, who had *been there* to see it done . . . and he was flatly refusing to tell her how to do it. She felt as if she were eight years old again, working out a difficult math problem and asking her mom for the answer only to be told she had to figure it out on her own. *Except this is a gazillion times worse!*

"I can't believe . . . Why won't you . . . Don't you *want* us to succeed?" she stammered pitifully.

It is not about wanting or not wanting. It is about the proper order of things, he answered with a finality in his tone that closed the door on further questioning.

Darcy stared at him in stony silence.

Tell me why you are going to see the Oracle.

Her cheeks burned with embarrassment. "It's stupid, actually."

Stupid? The Oracle does not accept stupid questions; it answers only questions of great importance.

"Well, okay . . . I wanted to know if I have to marry Prince Tellius like the prophecy says I do. I didn't know what I was doing when I invoked the Oracle. If I'd known what would happen, I never would have done it."

Why do you doubt the words of the prophecy? Were you not just lauding its clarity?

"It's not so clear about this. It says that the Intended—me—will marry the king when all is said and done, but it might not mean what everybody thinks it does."

How so?

"Some historians question the last four lines. They were lost in a fire long ago, and the prophecy was reconstructed. Tellius and I hoped maybe a mistake had been made. We wanted, at least, to know whether the marriage was absolutely necessary."

Hmmm. You believe Pateros, who gave the prophecy, would not see to it that an accurate copy was preserved?

"No, that's not what I mean—"

But yet you do.

Darcy bit her lip, Archaios's point hitting home. His tone was not accusatory, rather he sounded plainly logical. Still, his words made her feel guilty.

She wiped a tear that escaped her eye, and Archaios placed his massive snout next to her cheek and blew softly. *You should rest.*

She sniffed and wiped her nose. "What about the tsellochim? Are they moving again?"

Indeed, the black haze had dissipated, and distant black forms moved like ants up the mountainside now that the shadows were lengthening to nightfall. Archaios raised his muzzle to the air and sniffed, the feathers around his neck ruffling in the cold breeze. A deep boom of thunder resounded from somewhere off in the clouds. *They will not bother you this night,* he said. *You can sleep unafraid.*

Darcy wanted to ask him what he meant, but she was just too tired and afraid of being drawn into another discussion that would leave her feeling foolish and illogical.

That's what you get for engaging a three-thousand-year-old dragon in a history discussion, she chided herself.

Instead, she retreated into the cave. She couldn't hold onto the link any longer, so she dropped it, sure that Archaios would understand. She found her companions along the back wall of the immense cave, near where a natural spring bubbled into a cool pool. A pile of dried grass the size of a house lay on the floor of the cave, and Darcy figured it must be Archaios's bed.

The humans were asleep, stretched out next to each other like keys on a piano, huddled together for warmth. Darcy smiled at their remarkable trust in the beast at the entrance. *Or in me,* she thought. She was, after all, the only one capable of talking with Archaios, and she had directed them to follow him.

The narks stood by the others and watched her curiously. She supposed they wanted to know what Archaios had told her, but she just didn't want to feel the frustration and foolishness again, in explaining to them that Archaios knew how to close the gateways, but would not tell her how, and that he believed their journey to the Oracle was pointless.

She cleared her throat. "The tsellochim are moving again," she whispered, not wanting to wake the others.

"We know," Veli said. "But we won't have to worry about them tonight."

Darcy just nodded, too tired to ask why they were so confident, and shrugged her pack off her shoulders.

"You guys don't mind if I just go to sleep, do you? I know you must be wondering what—"

"Go to sleep, Darcy," Veli interrupted her. "You need it."

Darcy dropped her pack by the spring and scooted up next to Boitheia, not even bothering to kick off her boots. She was asleep almost before her head hit her arm.

When she awoke, the storm had darkened the sky so much that it could have been any time, day or night. Wind howled viciously across the mouth of the cave, and thunder boomed again and again, so loud she couldn't even hear the scrape of Tormod sharpening his axes. She was the only person left sleeping; the others had scattered about the cave.

The inside of their cave was remarkably warm. Archaios had moved inside during the night, and his body radiated heat. The warmth coming off him was so intense, she knew he must be capable of breathing fire, even if she hadn't seen him do it yet. He lit the cave with a soft, phosphorescent glow, the beautiful feathers under his wings and near the tip of his tail waving in the slight breeze from the storm.

Boitheia was curled up between Archaios's front feet with her head against his neck. Her mouth was moving and her hands gesturing as she had a one-sided conversation with the old dragon. Archaios didn't seem to mind. His eyes were narrowed thoughtfully and he dipped his chin from time to time.

The three narks cut impressive silhouettes against the mouth of the cave. They stood far enough inside that they wouldn't get too wet, but their hair whipped about their faces and their cloaks billowed behind them. Veli turned his light eyes turned toward her. Veli, not Yahto. She must have slept through the entire night and into the next day.

Darcy groaned at the stiffness in her back as she sat up, feeling well-rested after having slept the most hours she had since leaving the castle. She stood and stretched, waving groggily at Perry and Dean who were watching Badru sculpt animals out of handfuls of spring water. Darcy meandered over to the watchful narks.

A heavy blast of cold wet wind hit her in the face, and she could see the magic particles in it without even trying. She tugged on Veli's sleeve to get his attention, and he looked down and smiled at her.

"I wondered when you would awaken," he said, his voice loud over the wind.

"About what time of day is it?" she shouted back, her voice sounding rough. She cleared her throat.

"It is after the lunch hour," he replied. "If you're hungry, you'll have to eat something out of your pack, I'm afraid. We cannot forage in this weather, but we are thankful for the storm."

Darcy scratched at her left hand. "What's the big deal about the storm, anyway? Why don't we have to worry about the tsellochim in this weather?"

He looked at her out of the corner of his eye. "Do you remember what I told you on the raft two years ago?"

She thought back to their first night in Alitheia, when they had fled from the servants of Tselloch to a raft out on the sea. She wracked her brain. "We were safe out on the water, right? The Shadow couldn't reach us there."

"Good!" He gave her a proud smile. "The Shadow cannot abide water. Quantity and form make a difference, of course, but all water is harmful to them."

"What do you mean, 'quantity and form'?" Darcy squinted and stepped back as sleet blew into the cave mouth. She grabbed irritably at the wind and turned it back outside.

Veli raised an eyebrow but didn't comment. "Snow is uncomfortable for them and, though they can manage it, they will never go out in it if they can help it. Running water, on the other hand, is nigh impossible for them to touch, the same as a great body of water such as the sea."

"What happens to them if they touch it? Do they melt, or something?"

He laughed. "No, but it is very painful for them. It renders them inept and can even sweep them away. Thus, magicians who can manipulate water are most successful at fighting the tsellochim."

"But nobody was able to kill them until Perry came along, right?" Darcy looked over her shoulder at Perry and warmed when he glanced at her and smiled.

"Right."

Darcy tore her eyes from Perry and turned back to Veli. "What exactly *is* it about water, then, that they can't stand?"

"Rubidius believes it is because water, particularly running water, is pure; it represents life. The tsellochim come from a world of death, therefore . . ." He held out his hand, inviting her to form her own conclusion.

"And you and Archaios assumed this storm would sweep them off the mountain?"

"Exactly. In fact, we are almost certain it will. They will not be able to withstand this intensity for long, and it's likely to continue for some hours yet."

Darcy felt a swell of relief. "Do you think they'll give up?"

Veli hesitated. "Under normal circumstances, yes. But given who you are —"

"You think they'll try again," Darcy finished, her feeling of relief evaporating on the wind. "Well, at least it gives us some more time to get ahead of them."

He nodded, pleased with her optimism.

"Archaios can't stop them, you know, if they come through this way," she said, glancing over at the dragon. "The tsellochim, I mean. Pateros told him to keep the valley people from crossing the mountains into Mayim, but he's not able to stop the tsellochim. Why wouldn't Pateros give him the ability to fight them?"

"I suspect he didn't have to," Veli said. "The tsellochim can't abide water, and these mountains are notorious for regular, strong storms. The tsellochim would have no desire to risk traveling through without very good reason, indeed."

"And that's me, isn't it? *I'm* the very good reason."

Veli inclined his head. "As you say. But don't let it eat you up, my lady. The storms will continue to aid us as long as we are in the mountains. Actually," he smiled and crossed his arms over his chest, "I'm rather excited to explore this region. Very few Alitheians have traveled this way. We must be the first to come through this pass in over . . ."

"Five hundred years," Darcy finished for him, but she didn't share his enthusiasm at exploring uncharted land. "Archaios was told to guard the pass against travelers about the time the Shadow first appeared in Alitheia."

"How you doin'?" Perry said in her ear. Dean was hovering just behind them.

"Fantastic," she said dryly. "What's up?" She shot an apologetic look at Veli, but he waved her off.

"We were just thinking that we're probably going to be stuck here until the storm stops—"

"Which doesn't look like it's going to be anytime soon," Dean interrupted.

"And we are bored," Perry finished.

Darcy stared at them. "You're bored," she repeated. "You're not, like—gee, I don't know—just happy to be alive and feeling relaxed and maybe a little bit like a nap might be nice?"

"Nah, we slept for a long time," Perry said.

"*You* slept for a *really* long time," Dean added.

"And we're ready for a distraction."

"What do you want *me* to do about it?" Darcy asked.

"Didn't Lewis give you a poem he'd written before we left?" Perry asked. "We were thinking we might like to look at it."

She widened her eyes and smacked her forehead with her hand. They were right; Lewis *had* given her a poem.

"Oh my gosh, I totally forgot! Come on."

She jogged over to her pack and upended it, sending bottles, blankets, and various odds and ends scattering. At the very bottom was the crumpled piece of parchment with Lewis's scrawl on it. She pulled it out and smoothed it in her lap.

"Okay, let's see . . ." She settled back against the rock wall to read the poem. It was easy enough to see in the soft glow coming off Archaios's scales. She read it through three full times, frowning and trying to discern some meaning, before Perry and Dean got impatient.

"What's it say?" Perry asked.

Dean made a swipe for the page and she pulled it back, irritated.

"Hey!" he sniped.

"Chill," Darcy snipped. "I'm trying to figure out what it means."

"Well, let us read it over your shoulder, at least."

"Fine." Darcy adjusted the parchment so they could see, and they all read it together.

Wait a while
Wait and I'll
Come back to you.
In the end
In the end
One friend, not two.

"That's it?" Dean said. "What's the big deal?"

"I don't know," Darcy said, "but it's gotta mean something." She studied it again. "It sounds kind of . . . ominous, doesn't it? 'One friend, not two'?"

"It's something that hasn't happened yet," Perry said, running his hands through his hair and leaving it perfectly tousled. "I don't know how we can worry about it if we don't know what it means."

"Seriously, dude," Dean said, nodding. "Why does Lewis have to write things so cryptically, anyway? Why not just come out and write what he means?"

"This stuff doesn't come from him, you know. He just writes what comes into his head," Darcy said.

"Okay, then why does the magical voice in his head have to be so confusing?" Dean pressed.

"Sometimes you learn a bigger lesson when you have to figure it out for yourself," Darcy retorted.

"Ooh-hoo!" Dean threw his hands up. "Look who wants to be a teacher!"

Darcy punched him on the shoulder.

"Ouch! Geez, Darcy!"

"You deserved that, bro," Perry said, smirking.

"You don't have to be a jerk, Dean. I'm sure this is important!" Darcy chided him. "And *you* came to *me* looking for something to do, so don't blame me if you don't like it."

"Okay, fine, fine," Dean said, admitting defeat. "I was just trying to be funny; don't be so touchy!"

Darcy raised her hand again, and he flinched as Perry howled with laughter.

"Dude, man up!" Perry said.

Dean launched himself at Perry, and they rolled away on the floor together, each furiously trying to gain the upper hand.

Darcy folded the crinkled piece of parchment and replaced it in her pack, the words of the poem repeating in her mind. Who would be the one who wouldn't return?

Chapter 29

The Last Leg

Darcy awoke irritably, sitting up and reaching for her pack in the light of Archaios's scales. *Doesn't it know I'm coming as fast as I can?* she thought, finding a bottle of the bitter potion and taking several swallows. The storm had been raging for over twenty-four hours now, effectively halting any forward progress.

She emptied the bottle and shoved it back out of sight. She had only one left, but as long as they weren't too much further delayed, it wouldn't matter. She felt they were close now, but she hadn't told anybody else her suspicion. She didn't want to get anyone's hopes up only to discover she was wrong.

She wasn't sure how far they had left to go, but being up in the mountains made her feel much closer to her goal. The mountains seemed a mysterious, inconvenient, and thus adequate location for the lair of the Oracle, and she remembered learning that it moved around, never staying in the same place twice.

She tried to settle back to sleep, but sleep was evasive, and no matter how she twisted and turned, she could not regain a comfortable position on the cold floor. She tried humming to herself and counting backwards from one thousand. She even tried counting sheep, but nothing worked and she lay awake for the rest of the night. As the storm began to quiet, she heard the soft voices of the narks, their even, musical tones almost lulling her to sleep.

Around daybreak the storm was finally over and Fero and Wyn left with their bows and arrows to hunt some breakfast. They returned about the time everybody started to stir, with several pheasants and two rabbits already skinned and ready to be cooked.

Archaios lit a fire for them with one blast from his massive snout, and they all prepared to leave as the meat cooked.

"They're back at the village, just like we thought they would be," Veli's voice sounded from around the cook fire.

"The tsellochim?" She hurried over to him and squatted to receive a hot, greasy chunk of meat. She blew on it, shifting it from one hand to the other.

"Yes." He grinned. "We can see the haze hanging over the village."

"I have no doubt, however, that they will start up again once the sun begins to set," Daylan said grimly.

"Oh, certainly," Veli said. "But we have gained several days on them, at least."

They ate in silence, each ruminating on the day ahead. Darcy refrained from telling them her suspicion that they were drawing close at last. Instead, she finished her food, took one last drink of fresh water from the spring, and then shouldered her pack. The straps now rested on well-worn calluses, and she wondered if she would ever have smooth skin again.

That morning she'd connected the link between Archaios and the other adults, and she'd listened in on their questions about the lands beyond the mountain peak. Archaios had told them of wild forests and glacial valleys and warned them to stay clear of any centaur herds, as their migration time sometimes spurred clan warfare. Giants, he'd said, were solitary, simple-minded creatures, and most had moved far away from his domain in the time since the Shadow had come to the valley.

After breakfast, they gathered outside Archaios's cave and found the air to be crisp and cool even with the sun shining brightly.

The storm was the harbinger of autumn, Archaios said, raising his nose to the wind. *The air will soon be cold. Are you prepared for the weather to change?*

We have winter cloaks, Daylan replied through the link.

We've only been lugging them with us since July! Darcy thought to herself.

I wish you good travels, then, Archaios said. He turned his head sideways to gaze at Darcy through one eye. *I do not envy you for what you will find at the end of your road. I will petition Pateros for your safety and the safety of your travel companions.*

Darcy nodded. *Thank you, Archaios.*

The others bid the dragon goodbye, turning their backs on the cave and the valley of Fobos and hiking over the ridge to the game trail that continued on the other side. It crisscrossed down the ridge in a precarious descent until joining a swath of tundra grass about three hundred feet beneath them and turning northeast.

Beyond the narrow valley, the mountains stretched on in endless layers straight north to the horizon, and the vast blue sky kissed their peaks. Pockets of snow were visible on higher summits in the distance, and she shivered thinking of the winter that was on its way and would soon coat the entire mountain range in snow and ice. She hoped they would be well south, her errand with the Oracle fulfilled, before that time arrived.

"Well, Darcy," Daylan said, squinting downward in the bright light, "do we continue to follow the trail?"

"For now it's fine," Darcy said. Her internal Oracle pull was so strong now she felt it would be more direct to leave the path and cut northwest down the ridge, but the easiest way down the mountain was to take the path.

The switchbacks were much steeper on this side of the mountain, and Daylan called a halt shortly after they'd started their descent, securing a long length of rope between all of them except the oread and the wolf.

Terra and Lupidor were more than at home in this environment. Terra's face was vibrant, a lilt in her step. Her hair had grown long and wildly curly, mottled white and grey like the rocks. "Mountains are the bones of the earth, and every oread longs to visit them sometime in her life," she had said to Darcy that morning. She jumped from rock to rock like a mountain goat and amused herself doing flips and acrobatics above their heads. Every now and then she would pop into the ground and emerge minutes later looking content and superior.

The mountains were also the natural habitat of Lupidor's own people in Alitheia. He had never been this far north before, but he had gazed upon the mountains from a distance as a pup and felt the instinctual longing to explore them.

The rest of them, however, felt anywhere but at home, and it was with great relief they finally reached the bottom of the first descent and stepped onto the tundra grass, dotted here and there with low shrubs. Daylan untied them and rerolled his rope before beginning to lead them further along the path to the northeast. Darcy shook her head.

"No, I'm sorry. We have to leave the path now. That way." She pointed northwest. "I have to go that way."

They followed her line of sight. The route looked easy enough, even without a path. They would have to climb up a gentle slope and over a ridge that looked like a saddle against the horizon. Beyond that, Darcy felt sure they would continue northwest.

Daylan stepped back and swept out his arm. "Lead the way, Lady Darcy."

The trees had once again grown dense, but this forest looked much older than any that surrounded Ormiskos. The cedars were taller and more weathered, and although a dense undergrowth of ferns and moss covered the ground, no birch trees or flowers lightened the darkness. The fairies were evasive and shy, having never seen humans or narks before, and they looked much wilder than their southern counterparts.

This, Darcy thought, *is the sort of place Tselloch would hide, if it weren't for the rains.*

It did, indeed, rain almost every day, usually in intense rumbling storms, but none that lasted as long as the one they'd experienced in Archaios's cave. They rejoiced every time the rain came down, for they knew it put more distance between themselves and the tsellochim.

Lupidor and Terra scouted behind them from time to time, but the tsellochim were never close enough for them to see. Only when they climbed high ridges through a break in the trees could they look back and spot the black haze, always distant, but always there.

They traveled both day and night whenever possible to keep widening the distance between themselves and the shadow beasts. Now that they were back within the forest, it was only a matter of time before the tsellochim were able to move under the shadow of the trees during the day.

It had been two weeks since they'd left Archaios's cave, and they were very close to the Oracle now—Darcy could feel it with every step. The weather had grown much colder, her directions taking them ever northwestward, over ridge after ridge of mountains.

Their company had avoided the centaurs as Archaios had warned them. At their first glimpse of the wild horse-men, they had taken to ground in a grouping of boulders, feeling the earth tremble beneath them as a herd of hundreds thundered by. They'd continued on to find remains from a centaur battle: human torsos severed from horse bodies and piles of limbs and entrails, the rough-hewn banner of the winning clan flying over the pile of bodies. Poor Boitheia had lost her entire lunch and had to be carried away, pale and sweaty, by Wyn.

They'd been in the trees now for several days, and Darcy itched with impatience. *Just a little bit farther,* she chanted over and over in her head, only the thought of Lewis's poem able to distract her. *Who's not coming back?*

"We are almost there, aren't we?" Veli stated.

Darcy started, looking up to find him jogging beside her.

"Whoa." Darcy came to a stop, glancing over her shoulder at her companions strung out behind her, the humans looking distinctly annoyed.

"Have I been going that fast?" she asked, embarrassed.

"Indeed, for about an hour now." Veli stretched his back.

"I—I didn't know!" she mused, only now noticing that she did feel more winded than usual.

"It is okay, I expected this near the end." He glanced backward. "Wyn's been carrying Boitheia. The others won't admit they are starting to get tired, but I decided to take pity on them anyway."

"Thanks. I'm usually not much for jogging back home. I'm surprised I could even keep it up for an hour."

"You have gained much strength on this journey. Let us hope only that you have gained mental strength as well as physical strength." He looked sidelong at her.

"Because I have to face the Oracle," she muttered.

"Yes. And soon, it would seem."

Darcy covered her face with her hands, suddenly weary. "Oh, Veli," she sighed. "I just want to get this over with. And then we can head back and . . . and I won't have to feel afraid all the time of everybody dying anymore."

"Mayhap your meeting with the Oracle will be fruitful, and you will learn what you desire to know," Veli said, laying a hand on her shoulder. "I have hoped it would be so."

"Rubidius said the Oracle answers in riddles." Darcy dropped her hands and stared bleakly into the trees. "I need to keep going. I'm sorry, it's just that I can't concentrate on anything other than *it*."

"Then let us go, but perhaps a little *slower* . . . for the sake of your companions, yes?" He winked at her.

She laughed. "Oh, Veli, I'm glad you're here."

He grinned. "I'm glad, as well."

They walked together ahead of the rest, and Darcy found that as long as she kept moving toward the Oracle, she could engage in conversation.

The afternoon wore on, the ground sloping upward. In the early evening they came to a halt at the edge of a shallow precipice, at the bottom of which lay a valley basin, ringed on all sides by the cliff they stood upon. The entire basin looked to be the bottom of a gigantic sinkhole, several hundred feet across, one that had opened up in ages past. The cliffs ringing the sinkhole were only fifty to a hundred feet high, lower on the downward slope of the mountain. Still, the slope was steep, sheer, and likely problematic to get down and then back up again on the other side.

"Well," Daylan said, "we can go around, I suppose."

"No," Darcy said. The pull was so strong she could almost see her goal ahead, and it lay right in the center of the basin. "That's where the Oracle is. We have to go in. That is, *I* have to go in."

Tokala snorted. "Come now. You think we would accompany you all this way just to be left behind at the end? I want to see this Oracle for myself and, maybe, give it a piece of my mind for dragging us all the way out here to the middle of nowhere."

"Do we climb down now and take our chances in the valley tonight?" Tormod asked. "Or wait until morning when we have more time to scout it out? There doesn't appear to be a quick way out in a fight, and I don't fancy being trapped."

Daylan fingered his beard, looking over at Darcy. "How long do you think this is going to take?"

"I don't know," she answered honestly. "I just have to ask my question and get my answer. The center of the basin doesn't look too far away. Maybe we should just get it over with now." She bounced on the balls of her feet.

"We have a few hours until sundown," Veli added. "While Tormod speaks wisely, I would hate to allow the tsellochim to advance on us any more than is necessary. I agree with Lady Darcy; we should descend into the valley today."

Darcy shot Veli a thankful glance.

Lupidor bumped Darcy's thigh with his nose, and she opened up the link. *Yes?*

I will stay up top, he said. *If we have need of a quick escape, lifting me up the other side will be a liability.*

Lupidor, are you sure? I hate to think of you waiting all alone up here.

I will monitor the perimeter and howl to alert you of potential danger

"Okay," Darcy said out loud. She knelt and hugged Lupidor around his shaggy neck. "Be safe," she whispered. She turned to the others. "Lupidor will stay up here and watch the perimeter for us. If he howls, we'll know trouble is coming."

"All right," Daylan said, unwinding the rope from his pack. "That is wise. We'll be as quick as we can," he said to the great wolf.

Daylan secured the rope to an ancient cedar tree and they took the descent one at a time. Terra stayed topside until they all reached the bottom and then untied the knot and let the rope fall. She appeared on the ground with them a moment later. "Lupidor's off, beginning his first circle around the basin."

"Um, Darcy?" Dean called from behind her, and she looked back. She was already several paces ahead of them and moving fast.

"I'm sorry!" She dug her feet in and slowed down. "It's just hard to resist now."

"It's all right, we can keep up," Veli said. "Let's go."

Darcy was already moving again, the Oracle like a magnet in the center of the valley pulling her onward.

"These trees are younger than those up on the cliff," Tokala mused to Daylan. "I bet this was a sinkhole ages ago, and these trees grew in later than the rest of the forest, replacing the trees that were destroyed."

Darcy didn't take the time to admire the trees, her thoughts focused on one thing: getting to the Oracle and being done with all this.

The ground continued to slope downward, toward the center of the basin and, with a cry of relief, Darcy broke free of the trees into a large clearing pocked right in the middle. Small rocks dotted the grassy surface, the sides funneling up away from the center.

Her feet stopped moving; her palm stopped itching. She looked around at the rocks and grass, searching for it, but there was nothing. No strange entity, no engravings or monuments, no sign of any life at all, and yet all of the Oracle's energy was focused here.

Darcy took several steps forward and stopped again, listening hard. She could feel the curious gazes of her companions behind her.

"Are we there?" Perry called to her, but she ignored him, turning a full circle and searching for something, *anything,* that might be the Oracle.

"Hello?" she called.

The men murmured in low tones behind her, making her feel foolish.

Hello? Is anybody here? she threw out her link with all her might. Nothing.

She exhaled mightily and threw up her hands in frustration.

"*What?*" she cried. "*What am I supposed to do now?*" She took several jerky steps back toward the woods, passing her friends on the way as they stared at her, their gazes unnerving. She re-crossed the threshold into the trees, and it all came back: her restless pull toward the clearing, the itching in her palm, even a faint buzzing in her ear. She took two more steps, and the buzzing became so deafening that she doubled over, covering her ears with her hands.

She clambered back to the clearing, feeling relief—blessed relief.

I don't understand! she thought with despair, turning in circles. *What am I going to tell the others?*

A gentle hand touched her shoulder, and she jumped.

"Darcy," came Veli's kind voice. "What do you need?"

"I—I don't know." Angry tears came to her eyes, and she dashed them away in frustration, sniffing. "This is it, but . . . I don't know how to talk to it! I don't know what it looks like; I don't know anything!"

"It's okay," he soothed. "We're here. Why don't we set up camp so you can sit on it for a while?"

"Okay," Darcy sniffed again.

Veli went to the others and explained. Darcy couldn't hear what they said in response, but she could imagine their frustration. She sat with her arms around her knees as the others set up camp in the clearing. She didn't know if they were avoiding her or just giving her space to think. *They regret coming,* she thought. *It's laughing at me—the Oracle.*

She thought of Lupidor, alone in the forest above them, wondering where they were. She was too ashamed to call out to him, to let him know what happened.

Twilight dropped rapidly as the sun dipped beneath the trees above them. The days had grown noticeably shorter in the last two weeks, and Darcy dreaded every lengthening night that gave the tsellochim more time to move faster. *What will we do if they catch us here?*

Darcy stood and brushed off her pants, needing to move. She walked around and around the basin's circumference, the sun setting fully on her third cycle. The others had already gotten a fire going, and the day narks phased into night narks. She averted her eyes from Yahto, afraid of the censure she would see in his face.

On her fourth time around, she noticed Perry playing with the bone whistle, twirling it around on its thong in a bored sort of way, and she felt a stab of annoyance at his nonchalance. She paused in her circuit, wanting to go and take it from him, but Yahto got there first.

"Give that to me," the night nark snapped. "It is not a play thing." Yahto held it up to the flickering firelight, deep in thought. "Darcy," he called, turning to her with his back to the fire, his face a dark, expressionless mask. "Perhaps you could try blowing on this. Anything is worth a try at this point."

Darcy shrugged, and they started toward each other. She passed near the dip in the center of the clearing, and just before Yahto handed her the whistle, Darcy's left hand gave a stab of pain. She gasped and stopped, holding her hand in surprise.

Yahto slowly lowered the whistle, glancing at her hand. "What is it?" he asked.

The pain stabbed again, and Darcy cried out. The linen bandage felt wet, and she ripped it off. The sore had ruptured like a blister and a foul-smelling mixture of blood and puss was oozing out of it.

She and Yahto watched in disgusted awe as a fat droplet dribbled from her hand and hit the ground, rolling like a ball toward the center of the clearing where it touched the dimple in the ground and soaked in out of sight.

Darcy shouted in surprise as the ground dropped out from underneath her, and she slipped down a funnel of gravel toward the central pucker, which was opening into a yawning, sucking hole. Yahto dove after her and caught her in an iron embrace just before she slipped through, taking him with her. They fell together, as one, through the hole and into blackness.

CHAPTER 30

THE ORACLE

The earth closed above them. They fell forever, she and Yahto, but her clothes did not whip about her, nor did her hair fly wildly through the air. Were it not for the sensation of falling inside her chest, she would have thought she was floating instead. For a moment she hung suspended in time, aware only dimly of Yahto beside her, before a sucking noise preceded the end of their fall.

They landed—not gracefully, but not terribly, either; nothing like what she would have expected after a fall of that length. They landed on their feet and stumbled together. Darcy would have fallen were it not for Yahto beside her, holding her up.

Once she got her feet oriented beneath her, she disentangled herself from the night nark and took a look around. They were at the end of what appeared to be a long tunnel, a wall of solid rock behind them and a passage stretching out before them. Low murmurs and groans issued from the tunnel, and Darcy felt a stab of fear.

She cast a look at the ceiling above them. Also solid rock. She could see no sign of the tunnel through which they'd dropped, the only light coming from somewhere down the passage. Darcy turned questioning eyes upon Yahto.

"How did we get here if . . . if there's no passage above us?" she asked, her mind reeling. They had fallen for so long, they would surely be a hundred miles underground by now. But that didn't make any sense; that was impossible. "I don't think we're in the mountain anymore," she whispered.

Yahto glanced at the ceiling, looking composed, but Darcy could see the pulse in his throat beating rapidly. He, too, was afraid, but he was holding it together for her sake. Darcy felt sure that he'd grabbed hold of her so she wouldn't be alone down there. Her heart expanding, she reached for his hand impulsively, squeezing it in hers.

He cleared his throat and nodded toward the tunnel. "We must go forward," he said. He tucked the bone whistle into a pocket of his jerkin and squeezed Darcy's hand in return. "Come; I'm right beside you."

Darcy relaxed at his touch, which normally would have made her uncomfortable. Together they proceeded down the tunnel, and the murmuring voices became louder as they entered a gallery of sorts where a macabre display of ornaments and creatures were grotesquely exhibited in barred cages. Darcy's breath caught in her throat, her heart wrenching, and Yahto's grip tightened on her hand.

The creatures—all alive—looked ancient and withered, mumbling and groaning their misery, their cells barely large enough for them to lie down in. Some strange animals had extra limbs, some had protrusions coming out of their necks. There was a three-headed cow, a great lion whose tail was a hissing snake, blue pixies and fairies with extra wings, a gnome with three eyes, and some that looked normal, too, but despondent. None of them even looked up as Darcy and Yahto passed.

The objects about her were not caged, but Darcy would never have dared to touch any of them. Some were on display, while others were heaped in haphazard piles. There were so *many* of them—hundreds—and so odd, Darcy couldn't discern what any of them were for. Her eyes flickered over them as they passed. A thimble with a glistening drop of blood on its tip, a golden censer, a wooden horse with six legs and rubies for eyes . . .

"The Oracle has never taken money," Rubidius's voice resounded in her head. *"It is . . . a collector of sorts. Rare or valuable items, or creatures even . . ."*

"Payment," she murmured, swallowing hard, horrified at what the Oracle had required of others. *I don't have anything to give!*

They passed into a new gallery filled with rows of glass vials set into shelves in the rock, each identical in size and shape, roughly six inches tall and stopped with a cork. A roll of parchment sat inside each one. *". . . and if you have no physical object to give, it will accept promises as payment."* Here were the promises, recorded for all of time—hopes and dreams bottled up, never to be released.

They continued beyond the corked bottles into a gallery of barred cells filled mostly with humans, old and wild-eyed, looking like they'd gone mad. They came alive as a group and banged against the bars of their cages, begging desperately.

"I—I—I—I'll pay! T—T—Tell it, *please!*"

"I'm sorry! I'm sorry, so sorry, and I'm ready!"

"M—M—Me t—too . . ."

"I'll make the promise, I *will!* I didn't *know!"*

"I—I didn't *mean it!* I didn't *mean it!* Please tell it!"

Darcy cringed at their voices echoing off the curved ceiling and stone floor. The tunnel was so narrow that the prisoners' groping hands nearly brushed Darcy's shoulders, and she squeezed closer to Yahto to avoid them. The air was pungent with stink, each one of the prisoners showing the same sore in the middle of the left palm. The sores were open, as hers was now, dripping filth upon the floor.

Darcy whimpered and squeezed her eyes shut, letting Yahto pull her along, beyond the prisoners and into a cave at the end of the tunnel. They stepped into the chamber; the voices of the prisoners cutting off. Silence fell—a powerful silence.

In the center of the cave lay the source of the pale light that had trickled down the tunnel—a single upright stone pillar about four feet tall, its surface cracked with ancient runes and engravings.

The Oracle. Darcy knew it without being told. Never having imagined its appearance, its solid, faceless soullessness seemed exactly as she'd expected. The yellowish light seeped through its many cracks, casting the room in a sickly glow. It spoke in the enclosed space, its voice androgynous, like a sound of man, woman, and child talking all at once with pebbles in their throats.

"*You have come,*" it said, a ripple moving across its surface, bits and pieces of its rock face floating and rotating along its cracks. Its voice echoed strangely around the chamber, and Darcy waited for it to dissipate.

"Yes," she said, amazed at how steady she sounded. She released Yahto's hand and stepped forward.

"*I did not call him,*" the Oracle continued.

"No, he's . . . he's here to help me."

"*I see. What do you think of my collection?*" it asked, sounding amused and vain, as though testing her reaction.

Darcy recoiled in horror, struggling to compose herself, not wanting to anger the entity. "It's . . . you have very rare creatures, indeed," she said, but she couldn't help herself from asking, "The people at the end—who are they?"

"*Those who would not pay,*" the Oracle replied.

Darcy swallowed hard. "Some of them want to pay now, I think—"

"*They have only one chance to accept my terms. They belong to me now for all of eternity, ageing, but never dying. That is the fate you face, Darcy Pennington, should you also refuse.*"

She swallowed again, having no intention of not paying the Oracle.

"*Your question I have heard,*" it said. " '*What is the role of the Intended in regard to the prophecy of the Six, and is this role tied to a marriage with the king?*' "

Her words sounded ridiculous and juvenile when spoken back to her by the ancient entity, and she refused to look at Yahto for fear of seeing his disgusted face. Instead she waited in silence for her answer, her heart beating wildly in her chest.

The stone Oracle swelled, its cracks expanding, seeping more of the sick yellow light.

"*You, the Intended, have much truth to seek.*
Your path is not for the fainthearted or weak.
What was lost in the fire has now come to light,
Recovered, translated, against which you'll fight.
The words were restored, precise to the letter,
Their meanings should have been interpreted better.
Regarding the lines of the marriage and ring,
Ask yourself, Lady, who is the king?
And what is the ring that will mark you, in sooth?
In answering you'll find your way to the truth.
Now here's something more to help you understand
The words of the prophecy you now have at hand.
There shall be a wedding, not one, but two,
With the deepest color defining you.
Lady Darcy, Intended, you must look ahead,
Twice wed,
Twice dead,
Twice stained red."

The Oracle's riddle was emblazoned on her mind, every word clear as if she'd memorized it. Darcy held her breath and stared at the Oracle, waiting for more, for some interpretation of what it had just told her. But it said no more, deflating in on itself until it was once again the size it had been when they'd entered, the barest traces of light escaping through its cracks.

"That's . . . that's it?" Darcy squeaked. "That's not—"

Yahto placed a warning hand on her shoulder, but she shook him off.

"No. That's not an *answer!*"

The Oracle remained silent, and she stomped her foot in frustration. Rubidius had been right after all; the Oracle's answer was more confusing than her initial question. She wished now, more than ever, that she had never come. Would she, like Rubidius, be plagued for the rest of her life by a riddle she could not answer?

"Can't you just—I don't know—tell me whether Tellius is the king?" Darcy cried, grasping at straws, but she didn't care.

"*I have given you your answer,*" the Oracle said.

"Fine," Darcy snapped. "Can I go, then?"

"*You owe me payment.*"

A sick feeling of dread overtook her anger. "I don't have anything to give you, but I can make a promise, if you want—"

"*I have chosen my payment,*" the Oracle interrupted.

"What . . . what is it?" Darcy whispered, trembling.

A crack in the Oracle opened wider, and a thin shaft of light fell upon Yahto. "*I want the nark. I do not yet possess a nark in my collection.*"

Darcy's horror could not have been greater had the Oracle asked her to dig out her own eyeball as payment. She couldn't seem to force any words out at all, and instead she gaped like a fish out of water, her mouth working soundlessly.

Yahto shifted beside her, and she turned her wide, petrified eyes on him. He looked down at the shaft of light on his chest, his expression thoughtful, not concerned or even surprised. He turned his eyes up to meet hers, and something calculating in them frightened her.

She turned back to the Oracle. "I will *n*—"

Yahto, quick as lightning, clapped his hand over her mouth and pulled her tight against his chest. "Do not refuse," he hissed in her ear. "You have only one chance. If you refuse it, you will be trapped here forever. Is that what you want?"

She shook her head beneath his hand, and he lowered it carefully. "Yahto," she whispered, "I can't let it take you! This is my quest, *mine;* if anybody should stay here, it should be me!"

"Think of the prophecy, Darcy," he murmured. "You cannot stay."

Darcy frantically searched her brain for something that would change his mind. "What about Veli?"

Yahto's jaw tightened, a grim smile on his lips. "He made a decision without me, and now I make one without him. He would not allow you to come on this journey without us, and now I have decided just how much we will sacrifice for you. He would forbid you to remain here, and so will I."

"*You should know,*" the Oracle interrupted, "*that your friends are in grave danger. They will not be able to hold off the tsellochim for much longer.*"

It's lying, Darcy thought. *The tsellochim are days away.* But she knew what it was doing. Forcing her hand, just like Veli had forced Yahto's hand, and just like Yahto was now forcing Veli's. There was nothing Darcy could do. Her face crumpled and she melted into tears.

Yahto stepped forward toward the beam of light still trained on his chest, and it grew larger. "Lady Darcy accepts your terms," he said, "as do I. I will stay."

CHAPTER 31

THE WAY HOME

"*Excellent.*" The Oracle sounded wickedly pleased, and Darcy was filled with hatred. This was not an amoral entity, as Batsal had written in his histories; this was an evil entity, purely evil. But even as she seethed with loathing, she could not remove blame from herself. Yahto would be stuck beneath the ground with this horrible thing until the end of the world, and it was her fault.

Yahto's eyes fluttered in surprise as his body levitated into the air. He hung suspended there, spread eagle, his dark hair fanned out about his face, and an enormous dark hand reached out from the tunnel behind them and snatched him from the air. With a vast sucking noise, it pulled him to join the horrors in the gallery.

"*No!*" Darcy shrieked and reached for him. She hadn't even said goodbye . . . or thanked him. Her legs began to tremble so violently beneath her that she collapsed into a heap.

Her knees hit the ground, and it was wet. She was no longer in the chamber of the Oracle. A great commotion enveloped her, and large, fat raindrops mixed with sleet pelted her in the face. Her clothes soaked through almost at once, and a deep rumbling erupted overhead, like thunder, but different. The startled shouts of male voices cut through the driving rain.

Darcy couldn't focus. "*No!*" she screamed over and over again. "*Let me back!*" She pounded her fists on the ground, throwing up mud and slush onto her chest and face. "*Please!*" she wailed.

"Darcy?" Perry was at her side, shaking her violently. "Darcy, snap out of it!"

"She's back!" somebody shouted.

"But where is Yahto Veli?" Wal Wyn asked.

Darcy twisted her hands into her hair, covering her ears.

"*Darcy!*" Perry gave her another shake. "Come on, tell us what happened!"

"Quickly!" Daylan growled. "Badru cannot hold on much longer!"

Darcy looked up and tried to focus. Perry's hair was curling beneath his ears, and he had the scruff of a teenage boy long in need of a shave. Tormod, too, had a beard to match his mustache. Darcy looked at her own hands, startled to find her fingernails were so long they were curling.

Her head spun, confused. It was the middle of the day, though she'd left in the evening, and the sky was blocked out by sheets of icy water.

She couldn't stop crying, nor did she want to. Yahto and Veli were gone —gone the same as if they'd died. But they *hadn't* died; they would live in captive misery for the rest of time.

"Has she gone mad?" Tormod asked, squatting next to her. "Can she even understand us?"

She shook her head. "Yahto," she croaked.

"Yes?" Daylan leaned closer. "Where is he?"

She shook her head again. "No—he's—he's not coming back."

"Is he dead?" Daylan demanded.

"No . . . not dead. *He stayed!*" she wailed and covered her face with her hands.

She sobbed as they all went silent.

"It is just as the young lords insisted . . ." Daylan said, sounding awed.

"It is final, then. There is nothing more we can do here. We must leave!" Tormod shouted.

Darcy looked up despairingly from her hands, appalled that they so readily accepted that Yahto Veli was not coming back. She wanted to rail at them, but it wasn't their fault; it was hers. She had led him to his doom; she had left him behind. She looked from one sad face to the next, squinting in the watery spray. "How long—" she croaked out as she looked down at her fingernails again.

"You've been gone for seven months, Darcy," Perry said firmly. "It's April."

"Seven . . . *months?*" Darcy rasped. "You've been . . . How could you . . . survive, I—"

A shout sounded from nearby, and Daylan and Tormod leapt to their feet. "We'll sort it out later," Daylan growled. "Perry, Dean, help her. We need to get to the raft. It's time."

Perry and Dean each took one of her arms and hefted her to her feet. She didn't have the strength to walk, so Perry swung her up into his arms and carried her to where the rest of them were gathering.

There was no campsite; every pack they'd brought was secured to a broad raft sitting in the clearing. It had a single mast with a sail flapping in the wind. Darcy stared at it stupidly as Perry set her down on the rough-hewn cedar logs.

"What's—"

But Perry shook his head. "Hang on to this!" he shouted, showing her a leather strap looped around a log. Looking around, Darcy saw each of the others taking places on the raft and grasping similar leather loops, everyone soaked from the falling water and sleet shearing off the arc of water over the basin.

Badru was the last to board, and he stepped very carefully. He was soaked through with his arms stretched out before him, his palms up. As he settled himself onto the raft, he gave one quick nod and dropped his arms.

"*Hold on!*" Daylan shouted.

They ducked their heads as the water from above crashed down on them, the volume so great Darcy felt her body jerk upward in the current that formed around them. She held tight to her leather strap until the first gush of water had passed and she could breathe again.

More water flooded around them, rising fast. She looked over her shoulder to the north and saw a waterfall cascading over the lip into the valley like Niagara Falls. Hundreds of tsellochim surrounded the basin, clinging to the trees like enormous four-legged spiders.

The daylight hindered their movement, but the tsellochim advanced nonetheless. The ceiling of water no longer protected the valley and several shook themselves and began to pick their way through the tree branches. They moved from tree to tree without touching the wet ground, but the basin was filling fast, inching the water higher and closer to them.

Darcy felt the raft lurch off the ground, spinning around in the current until it stopped, pointing south—pointing home.

Badru concentrated hard from the front of the raft, holding the vessel steady in the wild current. The raft rose several more feet. Two tsellochim were now so close Darcy could clearly make out their forms, their fellows having given up and turned back to higher ground.

The raft approached close enough to challenge the shadow beasts who now had very little left of the tree trunk to cling to. Perry unsheathed his sword and stood, planting his feet and commanding, "*Come on!* Do it, if you dare!"

The tsellochim reared and hissed as his sword blazed with power and light. The water began to lap at their feet, and they leapt, as one, onto the raft.

Perry ducked and raked his sword across the first tsellochim as it plummeted toward him. It gave a keening shriek, sizzling where the sword had struck, the blazing trail eating away at its semicorporeal body until it was burned to ashes. The second tsellochim landed near Badru, shaking his concentration. The raft spun sideways as Badru sent a spray of water at the shadow creature. It hissed and shrieked, dancing away from the water stream, and Perry stepped forward, slicing off two of its legs with a single swipe.

Badru regained control of the raft as the tsellochim burned down to nothing.

Darcy slouched back, her brain still on overdrive, as her companions, too, began to relax. She barely noticed as their raft cleared the tops of the trees, sailing on the crest of the water.

The water spilled out over the lip of the basin and down an enormous rift between the mountain ranges. The forest in this glacial valley had been cleared, coming to an end just south of the basin, and they flowed down unimpeded through the channel. Tsellochim clung to the few remaining trees, hissing as they swept by, but none dared leap at them for risk of falling in the water. Darcy held her breath until they reached the natural valley beyond the forest, leaving the tsellochim far behind.

The glacial cut was steep, channeling the water into a raging river, but Badru continued to hold them steady, his focus never wavering.

"Where did the water come from?" Darcy asked Perry and Dean over the din of the rushing current.

"Winter runoff," Dean said. "Badru redirected it."

"And the forest . . . ?" Darcy asked.

"We cleared it," Dean said, adding, "*That* was fun."

"But *how*—"

"You were gone for seven months," Perry said. "We had a lot of free time on our hands."

"It wasn't seven months," she said, her brow furrowed. "It was . . . it was only an hour . . ."

Perry and Dean exchanged looks. "It was a long time, Darcy," Perry said.

"And it's a good thing you showed up when you did," Dean added.

"You waited for *seven months* . . . Didn't you think we were dead?"

"We would have . . . but we had the poem." Perry looked at Dean.

"Lewis's poem?" Darcy asked slowly.

" '*Wait a while, wait and I'll come back to you,*' " Perry recited in a near whisper. "The others thought you had died," he continued, "but Dean and I didn't believe it. We knew the poem was about you and that we had to wait." He hesitated. "And we knew Yahto Veli wouldn't be coming back," he finished. " '*One friend, not two,*' " he quoted.

"We sent a note to Rubidius asking what he thought, and he agreed we should wait," Dean added.

"Regardless," Perry interjected, "it got difficult. We almost had to leave without you and come back once we'd led the tsellochim off. They showed up about a week after you and Yahto disappeared. Lupidor warned us by howling, but we haven't heard from him since."

"How did you hold them off for so long?" Darcy breathed.

"They tried to fight us, but Badru and I gave them a run for their money. They backed off and waited for more to arrive."

"The storms helped, too," Dean said.

"Yeah, we had pretty regular rainfall, and Badru was already thinking about how to escape the basin. Terra scouted outside the rim and discovered this glacial valley, and Badru figured he could use it to channel water through," Perry continued.

"That's when he had us start clearing the trees," Dean said. "We only worked on sunny days so we didn't have to worry much about the tsellochim," Dean said. "You'd be surprised how many trees a nark can cut down in a day." He shook his head as if stunned.

"But we had no idea how long we'd have to wait," Dean added.

"What about the tsellochim?" Darcy pressed. "You fought them off the first time, but what about the next time?"

"Their numbers kept getting larger, but they knew we weren't going anywhere. It was late fall when they attacked again, and Badru and I fought them off. I killed as many of them as I could, and Badru created a dome of water over us, using some rainwater he'd kept stored. Then we just waited them out until the next storm."

"Then winter came," Dean continued, "with a whole lot of snow, and they didn't attack at all."

"Sure," Darcy said weakly.

"The snows only just started melting," Perry said. "I hated the idea of leaving you behind, but the tsellochim were getting ready, and . . ." he trailed off, looking at her apologetically.

Darcy swallowed and looked down. "Yahto stayed behind so I could leave." The words poured out of her. A shuddering sob threatened to escape her throat, and she fought it back before continuing. "He paid . . . my debt to . . . the Oracle." She lost her battle against more tears and dropped her face into her hand. "I didn't even get a real answer to my question," she sobbed. "It was all . . . for *nothing!*"

Dean and Perry were silent a long time, but when Perry spoke, there was no bitterness in his tone. "Darcy, if I've learned one thing, it's that there's a reason behind everything that happens in Alitheia. You got an answer, at least, didn't you?"

Darcy nodded miserably.

"What did it te—" Dean started, but Perry punched him hard on the arm, and Darcy was glad. She couldn't bring herself to repeat it.

The boys fell silent, the wind whipping their faces as the raft surged southward on the current. Darcy should have felt refreshed by the breeze, but instead it just echoed the chill deep within her.

That evening the raft lurched sideways as Badru directed the runoff to join with a real river. Darcy looked over her shoulder at the silhouette of the mountains as they left them far behind. Badru at long last let himself relax, lying back and immediately falling asleep. The narks took up positions at either side of the raft, holding long poles ready to keep the vessel from running into the shore.

Darcy lay back and stared at the sky, the words of the Oracle turning over in her head.

She awoke the next morning as the raft bumped into the shore. She blinked her eyes and sat up, feeling strange, as though something was missing. Her limbs were relaxed, no restlessness trembling through them. No buzzing invaded her ears, and the ever-present itch was gone from her left hand. She raised it to her face and stared at the large puckered scar in the center of her palm. It didn't seem fair—this was the only physical reminder of her trip to see the Oracle. She'd have rather left a limb behind than poor Yahto Veli.

She looked around. They were nestled up against the shore of the river in unfamiliar territory, the water broad and calm.

"Are we getting off here?" Darcy croaked.

"Just to refresh ourselves. We'll continue downriver as long as we can," Daylan said. He was already off the raft, kicking his boots off and changing into dry stockings.

"It's my fault," Terra said brightly from the shore. "I can't be away from the land for too long, but if I leave the raft, I'll never keep up with you. I'll just need to touch earth at least once every day."

"I'm not complaining," Darcy assured her, glad to have solid ground beneath her feet.

The rest of the group stumbled to the shore and scattered in pairs of two or three.

"Come on, girls," Terra said to Darcy and Boitheia. "There's a nice private little spot over here; it's not far."

Darcy shot a sidelong glance at Boitheia as they followed the oread nymph into the trees. The girl had said nothing at all the night before.

They reached a copse of trees, separating briefly to tend to their needs. Darcy finished and stood waiting for Boitheia and Terra. She drummed her fingers on her crossed arms, her right hand cold and beginning to prickle with icy jolts. Boitheia emerged from behind a tree and joined her in waiting

"Boitheia," she muttered, "I think we should get back to the raft."

"Okay," Boitheia said in a hushed voice.

"Terra?" Darcy called softly, to no response. She called again a little louder, "Terra?" She began to back up and then froze when she heard it.

A horrible gurgling sound issued from behind them. Darcy and Boitheia swung around, and there stood a six-foot-tall tsellodrin with Terra's tiny body impaled on his broadsword. Frothy blood dripped from her lips, the startlingly red droplets hitting the ground and disappearing into the earth like water. The oread's face beseeched them to run, but Darcy stood frozen, watching the life ebb from her friend's eyes.

The memory of Terra's words echoed through her: *"I'm only flesh and blood while I am topside, Darcy. As long as I return to the earth before my heart stops beating, I can regenerate."*

Darcy snatched her knife out of her sheath, took aim, and threw. It struck the tsellodrin squarely in the chest and sank up to the hilt. The tsellodrin stumbled backward, snarling, holding Terra high above the ground. Darcy screamed and charged at him, weaponless and desperate.

The tsellodrin caught her easily with a glancing blow to her chest that sent her sprawling onto the ground. Darcy's breath left her in a whoosh, and she lay helpless on the ground, wheezing and staring deep into the tsellodrin's fathomless eyes. Without warning, he lurched forward, dropping his sword with Terra still impaled on it. Darcy scrambled away as the tsellodrin's heavy form toppled to the ground. Boitheia stood over the sword in his back.

"Terra!" Darcy groaned, pulling herself over to the tsellodrin's fallen sword and rolling the oread over. The nymph's eyes were stuck open in shock, no breath coming from her lips. Darcy cried out and covered her face, sobbing hysterically.

Wyn and Fero burst through the trees and looked around, taking stock.

"No," Wyn said, stricken.

Fero set his jaw and stooped over her, gently closing Terra's eyes, and her body began to crumble into dust. "She is reunited with her element."

Wyn helped Darcy to her feet and peered at her neck in concern. "Where there is one, there likely will be more. We must get back."

Darcy stooped to retrieve her knife and hesitantly grabbed the sword that had killed Terra. It was a rough weapon, not at all beautiful like Perry's sword, but she felt it only right to claim it as her own.

"A tsellodrin," Fero informed the others as they returned to the water's edge. He lowered his voice. "Terra's dead. Darcy and Boitheia finished off the beast."

The others stood in stunned silence. Perry and Dean cast questioning glances at Darcy and Boitheia, but Daylan only nodded grimly. He seemed to compose himself, a weight of weariness on his shoulders that had not been there seven months before.

"Let's go," Daylan said.

They piled onto the raft and pushed off from shore as ten more tsellodrin stepped from the trees. The current swept the raft into the center of the river, and they left the shore behind in only seconds.

Darcy felt numb as the river bore them away, no tears left in her body to weep. The mood on the raft echoed her own, and as Badru guided the vessel, the rest of them sat staring with dull, glassy eyes. Each of their faces showed weariness and guilt, but none, Darcy knew, were as guilty as she. Two friends were gone because of her.

"Do we know where this raft is taking us?" she whispered to nobody in particular, hoping desperately for a swift journey back.

"It's taking us south," Wyn answered. "The river will eventually empty us into the sea, and from there we can find our way home."

Home, Darcy thought. *Ormiskos.*

CHAPTER 32

DARCY KEEPS A SECRET

Two weeks later, the stream emptied into the sea somewhere off the southern coast of Alitheia. Dean shot an arrow message to Rubidius telling him their whereabouts, and in three days they saw blue sails on the horizon.

"It's the *Cal Meridian*," Wyn confirmed. "We're almost home!"

They rendezvoused with the schooner as the setting sun glinted off the golden railing. Sam, Lewis, and Amelia poked their heads over the edge, waving at them with eager expressions, and Darcy broke down and cried. Perry laid a comforting arm around her shoulder while Dean patted her awkwardly on the back.

No one asked any questions when she got on board, and Darcy was thankful. She felt emotionally ruined, and Sam and Amelia just hugged her and let her cry. They already knew about Yahto and Terra from Dean's regular updates, but nobody pressed about Darcy's answer from the Oracle.

Captain Boreas gave Darcy his own quarters to share with the girls, and Darcy spent much of the voyage back to Ormiskos in the room's only bed at the other three girls' insistance. They talked only about frivolous things. Sam and Amelia gave accounts of the dance and etiquette lessons they had taken that year in addition to their work with Eleanor and Rubidius. Sam shared that all the young men at the castle seemed to be smitten with Amelia, but none moreso than poor Bayard. Boitheia smiled often as she got to know some other girls close to her age, but Darcy could never bring herself to smile or laugh with them. She felt like that part of her—the happy part—had died.

She liked to walk the deck when the sun was at its brightest. May had just dawned, and the weather was becoming noticeably warmer. The sun on her face helped her forget the cold of her experiences, if only for a little while. Occasionally she saw a golden eagle winging above them, keeping pace with the ship, but she ignored it. If it was Pateros, she had nothing to say to him.

They reached Ormiskos to find the sea wall completed and the massive gate thrown open to welcome them in. Darcy stayed below deck even though there were no crowds this time; she felt exposed and preferred to stay out of sight.

They docked at the castle, and Eleanor alone waited for them at the gate. She looked very old now. Darcy climbed out of the little skiff that had retrieved them from the *Cal Meridian*, and Eleanor threw her arms around her, weeping openly on her shoulder.

Soon she escorted them upstairs and someone helped her to undress and bathe. They cut her hair and her fingernails, lotioning and pampering her until she was as sweet-smelling and fresh as the day she'd left, but it meant nothing; Darcy was empty.

They left her alone in her enormous, feathery bed, and Darcy lay staring at the ceiling in misery. She tossed and turned, unable to get comfortable in the lavish bed after weeks of sleeping on the bumpy ground and the sawed logs of the bobbing raft. She could think of nothing except Yahto Veli suffering in a dank underground cell.

With a sigh, Darcy rolled from the bed and dragged her pillow and comforter to the floor. She lay down on the cold flagstones and covered herself with the comforter, resting her head on the pillow and feeling her shoulders relax, the mix of comfort and discomfort lulling her almost to sleep.

She heard a soft knock on the door adjoining her room to Sam's. "Come in," she called.

Sam opened the door. The year had been good to her. She had slimmed some, and her blond hair was long and healthy. Her face had thinned out too, as though her baby fat had melted away. Amelia followed her in, her heavy bangs swept off to one side. She still looked every bit as perfect as she had when Darcy'd left.

They schooled their faces to mask their surprise and pity at seeing Darcy lying on the floor and padded over to her, dragging two chairs close.

"We thought maybe you'd like us to read to you," Sam said softly. "You know . . . to help you sleep."

"To keep your mind off things," Amelia added.

Darcy turned her face to the ceiling and swallowed hard. Hot tears burned tracks out the corners of her eyes and down her cheekbones into her ears. "That . . . would be great," she managed.

"Okay," Sam said, and Darcy heard the soft flipping of pages and the crack of a book spine flexing. Sam started to read, and Darcy recognized the words as being from her own book of Alitheian nursery rhymes. Sam and Amelia traded off from story to story, and Darcy soon let herself drift to sleep in the lulling cadence of their voices.

A week later, Darcy was ready to talk. Lying on the floor of her room where she still slept, she told them everything that had happened since she'd arrived at the Oracle. Before their astonished faces, she recited the Oracle's answer:

"*You, the Intended, have much truth to seek.*
Your path is not for the fainthearted or weak.
What was lost in the fire has now come to light,
Recovered, translated, against which you'll fight.
The words were restored, precise to the letter,
Their meanings should have been interpreted better.
Regarding the lines of the marriage and ring,
Ask yourself, Lady, who is the king?
And what is the ring that will mark you, in sooth?
In answering you'll find your way to the truth."

She stopped, considering whether to continue reciting the second part, the words "twice wed, twice dead, twice stained red" echoing in her mind. She imagined Sam's and Amelia's horrified faces and, unable to bear them, decided to keep it to herself.

They sat in silence, Sam chewing her cheek and Amelia squinting, letting Darcy talk until she'd told them everything about her long journey. Hours later, Darcy finally reached the end of her story.

"I can tell you have opinions, so just tell me," she said propping herself up on her elbows to look at them.

"Well . . ." Sam seemed reluctant to spit it out.

"It basically confirms three things," Amelia jumped in, holding up her fingers to count off. "One, you *will* marry the king. Two, the last four lines of the prophecy are accurate. And three, you will be marked by a ring."

"But . . ." Sam sputtered. "It tells you to question two things we *thought* we had figured out—that *everybody* thought they had figured out!"

"Yeah, I know," Darcy said. "Who exactly is the king, and what is the ring?" She waggled her left thumb at them, the ring glinting in the low lamplight. "I'd always thought it was this, but maybe it's not."

"And where does that leave Tellius? He *might* be the king it's referring to, but then again, he might not be," Sam said.

"But who else could it be?" Amelia puzzled.

Who else, indeed, Darcy thought as she did her own puzzling over the *two* prophesied weddings, still choosing not to voice the rest of the riddle.

"There's one thing I do know," Sam said very business-like, but then she softened. "Darcy, you have to tell Rubidius. He's been waiting to see you."

Rubidius, Darcy thought, would be perhaps the most difficult person to face after this journey. He had been to the lair of the Oracle, and he would understand the state in which Yahto Veli was now living. She hadn't gone to see him yet, having stayed sequestered in her room and allowing only Sam and Amelia as visitors. But perhaps it was time to visit the old alchemist and try to get herself back together.

"You're right," she sighed. "I'll go tomorrow." She rolled over on the floor and buried her head in her arm. "I think I can get to sleep on my own tonight, guys," she said.

"Okay, g'night," Sam said, and they left her room.

Darcy steeled herself the next morning and knocked on Rubidius's door. She hoped that she wouldn't spend the entire morning boohooing all over his table, but come what may, it was time for them to talk. Her first knock unanswered, she knocked again—harder this time—and the door jerked open. Tellius stared at her in surprise as Darcy almost knocked him on the chest.

He was still gangly and awkward, even more so because he had grown another inch while she'd been away, but he held himself straighter as he stood. He was thirteen now, going on fourteen in the fall, and he had filled out a little. The puppy-dog awkwardness was diminished somewhat, and his hands no longer looked too large for his arms.

"Sorry," Darcy muttered, dropping her fist to her side.

"Darcy!" he exclaimed. His voice cracked and he grimaced, his ears going red. He glanced over his shoulder. "Rubidius, look!" he called, stepping back.

The old alchemist turned from helping Cadmus at the round table in the center of the cottage and he, too, looked surprised to see her. She raised her hand self-consciously and scratched at the back of her neck. "May I come in?" she asked.

"Yes, of course! Please." Rubidius pulled himself together. "Cadmus, Tellius, please leave us. That will be all for today."

Cadmus, now starting to take on the awkwardness of adolescence, gave a silent cheer behind Rubidius's back and bolted from the table before his tutor could change his mind. He wriggled past Darcy and Tellius, taking off down the hall.

Tellius was slower to leave. He lingered in the doorway uncertainly, opening his mouth to say something but hesitating. Darcy averted her eyes from his, only ready to talk to Rubidius today.

"Tellius," Rubidius said. "Please."

The young prince nodded in acquiescence and stepped out into the hallway. "I'm—really glad—you're back," he fumbled.

Darcy bit her lip and nodded, entering the cottage and closing the door in his face.

"Come." Rubidius pulled out a chair for her. "Sit, please." He waved over a pot of tea and two mugs. "I will admit, I did not expect you for some days yet."

"You think I'm weak, don't you?" Darcy whispered ashamedly. "Or cruel. You think it was cruel of me to leave Yahto there."

"Lady Darcy," Rubidius said firmly, starting to sound like his usual self. "I think neither of those things. What foolish notions you get into your head!" He sighed and poured her some tea. "I think you are quite strong, and I *know* you are not cruel."

She squinted at him.

"It is true," he chided her. "I didn't expect you yet because I thought it would take much longer for you heal enough to be able to talk to me."

"I'm not healed yet," Darcy said. "I don't know if I ever will be."

He nodded knowingly. "That is what the Oracle wants you to feel; it is one consequence of the journey you made. But it doesn't mean you cannot move on."

"But what about Yahto Veli?" Darcy cried. "Don't we have to rescue him?"

Rubidius looked troubled. "Rescue from the Oracle is—"

"Don't say impossible!" Darcy interrupted vehemently.

"*Improbable*," Rubidius said instead, peering at her. "But you should not concern yourself with it. *If* there is a way, I will find it, I promise you that."

"I tried to offer it something else," Darcy continued. "I offered to make a promise, but it only wanted Yahto."

"Yahto stayed of his own free will. He stayed to protect you and save you from certain death at the hands of the tsellochim. You had no control over the matter."

"But I did. If I hadn't invoked the Oracle—"

"Do not go down that road, Lady Darcy; what's done is done."

Darcy bit her lip, thinking. Finally she said, very quietly, "I'm going to find a way to rescue him."

"Yahto Veli is no longer your concern—" Rubidius began.

"No longer my *concern?*" Darcy seethed, her voice rising. "Yahto Veli is my *only* concern! He's my best friend in Alitheia and I'm not going to just —"

"Lady Darcy!" Rubidius barked. "I will not discuss this with you further. There is nothing more you can do for him. I want to know, now, what answer the Oracle gave you."

Darcy glared at him for minutes, her eyes narrowed, and he stared unwaveringly back at her. "Fine," Darcy sighed. "Can I write it down for you?"

He summoned a piece of parchment and a quill before her, and Darcy wrote out the riddle, certain every word was correct. She stopped again when she reached the last stanza, unable to bring herself to tell him. She put the quill down and handed the page to Rubidius. He read it slowly and carefully. Several silent moments passed.

"And this was the *entire* answer?" he asked her.

Darcy gulped, afraid he somehow knew she had left part of it off, but she nodded.

"Hmmm." Rubidius sat back and twisted his fingers together over his chest. "Well . . . it verifies that the *words* of the prophecy are accurate as they stand, as I expected. It is only their interpretation that is called into question. Of course, the Oracle also likes to cause confusion. It is very possible that our current interpretation is entirely accurate. The Oracle has allowed for it, in asking you to *question* everything, but—"

"*You* think the prophecy has been misinterpreted, don't you?" Darcy asked. "Just like the Oracle says."

"The parts about the king and the ring *are* somewhat puzzling," Rubidius said, "and I will admit there may be alternate ways of looking at those lines. We always assumed it would be a king in the line of Ecclektos and the ring would be the royal ring, but . . . there is something in the wording here . . ."

He looked very troubled, tugging his beard hard enough to pull down the corners of his mouth. He knew something, or at least he suspected it.

"What are you not telling me?" she asked, leaning forward.

"Hmm? Oh, nothing, nothing. I'm just thinking. I'm sorry I can't be of much help with this, but give me some time." He rolled up the parchment and sat back, regarding her.

"Lupidor made it home safely," he said after a moment.

"I heard," Darcy said, and silence fell between them again.

"Badru told me of the magic you performed outside of Fobos," Rubidius said.

"Oh . . ." Darcy had barely thought about it in the months that had passed since.

"It was a remarkable feat," he commented. "I'm very proud of you for wielding such great power with so little training, but it must have been very difficult for you."

"Yeah. I was so wiped out I passed out afterwards," Darcy said. "They had to carry me halfway up the mountain." Speaking of the mountain recalled something else to mind—something she'd only told the narks about after it had happened: Colin's apparition.

Rubidius listened with his eyes half shut. "And he had a scar on his hand like this?" he asked when she was finished, raising his left hand. Darcy stared at the puckered scar Rubidius, too, bore on his left palm.

"Yes, but he couldn't have—could he?"

"There are dark things at work here." He lowered his hand and furrowed his brow. "Thank you for telling me of this. I will . . . think on it."

"Okay." Darcy began to fidget. "Well . . . I guess that's all."

"Yes, of course. I will not press you to dig deeper at this time." He stood and walked her to the door. "And Darcy," he said before she left, "be encouraged. Yahto Veli is strong and resourceful."

Darcy nodded but didn't trust herself to speak.

She'd intended to go straight to her room after meeting with Rubidius but found it had felt good to get some things off her chest. Once out in the hall, she thought of Tellius's distraught expression and, feeling a burst of compassion for him, she strode down to the library and Tellius's room.

Once inside the library, she turned up the chandelier. The room was empty, and she still found it beguiling, even though it was where all her troubles had begun this year. She walked along the wall to Tellius's narrow staircase and began to climb.

The little gate at the top of his staircase was locked, blocking entrance to his balcony, and Darcy struggled over it in her long skirt, careful not to look down as she did so. Once over the gate, she straightened herself up and knocked on his door. It opened, and Tellius poked his head out.

"Oh!" he exclaimed in surprise.

"Hi, Tellius, I was thinking maybe you wanted to know what the Oracle told me," she said in a rush before she could change her mind.

"Yes, I do! That is . . . if you're okay with telling me." He looked anxious.

"Yeah, I'm okay with telling you."

"Sure . . . um . . ." He glanced back toward his room. "Let's go down into the library. Cadmus is in our room, and it's better if I sneak away." He stepped out and gingerly closed the door. He flipped a tiny concealed latch on the gate and opened it to let her down first.

Once again seated in the alcove where they'd first discussed the Oracle, Darcy recited for Tellius the first part of her answer. He reacted in stunned silence, his wide eyes blinking.

"So . . . I might not be the king it's referring to?" He scratched at his freckles.

"Nope, I guess not. But . . . you *could* be," Darcy said.

"But still . . . this is great!" He beamed. "We don't have to worry about being tied down anymore!"

Darcy felt much more wary about the answer, as Rubidius had said the Oracle may only want her to question things. "I wouldn't expect Rubidius or Eleanor to give you any more leeway," she said. "They'll still expect you to wait and see if you have to marry me."

He waved a hand dismissively. "It feels good to know we can just be friends without always thinking about . . . that."

Darcy allowed a small smile to light her face. "I suppose you're right about that."

She stood to go, satisfied now at having talked with everybody who needed to hear the story from her.

"Thanks for coming to see me, Darcy. I've been . . . worried about you." Tellius looked a little embarrassed, but Darcy was touched.

"Thanks," she said. "That's nice of you." She waved and moved toward the hallway, glancing once back over her shoulder at him before closing the door behind her.

EPILOGUE

WHAT DARCY SAW

Darcy woke up at Cedar Cove gripping the sides of her thin mattress in sleepy confusion for a solid five minutes before remembering where she was as everything from the day before rushed back to her. She rolled over and groaned into her pillow.

Torrin and Rubidius had escorted Darcy and her friends back to the gateway, the golden eagle soaring above them the entire way. She'd collided with her brother upon coming out of the gateway, swiftly covering his eyes so he wouldn't see the rest of her friends appear out of thin air.

Her father had been angry at their unexplained dash into the woods, and Darcy had burst into tears upon his reproach. Bewildered at her reaction, he'd insisted they all head back to Glorietta Bay where he forced Darcy to take a nap for being "over excited."

Now, as Darcy awoke Monday morning at camp, she stared with dull eyes at the ceiling. Her brother had already gone down to breakfast, and her parents were starting to stir. Darcy closed her eyes and pretended to sleep, hoping they'd let her skip breakfast.

They did. She waited several minutes after they left for the dining hall and then scooted off her top bunk and began to very slowly get ready for the day. A half hour later she wandered downstairs to look for her friends, not hearing the greetings others called to her as she passed. She wanted to be with them—with *only* them—but they were neither in the lobby nor the dining hall. She stood feeling rather cross by the lobby doors, when she finally heard a burst of laughter from a door ajar to her right.

She poked her head through the door and found all five of them huddled around the nametag table that must have been stored there since registration the first day of camp.

"That's great!" Perry sniggered. "We can write it on your bag too, and I'll do mine."

"Check it out!" Dean said, placing his completed nametag around his neck.

"What are you guys doing?" Darcy frowned, coming all the way into the room.

"Hey, Darcy!" Sam said brightly. "The boys are just playing a silly joke."

"Look!" Dean pointed at his chest where his nametag read "Elmer," pointing next to Perry whose nametag read "Fudd."

"We have a new counselor this year, and we thought we'd try to convince her that these are our real names." Perry grinned impishly. "You guys have to call us by these names all week, okay?"

Darcy looked blankly from one boy to the other, wishing she could laugh with them and angry that she couldn't.

"I don't understand," she said, "how you guys can *joke* at a time like this!" She speared Perry and Dean with a gaze. "Were we not on the same journey this year? Do you not remember that Yahto Veli is rotting in a prison right now and that Terra is *dead?*"

Their faces fell at her words, and she didn't care that she was being judgmental and harsh.

"I *told* you she wouldn't like it," Lewis muttered out of the corner of his mouth.

"Darcy," Perry said, removing his nametag and stepping toward her. "We're sorry! Look, we just wanted to make you laugh. You kinda need to, you know?"

Darcy shook her head and backed away from him, tears filling her eyes. "I just don't know how to move on from this. Don't any of you care about him?"

"Of course we do!" Sam looked shocked. "But there's nothing we can do while we're here," she said.

Darcy looked down at her hands. Like the coldness that remained in her right hand, the scar on her left hand had also remained, even after coming back to her own world. She stared at her scar and thought suddenly of the same scar on the palm of Colin Mackaby.

"Where do the Mackabys stay?" she asked. "Where's their cabin?"

"They're in East Mooring, why?" Perry asked. "What are you thinking, Darcy?"

She looked up at them, her eyes blazing. "I'm thinking there is one person here who might know something about the Oracle, and I'm tired of avoiding him. I'm going to ask him."

Sam gasped, and Amelia said, "Darcy, no. That's a bad idea."

"Then don't come with me!" Darcy called over her shoulder. She raced out of the room and banged through the door to the boardwalk, jogging down the trail that led through the campsites to the left of the beach.

"Darcy, wait!" Sam called from far behind her, but she picked up her pace and didn't look back. She wanted to do this on her own.

The colorful domes of the tents slid by as she raced down the wood-chipped trail. In this part of camp stood a few newer specialty cabins, one of which was called East Mooring. It was tucked back in the trees, invisible from the campground, and it had its own private dock and beach.

Darcy rounded the bend in the trail that led to the entrance of the Mackabys' blue-painted cabin, and she heard a loud thud and a shout of pain. She skidded to a halt and looked for a place to hide as the shouting grew louder, echoing out the cabin's screened windows.

"Where do you think you're going? Don't you turn your back on me!" Lawrence Mackaby's voice boomed.

Darcy stepped behind a tree trunk and peeked at the windows of the cabin. She saw Colin make a dash for the door, jerking to a stop as a pair of thick, tanned hands closed around his throat.

Mr. Mackaby picked his son up by the neck and threw him to the floor. He held aloft something small, thin, and white; it looked like it might be a cigarette. "If I *ever* find one of these in your possession again, *so help me* —"

Colin shouted as Mr. Mackaby kicked him so hard in his side that Darcy could hear the ribs crack from where she was hiding.

She put her fingers over her mouth in horror and made herself as small as she could behind the tree trunk as Mr. Mackaby stepped out of the cabin. He smoothed his hair with shaking hands and stalked down the trail away from where Darcy hid. Darcy stayed where she was, hearing the cabin door open and slam closed again. She peered out to watch Colin, wincing, make his way out to the private East Mooring beach.

Darcy crept closer to him, unable to arrest her curiosity or her concern. Colin sat at the edge of the dock, bent double, gasping and wheezing as though unable to breathe. Darcy turned to make a run for the first-aid station, but then she heard a pitiful whimper escape his lips. He was crying.

Unexpected compassion formed a knot in Darcy's throat, and she took a careful step toward him, reaching out a quivering hand. "Colin?" she whispered, barely audible.

Colin's head snapped up, and his gaze bore into hers. His eyes were vulnerable in the split second it took him to recognize her, and then his vulnerability turned to rage. He leapt to his feet, holding his chest with one arm. "Go away!" he shouted, starting threateningly down the dock. "Go . . . *away!*" His shout turned to an enraged scream.

She froze. Colin raised his left hand, and she stared, riveted, at the clean, unmarred flesh of his palm. He slowly pulled his fingers into a fist and advanced on her with a snarl.

Darcy turned tail and ran.

The Gateway Chronicles

Book 3

The White Thread

Chapter 1

The Disappearance

Confounds Law

ide as she took
an old picture,
e confirmed it

camp at which his family was staying, but an area-wide search has turned up no leads. No residents in the nearby town of Logger's Head recognized the boy. Police task forces have scoured the woods for miles around the camp with body-sniffing dogs, but no traces have been found. Police now fear a possible kidnapping and request that locals report any suspicious vehicles or persons. A hotline has been set up at the phone number listed below, and the Mackaby family is offering a reward of $50,000 for any information leading to the recovery of their son . . .

Darcy scanned the rest of the article, but it was nothing more than a description of Colin and what he had been wearing on the day he had disappeared. She leaned her head back against her headboard, her heart thumping noisily within her chest. "Oh, Colin . . . what have you gotten yourself into?" she murmured.

CPSIA information can be obtained
at www.ICGtesting.com
Printed in the USA
LVOW01s0430160816
500531LV00006B/19/P

9 781612 133270